PRAISE FOR *Not the girls you're looking for*

"...gaging and unexpected, ...-y and full of verve, this a ...mart swan dive into all the ...iness of best friendships ...new romance, fitting in ...and growing up."

—... Cotugno, *New York Times*–...lling author of *How to Love*

"...s hilarious as it is ...arming, this beautiful ...ut family, friendships, ... amazingly complex ... girl will leave you ...ging for more."

—...andhya Menon, ...*k Times*–bestselling ...*When Dimple Met Rishi*

"...nse, emotional debut ...ding one's place in the ...d throwing off labels ...d by other people."

—... Meadows, author of ...*efore She Ignites*

"...aad is exactly the ...on has been looking ...ss and beautiful Arab- ...uslim ready to take the ...orm. Sparkling with ... and vulnerability, ...t will make you ...and cry."

—...hena, author of ...*ke That*

"Deftly written and darkly funny, *Not the Girls You're Looking For* is an unflinching portrayal of what it's like to be a girl who refuses to be boxed in. Lulu and her friends are fierce, flawed, feminist, and full of heart—not to mention utterly unforgettable."

—Katy Upperman, author of *Kissing Max Holden*

"Fiercely unapologetic and unapologetically fierce. This is exactly the kind of bold, messy, girl-driven, friendship-centric narrative that I have indeed been looking for."

—Laurie Elizabeth Flynn, author of *Firsts*

"A sexy, multifaceted, and beautifully complicated debut for anyone who has ever struggled with friendships, religion, and love. A must-read!"

—Nisha Sharma, author of *The Perfect Ending*

"*Not the Girls You're Looking For* are exactly the girls you're rooting for. Lulu is fierce, loyal, and a main character you won't soon forget. An honest slice of teen life from a teen character you need to know."

—Sara Farizan, author of *If You Could Be Mine*

For Steven—
You definitely told me so.

A FEIWEL AND FRIENDS BOOK

An imprint of Macmillan Publishing Group, LLC

175 Fifth Avenue, New York, NY 10010.

NOT THE GIRLS YOU'RE LOOKING FOR. Copyright © 2018 by Aminah Mae Safi.
All rights reserved. Printed in the United States of America.

Our books may be purchased in bulk for promotional, educational, or business use. Please
contact your local bookseller or the Macmillan Corporate and Premium Sales Department
at (800) 221-7945 ext. 5442 or by e-mail at MacmillanSpecialMarkets@macmillan.com.

Library of Congress Cataloging-in-Publication Data is available.

ISBN 978-1-250-15181-0 (hardcover) / ISBN 978-1-250-15180-3 (ebook)

Book design by Liz Dresner

Feiwel and Friends logo designed by Filomena Tuosto

First edition, 2018

10 9 8 7 6 5 4 3 2 1

fiercereads.com

Not the girls you're looking for

Aminah Mae Safi

Feiwel and Friends
New York

1

Rakish

Lulu swatted her way through the unfamiliar coat closet. After tearing down several of what felt like rather expensive fur coats and a couple of potentially cashmere jackets off their hooks, she managed to hit her head against a dangling light switch chain. She swore. Not that there was anyone left to hear her. She pulled the switch, located the closet door, and made her swift exit. She looked left, then she looked right. The coast was clear. She took a deep, relieved breath. What a night it had already been.

Of course, that's when she heard the tutting. Across the hall, Dane Anderson perked up from his lean against the wall. He was the sort of boy who was extensively practiced at leaning against things—walls, lockers, overly large trucks. He was an expert leaner. The only light in the hallway was that streaming out of the closet, and as Dane moved toward her, his face shifted from the shadows to the light.

Lulu stopped straightening out her clothing. She was acutely aware of every tousled hair on her head. She could feel the back zipper of her skirt disobediently tickling her hip. She assumed her shirt was buttoned back up incorrectly, because that was the sort of luck she had. But she'd be damned if she let her nerves show. Not to him.

Because nature had already given Dane Anderson plenty. His sandy brown hair waved beautifully, effortlessly. His warm, friendly eyes were heavy-lidded and half-open. Whether that was from alcohol or the sudden light, it was difficult to say. The sleeves to his oxford shirt were rolled lazily up to reveal his suntanned, muscular forearms. The top of the shirt was unbuttoned so as to display his crisp white undershirt. His throat bobbed. "*Qu'est-ce qui se passe avec toi?*"

Lulu blinked. What was going on with her? Nothing. Nothing at all. The hallway filled with her silence. She stole a glance at the stairway. She could hear the muffled din of the party below.

Before she could move, Dane took a step forward and put his hand on the wall, his arm blocking her path to escape. "You gonna answer the question, honey, or do you need it in English?"

Lulu's heart hammered so hard that her pulse rang in her own ears. Retreating back into the closet wasn't an option. Not with Dane. Not when they were so alone. But he wasn't one to fight fair, either.

"Nothing's up with me," she said.

"I can see that." Dane eyed her from head to toe, back to head again. His gaze lingered in the middle.

Lulu took a shallow breath. Then another as her stomach clenched. She had to find some scrap of truth to throw his way. "I fell."

"Fall in all by yourself, did you?" A grin pulled at Dane's mouth. It was a Clark Gable kind of grin—all charm and menace. Another gift of his birth and breeding.

"Maybe. Why do you care?" Lulu looked him dead in the eye. That was her first mistake. Dane had beautiful eyes. They were brown with flecks of green in them, dusted with thick lashes. Lulu gripped the wall behind her, a spin overtaking her head. It was all the alcohol she had drunk. Alcohol spins. Not beautiful, terrible boy spins.

Dane closed the gap between their bodies to next to nothing. Lulu—God help her—flattened her back against the wall. Dane had never been unaware of the effect he had on women. Lulu had never been unaware of the effect Dane had on her. In that, at least, they were equals.

"Why don't you like me, Lulu?" Even slurring slightly, he sounded like he had a thousand years of good ol' boys behind him, like he could carry a thousand more after him. There had been four generations in his line—he, after all, was only Daniel Dodge Anderson IV. But his voice bore the weight of a never-ending, never-broken string of gentlemen. A voice of infinity. "Why can't we be friendly?"

"You know why." Lulu gritted her teeth.

Dane's expression stretched into a full-blown, Cheshire cat grin. The world tilted on its axis slightly. Lulu could have had a crush on him for three weeks straight if she'd wanted, at the mere flash of this smile. In fact, at some point in her freshman year, she had. And that was two years ago. Lulu willed her breath even and buried that feeling away as deeply as she could. Lulu didn't think about freshman year, if she could help it.

"Explain it again." His breath fanned across her cheek as he leaned in.

Lulu's mouth fell open, ever so slightly. Why couldn't *nice* boys smell like peppermint and gin?

Lulu offered up a silent prayer to whoever watched over the dignity of girls like her. Soft, cold lips whispered against hers when a series of repetitive thunks echoed up the stairs. Dane looked up—toward the sound. Lulu didn't think; she simply took advantage and ducked under his arm. She fled toward the stairs.

Unfortunately, Lulu hardly looked up as she ran away from Dane. She smacked right into a tall, lanky boy—more limbs than anything else. Limbs

3

she fell into, like some horrible moment in a rom-com. She disentangled herself with much more effort than it should have taken.

Lulu clenched her hand into a fist. The boy raised his arms as if to say, "Whoa, lady. Not my fault." Fine. Not his fault. Nobody's fault but her own. She relaxed her hand; the boy nodded like he appreciated the restraint.

Lulu leaped down the steps—two at a time—toward the safety of the ground floor. Toward people. Toward Audrey and whatever lecture was in store from that quarter. From above, Lulu heard the boys' subdued voices. She didn't stop moving until the sound was a distant memory. Until the cacophony of the kitchen swallowed her up.

―――――

In hindsight, Lulu ought to have fixed her shirt before looking for Audrey.

Audrey Bachmann took in Lulu's state of undress and in less than half a second had pulled Lulu out of the kitchen and into a quieter, less populated room. Audrey might have been holding a red Solo cup, but her white and pink floral sundress was still spotless and unrumpled. Her face was flush—she must have only been half a drink into her evening—but her fair hair was still smooth and neat.

"Hold this." Audrey handed Lulu her drink cup. She pinched a lock of Lulu's hair between her fingers, then dropped it with a sigh. Audrey fussed over the buttons on Lulu's shirt—unbuttoning then smoothing as she rebuttoned.

Lulu swatted away Audrey's hands. One mother was enough.

"Aren't you going to let me lend a hand at all?" Audrey's voice was more of a screech and less of a question.

The wild hammering in Lulu's heart had faded to nothing. Her head swam. Relief hollowed Lulu out, leaving her dizzy. Behind her was an inevitability she'd avoided for now. Ahead were only consequences and a lecture.

A desire to lash out tore through her, obstructing any number of reasonable thoughts in her head. "No."

Audrey jerked so hard on Lulu's shirt that the drink in Lulu's hand jostled. Sticky pink liquid splashed across both of their clothes. Because of course it would.

"Fantastic," muttered Audrey. "Now we'll for sure smell like liquor when we get back to my house. You better pray my mother isn't awake."

"You could've set your drink down."

Audrey's lips pressed into a firm line. She snatched the cup from Lulu's hands and threw back the rest of her drink in one swallow. "Fine. I'm getting a refill. Deal with your boy drama all by yourself."

Lulu winced as she watched Audrey turn on her heels. That wobbly, hollowing nothing surged again. Lulu didn't want to be responsible for Audrey spiraling tonight, too. "Wait," she called.

Audrey whipped back around.

"I got stuck in a hall closet with Brian," said Lulu.

As anticipated, Audrey wiped her hand down her face in pure exasperation. "How stuck?"

Lulu ran through any number of explanations she could have given. Entangled in his arms and mouth. Pressed up against coat hangers and a wooden closet rod. Pinned by her own curiosity but not by any real interest. She settled on, "Very."

Audrey reached out and smoothed the front of Lulu's shirt, then tugged the bottom hem. This time, Lulu let her.

"What the *fuck*, Lulu?" said Audrey, nearly at a whisper. Audrey didn't say curse words at full volume if she could help it.

"I was promised a telescope."

"Naturally." Audrey tried to take a drink out of her cup, then scowled. She must have forgotten she'd finished it. She set the empty cup onto a sideboard with one of the provided coasters there. She turned her glare onto Lulu. "They're not all your big brothers. You have to be careful."

Lulu giggled, as though she were teetering off the edge of a cliff and laughter would steer her away from a plunge. Her brothers weren't here right now, thank God. They were away at school. "It was only Brian."

Audrey arched a perfectly manicured eyebrow. "Did anyone see you?"

Nearly. "No."

Audrey pinched the bridge of her nose. "Thank goodness."

The sting of Audrey's judgment lit a fire in Lulu's temper again, at least keeping her away from that awful, flooding nothing. "Well, screw you, too."

Audrey closed her eyes for a moment. She took a deep breath before she reopened them. "I'm looking out for you, you know. Keeping your reputation intact."

"Joke's on you, 'cause I don't have a tactful reputation." Lulu forced out a single laugh.

Audrey raised her eyebrow again. "As soon as you're finished throwing your little theatrics, I'm going to get another drink." That was pure Mrs. Bachmann, Audrey's mother. Audrey looked down her straight, aquiline nose and everything.

"I'm only getting started." Lulu put a hand on her hip. She had never been cowed by that look when Mrs. Bachmann gave it, and she wouldn't quaver before it now. Except as she jutted her hip, Lulu's jelly legs finally gave out. She wobbled once, then simply toppled to the ground. She landed with her legs splayed and her tailbone potentially bruised. She could already tell she was going to feel wonderful tomorrow, even if the liquor was taking the edge off tonight.

Audrey sighed. She bent over, holding out her hands. Lulu pushed herself up halfway, then accepted the offering. Audrey yanked Lulu to her feet.

"I need a fresh drink," said Audrey at the same time as Lulu said, "I need some air."

The two stared at each other for a long, silent moment.

"I just need to breathe, Audrey Louise," said Lulu. "I'm not sick or anything. Closets aren't as roomy as they look. Swear." Lulu held out her pinkie.

Audrey groaned but locked it with her own. They touched thumbs and twisted their hooked pinkies apart. That was still sacrosanct between them.

"Be good," Audrey said, her tone still sharp. Judgment came so easily to her.

"I always am." Lulu was sure of her success. It's not like she could get into much trouble outside.

———

The back corner of the large, rectangular pool was banked by reclining chairs—not the blue kind you'd find at a community pool. These were impossibly white and elegantly shaped. Still, they were slatted, and Lulu anticipated the wide, cherry-red stripes that they would imprint onto the backs of her thighs. She sloshed her foot through the pool briefly before she flopped onto one of them. She sprawled out, trying to relax. A littering of plastic cups indicated that whatever crowd had been out here had already migrated back in again, deterred by the wet, heavy air of Southeast Texas.

Wet, heavy air that was becoming a problem.

Though the season was technically fall, summer lingered. The humidity that stifled her breath also pushed her previously tamed mane outward into puffy spirals. She was not Lo—and everyone called Dolores Campo *Lo*—who never let humidity alter her appearance. No, Lulu's hair would be ruined. A necessary casualty of the evening, along with her tailbone and her pride. Lulu closed her eyes; she was going to ride the melt. At least until the spinning stopped.

A scraping noise sounded—metal on concrete. Lulu's eyes flew open. Around the corner of the pool and three chairs over from her, the boy she'd run into upstairs was adjusting the back of one of the recliners to a more upward position.

Or, he was trying to. The metal must have been stuck in its hinges, rusted over from the humidity. Lulu watched as he dragged the chair back and forth, trying to jiggle the joint free. But the chair would not come unstuck from its current position. That piercing, grating noise continued.

Lulu coughed. The boy's head snapped up. His eyes widened momentarily with recognition. He must have thought she'd been passed out. He must have wanted to avoid any interaction. Lulu swiped her teeth with her tongue, waiting. He eyed her, then the chair in his hands, seemingly unsure of what he should do next.

Lulu pointed two chairs over from herself. "That one's already in the upright-and-locked position."

The boy stood frozen like a deer in the headlights. Or a cartoon rabbit caught in the gaze of a hypnotizing snake. Lulu didn't look away. She bit the inside of her mouth to prevent a smile from creeping across her face. Finally, she raised her eyebrows. That broke the spell. He moved to the chair she'd indicated. Lulu turned back to face the pool.

Out of the corner of her eye, she continued to watch him. He stretched his body out along the lounge chair, crossing his long legs, one over the other, and resting his hands behind his head. There was no fluidity in his movements. His height must have been newly acquired. He wore a short-sleeved undershirt as a shirt. A patch of skin flashed for a moment above his jeans—soft and pale. A curious impulse flashed: to reach out and touch him there. Who knows what would happen if she did. Lulu rolled her hands under her. She could still hear Audrey's piercing shrill ringing through her head. No need for another lecture tonight.

"Good call." His deep, gravelly baritone had no slur whatsoever. "On the chair."

"Yes," Lulu deadpanned as she recovered her wits. The tone of his voice had hummed through her. *Keep it together for five minutes, Saad.* "They tell me that all the time. So many good calls."

"Full of wisdom?"

A low laugh built in Lulu's throat. "A font of it. They will remember me as Lulu the Wise."

"Lulu," he said. "That's got to be short for something."

Lulu sighed. "Leila. It's short for Leila."

And, right on cue, the boy began to wail, "Layyyylaaaaa," like he was Eric Fucking Clapton. He looked over, a grin spreading across his face until it crinkled into the corners of his eyes. He caught Lulu's eye. The singing immediately stopped. "Bad call?"

"Absolutely horrendous."

"Horrendous? Why horrendous?" But there was no demand in his tone. "Please."

Lulu turned over onto her side to face him fully. He just looked at her, his face wide and open. Her pretty smile fell. Raw honesty wasn't something Lulu got much of in her neck of the woods. She stared, waiting for the sarcastic bite, the playful joke to his words. The light from the pool glimmered across his face. And his round, unflinching eyes just kept on staring. As if the rabbit could transfix the snake.

"I've never wanted any man on his knees, not really. Or worrying some kind of ease, or whatever the lyric is. I dunno. I don't wanna be Leila, or Carmen, or Belle de Jour. I just want to be me. Without some dude strumming a guitar or writing an opera or filming a movie trying to tell me how to do that. The singing reminds me that no matter what I go by somebody is gonna step in and remind me what some obsessed asshole thinks of my name. Reminds me that Clapton's Layla is cruel and Bizet's Carmen dies. So Lulu. That's me. It's mine. And it's just as real as any other fiction. No serenade required." Lulu took a deep breath. She'd managed to run out of air by the end of her confession. She didn't expect him to understand, because the only person who really got it was Lo.

"Okay, Lulu," he said. "I'm James."

Lulu held out her arm and gave a pretend handshake in the air. "Why don't I know you?"

"Just moved back from Florida."

"I'd never have pegged you for a Florida type."

His mouth twitched upward. "And I'd never have pegged you for a Buñuel type."

"What's a bunwell?"

"Luis Buñuel? You know, the director of *Belle de Jour*, the movie you were just complaining about?"

Recognition flitted through Lulu's mind. Damn. "Not a fan. Or a type. I've just been taking French forever. And you know how French teachers are: they don't want you only to speak French, they want you to know what it is to *be* French. Hence the French opera and the French cinema. And sometimes French rap." Lulu nodded seriously and furrowed her brow with exaggerated severity.

"Guess it worked, though. I mean, you made an artsy film reference at a house party."

"God, you're depressing," said Lulu, but without any real conviction. "I hated the movie, but sometimes things you hate stick with you, you know?"

Lulu waited for an answer. Frogs hidden in the grass around the pool croaked in a vibrating, syncopated rhythm. A slow, heavy breeze blew through humid air. Better than nothing, but still sticky and frizz-inducing. A whispering, slithering sensation crawled up Lulu's spine. She ought not to have confessed to him. She ought to have stayed hidden. She stared at the pool until her gaze went fuzzy and wide. Her vision transformed into a blur of blue and white light.

"You're different."

The pool snapped into focus. She turned to James. Keen, wide eyes watched her.

Lulu took a deep breath, because Emma would have told her to take a deep breath. Emma Walker was always reminding Lulu to take deep breaths. But the deep breaths weren't helping, and she wasn't going to play this game and lose in public. She stood up, gripping the back of the nearest chair to steady herself. "Oh, what. Am I not like the other girls?"

"That's not what I said." James frowned.

Good. Lulu was snatching the conversation out from under him. He didn't know it yet, but from watching his face, he sensed it. Lulu backed away from him. "Isn't it?"

James stood. He stared for a long moment. "You're twisting my words."

He didn't know the half of what she was capable of twisting. Lulu took one more step back. She could picture Emma's disappointment, Audrey's judgment, and Lo's joy at the plan forming in her mind. "You said I was different. Not like the other girls. Not like everyone else you saw in there, including my best friends. *Different*. Isn't that right?"

"Yes. No." James took a step toward her, between her and the edge of the deep end. "That's not what I meant."

"Explain it to me, then. Since I'm too stupid to understand." Lulu smiled so she could bare her teeth.

James crossed his arms. "You know? I don't think I will."

And that was it—Lulu's cue.

Lulu took two steps forward and she shoved James hard. Somehow he didn't expect it. And then everything happened in slow motion. Lulu watched as he lost his balance and flailed once—no, twice—then splashed into the pool behind him. She smirked.

Oops.

Lulu watched for James to come up for air, but she didn't see him. It was the deep end, after all. Maybe he had to swim to the surface. But she didn't see any bubbles anymore. Lulu waited a beat. And another. He couldn't have hit his head. The pool was too deep here, at least eight feet. She'd only been trying to push him away. Not harm him. She couldn't kill a boy. Not tonight. And not this one.

He still hadn't come up for air, though.

Lulu swallowed. She hadn't marked the time when she'd pushed him in. Not that she remembered the difference between a normal amount of time or a not-normal amount of time to be submerged in a pool. That slithering down her spine made a tight grip on her breath, made her fingers tingle, made her head spin. There was only one thing left to do.

Lulu dove in.

She saw James at the bottom of the pool—his limbs sprawled out and his head down. Lulu grabbed for him and swam to the surface, kicking with all her might. She gasped when she reached the top. He was much heavier than she could have anticipated. Dead weight. Except he wasn't dead. He couldn't be dead. It was not possible for him to be dead. No one was dead. Except the already dead people, wherever they were.

Treading water in the middle of the pool, Lulu didn't know what to do. He hadn't gasped at the top. She didn't see any blood—so maybe he hadn't hit his head. Everything was fine. Tonight was going swimmingly. Lulu choked on a laugh. Chlorinated water burned through her nostrils.

Why, oh why, hadn't she paid attention the day they did CPR training. All she remembered was laughing as Lo licked the mannequin in front of the class. It had seemed terribly funny at the time. Not so, anymore. Lulu swam for the closest edge, the oversized boy filling her arms. Lulu didn't know how she was going to hoist him over the tile ledge onto the concrete.

That's when James's head snapped up and he looked straight at her. "Never be a lifeguard. I would've been dead sixty seconds ago."

Lulu had heard the expression "seeing red" before. But she'd never before had red flicker into the edges of her vision. Never known that her rage could light through her in that way. She scrambled out of the pool. James followed. He was laughing. She'd nearly killed him and he was laughing. Lulu put her hands on her knees. She almost vomited. She took two deep breaths. The nausea dissipated a little. One more deep breath and she found her footing again.

"You!" she screamed. She tried to think of all the curses she knew in all the languages she knew them. But her mind blanked. All she could get out was, "You!"

He was laughing harder now. Lulu didn't think; she started swinging.

"How. Dare. You." She was punching wildly, but effectively. "I am going to kill you. Murder you. I thought I *had* killed you."

James had, by this point, put his arms up to cover his face. "Ouch! It was only a joke."

He backed away, making space between them. Lulu didn't give chase. She stood there sopping wet and breathing heavy, her hands balled into fists.

"Fair's fair. You pushed me into the pool," James said.

"And there's no way you did anything to deserve that!" Lulu's voice echoed into the night.

James remained silent on that point. The sound of dripping reverberated across the lawn. Lulu looked down. She was all wet. This was going to be difficult to explain. Particularly to Audrey's mother. To any mother.

Lulu did what she could given the situation: she gave him the finger. Then she stalked away with as much grace as she could muster. She could hear the sad sloshing against the pavement as she walked. It did not feel dignified. At least she hadn't stuck out her tongue. That would have brought shame onto the family. She was her mother's daughter; there were standards to be upheld. Lulu dripped her way through the house, grabbing her purse in the kitchen and heading out the door. Everybody stared. Lulu didn't blame them. She held her chin high, though. At least she didn't need to text Audrey to meet by the car. Rumor had worked faster than data service.

Once Audrey caught sight of Lulu, she screeched, the disbelief raw on her throat. "You had better hope my mother is asleep."

Lulu's hopes came to nothing. Mrs. Bachmann was wide-awake for the girls' entrance. The night did not get any better from there.

2

Sins of Omission

Sealy Hall was situated on the edge of a Houston neighborhood filled with stately homes, long winding driveways, and expansive manicured lawns. The kind of place where homeowners were routinely complimented on landscaping that they refused to do themselves. The school itself was a local institution—storied cloisters, a quadrangle, a chapel, and a dining hall—the real deal. An aging public school even sat catty-corner, perfectly situated to offset Sealy Hall's institutional authority. That was a joke Lulu regularly told herself: she'd been institutionalized. She was being shaped into the spitting image of success.

And voluntarily, too.

She didn't have the requisite last name, but she was being taught the rest. Many would be resentful of this. But Lulu knew her options in this world. She was the daughter of an immigrant and a Louisiana woman. Blending wasn't a party trick. Blending was survival. Lulu took what Sealy Hall had to offer, with her eyes and hands open wide.

The dining hall—not a cafeteria—sat at the bottom of the student center—an expansive space filled with intimate round tables. To foster discussion and camaraderie, that's what the pamphlet said. The perfect size for gossip, was more of Lulu's experience with the layout.

"And then, I swear to God, I saw her give him a hickey. He's going to have a purple mark on his neck for at least a week." Lo—and nobody dared to call Dolores Campo *Lola* or, shudder to think, *Lolita*—sat cross-legged in her chair. Lo habitually took up more space than her body required.

"We saw it all happen Saturday night. We don't need a blow by blow." Lulu stole a french fry off Audrey's plate and ignored the resulting grimace.

Lo, however, was a hurricane. She could not be stopped; she could only be weathered. She pushed her hands through her hair, deliberately mussing her tousled mane. "It's not a blow, Lulu. It's a suck. That causes capillary bruising. It's just physics plus biology."

"Literally. How fascinating." Lulu tried to take another fry but was blocked by Audrey's strategically placed elbows.

"Lulu's just upset because she made out with Brian Connor this weekend." Audrey's eyes lit up with an inaudible laugh.

One pilfered fry and Audrey had turned traitor. To think Lulu had taken the fall for her this weekend. Lulu took a deep breath. She hadn't cared that night, not really, and she wouldn't care now. Or at least, she cared in a different way than most people would anticipate. So she lied without ever actually lying. Her mother would call that a sin of omission.

Lulu snorted. "Whatever."

Lo arched an eyebrow. "Whatever?"

Emma Walker—two chairs over from Lulu—quietly watched her two friends. Her eyes flitted back and forth, taking in the scene. That was how Emma gauged threat levels.

"It was an accident." Lulu hoped a shrug might shake Lo off. It didn't.

16

"Then you're kind of accident-prone, Daphne." Satisfaction slid across Lo's face.

Lulu didn't hesitate. "It's danger-prone. If you're referencing *Scooby-Doo*. It's 'Danger-Prone Daphne.'"

That was as close to a "fuck you" as Lulu could get while they were still moderately supervised by the faculty. Lo knew it too, because her eyes narrowed and her chin tilted down. She was ready for a fight. Excellent. So was Lulu.

"Why'd you do it anyways?" Emma asked, in a soft tone that still managed to carry across the table. She didn't have to speak loudly to be heard, somehow, even among this group.

Of all the friends, Emma Walker blended into the background the best. She took easy refuge in the shade of their personalities. Her romanticism—fed on a diet of fairy tales, Disney princesses, and Molly Ringwald movies— was of the incurable variety. And she stayed in the safe, comfortable groups of girls she had always known whenever they went out. Or stayed in. Or just sat in the dining hall for lunch. She was a creature of careful habits. She composed perfect bites of her lunch, cutting her cafeteria pizza into neat little squares.

"He was there. I was there. It just happened, you know?" Lulu shrugged. A safe truth.

Lo laughed, dry and full of pretention. "God. Lulu. You mess."

Lulu glared. "Better than constantly taking someone's sloppy seconds."

Audrey gasped. Emma held her breath.

Lo, however, laughed again. "Touché. At least I'm not the one who got grounded for falling into a pool."

"I did not fall," said Lulu. "I pushed a boy in. He looked like he was drowning. I *tried* to save his life. I definitely did not fall into a pool."

"You still fell for his wily ways," said Lo.

"Like you could tell the difference between a fake drowning and a real drowning." Lulu rolled her eyes.

"Maybe." Lo turned away from Lulu's incredulity. "And anyway, you getting grounded is the worst because there's a battle of the bands this week. It's gonna be epic, y'all."

Lo leaned back magnificently, but as the front legs of her chair kicked out, the back of it ran into an unsuspecting freshman girl. Lo, of course, landed back on her feet. The poor girl, however, toppled over with a near-comedic finesse—arms akimbo, legs sprawled, the remains of a cornbread muffin flying. For a moment the area around the table went as silent as any room Lulu walked into the day after she'd had a particularly notable hook-up.

Emma was the first to reach out. "Are you okay?"

"It's fine." The girl, still plopped on the floor, began by straightening out her bangs. "I'm fine."

"Of course it's not fine. Lo's an absolute brute." Emma tsked.

"Hey!" cried Lo, but she was ignored.

"She legit has no sense of where she is in space at all. Ever." Emma reached her hand out farther.

This time the girl took it. She got to her feet and straightened her skirt. The corners of her mouth had turned up into a hint of a smile. "Thanks."

Emma smiled, bright and earnest. "Anytime."

The girl walked off, meeting back up with a friend a few paces away. She exited the dining hall, turning around once to meet Emma's eye.

Lo tapped her finger against the table. "As I was saying. Before I was interrupted."

Lulu and Audrey shared a quick glance. Lo could be so self-important.

"Nina Holmes told me about the Battle of the Bands." Lo's eyes, gleaming with possibility, danced around the table. When they stopped finally, they rested on Lulu. "And you're going to miss it."

Lulu refused to be cowed by this. "Didn't Nina puke all over the lawn on Saturday?"

"Yes, but this was before the puking, not after." Lo slurped her Coke.

Lulu did her best to stand her ground. "Whatever."

Lo didn't break her focus. This expression—where her eyebrows pushed together and her mouth found a firm line and her eyes locked onto their target—was why so many people would follow Lo anywhere. Or run from her when they saw her headed their way. "Figure it out, Lulu. We're all going on Thursday. You're clever enough to get out of anything. Including a grounding."

Of that, however, Lulu was not so sure.

———

If asked, Lulu would have admitted that the purpose of being grounded was inconvenience. Trouble now meant a loss of privilege later. It was, in many ways, the perfect punishment for the sins of instant gratification. But this particular grounding had come at an especially inconvenient time. And the way out was murky.

The youngest of three, Lulu often went to her father to get her out of trouble. But Ahmed Saad didn't know she was grounded this time. This was partly because Lulu's mother, Aimee Saad, was quick to punish but slow to tell. The effects of her own upbringing, no doubt. This was also because Aimee had learned the hard way about Lulu's persistent commitment to reversing her punishments.

Desperate and wishful of a distraction, Lulu swiveled back and forth in the desk chair in her room. But Lulu should have been more careful. Once, her grandmother had told her wishes were the province of the jinn and, like gifts from faeries, were not to be trusted or taken so lightly.

"Lulu, phone," said her mother, waltzing into Lulu's room like she owned the place. Considering her name was on the mortgage, she did own the place, but it didn't soothe Lulu's injured pride to think about it that way. Her mother laughed, as though the voice on the other end had told a joke, then held out the phone for Lulu to take. Lulu noticed a newspaper in her mother's other hand.

"Who is it?"

"It's your grandmother."

"Which grandmother?" It was a petty question, and Lulu knew better than to ask it. But a pit had fallen into Lulu's stomach. She took back her wish for a distraction. She tried to look busy with a textbook.

The only reason Aimee's people had tolerated her unorthodox marriage to a Muslim and an immigrant was the stern-fisted will of Lulu's other grandmother. Mimi the Matriarch—a Louisiana spitfire if there ever was one—had held her family together, if not always with love then with purpose and determination. It hadn't quite been kindness. She had refused to acknowledge arguments from either side. To Mimi, family was family. She'd hear of nothing else but mutual toleration. The Saads would be invited and they would stay silent and behave while the Natales fed them a feast of seven fishes and hundreds of insults. When Mimi had died, Aimee's people had stopped inviting the Saads for Christmas. When Mimi had died, Aimee took off the gold cross she'd worn at her neck since first communion. She had never put it back on again. When Mimi had died, the rest of the Saads knew not to bring her up unless Aimee did so first.

Lulu's mama stared. The laughter was gone now. "The only grandmother you've got left, darlin'. Your *bibi*."

Lulu swallowed the guilt collecting in her throat. Her mother didn't even speak Arabic, and yet Bibi was always making Lulu's mother laugh. There was a strange camaraderie there she didn't understand. Lulu took the phone. Her mother turned and left the room, leaving the door open as she went.

"Hello?"

"Halloo," bounced back a thickly accented echo into Lulu's ear.

"Hello?" There were times when Lulu could only be relieved at having no obligation to say anything other than hello and good-bye to her father's mother. She'd already lived through the dark side of a family that perfectly understands one another. Other times, like today, regret that she couldn't communicate a full sentence with her grandmother overshadowed all of Lulu's thoughts.

"Halloo!" Static traipsed across her grandmother's answer.

Lulu cradled the phone to her ear with her shoulder. She grabbed a pen and began doodling across her arm. "Bibi?"

"Hallo, Bibi!" the crackled voice responded, distorted across continents and wires until it ought to have been unintelligible.

Lulu thought a good deal on the repetitive nature of her phone conversations with her family overseas. She'd narrowed down the potential culprit to any of these: poor transmission, linguistic barrier, or a cultural difference in handling the telephone. Maybe all three. A large piece of her needed a definitive answer. But, truth be told, she'd never asked anyone else if their experience was the same. Anytime she got close, the question sounded so foolish. So she'd stayed silent, waiting to see if she could figure it out on her own.

"How are you?" Lulu swirled and whirled the pen across her arm, leaving a trail of ink in its wake.

"*Kefiq ya, habibti?*" Love and care radiated out of her grandmother's voice. She had a warm, gruff cadence.

The pen caught on Lulu's forearm, skidding across her skin. Lulu set it down. *"Zienna, Bibi. Wa anti?"*

The Arabic phrases that Lulu knew mostly related to food, and she could, in fact, only speak a little Arabic. Every once in a while, Lulu remembered how to tell someone if she was hot or cold. She knew a choice selection of curse words picked up from the other Arab American boys who were, to her, something between friends and cousins. Her brothers had taught her how to say "eat shit." And there was one word that she only heard in whispers; it came with knowing looks and expectant glances. Lulu pretended never to know it, not even to hear it. She buried that word in a place she hoped she could never find again.

This knowledge base, apparently, had been enough to satisfy a grandmother who lived thousands of miles away. Lulu hadn't stopped waiting for the day when it wouldn't be enough. Lulu could overhear her grandmother repeating Lulu's words to the room at large. She wondered how many relatives surrounded the phone call. Lulu's chest went tight.

"Alhamdulillah, hayati," crackled Bibi through the receiver. *"Hathe amtich, hathe amtich."*

The phone was passed around, relative to relative—aunt to cousin to uncle to cousin again. Each time Lulu had a nearly identical conversation as the one before, with each phrase and each question repeated like a glitch in a video game. Depending on the new speaker, the language of the conversation jolted from English to Arabic and back again, with Lulu attempting her best Arabic, while her relatives with an actual mastery of English shamed her.

"Hallo, Lulu!" A small, breathless voice had taken charge of the phone. This was Lulu's baby cousin, Rana.

The Saads didn't have many girls. They were rare to the family, and therefore all the more precious. There wasn't a girl born into the Saads or one of its tributaries that did not take advantage of this. That's why Rana could grab the phone right out from the hands of her older cousin.

"Hello, Rana," said Lulu.

Rana's breath was still catching up with her words. She must have run across the room to take the phone. "I'm going to e-mail you."

Lulu laughed. "All right."

"Good!" said Rana. "Oh, here is Bibi."

Lulu barely had time to recover from the tempo switch.

"Halloo, Bibi!" Lulu's grandmother was back on the line.

Thank goodness Rana had warned her before handing over the phone. Truthfully, Lulu couldn't always tell when the phone switched over between speakers. In her mind they were all disembodied voices. Not that she hadn't been shown pictures of her relatives, but the voices were separate from the faces, which in turn were entirely separate from the family histories related by her father.

The only person who stuck out in her memory as complete—a face, a voice, and a story—was her grandfather, and that was only because she had the glimmer of a memory of having met him as a tiny child. The story of that was a famous one, told so often that Lulu was sick of hearing it.

"*Ahibich, 'azizati. Ahibich,*" said Bibi.

"Miss you," said Lulu. "Love you."

"*Ma'asalama 'oyooni. Ma'asalama.*"

"*Alaykum Masalam, Bibi.*" Lulu heard the phone click shut. That was it. Lulu set the phone down next to her in the chair. But that wasn't enough. She took it and buried it under her leg. The plastic bit into her thighs. Uncomfortable, yes, but at least she didn't have to keep looking at the phone. It was as though the device had grown eyes and was watching her. She didn't want to be seen.

Not a moment later, her mother popped back into the room.

"Your father left this for you." She handed Lulu a folded section of newspaper. From the stilted, direct movements she used, she still hadn't forgiven Lulu for bringing up Mimi. She would, eventually. She always did. "He set it by your place at breakfast, but you left it."

Lulu stared blankly for a moment. Recognition dawned as the headline came into focus. Lulu could only see the words *Iraqi* and *art collection*, but they were enough. Lulu reached out to take the paper. "Thanks."

Her mother leaned down. Lulu roughly kissed her on the cheek—more velocity than affection. Then Lulu bent her head over the newspaper. The door to her bedroom clicked shut.

Once alone, Lulu set down the article. It could wait. She placed it atop a stack of similar articles, all patiently awaiting her attention. She told herself she'd get to them. And she meant it, too. She looked out the window. The sun would set soon. Time would keep going on with or without her.

Lulu reached for the phone under her leg. She had a quick call to make.

———

Liza Pazornik—a senior girl of the ambitious variety—had not gotten to be editor in chief of *The Sealy Examiner* by sitting on her laurels or by being gullible. But she played into Lulu's plan beautifully, if unwittingly.

Having just lost the cell-phone connection with Lulu—a staff member— giving her a good story tip, Liza called back at the landline number listed in her copy of the school directory. Lulu's dad picked up. Liza informed him she had a possible newspaper assignment for Lulu. He passed the call along gladly.

Lulu took the call from Liza with as much surprise as she could muster. She suppressed the triumph that ran through her. She walked out of the room as she normally would have, had the call been truly unexpected.

She'd have to play this as cool as humanly possible.

24

A couple of minutes later, Lulu reentered the living room. She held her hand over the phone mic. She cleared her throat, a notch louder than necessary but not suspiciously so. Her mom looked up. Her father kept his eyes on his opened newspaper.

"Baba? I've got a newspaper assignment," Lulu said. "A last-minute one."

Ahmed turned the page with a crinkling swish. He must have been one of the only people left who read a real newspaper anymore. Said he only liked the news if it got his hands dirty. Aimee froze—she had been working through a stack of papers from where she sat on the couch.

Lulu didn't flinch. "I need to cover this Battle of the Bands tonight."

Aimee's face went rigid.

"For school," Lulu emphasized, trying not to gulp. She kept a tight hold of the phone. Yes, she had called Liza with the hot tip for the story about covering the Battle of the Bands. And yes, she had purposefully hung up so that Liza would have to call the house line rather than Lulu's cell. But those weren't details her parents needed to know.

Ahmed turned a page in his newspaper. Without looking up, he said, "Of course, habibti."

Aimee coughed. "Honey, do you really think she should go out on a school night?"

Ahmed put down his paper and appraised his youngest. "Where do you need to go?"

He had no softness to his voice. His tones were all consonants, clipped and hit hard. To his credit, he'd grown up speaking a dialect of Arabic that necessitated the use of such sounds. But the annunciation did not lend itself well to English, not when attempting kindness or sympathy. English, unlike Arabic, was not a poetic language. English had been cobbled together by too many unknown parents, too many unsure users. English lacked the single word that differentiated an attacking lion from one at rest. Nor did English have the capacity to relay the succinct, linguistic separation of a maternal uncle from a paternal one. English was not a thoughtful language. Ahmed was kind, though his English was not.

"Between Montrose and downtown," said Lulu.

As Ahmed looked at Lulu, sweat built up in her armpits. She hailed from a nice enclave inside a much larger city. Sometimes that made getting out a little tricky. She was headed to the less savory edge of the arts district. "I can call Audrey, see if I can take her, so I won't be driving alone," Lulu added. That had been part of her plan all along, but it sounded better if she suggested it as a solution to her father's hesitations rather than as her own particular desire.

"Okay. You'll be back," he said.

"Yes." Lulu preferred to start out in agreement.

"Nine thirty." He nodded once.

"Yes, but, Baba, the band goes on at nine." Lulu tried to keep the wheedling out of her voice.

For a long moment, the only things in the room that moved were Aimee's eyes, which ping-ponged between Lulu and Ahmed.

"All right. Ten thirty," Ahmed said with finality. "And don't forget to take your mobile phone."

Lulu crossed the room, leaning over to give her father an unnecessary squeeze. He accepted it heartily. As Lulu looked back over at her mother, she made sure her smile was wiped clean off her face. If there was one thing Aimee hated, it was one parent overruling the other in front of one of the children.

Of course, Lulu knew this.

That thought caught in the back of Lulu's throat for a moment. She swallowed it. Lulu took her hand off the phone and put it back to her ear. "Liza? I can do it."

Ahmed continued smiling behind his paper, as though he had done a good deed. Aimee gave Lulu a long, hard stare, straightening her work papers into a neat stack on the coffee table. There was an unsettling quietness to the movement. Winding up her mother had yet to pan out as a good idea. Aimee wouldn't forget.

But it was Thursday and Lulu had gotten out of her punishment. She wouldn't let the lingering image of Aimee's promising grimace invade her joy. Instead, Lulu stayed on the phone with Liza as she walked out of the room. After they'd run down the necessary information, Lulu went and grabbed her phone off her mother's desk. She texted only one word to Audrey—*Jailbreak*.

3

Somebody's Yoda

Her shoes riding shotgun, Lulu curled her bare feet around the gas and clutch pedals. Warm, humid air invaded the car through the open windows. She inhaled the sweet, wet air deeply. The back of her thighs were slicked up with sweat against her vinyl seats, but she didn't mind. Lulu loved to drive. She loved the single-purposed focus she had when she sat behind the wheel. So few things in her life gave Lulu that clearheadedness. That driving barefoot was illegal in the state of Texas only heightened the thrill.

Houston itself was not a beautiful city. It was a resilient one. If Austin was the crown jewel of Texas, and San Antonio was its tourist trap, and Dallas was where bankers and stereotypes made dividends, then Houston was the begrudging East Texas swamp that nobody wanted to acknowledge as mattering. But Houston did matter. The kind of swampy city that withstands mosquitoes and floodplains and hurricanes—not unlike New Orleans or Versailles. Except not a quarter so architecturally fine. Not a third so bent on flashing itself for the crowd. No. Houston was built on oil and energy, on rolling up your sleeves and doing the kind of work that was necessary, if not actually good.

Lulu honked twice as she pulled up to Audrey's driveway, taunting Mrs. Bachmann with her conspicuous display of freedom. She only did it half on purpose.

"What's up, slut?" Audrey slid into the car, shoving the shoes onto the floorboard and turning up the radio all in one fluid move.

Lulu cringed, but said nothing. Audrey was already talking a mile a minute. Thanks to the volume of the radio, Lulu could barely hear Audrey over the sound of the bass thumping.

"I thought you were going to be grounded until Halloween at least," Audrey finished.

"No thanks to you." Lulu waited a moment, then ticked the volume back down a few notches.

"Next time, if I'm the one taking a drunken swim, feel free to lay the blame at my doorstep," said Audrey.

"It wasn't a swim!"

"Of course not." Audrey turned the radio back up.

All things considered, she was taking Lulu's accusations startlingly well. Lulu turned the volume back down. "You're in a bubbly mood."

"I swiped my sister's ID on my way out. Sucker." Audrey smiled an irreverent smile. There was a clear, secretive pleasure written across her face.

"I mean, really, who's going to believe we're twenty-two? Or that you look anything like your sister? You two barely pass as cousins." Lulu went on unnecessarily. "No one, that's who. Besides, they're letting sixteen and up in for this gig."

"It's a matter of principle." Audrey crossed her arms.

When it came to Audrey and her sister, everything was a matter of principle. Lulu shrugged. What Lulu knew of sisters, apart from Audrey, she had taken from fiction. Lulu suspected that Audrey found her sister to be a Mary Bennet—priggish and pedantic—while Audrey's sister probably thought of Audrey as a Lydia Bennet—thoughtless and selfish. Or maybe they were Amy and Jo March, and this was all about a burned manuscript and an heiress of a boy. Lulu found the idea of sisters fascinating, but her only vocabulary for the relationship was borrowed. She did the best she could to follow, given the circumstance.

Audrey turned the radio back up. Lulu flicked Audrey's fingers, like swatting a fly, and turned the radio down. Audrey sighed. After waiting a beat, she raised the radio volume in one grand, sweeping effort. "So where to first?"

"Emma's, then Lo's." Lulu punched off the radio with her knuckles. Her ears vibrated from the aftermath of that decibel level. "Then I'm thinking tacos. We haven't had tacos in forever."

"Two weeks. Yes, that was *forever* ago." Audrey used as much condescension as she had in her. And Audrey had been bred to hold plenty of condescension.

Lulu laughed. Her freshly won freedom made her gracious enough not to hold a grudge. She had taken the blame for the night of the pool incident, getting Audrey off nearly scot-free. But Audrey would do the same for her, even if Audrey knew the world to be a certain way. A way that didn't hold water, but still.

Lulu made an unprotected left turn, and Audrey swooped in to turn the radio back up. Lulu paid these antics no further attention. They constantly danced around like this, attracting each other with what ought to repel. The two girls chatted and laughed until they became four. How any of them could hear one another, over each other, or the music, or the wind coming into the car as it sped along, was anyone's guess.

———

The venue for the Battle of the Bands was going for a kind of cool, industrial loft look. It was on the edge of downtown without being in downtown. It was near the gay bars without being one itself. Almost in the arts district, but not quite. It was hopelessly in between, desperately on the edge. And tonight it was too full of a hopeful, underage crowd to achieve its most basic, casually cool aim. The bathroom echoed this attempt at a hipster vibe—concrete littered with fliers. Plus a faint odor of vomit that would never wash out.

Lulu rubbed her shoulder. She had been dragged—literally—into the bathroom by Lo. A sophomore girl at one of the sinks was attempting to wash off the UNDERAGE that had been inked across her hand. After a brief tussle with the venue-provided soap, the girl finally gave up hope and shuffled out of the bathroom, defeated. Lo watched her sad exit with narrowed eyes.

Lo muttered her disdain under her breath. A stall opened up, and Lo pulled Lulu in with her. She whipped out a travel-sized bottle of makeup remover and grabbed for Lulu's hand. But Lulu yanked away.

"Dude, no." Lulu's voice was stern, probably louder than it needed to be. "My mom knows where I am and what I'm doing. She'll be expecting a hand mark."

"That's no fun." Lo ostentatiously pushed her hands through her hair, which still looked perfectly tousled despite the humidity. As always.

Lulu's own hair looked like it had gotten into a tussle with a badly behaved house cat. She didn't know how Lo did it. Nobody did.

Lo took the bottle of makeup remover and tilted it toward a wad of toilet paper, which she in turn put to work against her own hand. The ink across her hand dissolved quickly. There wasn't a single red mark left over to show visible evidence of scrubbing. Lo was a pro.

"I can't believe she tried scrubbing. With the soap!" Lo's voice was a harsh whisper. "And like right at the sinks, in front of everyone. You can see that sink from outside. What an amateur!"

Lulu shrugged. "You could adopt her. Teach her your ways."

"I don't babysit." Lo wiped the residue of the makeup remover with an individually packaged face wipe. Lo was also thorough.

"It wouldn't be babysitting. You'd, like, be her Yoda. Everyone wants to be somebody's Yoda," said Lulu.

Lo gave Lulu a scathing look. Lulu knew where this was going.

Lo threw the makeup wipe away in the tampon bin. "No. Everyone does *not*. You're such a freak."

"Seriously?" Lulu could have sidestepped the ages-old argument, but Lulu didn't particularly enjoy avoiding a fight with Lo. They were verbal sparring partners. They learned from each other, honed their individual arguments so that when they faced real opponents, these others didn't stand a chance.

Lo squatted down to pee. "Seriously. Why the hell would you be Yoda, when you could be Boba Fett. The man survives the sarlacc's pit. He's got the, like, sickest helmet, ever. He's a bounty hunter; he's definitely in it for the money. And he doesn't waffle like Han does."

"Waffle?" Lulu's voice echoed well beyond their stall. "You call turning to the aid of the rebellion, being the sole reason Luke can safely blow up the Death Star, *waffling*?"

Lo pulled her skirt back down and flushed. "Boba Fett knows what he wants. And he gets it. Including Han."

"Who he could've killed, but didn't. What do you say to that?" Lulu put her hand on her hip, partially blocking the stall door.

"That says, that even when a fellow runner turns, Boba still has a code he lives by. That's what I say to that." Lo sniffed, fully satisfied that her point had ground this argument to a halt.

"Anyways." Lo tapped her upper thigh, a metallic sound tingling slightly.

"Find me if you need me. I always bring backup." She pushed Lulu out of the way to open the stall to the door, majestically exiting as though everyone's eyes would be on her. And to further Lulu's annoyance, they all were.

Squeezing out of the bathroom and into a hallway, Lulu shuffled by a girl who was crouched on the floor, crying. The girl's makeup drizzled down her face, and Lulu couldn't believe someone was already having such a horrible time. She looked a little bit like Nina Holmes. But Lo yanked Lulu onward before she could be sure. Lulu yanked back. Lo gave up then, abandoning Lulu to the crowd. Lulu passed a couple kissing. The two boys were of a similar height, similarly sized shoulders—one fair and the other dark. They made a cute couple. Then again, Lulu was disposed to like mixed couples, being the product of one herself.

Alone, Lulu pressed forward into the open floor space. She scanned the darkened dance floor, none of her friends in sight. As she turned, she saw Dane Anderson holding two open beers and smiling with delightful malice.

"Look who it is." He flexed slightly as she eyed the drinks. "I didn't know they let you out unsupervised on school nights."

"I didn't know they let seventeen-year-olds drink in clubs." Lulu gave a mean, flirtatious grin. Mostly to keep from staring at his now-taut arms.

"Fun fact: they do let twenty-two-year-olds drink." A smug satisfaction coated Dane's face. He reached out and draped his arm around her.

"God, Anderson, you're going to spill beer on me. What?" His name rolled off her tongue like one of her favorite swear words. Lulu crossed her arms in defiance. She made no move to shove him off, as that seemed to be the object of his taunting. Instead she stood there, feeling the pressure of his frame against her body.

"What do you mean, what?" He slung her closer, sloshing some beer onto her shoulder.

"I mean *what*."

A few people glanced over now. Lulu couldn't recognize them in the obscured lighting, but she felt watched. Lulu ran her hands through her hair, attempting to smooth any flyaways.

"Do you?" Dane had a grin that rewrote reality.

Lulu leaned in, like she was only going to smell the fresh-baked pie but not eat it. There it was—that gin and peppermint again. She caught the faint scent of smoke. "I do."

"Damn, Lulu. You look good tonight."

Lulu stiffened. She forced herself to lean away from the almost certain peril. "Do I? I hadn't noticed. Your observations are necessary and appreciated as always."

"Christ, are you on your period?" Dane rolled his eyes, and his beautiful face contorted into an ironic sneer. In a just world, he would have looked uglier.

Lulu remembered afresh why she had put up a wall of defense between herself and this boy, all those years ago. Her body often forgot, but her mind wouldn't. "No, are you?"

Dane clutched Lulu closer, crunching Lulu's shoulders as more beer dribbled down her arm. "Great. Then we're good to go."

Lulu grabbed his shirt where the lapels of his coat ought to have been. She could feel his chest underneath her knuckles. She watched the confusion cross his face, which nearly brought on a smile that would have spoiled the entire affectation. For added drama, she put a swooning hand across her forehead. "How did you know? I can't live without you. Take me now."

She bowed backward, across his still-outstretched arm, in a posed faint. For a moment, Dane Anderson stayed impossibly still.

Lulu popped upright, laughing. "Get over yourself, Anderson."

"You think you're so clever, don't you? I'll bet you think you're special, huh?" There was an edge to Dane's voice. A tension Lulu couldn't quite read. His eyes narrowed, the unnatural lighting catching his too-long lashes in their blue tint. His looks and his power would ruin him, if they hadn't already.

He was a boy made to be conquered, maybe even saved. But not by Lulu. She was neither a knight nor a Nightingale. She was a girl made to be selfish. She would have her own adventures. "Don't worry, I don't think I'm special. But I'm not stupid, either. I know what you try."

"Honey," he said, "if I'd ever tried with you—"

Lulu placed the tips of her fingers across his pouting lips, staying their movement. So soft, and yet so pliant to such meanness. She removed her hand quickly. "Do yourself a favor. Don't finish that."

Lulu made a move to swing out from under his arm, but he leaned in close to whisper into her ear, blocking her face from view. "Oh, Lulu. Innocent little Lulu. I don't need to finish it. I can tell. You've got the imagination to fill it in perfectly." He touched her temples.

Lulu stood so still she thought her pulse paused along with her. "You're a douche, Dane." She pushed out from under him, but she needn't have. He released her immediately, making Lulu wonder if he'd been holding on all that tightly to begin with.

———

Emma stood close to the stage, like this was a garden party and she could reserve a nice seat for herself. Emma was an inherently endearing sort. She and Lulu had been friends since freshman year, but they'd known each other since they were eleven. It had taken Emma three years to be pulled into Lulu's orbit. And even then it was only a mutual newspaper assignment where Emma had been the photographer. That they were an odd pair of friends made their bond inevitable, like a milkshake with french fries.

35

Emma tilted her head as Lulu approached. "Was Dane bothering you?"

Lulu snorted. "Man, you are such a shutterbug. You miss nothing, do you?"

Emma touched the camera around her neck as though to double-check she still had it. She had agreed to take photos for the article Lulu was now writing. "That's not an answer."

"Don't worry about it," said Lulu. "I can handle Anderson."

Emma frowned. "Nobody should have to handle him."

"True," said Lulu. "But forget him. Because you, oh wondrous photographer and friend of mine, you staked out a fantastic spot."

"Thanks!" Emma's responding smile beamed with pride. Emma didn't crave approval, but she thrived under its care.

"But you do know the stage is that way." Lulu pointed behind them. She waited to see what Emma would do next.

"Obviously." Emma shrugged with such a forced nonchalance that Lulu had to swallow her laugh in a cough.

"Whatcha been looking at?" Lulu batted her eyelashes and offered a charming grin.

"Nothing," said Emma, far too quickly. She was hiding something.

Lulu looked around, trying to find the source of Emma's interest. "Not the stage, that's for sure."

"No." Emma squirmed slightly—clearly desperate not to be caught. "But why would I look at the stage when there's nothing on it?"

Lulu scanned the crowd and stroked her chin with her thumb, like a pensive villain. "Hmmmm, let's see. I spy, with my little eye…"

"No! Don't!" Emma yanked Lulu's hand off her chin. The camera jostled.

Lulu couldn't contain the laugh she'd trapped in the back of her throat any longer. "Please, let me have a little fun."

"Is that all you care about?" A worried edge crept into Emma's voice.

"What's wrong with having fun?"

Emma paused, her mouth twisting to the side of her face. That was how Emma planned her carefully chosen words.

If that wasn't a case in point, Lulu didn't know what was. "See, you can't think of anything, can you?"

"Please," said Emma in her quiet, resonant way.

Lulu opened her mouth, but the next words were not her own.

"Lo. Lo Campo. Stop this instant. You are all of fifteen seconds away from dislocating my shoulder." Audrey skidded to a halt beside Lo. She nearly tackled Lulu in the process.

Lo let go of Audrey. She held a drink in her hand, and her eyes flitted between Lulu and Emma, but Lo said nothing on the subject.

Audrey rubbed her shoulder, her jaw set into a hard line. "Much appreciated."

Lo rolled her eyes. "Please. You're such a baby."

"You *are* stronger than you think," said Emma, in a calming tone.

"True," said Lo. "There's Nina; I'm going to say hi."

And Lo was off again, away from the stage. Lulu turned her head to follow Lo's movements, and she discovered Emma's direct line of vision. The plot thickened. Brian Connor stood beside a fresh-faced freshman girl, whose name Lulu couldn't quite remember but who always wore her hair with a thick fringe. The one who'd fallen by their table that week, thanks to Lo's chair tilting.

The only two things anyone needed to know about Brian Connor were that he liked fast cars and smoking weed. No wonder straitlaced Emma was embarrassed. Plus she knew Lulu had recently made out with him in a hall closet, and Emma was an entirely honorable sort. He was an unusual target for Emma's lust, but maybe she liked boys who talked a big talk about engines. It's not like Lulu had been able to pin down Emma's interests definitively before.

Then Lulu was granted the pleasure of spying Dane Anderson as he pulled that heavily fringed freshman away from Brian. Anderson employed his signature move, a casual low-slung arm around the waist. The poor girl had no idea what was about to hit on her.

"Why are you frowning?" asked Audrey, interrupting Lulu's thoughts.

"I'm not frowning." Lulu rearranged her face into a smile.

"Yes, you were. You were frowning. And looking that way. Y'all both were, actually." Audrey pointed her arm toward Dane in a manner so unsubtle, it was practically a wave.

Emma turned abruptly, her eyes wide.

Lulu cringed. She had come to expect a lack of discretion from her friend when alcohol was involved, but every once in a while, Audrey could still surprise her. "You maniac. You nearly took Emma's eye out with your arm."

Emma shook her head. "It's all right. I'm all right."

Lulu put her hand on her hip. "No, it's not. Audrey Louise, aren't you going to apologize?"

Audrey, however, had stopped in her spot, staring. She sighed a great sigh. "Scumbag Luke. He's here."

"No," said Emma at the same time Lulu said, "Where?"

"There." Audrey pointed, with no more diplomacy than before. But Lulu wasn't fazed in the slightest by the rudeness this time. Nor was Emma. They both stared openly.

Lulu turned to watch Lo, who had found Nina in the crowd. Nina wasn't by her boyfriend, and Lulu had a sense of why she had been crying in the bathroom hallway earlier. Every moment or two, Lo's eyes casually flickered over to where Luke stood. Lo was slowly herding her group toward him.

"Shit," said Lulu.

"Agreed," said Emma.

There were only three things that anyone needed to know about Luke Westin. The first was that he had the kind of hair a girl would want to run her fingers through—soft and thick and perfect. The second was that he played shortstop for the public school down the road. And the third was that he was the kind of guy who confirmed every stereotype about Texas that Lulu had spent her whole life struggling against. For the first two, Lulu could understand how Lo might find him interesting. But for the last one, Lulu went over and grabbed Lo's arm in a vise grip and pulled her aside.

"Lulu. What are you doing." Lo had a calmness about her, like she was trying to stop Lulu from behaving stupidly, rather than the other way around.

"Come on," said Lulu. "Don't go over there."

"Over where?" asked Lo.

"Don't play dumb with me." Lulu nodded toward Luke.

Lo leaned into Lulu's space, speaking so only they two could hear. "I'm only gonna say this once. I don't tell you whose mouth to stick your tongue in. So don't tell me what to do with mine."

"But he's so—"

"I know." There was a certainty in Lo's eyes that Lulu couldn't ignore, no matter how much she might have wanted to do so.

No matter how many times Lulu reminded her friend that Luke had a girlfriend. That Luke was the worst sort of boy. That he was Scumbag Luke. It never sank in. Or, worse, it did sink in and Lo simply didn't care. Lo was drawn to the darkness like a bad after-school special.

"Doesn't it bother you?" Lulu could have been referring to anything—the awful things that came out of Luke's mouth, that he dated while dating, that he rarely acknowledged Lo in public unless he was drunk. Lo shrugged as her answer.

"I mean, you don't have to prove anything," said Lulu.

"Maybe I do have to. Nobody else is going to climb the social pecking order among the four of us. You don't. Emma won't. Audrey can't," said Lo. "Or, maybe I get my kicks knowing Luke doesn't want to want me but I can still make him anyways. I get to watch his hate fight with his lust."

Lulu didn't like it, even if Lo could take care of herself. "I'm not sure which is worse: your cynicism or mine. I could never date someone only to make them want me. I'd rather be alone."

Lulu laughed as Lo raised an eyebrow. "Which is why I make out with them all and wind up abandoned in upstairs closets. It's a romantic life, but somebody's got to live it."

Lo raised her glass. "To the romantic life." She downed the rest of her drink in a gulp and tossed the cup to the floor. A magnificent departure, if ever Lulu had seen one. She catalogued it in her memory as an excellent maneuver of both power and style, though Lulu would cut off all her own hair before she'd admit that to Lo.

Lulu loved to dance. While the beat of the band thrummed in the background, she could be free. And if she could only hear music in her head, she didn't feel afraid of making a fool of herself, either. She wasn't a particularly talented dancer. But neither was she in any way lacking. She loved the thoughtlessness of her body under the sway of a song. The feeling was sensual and ridiculous, frivolous and powerful, and she flourished in such soil.

Emma *would* stand off to the side, overly aware of her body and swaying lightly. Poor Emma. She'd start taking pictures soon to avoid any further obligation to the dance floor. What Audrey lacked in fluidity, she made up for in sheer effort. Lulu loved the energy behind Audrey's stilted labors. Lo was the true dancer. She ought to have been there in their circle to put them all to shame. But Lo wasn't with them right now. She was off with Luke. The other three girls were left to their own devices. Sweat stuck Lulu's shirt to her back and matted down bits of her hair. She lifted her elbows, trying to circulate air under her armpits, but to no avail. She pulled at her shirt, but that only further suctioned fabric to the sweat down her spine.

"Water?" Lulu's voice carried barely beyond a murmur, though she shouted. Audrey shook her head no. Emma, who was now taking photos, also declined. Alone, Lulu pushed her way through the undulating crowd. She approached the bar and received a skeptical appraisal by the bartender.

Lulu put her to rights quickly. "Water, please!"

The bartender nodded. Lulu bobbed her head and thrummed her fingers against the bar as she waited. Lulu looked over. She saw a lanky, boyish figure across the way. And while Lulu often appreciated a tall, lean body and a head of tousled hair, there was something else about this one in particular. Something familiar. Something, somehow *known*. She couldn't quite place why. Then the boy turned and met her gaze.

Hell and damnation.

The last time she had seen him, she had been screaming and drenched in pool water. It was James the Falsifier. The instinct to turn and run flooded through Lulu, but she wasn't a coward. She'd face him again. Even if she didn't want to. Besides, it wasn't like she had been honestly staring at him. Not *staring*, staring. Not that she was going to explain that to him. But he was moving rapidly toward her, and explanations were becoming unavoidable. Lulu looked at the bar, hoping her drink was ready. But the bartender was nowhere in sight. She'd been forgotten. She'd have to handle this all on her own.

"If it isn't Cinderella." James smiled as he reached her.

"Cinderella's a blonde. She also lost a shoe. I would never lose a shoe."

Lulu couldn't let him go unpunished. "And besides, Ariel was the one who saved a drowning fool."

James's teeth looked stuck in their too-bright smile. "I meant. I mean. You ran off. At midnight. It was a metaphor."

"It was eleven."

James's smile fell. He stared, with his big, brown eyes. Doe-like. And before she could regret it, or even think the better of it, Lulu said, "I'm writing an article."

"About youth culture?" He smiled again, like he'd told a funny joke. Like he was someone who didn't give up hope. James reminded Lulu of things best forgotten, of the cost of survival and the price of high living.

Lulu had paid the price by trading in her tongue. Lo had cut out her heart. Audrey, who had been born into this world, had no ability to see beyond its borders. Emma alone seemed untouched by any kind of deal with the devil. But Lulu didn't believe that to be true. Nobody could go without paying the price. The prize of being accepted into the fold of the one-day rich and powerful was too tempting, too all-encompassing. Emma's bargain must have been the worst of all to stay so neat and invisible.

"No. I'm reviewing the band."

The bartender caught Lulu's gaze then, perhaps sensing the tension radiating off her body. She nodded, like that was reassuring. Lulu sighed, though the noise was lost in the ambient sounds of the venue.

"How do you like the band?" James asked.

It was a taunt. Lulu had been taunted well enough by her older brothers to know one immediately. She didn't need to prove she knew the band's name. This was her scene, and not his. "I've always liked *the band*."

"Why'd you bother to come, then?" He tilted his head, and a bit of his hair sagged into his eye. He pushed the unruly lock back. "I mean, if you'll like the show regardless, why review it?"

With that, Lulu found her venom. "Because I'm good at my job. That's why they gave me the assignment. I'm not sure where you got the idea I'm rainbows and sunshine but I'm not some magical fucking princess who can't form a serious opinion just because I'm having a good time. I know the difference between fun and good."

The air between them shifted. The lingering tension that had been there was now sharper, a live wire. The fin in the water belonged to a circling shark.

"What's your favorite band?" he asked, crossing his arms over his chest.

Lulu barked a laugh. "Of course you'd ask that."

James narrowed his eyes. Good. Then she wouldn't be distracted by them and their naturally helpless expression. Though they crinkled rather adorably in their new position.

"Please, then, Oh Magnificent Queen of the Universe, tell me what else I should have asked?"

Lulu nodded, like she took his epithet at face value. "You could ask what I'm listening to right now. I mean, it's still obviously a line to be judgmental, but at least it doesn't require the same kind of ponderous pretension of picking a favorite."

Lulu watched, waiting. She enjoyed testing people's mettle. It gave her a lay of the land. Not that she wanted to survey James's land. At all. Not even a little bit. James's face fell into that trapped expression she'd seen however many nights ago by the pool, when he couldn't unstick the lawn chair.

"Are you always this aggressive?"

"Is asshole your default setting?"

"What? No," James said, his voice considerably more quiet.

Lulu read his lips more than she heard the words. "No? Because, honestly, it seems that way."

He opened his mouth. Lulu raised her eyebrows, challenging. She expected a frown. Instead, he smiled and Lulu mistrusted herself, watching his mouth move like that.

"You're right." And with a light shrug, he made his exit. "See you around. Maybe."

Lulu let out a high-pitched grunt followed by a stomp, which only served to alarm the bartender. The bartender, finally having gotten all the other drink orders together, tossed Lulu a bottle of water. Lulu paid and stalked away, back to her friends in the crowd. How dare James take the last word. How dare he. Lulu joined her friends in the crowd again, but she could not muster her earlier enthusiasm. The poor performing bands would suffer the price in her review.

And when Lulu got home, she had more good news delivered to her.

"We're going to the Alkati house this weekend, habibti," said Ahmed, still sitting in his same chair, but now reading a book instead of a newspaper.

"Why?" asked Lulu.

Ahmed looked up. "Ramadan is Sunday."

Lulu closed her eyes. "Wonderful." She trudged upstairs, desirous of the oblivion of sleep.

4

Tolerable, We Suppose

Try as she might, Lulu couldn't drown out all the noise of her surroundings—a house filled with people and music and food and an endless flow of sugared tea. The Alkatis had a curated kind of home, including a collection of rugs that had been in the family for more than four generations, a Damascene desk set, a large wall of inlaid imported tile, and several old silver coffeepots. Here was a party that had all the necessary fanfare to accompany the observance of Ramadan, which had begun at sundown.

Lulu thought she heard a phrase that sounded suspiciously descriptive of her dress coming from the direction of Auntie Salwa. But it was in Arabic, and just because she'd heard the word *red* and her dress was red, that didn't mean anything. She could be imagining the comment. If she was only imagining the comment, she didn't need to do anything in response. She'd heard the word *tight*, too, but her dress wasn't that tight. Snug, more than anything. She could sit in it comfortably and everything.

Besides, Lulu wouldn't risk drawing notice to herself; she kept her eyes steady, focused on the full plate of food in front of her. Beautiful desserts, piled high and with great care. Grape leaves stuffed with rice and meat. Rice that had been purposefully burned to the bottom of the pan—so it was golden brown and deliciously chewy. Lamb and beef and chicken and fish all accompanied by grilled onions and tomatoes. Hot pink pickled radishes, and some blessed guest had actually brought the crisp, sour plums that made Lulu's mouth water. If nothing else, Lulu would not go hungry on this night. She took a bite of the plum.

Lulu ought to have developed some kind of equanimity around these kinds of parties. But she hadn't. A wave of nausea flashed, then was gone. Social discomfort was not something that came naturally to Lulu. She picked at her blue nail polish—the same shade of blue of the evil eye guarding the door to this house. Lulu suspected she was more likely a thing to be warded off rather than a person worthy of its protection. At least here.

Her mother sat surrounded by women chattering in Arabic. Lulu knew her mother didn't speak a word. The women, too, shared in this knowledge. As they were putting forward their most proper efforts to snub Mrs. Saad, they continued. Spiteful of their intentions, her mother maintained a placid expression on her face. She gave off the air of one who would not care for the conversation, could she understand it. She was the face of Southern equanimity, and underneath lay a frozen tundra of disdain.

This attitude did not help endear her to the other women.

Auntie Salwa was the heart of the group. Their ringleader and their champion. She had two sisters—one recently emigrated and another who had citizenship while her children did not. The Nasser sisters had been famous Baghdadi beauties. Farrah Nasser—the middle one—still clung to the vestiges of her glory days, with her dark hair curled into the large, fashionable waves of her youth. Auntie Farrah was an expensive relic who sat dutifully beside her eldest sister.

Whatever nature had given Salwa Nasser in terms of hair color, Lulu was fairly sure it wasn't the champagne blond she now wore. Auntie Salwa smoothed and waved her hair in the current style. Her looks were an exercise in self-preservation—she had the skin of a woman who had, throughout her life, assiduously avoided the sun. Auntie Salwa was proof that with diligent work, beauty did not have to fade fully.

The third sister was younger than the other two, but her face had the weathering of the eldest. She had emigrated from Iraq a few years prior, and she had only been in the States a few months. Her English was as stilted as Lulu could ever hope her own Arabic to be. She wore a hijab and jet black kohl. It was a fierce kind of makeup that Lulu often emulated and admired, though she had trouble remembering the third sister's name. She had a quiet, steady presence, much like Emma. The third sister sat four seats away from Auntie Salwa, her expression thoughtful.

Iraqi women did not change their surnames at marriage. So they were the Nasser Sisters—through war and marriage, through immigration and resettlement—and they belonged to one another as much as they belonged to anyone. And Aimee Saad, who could win many a courtroom battle, would not let them get the best of her.

Lulu picked at her nails again, accidentally flinging a peeling of polish across the dark wood of the table. She looked up; no one had noticed. She didn't know whether to be disappointed or relieved. Still, she kept her face like a death mask, taking a cue from her mother and refusing to let slip her personal turmoil.

"Lulu!" a voice shrieked.

Lulu looked up. Dina Alkati had positioned herself beside Lulu's chair—her arms wide open. Lulu leaped up immediately, embracing her as the unlikely white knight she was. But the movement drew attention from the rest of the table. Dina's mother stared Lulu down with hawkish eyes, not unlike her French teacher, Madame Perault. Auntie Salwa—Dina's paternal aunt by marriage—offered a tight smile.

Lulu couldn't mistake their meaning. She was an intruder in their midst and only half of what was considered respectable. Lulu ought to have been glad of any toleration at all, a magnanimity which her mother clearly did not receive. But Lulu could never be grateful for hardly restrained resentment. Lulu bared her teeth at them in response—a pretty smile that would not touch her eyes. They returned the expression, their eyes as alert as her own.

"Dina!" Lulu's voice went overly bright, matching Dina's tone, as though they were competing for the most sincerely executed deceit. And maybe they were.

"How are you?" Dina asked.

Lulu marveled at the way Dina could draw out her *r*'s so they conveyed such false feeling. Lulu didn't only dismiss Dina's sincerity; she dismissed Dina on the whole. Yet Lulu was awed by that girl's ability to fake emotion so painstakingly. Lulu, herself incapable of doing anything halfway, couldn't help but admire Dina's level of commitment. Even if Lulu did have visions of throttling her by the beautiful gold chain hanging around Dina's neck.

"So good. How are *you*?" Lulu raised her eyebrows, a knowing smirk playing across her face.

"So good. My cousin is engaged! To Ali Hassan—his family owns that large building downtown, you know. He told me he's going to get her a Jag as a wedding present, instead of jewelry. Alhamdulillah, we're so happy. You remember Tanya, don't you? Oh my gosh, I *love* your shoes." Dina pulled Lulu along to the upstairs hallway where the rest of her generation had congregated.

"*Mashallah!*" Lulu wrapped her arm around Dina's waist, not unlike the first slithering moves of a python. "And thank you! I love yours!"

"Mashallah—look at you! So sweet of you, I'll have to tell her you said so. But your shoes have bows. I super love bows. Don't you love bows?" Dina flicked her beautiful carpet of hair.

Lulu squinted, resenting the movement. Lulu might be vain about her hair but, she was sure, her own vanity was hardly like *that*. Her pride led her to believe her displays were more founded, less showboating. Lulu would have been horrified to learn that her own hair flicks looked exactly the same as Dina's—she performed the move with equal finesse and panache. It was a movement passed down from one Arab girl to another, until it seemed, to outsiders, like an innate trick of these women. That it was a practiced art that they taught one another, both in social warfare and intimate preening, was unfortunately lost on a casual observer.

"I do love bows. That's why I bought these shoes." The feigned bright-ness in Lulu's voice faded. Her plastered-on smile wavered.

Dina laughed, all charm. "Lulu, you're so funny."

Not having meant comedy of any sort, Lulu could only politely hold on to her smile. She caught sight of the conglomeration of those her age, above the landing on the stairs. Eyes flickered toward her. They were segregated by gender as they stood, though no more segregated by gender than the cafeteria at Sealy Hall and definitely less rigidly. Lulu couldn't have said when she'd noticed that people segregated themselves that way. Only that once she had, she couldn't stop seeing it everywhere she went. She didn't dare air these ideas aloud. She already felt enough like the living embodiment of contraband. No need to prove everyone correct.

Lulu scanned the crowd for Tanya, but she wasn't there. A pity, since Lulu enjoyed Tanya's company. Miriam was nowhere to be seen, either. Ali and Thabit and Omar were all listening to a story told by Mustafa. He gave her a smile over their heads. Lulu pretended not to notice it. She was used to pretending not to notice Mustafa.

Mustafa was handsome. Or, more to the point, he was "that handsome

Mustafa." He had a crinkle in his eyes when he flashed his matinee idol smile. With his close-cropped hair, he'd never be mistaken for a boy. No, despite being Lulu's age, he was what mothers and aunties liked to call a "young man." Or, more specifically, "that handsome young man." Even her own mother called him that. They were trying to make a point, those mothers and aunties.

Lulu politely ignored it.

Were he not the sort to be regularly pulled aside for random TSA security checks, Lulu would have called his looks all-American—such was the intensity of his fresh-faced, amiable appearance. Lulu could rarely look at him without receiving the sudden impulse to lick him. She did her best to keep a lid on these feelings.

The expats and immigrants had brought to this country their sense of communal parenting. Lulu couldn't risk an encounter with Mustafa; she wouldn't risk it. She valued her privacy too much to throw it away on a pair of fine eyes and a stunning jawline. People died for her to have such independence. People in her own family. Her father had given up his homeland so she could be free to shut the door to her own room. So that there was a space that was hers and no one else's. Perhaps when she wasn't looking, Mustafa regarded her with her same brand of curious lust. Who knows. Lulu wouldn't be the one to wait around and find out.

"Look, here's Tamra!" said Dina as another girl approached.

This new girl enveloped both Dina and Lulu in a hug and a proper three kisses on the cheek. Tamra Alkati was Dina's paternal cousin and Salwa Nasser's youngest daughter. Between the two girls, Lulu would always pick Dina, who was more of an adoptive, distant cousin and less of an acquaintance. Tamra had little of this familiarity with Lulu and none of the friendliness of her older sister, Tanya.

Also, Tamra was beautiful in the same way Lo was beautiful. In the way, Lulu assumed, her mother, Auntie Salwa, had been beautiful. Except, Lulu didn't know enough of Tamra to humanize her. In a friend, uncommon looks were a mere fact, like dark hair or a loud laugh or an allergy to the local oak trees. In an acquaintance, such looks were insufferable.

"Did you hear my sister is getting married? We're all so excited!" Tamra beamed.

It finally sunk in then—why Tanya wasn't socializing here, upstairs. She'd moved on to adulthood. She was in her midtwenties now, after all. She'd been flitting between the older children and the adults for years. This cemented it.

"*Mabrook!*" Lulu pulled on her most winning smile.

She and Tamra stood like that, smiling at each other as they sized each other up again.

"It's been soooo long since we've seen you. You never come out anymore!" Tamra reached out and pinched one of Lulu's cheeks. Tamra had nine months more on this planet than Lulu, and she'd never let Lulu forget it.

Lulu gritted her teeth, still holding the smile. She had been invited out with these girls regularly for a time, usually through her parents. And they had spent most of these evenings smiling and chiding her, welcoming her into the fold, only to increase Lulu's discomfort. They didn't like her. Or, at least, they didn't trust her. Lulu didn't mind—she didn't trust them, either. But they were all too bound together to air any of these grievances aloud. They all talked around what they could not talk about. Lulu had taken to avoiding them. Except for Miriam, who Lulu didn't see.

"Will you come out with us the next time?"

"*Of course* I will, *inshallah*. I've missed it. It's been so busy! I've been so busy!" Lulu's face hurt from the effort of smiling. "You know I love dancing."

"I'm sure. You're always busy. I was just telling Dina how much fun we had last time. You know Mustafa? I was telling Dina how he said the funniest thing. And do you know what it was? He was saying that he wasn't going to fast this year on account of basketball. Isn't he funny?" Tamra, who had been facing her cousin during the entirety of this speech, trained her gaze directly onto Lulu. "Oh, but you don't fast, do you, Lulu? Inshallah next year, habibti."

Lulu took a sharper-than-necessary inhale. "I do, actually. Excuse me."

Tamra hummed a tiny noise, then turned her attention back to Dina. Lulu headed to the bathroom, choosing to wade through the crowd of people downstairs rather than use the closer one upstairs. Everything upstairs had been like a carnival fun house. Lulu didn't appreciate the reflections she saw, even if they might have been distorted. That any of it could belong to a likeness of her made her irritable.

She was waylaid a handful of times by adults as she passed until she ran into Sheikh Fadi. He ruffled Lulu's hair and kissed her hand like her own grandfather would. He had the air of a man who had once been quite something in his prime, but his prime was now sixty years behind him.

"Ey, habibti," he said. "*Wenu* Baba?"

"My dad's talking with Amu," she said. "How are you, Sheikh?"

"Sheikh, sheikh." He shook his head. "And what is sheikh without tribe?"

Lulu clucked her tongue. "We are your tribe, Sheikh, you know this."

And it was the truth. Sheikh Fadi had spent his twilight years in the States, issuing fatwas to help settle community disputes in the city. He gave advice on anything as petty as a car wreck to issues as large as business partnerships going awry. He was the head of their amalgamated tribe, and he used his honorific to keep the peace.

"Ey." Sheikh Fadi waved Lulu off. "Miriam is outside, *yallah* habibti."

Lulu nodded as he shooed her farther out of the house. Sheikh Fadi understood people on a level that Lulu found nearly auspicious. She made it through the sliding doors at the back of the house. It was still too warm for there to be any refreshment from the outside air, but she charged farther into the backyard in any case.

———

A light breeze played through the humid air. Lulu teetered on a swing in the backyard, far from the crowd that maddened her so, balancing her seated form on the tip of her sneaker. She heaved a great sigh, slumping her shoulders up against the chains of the swing in the process. She watched the way her arms dangled at her sides. They almost looked like part of someone else's body, someone else's life.

"It's insane in there, isn't it?" said a muffled voice.

Miriam Razi was trying to furtively light a cigarette while she spoke. She and Lulu had grown up together. Though they had never been the best of friends, they were comrades-in-arms in these situations, and they bonded together over their war stories and battle wounds. They were both half-Arab, and they clung to each other for support. Miriam successfully lit the cigarette and took a deep inhale.

"Seriously. Aren't you afraid Ame Nadia is going to walk out here and find you? Or someone will report on you to her?" Lulu stole a few glances around them. This corner of the backyard remained empty and obscured from anyone's view.

With the reference to her mother, Miriam snorted, then exhaled a stream of smoke. The way Miriam's features relaxed made Lulu glad she didn't smoke. She didn't want to become dependent on that kind of catharsis. Though at the moment, it did look wonderfully freeing.

"Nah. They never come out back here, and anyways, the men have started up with the nargileh, so if I stand by my dad for a bit, I'll smell like smoke anyway."

"Not on your breath."

"Ah, you see. That's why I've brought backup." Miriam pulled out a layer of raw onion and a piece of feta cheese that she'd wrapped up in a bit of flatbread.

Lulu laughed. That, she knew, would obscure the scent well enough. "You're a professional."

"God, you have to be, don't you?" said Miriam on an exhale.

"Pretty much."

"How was *Dina?* And *Tamra?*" More smoke snorted out of Miriam's nose, like a giggling dragon.

"The same." Lulu shrugged it off, but badly. Her voice sharpened slightly as she continued on with what she had earlier maintained she would keep only to herself. "Can you believe it? Tamra actually had the balls to ask me if I would fast? As if I don't do it every year. As if this whole shindig isn't supposed to be marking the beginning of Ramadan. As if."

"Jesus." Miriam clucked distastefully. "I mean, I don't. But Jesus."

"I know," said Lulu.

"Well." Miriam picked at her teeth as she appraised Lulu. "I could be like my mom and tell you she's just jealous of you." She tipped the cigarette in her fingertips toward Lulu.

Lulu declined the offer. "You know she's not, though."

"True. But there's something about someone going that far out of their way to make you miserable."

"There is, isn't there?" said Lulu.

Miriam's eyes lit with a humor Lulu understood all too well. "I mean, if she didn't, I don't know. I wouldn't feel special anymore."

"God, that's depressing. Isn't it?" said Lulu.

Miriam shrugged. "Maybe."

At that moment, they heard a yelling, singsong voice vibrating in the distance. It sounded like it was moving toward them, and rapidly.

"Oh God, is that your mom?" Lulu eyed Miriam's still-lit cigarette.

"Shit. She calling my name? She is, isn't she? She's the only one who can make my name sound like one of those goddamn tongue trills. She's not even Arab." Miriam hastily stubbed out the cigarette, trying to dig it a small burial hole with her shoe, then popped the whole bread-onion-cheese wrap into her mouth. She chewed, shouting in barely intelligible words back to the voice. "Coming, Mom! I was on the swing!"

Lulu laughed at the sight of her. She wondered how Miriam would fare at passing off the cigarette smell to Ame Nadia. Lulu had a pang of her own worry at being discovered smelling like smoke. But she knew she too could shrug off the blame of the smell onto the men who smoked, and her mother would be none the wiser. Indeed, Aimee might pity poor Lulu for having to put up with such a stench all around her.

Lulu's teetering grew into a full swinging. She pumped her legs faster, pushing her body higher. Swinging gave her the elation of a pilgrim in the Holy Land, allowed through the gates of Mecca and filled with joy. But Lulu lacked any knowledge of the rites she needed to perform—a girl allowed to participate in cotillion but who had never been taught to dance. A stranger in a familiar place. And as she swung herself to the precipice of the swing's arc, she leaped. Her body soared through the air and she landed on her feet. She always landed on her feet. She couldn't have thought of another eventuality.

Lulu went back into the house, her best and most winning smile pasted across her face. She would not be defeated. Not even by her own ire. Not this time, at least.

5

Hunger Pangs

The strange yellow light from the street lamps outside poured through Lulu's window the next morning. Still half-asleep, she could smell the beginnings of breakfast cooking downstairs, sweet coconut oil mingling with onions and tortillas. The scent was simultaneously intoxicating and nauseating. Lulu's door cracked open with a slow creak. Aimee's head peeked in.

"Coming down, darling?" her mother twanged—Louisiana nasal peppered with twenty years in the Lone Star State. Her own personal accent.

Lulu grunted, and her mother abandoned the door, leaving it wide open. The light from the hall pulsed in Lulu's eyes. As she rolled out of bed, she smacked her lips—her mouth tasting stale and unclean. She trudged down the steps, smushing her body into a seat when she reached the table. No god was worth this.

Her baba, chipper as can be, looked over his newspaper and said, "How's school, habibti?"

"No." Lulu shook her head.

"Come and get it!" Aimee called, interrupting the tender moment.

Ahmed got up to grab himself a helping. Lulu sat there, contemplating the existential purpose of her plate.

Aimee sat down in her usual place and coughed lightly. She didn't fast, but she ate early-morning breakfast in solidarity. "Food is ready, darling. You ought to go grab some before the eggs are cold. There's cheese to the side of the burner if you want any."

Lulu grabbed her plate and stood up, pausing through her momentary confusion, then walked into the kitchen. She flopped the food onto her plate with the provided spatula. She lumped some cheese on her dish. She sat herself back down, and had to rest her head in her hand before attempting to eat the food in front of her. Her stomach growled and revolted, all at once.

"What subjects do you have today?" Ahmed Saad was a dauntless man who had survived a dictatorship and a war zone. His daughter's predawn mood did little to discourage his naturally gregarious morning manner.

"All of them." Lulu shoved an enormous bite into her mouth in an attempt to end the conversation. All she wanted was silence and sleep.

"Do you have tests?" he asked.

"No." Lulu continued shoveling food into her mouth in a perfunctory manner—all for a future need of fuel and none for any pleasure. "It's a quiz."

"What quiz?" he asked.

"History."

"What unit do you study?" Again from her baba, because her mother had the good sense to speak as little as possible to Lulu before dawn.

"I don't know." Lulu didn't want to think about the answer. But she took in her father's expression, and she had to find a better response than the one she had already given. "Somewhere right after the War of 1812."

"Ah, fledgling democracy. Such a fascinating thing." Her baba spoke in a tone that indicated he teetered on the precipice between at least two different histories. Either way, a lecture was at hand. He was, after all, Professor Saad.

Lulu held in her groan. Or at least, she hoped she had. "I guess."

As a little girl, Lulu had listened to the way her father's rumbling voice would rise and fall with the triumphs and woes of historical players, as though histories were fairy tales. She'd been taught these stories rather than those of dragon slayers and white knights. This morning, though, Lulu gripped her head to steady the dizzying sensation she was experiencing. She didn't want to think about US History. Or any history.

"The birth of American nationalism, to have won 'The Second War of Independence,' though, who can really say if they did. More like a three-way draw." Her father was quite excited. And he was only warming up. His lecture could travel anywhere: the historical significance of the nationalist fervor of the nineteenth century, a desire to correct anyone who called the War for Independence the "American Revolution," or how most Americans didn't remember that at one point they had, in fact, gone to war with Canada.

Lulu had heard each of these enough that her patience with them was, on her best days, thin. She pushed the food on her plate around with her fork. Her stomach clenched with morning hunger sated earlier than antici-pated. "I know."

"The real losers, though, were all the American Indians who lost their autonomy in this quest for territory, nationalism, and the beginning of feel-ings of manifest destiny."

Lulu took a final bite of her breakfast. "I know."

"It's why the border at Canada is demilitarized."

Lulu slumped over herself. This was a battle she wouldn't win.

"For heaven's sake, Lulu, sit up. Sometimes you are so dramatic," Aimee said from across the table.

Lulu sat back up. Ahmed continued to tuck into his breakfast, apparently undisturbed. The lecture, at least, had been forestalled.

———

That morning in US History, Lulu learned genocide could earn a president a spot on the currency if framed properly. In English, Lulu learned that the eyes of Dr. T. J. Eckleburg were always watching. In physics, she learned that she was constantly pushing up against sound waves. In French, Lulu learned exactly how her hunger could get the better of her.

A hand slapped down on Lulu's desk. She jolted. An owlish face hovered above her. Madame Perault was what one would picture in a French teacher—exacting and politely aggressive, with a perfectly tame coiffure and red nails sharpened as though they were talons. Lulu wasn't intimidated by many people, but Perault frightened her on a primal level.

"What's going on?" said Perault in her native French.

"Pardon, madame?" Lulu swallowed hard, but she didn't break eye contact.

"Your book. Where is your book?" Madame Perault maintained her steely, wide-eyed stare. She tapped a single nail across Lulu's desk. *Rat-a-tap-tap.*

Lulu shuddered. Being hungry led to all sorts of carelessness. Not that she could explain that to Perault. "I left it."

"And so you think you can leave your book whenever you like? And me, what would happen if I left my materials for class, eh? What kind of class could I teach then? Do not you think it is acceptable to leave your books for class, no?" Perault went on, still in French.

Unanswerable questions were a strength of the French language and a decided advantage in this world for the native French instructor. Lulu half gurgled a noise as she grappled for the proper word in French to answer a negative question. Still, Lulu maintained eye contact. It was better that way.

Perault squinted. Desperate, Lulu shook her head.

Perault's nail, mercifully, stopped tapping. She stood, then waved her hand in Lulu's direction. *"Alors, partagez avec votre voisin."*

Lulu sighed as she looked over to her neighbor. Dane Anderson currently sat sprawled across his chair, his leg carelessly intruding into Lulu's space. Lulu eyed the offending limb with a narrowed gaze. She couldn't believe he was on track to graduate in the spring. He must have been hanging on by a mere thread. And a year behind his peers in language class. Lucky him, he only needed three years' credit of French to graduate. Anderson caught Lulu looking and despite her scowl, or maybe because of it, he winked.

Lulu turned away. Attempting to reclaim her space, she kicked her book bag over, toward his leg. Her bag wobbled instead, toppling back onto her feet after ricocheting off Anderson's impossibly, annoyingly steady calf. Lulu wanted nothing more than to grunt out her frustrations, but she suppressed the noise before it could escape and draw further attention from Madame Perault.

"Share with me?" Lulu asked.

"Sure," he said, in a way that implied her request hadn't been for a book at all. Dane stretched out, long and lean. He arched his back against his desk chair, exposing a sliver of stomach and a dusting of hair that Lulu wished she had never seen. Some parts of Dane Anderson's body ought to come with warning labels. Most parts, honestly. Lulu was too hungry to deal with this sort of visual onslaught. It was cruelly unfair that one kind of fasting made her other appetites that much more gluttonous. Not that she was supposed to entertain any physical appetite, while the sun was up.

As Perault's lecture began, Lulu leaned over Dane's desk. He flicked

Lulu's arm. She ignored it. A few moments later he flicked the spot again. Lulu pulled her shoulder away pointedly. Dane flicked her ear.

Lulu turned to him, a wide-eyed imitation of Madame Perault's owlish expression. "Seriously?"

He grinned. "It was funny."

Madame Perault looked up and locked eyes with Lulu. "What's going on?"

"Nothing, madame." Lulu arranged her face to perfect passivity. "I was showing him about the verbs, madame."

Hawk-eyes appraised Lulu, but Perault moved onward, sweeping through the class. Lulu breathed the tiniest sigh of relief before succumbing to her angry thoughts. Whenever Lulu was caught talking to a boy, she was at fault. She tensed her grip around her pen. Next to her, Anderson didn't look remotely chastised. In fact, judging by his casually crossed arms and the rakish lean to his back, he sat quite satisfied.

Despite the uncertainty of her safety, Lulu leaned over the book again. She was trying to follow along with Perault's lecture. Trying and failing. She was nearly as close to Dane as she had been that night in the hallway two weeks ago. Dane Anderson was everything Lulu was supposed to want, and she had enough experience to know better than to try.

Unfortunately, there was a perverse, inverse relationship between what her head knew and what her body responded to. He was a hot pan and she was curious enough to see what would happen if she touched it. *Danger* flickered in all-red letters across her mind. She felt herself lean in farther, and she knew she wasn't getting any better of a look of the text in the book.

"Get a good eyeful?" he asked, a whisper in her ear.

Lulu jumped. "Pax, Anderson. French class truce?"

Dane flicked the edge of her hair. "*Peace*, I hate the word."

Lulu pulled her hair back with a spare rubber band on her wrist. "Please don't quote Shakespeare. You'll hurt yourself."

"I was quoting John Leguizamo." Dane pulled at the end of her ponytail. "But I understand. Playing hard to get."

Lulu forced her attention forward—on Perault and the lecture at hand. A small bit of folded paper popped onto the top corner of Lulu's desk. She covered it immediately with her hand. She didn't need to turn to see who had written her. Neatly, and nearly microscopically, printed across the bit of paper were the words: *What up btwn u and Denair?*

Lulu quickly scratched a message on the back of the same paper. Perault turned then, and Lulu made to look like she was taking a grammatical note in her notebook. Perault swept by, continuing her lecture.

Lulu released a breath she didn't know she was holding and flicked her response perfectly back onto Dane's desk. *Who?*

Dane tossed his response into Lulu's lap. Perault's lecture carried her toward Lulu's desk, and Lulu was forced to crumple the note into the waistband of her uniform skirt to hide the evidence. Perault, ever keen, sensed rather than saw that misbehavior was afoot. Lulu had to answer several questions perfectly before the teacher would leave her alone.

Ur heartless. My buddy James. He looked smitten at the bar.

Anderson couldn't mean that as a compliment.

Lulu wrote back on a new bit of paper, in her prettiest, loopiest handwriting. *Maybe. Or maybe I'm the smitten kitten.*

Admitting to liking a near stranger she would likely never see again seemed safer than having to go on the defensive about how she handled her physical and not-so-romantic entanglements. Her track record there wasn't a defendable position, not as a girl. Dane's was worse, mind you. But it didn't matter. Dane Anderson had the high ground in the fight because he was a boy, and Lulu was stuck in a muddy, swampy, wide-open field of girlhood.

She was easy pickings and they both knew it. And Anderson seemed determined to keep turning their conversation toward an argument so clearly stacked in his favor. Lulu's resentment of this ran so deeply within her, she almost didn't notice the feeling.

Doubtful. Ur not the type.

That blow landed. Lulu wanted to inflict discomfort, if not pain, right back. *Why? You jealous?*

Dane leaned across her book again, and started writing. He blotted it out immediately, then rewrote his retort, but not before Lulu caught a glimpse of the words *please* and *delusional.* Lulu frowned, turning her attention away from him. As Lulu kept watch on Perault, Dane ripped out what he wrote. Then, instead of passing it to her, he slid his response under her leg. Lulu jolted from the contact. She hunched protectively away from Dane as she retrieved the note. This wasn't a game she wanted to play anymore.

Nope. Ur lying.

In her usual temper, perhaps Lulu might have backed down. But she was seven hours into her first day of fasting. She dug her heels in; she would not lose. The edges of Dane's mouth pulled up with sardonic pleasure.

Lulu only knew of one way to wipe the expression off his face. She dropped her next note at his feet. *Gimme his info.*

Dane raised an eyebrow, but he quickly fetched the information on his phone. Lulu quietly grabbed the phone out of his hands, then, placing it beside her own phone, began typing.

Hey it's Lulu wanna grab some coffee sometime?

Her indignation still flooding through her, Lulu stared at Dane, flashing him her phone and the message's recipient. At that, Dane's face fell slightly. Clicking her phone locked, she taunted him with a smirk.

That's when her phone buzzed in her lap. Lulu turned away, giving Dane no chance to see the panic that flooded through her at that moment. She had asked someone she hated on a date to prove Dane Anderson wrong on a point of honor that she couldn't quite understand anymore. She had, for a moment, a faint hope that she'd be rejected.

Sure. Tomorrow?

Lulu thought she might be sick, but that was probably just a hunger pang. She confirmed the appointment. Perault approached then, and Lulu clamped her legs shut to hide the phone in the folds of her skirt. She winced from the pain of the casing jamming into her knee. Perault's face froze into a hard stare. Lulu prepared herself for what seemed inevitable. Instead Lulu's essay slapped hard against her desk. Perault moved on to the next paper in the stack. Lulu could have melted into her desk in relief. At least one thing had gone right.

The bell rang and the room filled with the sound of books, papers, and book bags chattering together as their disgruntled owners slinked out of class.

"How'd you do that?"

Lulu looked up to find Dane peering over her shoulder at her grade. Lulu straightened her spine purposefully. "Do what?"

"Get a near-perfect score on that composition," he said.

"Jealous?" Lulu smirked.

Dane smirked back. They stood there for a long moment, neither one conceding to the other. Eventually Dane shrugged, turning and walking away. As she watched him walk down the hall, Lulu wasn't sure if she was grateful or disappointed. She did know this, though: she was going to have to pay for her pride.

———

The first three days of Ramadan, she knew, were the worst. And yet, sitting at the cafeteria table and watching Audrey bite into pepperoni pizza, dripping meat grease onto her plate, was nearly more than Lulu could bear. Lulu thought about licking the orange-coated crust crumbs that had fallen onto Audrey's tray. Lulu didn't like pepperoni, didn't even eat it. She also wasn't sure how clean that tray was. It didn't matter. The crumbs still tempted. She licked her lips.

"What's everyone going as for Halloween?" Lo sat between Audrey and Emma at their usual table.

"Early much, Lo?" Lulu leaned against the table. Every year the senior girls would throw a Halloween party, effectively highlighting the fall social calendar in a way that weekly football games could not. Not sanctioned by the school, the tickets were sold exclusively by the seniors to Sealy Hall students. The venues themselves were only available with the promise of parent chaperones. The event had proved, year after year, a guaranteed recipe for both delight and disaster.

Lo stared at Lulu. "Halloween is this weekend. And y'all all owe me for the tickets."

Lulu's elbow slid down with her expression. She didn't have a costume in mind and, worse, she'd have to get through the night without a friendly drop of alcohol. Not eating lunch was one thing. But with this, her friends would all be cavorting around like idiots and she'd be forced to remember every detail of it. Guilt chased on the heels of such a thought, but that didn't stop Lulu from wishing she lived in an alternate universe, one where Ramadan had started a week later in the Gregorian calendar.

"Anyway. I'm going as a ladybug. Isn't that cute? I found a tutu and everything," said Lo.

Of all the ways Lo would be likely to dress for Halloween, *cute* would hardly be the word to describe her costume. But the entire table—Lulu included—agreed that a ladybug was an absolutely adorable idea.

"I'm going as Dorothy," said Emma, with unusually declarative force. "I found a pair of sparkly red shoes, and I have to wear them. They're insane. What about you, Lulu?"

Lulu was too distracted by the conglomerated smells of the cafeteria—Frito pie and pizza intermingling with the scent of instant soup and the remnants of spicy fries. She'd give the tip of her right thumb for a bite of Frito pie. She heard a whimper and looked around the table before she realized it had come from herself. She shrugged. "Something slutty."

The table laughed at that.

Audrey's face betrayed her worry. "You all right?"

"Yeah, first day's always the worst," said Lulu.

"I know. I mean, I don't know, but I'm sorry." Audrey paused, frowning. "I wish I could give you a bite."

"Unfortunately, that would be the opposite of helpful."

"I hate seeing you like this," said Audrey.

"I know. I'll be better in a couple days. Promise." Lulu's pasted-on smile faltered as she remembered she still had a dare of a date to go on.

6

You Can't Just Ask People Why They're White

Lulu peered over the railing of the coffee shop. Below on the ground floor, tables of teen boys sucking on their vape pens were interspersed among those filled by older, literati-inspired men sporting fedoras. The wood—of the railing, the bar, the tables—was warm, and the fragrance of the café-cum-bar had a decidedly masculine flavor. She'd been here once before, with her friends. They had not lingered.

This time, she was on an accidental date and it was already a disaster. Nobody else seemed to care about the strange, suffocating quality of the air. Lulu coughed lightly. She scooted forward in her too-large chair, which wobbled unsteadily toward the balcony edge. She gripped her mug a little bit tighter.

Across from her sat James, his limbs trying to find any sort of normal position at the tiny table. He cleared his throat. "How are things?"

Lulu flipped her sandal up against her heel, making a faint clicking noise. "Good. You?"

"Good."

Lulu didn't have anything else to add. She looked back over the balcony, nursing her chai latte and shielding her face with her mug all at once. At least it was after sundown. She took a fresh sip.

"So. Quick question. Why'd you ask me out?" James had that keen, wide-eyed look of his. The one that irresistibly drew the truth out of Lulu. "Because I've been under the impression that you hate me."

"I mean. I do." Lulu watched as he spewed latte back into his mug. "See. Dane Anderson. We have French together." Lulu paused, deciding to take a different tack. "How do you know Dane?"

"Grew up together, before I moved to Florida. Our sisters are still friends." James shrugged. "Dane's all right. He's just an asshole."

Lulu barked a laugh. This kid didn't know the half of it. "Dane gave me your number on a dare. So I asked you out mostly to prove I would."

"Wow. Awesome." It was James's turn to hide into his mug. "Remind me to thank him. Do you even want to be here?"

Lulu took another sip. "You know. I think so."

"You think so?" James's mouth flattened into a line. "I wait seventeen years for a girl to do the asking, and she only maybe *thinks* she wants to be here. That's super."

"Haven't you been asked out by a girl before?" Lulu ought to have stopped there but James's sarcasm had bitten into her conscience. "I would think with your general smooth-talking, all the ladies would come-a-runnin.'"

"You're just a ray of sunshine, aren't you?" asked James.

"What can I say? You bring out my sunny side." Lulu flourished her words with a horribly winning smile. "Why'd you pick this place anyway?"

"Made me think of you," James said, his voice quiet.

"Of me?"

James took another sip of his coffee. "Yeah, why not."

"What made you think of me?" This answer could change the entire evening. They were on the precipice of a great unknown. Lulu leaned in.

James must have sensed it, too. He put down his mug and said, as though she were the only person left in the room, "Tonight they've got their weekly belly dancers. I haven't seen them yet, but I've heard they're really great. Like, best in the city."

"You brought me here. When I asked you out. To see belly dancers." Lulu nodded as she spoke.

James returned the nods, all friendly-like. Lulu stared at him, waiting to see if that was all he would do. Apparently it was.

"And you don't see how offensive that is." She tried to take a deep breath. "Seriously?"

"I mean." He looked left and right, to see if perhaps the balcony or the narrow passageway might come to his aid. "I don't think so, no."

Lulu used her calmest tone, but it was a thin layer of ice over a riotous sea. "You thought this was a date, so you took me to see a half-naked woman dancing around? From my 'culture'? Because it reminded you of me?"

"Turns out this isn't really a date," he shot back. "I still think you would enjoy it. Since, you know." But his voice had trailed off.

Lulu could have thrown the last of her hot drink into his lovely, pleading eyes. She was always captivated by the worst kinds of boys. "Since I know *what* exactly? Since I know I'm Arab? Or, since I know I get to stuff tips into the dancers' waistbands?"

That wasn't what bothered Lulu. She loved watching belly dancers. She loved the rhythm of their bodies set to the music. As a little girl, she had thought the movements beautiful and free. But Lulu had gotten older and learned that the sashes and bells on a dancer's body were as much about drawing attention to flesh as to movement. A dancer's own sense of pleasure was beside the purpose. That a woman had talent in dancing the Dance of the Seven Veils did not bother Lulu. It was what came after. The leering, lingering looks Lulu would receive. The hope that she, too, would dance for the pleasure of another. The sense that her body had become public. The knowledge that her body was suddenly not her own.

"How d'you know that?" James interrupted Lulu's thoughts.

"Because, as you already have so wonderfully insinuated, I've seen belly dancers before."

"These could be classy belly dancers. Maybe they don't take tips." There was an evident defiance inside him that Lulu could at once despise and respect.

"Fantastic. Classy ones." Lulu wouldn't let herself speak anymore, so unsure was she of what might come out of her mouth.

"So, um, to be clear. Under what...circumstances...have you seen belly dancers? I mean, why have you seen them before?"

"Because, I'm Arab." Lulu arched her eyebrows. "Isn't that the obvious answer?"

James looked around himself, like he was planning his escape. "Is that a trick question?"

"You're unbelievable." Lulu took a last, enormous swig of her drink. She stared him down, willing him to answer differently, hoping he could possibly have *something* to say for himself. But he couldn't and he didn't.

"I've changed my mind," she said.

"How so?" His eyes brightened, possibly hopeful that she might be calming down.

"I definitely don't want to be here." Lulu slammed her mug on the wood. At that moment, she'd rather take her frustration out on the table than on his face. Though, truly, his face made a tempting target. Several nearby tables turned and stared at them.

"Do you always blow hot and cold?" He broadened his narrow frame at that. "I mean, I didn't fly off the handle when I found out you asked me out *on a dare.*"

Lulu thought she saw tiny spots clouding her vision. "I don't blow anything." Lulu got up. She stuffed a handful of cash on the table. And then she was gone.

———

"Ugh, I mean can you believe it?" Lulu, in a squealing tone, was recounting to Audrey exactly how not over the previous night's events she was.

"No, I can't." Though Audrey had agreed she couldn't believe the story at least three times already.

"Belly dancers!" Lulu said. "Belly dancers!" There were only ten minutes left in the lunch period, and Lulu meant to use all of them on the topic. Lulu slammed her locker with a force that rattled two doors down.

Her locker neighbor, Atman Rai, looked up at her, entirely startled. She glared at him, which she knew he most certainly did not deserve. He scuttled away, and Lulu was left to lament that she had doled out her revenge on a boy who neither deserved it nor understood the source of her wrath. She groaned, rolling her back up against the lock.

"Lulu." Audrey leaned against Lulu's locker, trying to keep their conversation between them two, despite the bustle of the hallway around them.

Lulu heard the tentativeness in her friend's voice. Her wildness quelled at that, anticipating some censure was around the corner. "Yes?"

"I love you. You know I do."

If that wasn't a preamble, Lulu didn't know one when she heard it. "But?"

Audrey took a deep inhale. "And I say this as someone with an obsessive crush."

"Seriously?" Lulu crossed her arms over her chest.

Audrey responded with her calmest, steadiest tones. "Lulu. Let me finish."

"Fine." Lulu uncrossed her arms.

"Anyways—I say this as someone with an obsessive crush. And who takes a lot of things probably a little too seriously—you're being kind of sensitive."

"I am not!" Lulu kicked the bottom locker that did not belong to her. It didn't deserve her ire any more than her neighbor, Atman, but, luckily, she felt less guilty pelting inanimate objects with her temper.

Audrey made a disbelieving face. "I mean. Come on. It's only belly dancers, Lulu. You seem—really rattled by it? I mean, he's just some guy. He must have a crush on you. Pulling pigtails, etc. You probably intimidate him, you know? You are kind of intimidating. He goofed."

Lulu suddenly felt small and wrong for kicking the locker, for slamming the door, her anger, all of it. She heard her own voice catch. "I hate him."

"I know, honey. I know." Audrey offered a comforting pat.

Lulu leaned back onto the locker, accidentally jamming the lock into her spine with the force of her action. She winced. "But?"

"But, with you, hate and attraction go hand in hand."

Lulu opened her mouth and closed it. Audrey was wrong, and yet, Lulu couldn't find the words for why. They were on the tip of her tongue, but never fully formed. All she had was the ability to tell this story over and over again, until maybe someone understood. Until that person could point out the piece that unlocked the anger and turned it into action. How could Lulu have known that Audrey wasn't that person? Audrey was, after all, the smartest person Lulu trusted.

"Lulu," Audrey said. "Breathe, honey. You wouldn't be so rage-y if it weren't the truth."

That took the air out of Lulu's anger almost immediately. She didn't have any words left. Audrey's version of the truth was the one Lulu feared most. It froze Lulu, creating a sensation that a deep hollow had been scooped out of her chest. Lulu rubbed at the sore spot in her back, where she had hit the lock. She hoped it wouldn't bruise.

"Come on. Let's not think about it anymore," Audrey said.

Lulu had heard Mrs. Bachmann say the same thing when Audrey was upset. It was an unsettling vision of the future. "Easy for you to say." Lulu picked up her bag and slung it over her shoulder as she stood.

She and Audrey headed down the hall.

"True. I only have to say it and not do it. But you know what, I get how you feel. All the time." Audrey preened with this wisdom.

But Audrey didn't get how Lulu felt. And Lulu was too worn down to argue the point. Too unsatisfied by the turn of the conversation. Lulu followed where Audrey would inevitably lead. "Clark?"

"Obviously."

"He's an idiot," Lulu responded robotically.

"They all are, Lulu. They all are." Audrey smiled.

Lulu faked a laugh, hoping it would alter the expression she felt forming on her face. She wrapped her pain into the hard casing of humor. "I think it's so much worse because I'm so hungry. I could eat a horse." She thought her hunger during the day would have abated by now. She'd been mistaken. Hunger didn't abate; the pain of it simply dulled.

"God, that has to be the worst." Audrey scrunched up her face, sympathetic and slightly disapproving.

"Sometimes it is." Lulu shrugged. She couldn't explain fasting to someone who'd never done it. There were only so many words for the experience that weren't trite or repetitive.

"When isn't it?"

"I guess, when I know it serves a higher purpose." The sentiment tasted foreign on Lulu's tongue. She didn't know how else to express the feeling, though. She'd have to resign herself to sounding a bit devotional, even if it wasn't her exact truth.

"When's that?" Audrey pulled out a stick of gum and started chewing it. Audrey knew better than to offer a piece to Lulu, but she did so anyway.

Lulu declined with the shake of her head. "Like, I could eat anytime, right?"

"Sure."

"But some people can't. This ends in a month. For some people, this never ends. They're always this hungry. I mean, getting anything done is a struggle during the day. I can't imagine if this were my life. All the time. Always hungry." But that wasn't it entirely, either. Lulu also knew her family half a world away fasted. Fasting tied her to them in a way she needed. They did not share a homeland. They did not share a time zone. But this, this hunger, they shared. This time on the ever-moving calendar, they shared.

"That's some serious shit, Lulu."

"Sorry." Lulu shrugged.

"Nah, it's cool. And here I thought it was tough giving up chocolate for Lent." Audrey stood by the door to her next class.

Lulu leaned against the wall, clutching a book. "I can eat as much of that as I want. As long as the sun's not up." She winked.

Audrey laughed. "You are the funniest person I know."

"I know." Lulu shrugged her shoulders.

"And modest, too." Audrey swatted Lulu's arm.

"Modesty's overrated, Audrey," said Lulu. "Hey, are we going Halloween shopping today?"

Audrey grabbed at the doorknob, holding the door open to the classroom. "Let's go Friday. After school."

Lulu frowned. "Cutting it close, isn't it?"

"Yeah, but I've gotta get this lab analysis done tonight. Plus we've got a quiz tomorrow in US History." Audrey continued holding the door open as half the students in the class and Mr. Medina walked through.

"Ughhhh. Quizzes." Lulu rolled her eyes.

"Tell me about it," said Audrey.

"Is there somewhere we can run away to? Where there's no quizzes or boys or anything stupid ever again?" asked Lulu.

"Doubtful. Besides, if we miss Halloween, Lo will kill us. For sure."

"How did you ever get so wise?"

"Looking after your ass for three years," said Audrey.

"Shut up," said Lulu.

Audrey laughed and flitted inside. Lulu, seeing how deserted the hallway was by this point, took her leave quickly. She hustled to her next class, barely making it to her seat in time for the bell.

7

Costumed Drama

One purple wrap dress, a pair of red hot pants, and a ribbed orange turtleneck later, the girls were happily driving away from the thrift store with the spoils of their shopping excursion. They found two pairs of coordinating combat boots and made their way to Nina Holmes's house to pick up a wig for Lulu to borrow. A stop at a costume store procured the toy weapons and accessories they would need for the night. Once at home, Audrey got out a pack of multicolored permanent markers and two pairs of thick false eyelashes. After sundown, Lulu picked up an enormous burrito and scarfed it down as they readied their costumes. They were armed for the night before them.

"Don't move, okay, Lulu? I've almost got it." Audrey bit her lip in concentration.

Lulu sat on the floor of Audrey's room with her eyes closed.

Audrey held a pair of tweezers, which, for their part, held one set of false eyelashes. She blew a stream of air across the base of the lashes, trying to get the glue tacky, and then placed the strip along Lulu's lash line.

Lulu did her best not to wince. She wouldn't usually trust Audrey so close to her eye, especially with glue and a sharp, pointy object. But Lulu wore her glasses rather than contacts that night. And Lo was taking her time doing Emma's makeup. Lulu's options were between her own blurred vision and Audrey's lack of coordination. She'd picked Audrey, by a slim margin.

"Okay. Stay like that," Audrey commanded. "They're both on, but don't open your eyes yet."

Lulu tapped her bare foot against the floor. "Sure, sounds fine to me. Do you want me to do yours when I'm dry?"

"Yes, please. I've never been able to get them on without losing half of my lashes in the process," Audrey said.

Across the room, Lo snorted.

"Be nice," said Emma.

"Who, *moi*?" asked Lo.

Lulu heard a scuffling tumble, and assumed Audrey must have chucked a pillow at Lo's head. Lo must have retaliated with a makeup brush because she heard its distinctive thwack on the wall nearby. But, as her eyes were closed, Lulu couldn't be sure.

Lulu held up her arms. "Y'all. Drying over here. Please don't cause a wardrobe malfunction."

"That is so not what *wardrobe malfunction* means," said Lo.

"You guys hush," said Emma in an unusually direct way. This was not her normal appeal for peace. Her voice vibrated with too much energy. Her fingers tapped against the floor with too much urgency. "You know—"

But Audrey was already talking over her. "Guess what? Tonight, I'm going to go for it. Clark Kelly. It's do or die."

"Attagirl!!" Lulu squealed, bouncing in her cross-legged position.

"Finally," said Lo.

Emma said nothing, her voice having stopped where it caught when Audrey spoke over her.

Not that Audrey noticed this. "I know I am going to be brave. Brave like you, Lulu. Except more like me."

"Audrey, that makes zero sense." Lulu squinted her eyes, testing the glue. She felt the lashes shift slightly and made her face placid again.

"I mean you're brave. But I'm not gonna be like how *you* would be brave. I don't want to make out with, I mean, *anyone.*" Judgment rattled through Audrey's voice.

"I'm going to pretend there wasn't a veiled insult in there somewhere, Mrs. Bachmann." Lulu tapped her fingers at the base of her lashes. They were so close to dry.

Lo laughed. Emma forced a chuckle.

Audrey smacked Lulu's arm. "Ugh, you suck. I am nothing like my mother. You can probably open now."

Lulu fluttered her eyes open, admiring herself in the mirror propped up against the wall. "Oh, perfect, Audrey Louise! We're gonna look so good. I mean we already look so good, but with the costumes on, it's gonna be epic."

"I know, my turn." Audrey stepped in front of Lulu, blocking the view to the mirror.

"And Emma is done!" said Lo, with a flourish of her makeup brush.

Emma gave a milquetoast smile.

"Oh, come on, it's better than that." Lo put her hand on her hip. Her own makeup was, of course, already complete.

At the sight of Lo's disbelief, Emma laughed and was more herself again. Emma finished by twisting her hair into two braids. Lulu placed Audrey's false lashes without incident. Audrey cut the sleeves off Lulu's sweater. She and Lulu drew matching bicep tattoos on each other, though Audrey's drawing was slightly cleaner and more neatly done than Lulu's. Fully composed, they all appraised themselves and one another in the mirror as they jockeyed for space.

Lo blew an air kiss at her reflection. "Now or never." She grabbed Emma and pulled her out of the room.

Lulu hooked Audrey's arm through her own. She felt ready for whatever the night would bring. "Let's."

Lulu parked, and her carful of girls unloaded. Lo wore the ladybug costume, with a tutu that encircled her hips, creating a protective buffer between her body and the rest of the world. Emma's hair was sweetly plaited into two French braids, her blue-checkered dress flouncing as she walked. She made a convincing Dorothy. Audrey, with her white thigh highs, combat boots, fake tattoos, and curled hair, looked the least like herself. She had a powerful aura in her disguise, though none of them were sure as to whether the effect was real or not.

Lulu hopped out of the driver's seat last, her body humming with excitement. Her hands moved over her hips as they tested the edge of her impossibly short shorts. Half an inch less and she'd be out of them. But she'd bought them and put them on, so there was no sense in worrying about it now. She fingered through her bobbed wig. The plastic strands snagged when she reached the bottom. She resmoothed out the edges and left the wig alone. Nothing she could do about that, either.

At the door, Lulu took the lead, giving off the best, and most sober, first impression to the authority figures waiting there. The four were admitted without incident. Lulu scanned the scene. The music was loud, too loud for talking. The bass thumped into Lulu's chest. The hook whined through her ears. Lo had already grabbed Emma, swooping her body to the right. Emma giggled and swayed, having the opportunity tonight to drink rather than stay sober and drive. They settled in a spot near the thick of the crowd. Audrey trailed behind them. But Lulu preferred to take a lap first. She would have preferred to take it with Audrey, but she squished through the pressing of bodies alone, giving her greetings where appropriate. Nina was there already, dressed as a disco ball in a spangley leotard.

"Thanks for the wig!" Lulu put a hand on her hip, appraising. "Aren't you festive."

" 'Tis the season." Nina gave a twirl. Not that she had anything to twirl other than the leotard. She leaned in and spoke at a serious whisper. "Don't look now, but you've got a lurker right behind you."

Lulu, of course, had to look right now. She stopped midclap to turn. Brian Connor stood alone in the crowd—rare for a great sharer of weed—and like a flash Lulu had a plan for the night. Halloween was, after all, good for a little subterfuge. "Hold that thought."

Nina, who was born for mischief, winked.

Lulu sauntered over to him, an impish thought in mind. "Hey, Brian."

"Hey, Lulu." He returned her smirk, clearly hoping it looked as charming as her own did.

Lulu's smile broadened. "Are you going to ask Emma to dance?"

Brian shook his head a little, like he'd misheard her. "Am I what?"

True, Lulu couldn't be entirely sure if Emma had been looking at Brian at the Battle of the Bands, but this ought to be the best way to find out. Lulu scanned the crowd and found Emma, who returned Lulu's enthusiastic grin. Emma—who rarely grinned across rooms like that—must have been having a marvelous night already.

Lulu arched her eyebrows at Brian. "Ask Emma. To dance."

Brian, reading meaning where he was ready to see it, smiled over Lulu's head. "You know, I think I might."

Laughing, tipsy Emma swayed as Brian approached. Brian was quick to lend a hand to catch her. But he didn't release her once she'd steadied. Confusion danced across Emma's face. He led her onto the dance floor. Lulu could somehow hear the squeaking resistance of Emma's shoes against the linoleum floor. Lulu took a step forward, conscious of a misstep on that front, when a hand shot out and grabbed Lulu's forearm in a vise grip.

Audrey, whose face had gone a bit slack, held on to Lulu as if she could not support herself. Lulu looked around until she saw Clark Kelly hanging on to that freshman girl with the fantastic bangs. And he was enthralled by her.

Lulu should have learned the girl's name by now, but instead she thought of her as Bangs. The freshman had borrowed one of her friend's cheerleading uniforms as a costume, and every time her hips moved with the music, Lulu thought she nearly saw a flash of her underwear. Lulu pulled down her own shorts, which covered little more than underwear themselves. The grip on Lulu's arm disappeared. Then Clark leaned down to Bangs's mouth, and Lulu didn't have to watch the rest to see what would happen next. Lulu turned quickly to gauge Audrey's feelings. But Audrey had disappeared.

Lulu spun around once in a circle, hoping Audrey was still behind her. Who she found instead was Lo, rubbing at the inside of her thigh.

"Damn. That was my favorite flask," Lo said. "My only flask, point of fact."

Lulu wiped a hand across her face. "You fit a flask in that costume?"

Lo shrugged. She lifted up her ladybug skirt to reveal shorts underneath. "I always bring a backup. You know that."

"Audrey will bring it back." At least, Lulu hoped she would.

"She better," said Lo. "Or she's gonna owe me one."

"That is so besides the point." Lulu squinted, trying to scan the crowd, but Audrey was already lost to the sea of movement and the darkness of the room. Lulu looked over to Emma and Brian then. Her eyes narrowed, watching them. Something was off. For every move Brian made forward, Emma pulled back. Then Brian's mouth was on Emma's, and in the dark Lulu couldn't tell if her friend had gone slack into his arms or melted into the embrace. She couldn't remember if Emma had ever kissed a boy before.

Lulu felt a tap at her shoulder. Hopeful it was Audrey, she whipped around. But it was only a sophomore boy. One of the more attractive ones, as far as that grade went. He asked Lulu to dance, and Lo, at the ready, declined on Lulu's behalf. Lulu made an apologetic face. The boy, with what can only be described as a taste for masochism, stayed beside the two girls. When Lulu turned around, Emma was no longer on the dance floor. Brian, now alone, had been abandoned.

"A sophomore, really? You could so do better." Lo made an elongated O with her mouth, wiping some errant lip gloss off the side of her lips.

"Lo, he's cute. And, whatever." Then Lulu leaned in so that only Lo could hear. "Nothing was gonna happen."

"I'll believe that when I see it. Besides he's *so* not cute. Pasty levels of pale."

"He's not deaf." Lulu pointed to where the unsettled boy hovered.

"Are you still standing here?" asked Lo.

The boy jumped, like a startled woodland creature. Lo meant for him to scamper off, but he either didn't take the hint or was too frozen in the beam of Lo's displeasure to move.

"We said no, thank you. You want an engraved rejection?" Lo asked.

The boy didn't move. Definitely frozen in fear, then.

"These are not the girls you're looking for." Lo waved her hands with a beautifully executed flourish.

The boy's whole face flushed a deep magenta. He scuttled off. Lo turned to face Lulu. If it were a blinking contest, Lulu would have lost immediately. Lulu felt her eyelashes coming unstuck with the heat, which only made her flutter them more exaggeratedly. She pressed a finger to the ridge of her lash line. Lo twitched, watching Lulu's makeup succumb to the inevitable. Lo's makeup knew better than to be so disobedient.

"I can accept and reject my own dance offers." Lulu didn't appreciate Lo's interference. Sure, the boy was pale, but he had an adorable dimple on the right side of his mouth when he smiled.

"I was giving you a taste of your own medicine. Why were you pushing Brian onto Emma?" Lo swiped her finger around her mouth again, even though her lip color hadn't run in the slightest.

Lulu understood Lo's meddling now—it was of her instructive variety. "I was not *pushing*. Just, you know, hinting."

"Audrey is less subtle with a hint." Lo dabbed the sweat under her eyes so it neatly collected into her tear ducts at the inner corner, then blinked the liquid away, creating no mess at all. Whenever life went haywire, Lo took the extra time to perfect herself. "It's not polite to shove your leftovers on your friends."

"Whoa. I saw her checking him out at the concert last week. I was trying to help. But fine. Make me the asshole."

"I see." Lo arched a single eyebrow. "How 'bout we find you someone other than a sophomore for tonight. I mean, really."

Lulu squirmed under Lo's appraisal. "I just want to have fun."

"I know, lovey. I'm trying to facilitate that for you. Exactly like you did for darling Emma." Lo's words began to slur and her movements exaggerated into Lulu's space. The effects of alcohol were showing.

"Then come dance with me." Lulu pulled Lo by one arm, before her friend could return to any further makeup inspections or personal criticisms.

"Please." Lo stuck her hand so into Lulu's face that Lulu had to duck not to have a palm shoved up her nose.

"Come on." Lulu yanked her friend again.

Lo protested with a delightful pout, dragging her heels until she forgot she wanted to. Lulu managed a minute of dancing before a member of the soccer team pulled Lo away. Lulu wasn't sure which one, in costume. The best features of any of them were their legs anyway, so Lulu rarely wasted her time looking at their faces. Alone, Lulu scanned the crowd around her, hoping to spot Audrey. She turned around, several times, finding nothing. Until on her final spin, she found herself face-to-chest with Dane Anderson.

"Well, hello," he said, smiling down at her. "What do we have here?"

"Velma Dinkley. And you are?" Lulu asked, partly out of obligation but mostly out of a need to have anything intelligible to say to such a distracting version of him. She knew it didn't matter what Dane's costume was meant to be, as the whole point of his attire was to walk around shirtless, exposing his perfect abs all night, inflicting them on an unsuspecting populace. She hated the sight of them, particularly as they incited her to reach out and rest her hand carelessly across his stomach.

Half-dressed as he was, Lulu could hardly pretend not to appreciate his bared body. But neither could she pretend she wasn't disgusted by his sense of total self-assurance. He was a boy, weaponized. Worse, she knew he'd done it on purpose. And worse still, she keenly felt how well his tactics were working. She was glad to be sober tonight, after all. She didn't think about how woozy an entire day of hunger had made her, sated as she had been by her large, but not quite large enough dinner. She especially didn't think on how depleted her willpower had been from a day already spent in physical denial.

"Hmmm, I could be Freddie if you like." His words were slurred and his voice purred with a purposeful aggression.

"I don't like." Lulu spoke her mind, though her body moved to disagree. She blinked one too many times to be convincing. "Besides, you'd need to find Daphne if you're going to be Freddie."

Lulu, trying to focus anywhere but on his perfect stomach, looked up.

He tossed his hair with a beautiful flip. She was reminded of the one time she'd played basketball and had caught the ball squarely with her face. She tried to remember what she'd been doing only a moment before, how to get away from temptation incarnate. But Dane quickly intruded in on her space, stepping right in front of her and continuing the conversation he meant to have with her.

"Nah, I think Freddie always secretly harbored a crush on Velma. He was just too manly and in need of a trophy girlfriend to admit it." Dane brushed his elbow up against Lulu's. His skin was already damp with sweat.

"If he was so manly, then why did he wear an ascot?" Unfortunately, her own mention of neckwear made her stare in the hollow at the base of Dane's throat, right where his collarbone started. She couldn't trust what her hands would do anymore. Lulu crossed her arms.

"Come on, Dinkley, dance with me." He tugged until her arms uncrossed.

"Anderson, that's not my name." She wanted to roll her eyes at him, but all her energy was reserved for continuing to look him in the face.

"You can pretend you don't hate me for one dance." He grabbed her hand, pulling her toward him. "You won't regret it."

Lulu allowed herself to be led back into the throng of the dance floor. She winced as her body slammed into his. "Wanna bet?"

Pressed up against him, Lulu could smell the peppermint and gin on his breath again. She could feel his stomach up against hers, while his hand slowly slid down her back. But she looked up into his eyes and they were hazy and vacant. She turned around so he was mashed up against her back. He waited a few beats and pivoted her so she faced him directly. Avoiding eye contact, Lulu pressed herself closer into his frame so her head sat against his shoulder, using his body as a makeshift shield against his lure. Dane didn't do anything to move her from this position.

His momentary patience would be her undoing.

Lulu lost herself in the music, the rhythm of it. His body moved and hers responded. If she was in control of herself at this moment, she didn't know it. Her fingers gripped into his bare back reflexively. In that instant, everything shifted. He pressed his tongue clumsily into her mouth as his lips crashed up against hers. Lulu felt her sobriety then—too alert to disconnect from what was happening, too capable of feeling every brush of skin up against skin to not keep going. Her thoughts were a panicked blur—trying to figure out how she could pull out of this position, trying to figure out how she could pull him deeper into the corner of the room.

Lulu's hand grazed Dane's flexed stomach. Immediately responding, Dane's hand snaked up the front of her shirt, grabbing for her chest. She pushed it down, but he continued unabated. She didn't know how to make his hands stop so she pressed her mouth onto his more firmly and pulled his body toward her, forcing their chests flush against each other. But his strong arms maintained control of the situation in a way Lulu was unprepared to deal with. His other hand groped her mostly bare thighs, finding their way under the edge of her minuscule shorts. His fingers prodded along slender muscle that joined her thigh to her groin. This had to stop. She didn't know how to make him stop. He would go where he wanted. One yes had become a surrogate for all yeses. Lulu had to get out. Nothing else was working; she shoved her hands hard up against Dane's chest.

"What?" Dane's eyes were still hazy, looking at Lulu with a pressure she found troubling. He leaned his head in toward her.

"No." Lulu pulled her head away, wiping the sides of her mouth with the back of her hand.

"What?" His voice didn't carry over the music, but Lulu could read his lips and feel the surprise rippling across his body. He hadn't let go.

"No." Lulu shook her head, trying to disentangle herself.

Dane gave Lulu a hard stare. She did her best not to flinch. Disappointment and annoyance danced across his face. He shook his head, dropped his hands, and turned on his heels, stalking away without anything else to say.

Lulu looked around. No one else seemed to notice what had happened. They were, themselves, lost in their own miniature dramas. She was glad to not have had an audience. The dance floor began to close in on her, and she didn't think she could breathe. She pushed her way to the back door, desperate for air.

Outside, Lulu crouched low, her back against a concrete platform at the rear of the building. She'd escaped the dance floor as her vision blurred. The area was isolated, and she found solace in the idea that she would not be found. An acute pang in Lulu's chest threatened to split into a giant chasm. She had done what she had sworn to herself she would never do. She had given Dane all the power, and left none for herself. She had violated her only rule—Never Dane Anderson. And he had proved her right for making the rule in the first place. And she had proved his taunting right. Lulu took deep, deep inhales. But they didn't help. She had done this to herself. She closed her eyes, but that only intensified her feeling. She felt her cheeks—they were wet. Unbidden tears streamed down her face.

She sat there as silent sobs shook her body. Lulu curled into herself. A few more minutes and she could get this out of her system. Her body fought with her desire to master her emotions. But her body wouldn't win. Her breathing steadied again. She was already wiping under her eyes, trying to minimize the evidence of her feelings.

Then she heard a light cough. Lulu whipped her head around and, catching sight of the source, groaned.

Sitting beside the door, in the space where the door would swing open and cover, was James. Lulu stared, wide-eyed. Her secret was now also his.

That did not settle well with Lulu. He cleared his throat, and then, with unsure movements, scooted halfway between her perch and his seat by the door.

"Are you okay?" He paused, arresting the boyish hopefulness in his face.

"Yeah." Lulu beamed an overly bright smile, her blotchy face be damned. "Super."

But her sarcasm did not deter him. He moved, slowly, closer.

"Do you wanna…" James clearly had no idea how to finish the last of that thought.

But Lulu knew how to end it. "Nope."

A silence loomed over them, threatening to never end.

James stood and started feeling through his pockets. "We went out for barbecue earlier."

Lulu didn't understand the gibberish he was rambling. She wanted him to go away, and leave her alone, like she'd never been found to begin with. He didn't even go here. *How did he possibly get a ticket to the party*, Lulu wondered. She fought back more tears, these of pride.

He wasn't looking at her, though. Finally, he seemed to have found the object of his search. "And they always give us these." He closed the space between them in two perfunctory steps, handing her a small square packet.

Lulu saw what he offered—a moist towelette. She stared.

"I thought. You wanted to clean up. I think. I don't care. I thought you might want it." He must have noticed her wiping up her face.

Lulu didn't know what to say, so she took it. He sat beside her without further comment. She mopped under her eyes, clearing what must be a mass of mascara and eyeliner pooling there. She slapped her cheeks lightly. She took a deep inhale and turned her face to him—her sparkling, charming smile plastered across her face again.

"How's it look?"

"Better. I think. I mean, your nose is red. But the rest of your makeup looks good."

Lulu ought to have been affronted by the honesty, but she wasn't. She appreciated it. "It couldn't. Not after."

James tilted his head, then, motioning to her. "May I?"

"What are you going to do?" Lulu leaned away, mistrusting both him and herself in such a moment.

He curled his fingers back, unsure. "You. You have a … thingy. Just there." He touched a lock of her wig resting by the outer corner of her eye. His hand retreated. "I'm sure you can get it."

There was a vulnerability in him in that moment that Lulu couldn't resist. She tilted her face toward him. "This help?"

"Sure," he said, his voice maddeningly steady.

James clamped his lips as he made a hesitant move toward her. Lulu closed her eyes. She felt a light tickle at her temples. Curiosity got the better of Lulu. Her eyes flashed open, and they made direct contact with his. Lulu shut her eyes again quickly.

He stayed his movements. "Hold still, please. I'm not sure what this is. I think. I think it's fuzz." His fingers grazed the edge of her wig. They pulled delicately through her false hair. "Got it."

Lulu's eyes fluttered open. She cleared her throat. "Is it better?"

He placed one set of her false eyelashes into her hand. "Wasn't all that bad to begin with."

Lulu couldn't look him in the eye anymore. The moment was too strange, too intimate. Looking down, she caught sight of a sliver of his exposed stomach, between his shirt hem and his pants. He didn't look particularly muscular there, but she envisioned the ways she might graze her finger across the patch of skin. Then she froze. An image from earlier flashed into her mind. All she could think about were strong hands moving across her body against her will. All she could think about was remembering to breathe steadily again.

"Lulu," he said.

She looked up. His face hovered beside her, staring at her. Concern played across his face. She leaned in, ready for the comforting feeling of lips against her own. But instead of leaning in, he stood quickly. And, without further ado, he fled.

Lulu hardly could process what had happened, when Lo flew out the back doors. "We have to go."

"What?" Lulu was still in a mental haze. She couldn't react as quickly as Lo needed.

"Audrey."

In that one syllable Lulu knew what had happened. She could have kicked herself for getting so wrapped up in her own silly drama that she forgot about Audrey. The sinking feeling in the bottom of Lulu's stomach returned with a vengeance. "Oh no."

"Oh yes," said Lo. "You go by the car. I'll get her."

"You?" Lulu asked.

"Shut up and go." And Lo was off again, as quickly as she had appeared.

————

At the sight of Lulu still standing by the back door, Lo's eyes went wide. She was stooped under the limp weight of Audrey. "I told you to wait by the car."

"And how are you planning to get her to the car without the chaperones seeing? You need two people to get her to the edge of those trees." Lulu pointed to a copse along the perimeter of the building. Then she hoisted up Audrey from the opposite side as Lo.

Lulu looked over her shoulder in case of a supervising eye, then, seeing the coast clear, walked a path closest to the shadows and the trees. It took a minute to finagle the door open without causing the car to beep. But eventually, Lulu got it, and without dropping Audrey in the process. She and Lo shoved Audrey into the car, propping her up against the door frame. Audrey slumped down across her crossed forearms. Lo shoved Audrey up, pushing her back, then sat herself in the passenger seat. Lulu started the car and drove off into the night.

"God, what happened?" Lulu fired at Lo, trying to assess the damage.

Lo raised her eyebrows at Lulu. "I never got my flask back."

"Do you have it now?" Lulu did her best to steady herself as she drove. She couldn't risk being pulled over with her friend sitting in her back seat in such a state.

"No, she left it somewhere in the hall. But I'm pretty sure she drained it."

Lulu groaned. "Jesus, what was in it?"

"Everclear," said Lo. "And now I'm totally out of booze."

Lulu glared at Lo. "Perspective."

Lo shrugged.

"Did you know," Audrey mumbled in the back seat, trying to prop herself up unsuccessfully.

Lo turned around. "Do I know what?"

"Did you know." Audrey tried staring at her friends, but her eyelids were too much of a burden for her current state. She blinked heavily several times, then squinted. Eventually, she found her point again. "That. The air speed velocity. Of an unladen swallow's 'bout whether or not it's carrying a coconut. Coconuts. Nuts."

"No, it's not," said Lo. She caught Lulu's glare and barged on, regardless. "Seriously, if the swallow is unladen, it, by definition, is *not* burdened with any cargo. What really matters is the velocity of the wind. Then the bird has to be converted back in terms that can be understood as ground speed. Plus, the speed and velocity of an object are *two different equations*. Related, but different. You so know that, Audrey."

Audrey smiled, then went limp.

Lulu breezed through a list of profanities, thankful again that the sun was down. "How the hell are we supposed to get her up and home? I mean, do we need to take her to the hospital?" Panic rose in Lulu's throat. It took more and more energy to steady her own breathing.

"I don't know. What about to your house?" Lo said.

"God, no. Not if we called on Audrey's behalf. Especially not after the swimming pool incident. Mrs. Bachmann will see through that immediately. Plus, if she's asleep, then we'd for sure wake her. And then she'd want to talk to Audrey."

"Bad idea." Lo nodded.

As if on cue, Audrey's face squeaked against the windowpane—cheek slipping down glass.

"Can you get back there and wake her? If she doesn't wake up, I'm going to the hospital."

Lulu expected more of a huff, but Lo crawled through the center console and into the back seat easily and without fuss. She shouldn't have doubted her friend. Lo lightly slapped across Audrey's face in an attempt to jiggle her awake. Audrey moaned once roused.

"Quick. What's the square root of pi?" Lo asked.

"1.772," Audrey answered in a murmur, but at least in an immediate one.

Lulu breathed out a sigh of relief. "Is that right?"

"How am I supposed to know? Audrey's the math wiz."

"Jesus, Lo. Ask her a question you know the answer to!"

Lo rolled her eyes but acquiesced to Lulu's barked request. "Audrey, who do you wanna be when you grow up?"

Audrey gave another quick murmur in reply. "Not my mother."

"See, she's fine," Lo said.

Lulu couldn't possibly argue with that kind of logic, so she didn't try. They drove silently the rest of the way to Audrey's house, tense with the anticipation of what they might find there. Soon they were parked. Lulu hoisted Audrey by her shoulders. Lo grabbed her feet. Audrey's head lolled about disconcertingly, but her eyes were, at least, open. The kitchen door, which they predicted would be unlocked, creaked slightly, but otherwise the house was soundless and asleep. Every breath that was too loud gave Lulu pause, but Lo kept moving slowly and steadily until they all reached Audrey's bedroom. Lo let go of Audrey's feet onto the bed, and Lulu lost her grip on their friend, nearly dropping her on the floor. Lulu shot daggers out of her eyes. Lo ignored her.

"Audrey, honey. Audrey," Lulu whispered. "How're you feeling?"

Audrey's eyes were still slits. "No good," she mumbled.

"Okay, let's go over here," Lulu carried her friend over to the bathroom and set her head against the toilet.

She went in and out of the room, pulling pillows and covers from Audrey's bed as Lo watched over Audrey. Lulu rushed back in, pillows in hand, when she heard Audrey retching. Lo held back Audrey's hair, stroking her back.

"See, she's fine," Lo said. "Her stomach's pumping itself."

"You have the darkest optimism I've ever seen."

"Aw, thanks." Lo gave a sloppy grin.

Half an hour later, the damage was done. Lulu attempted to get Audrey to gargle with mouthwash but ended up with a good amount across her face from Audrey spitting it out at her. Lo did her best to help Lulu ready Audrey for bed, but her movements were far less coordinated than Lulu's. In the end, Lulu wrangled Audrey out of her dress and into a pair of shorts. She set up a place for Audrey to sleep by the toilet, propping her friend up on her side for good measure. That should do for one night.

As soon as Audrey was settled, Lo grabbed one of the pillows and blankets permanently dotting Audrey's floor. She curled up and went immediately to sleep, her makeup still on her face and a tutu still wrapping around her hips. After washing her own face off, crawling into an enormous T-shirt out of Audrey's dresser, and climbing into Audrey's bed, Lulu had a single thought—she never wanted to celebrate Halloween again.

8

Woke Up Like This

Audrey groaned. She winced as she opened her eyes. Morning had come and, in Audrey's case, had come viciously and without warning.

"Look. Sleeping Beauty's up," said Lo.

Lulu entered from the connected bathroom, adjusting her contacts. "How you doing there, killer?"

To that, Audrey could only grunt.

Lo laughed. "Dude, you owe me a new flask. And a bottle of Everclear."

"Everclear?" Audrey's voice sounded graveled and throaty—like she'd gone through half a pack of cigarettes last night.

"Yeah. What did you think you'd been drinking?" Lo said.

"Vodka?"

Lo laughed again.

Lulu gave her an ominous look. "Lo—lay off. It isn't funny."

"At least she didn't drink that much Everclear on purpose last night." Lo went into the bathroom, then with a few clattering noises, reentered the bedroom. She shoved a pill cocktail into one of Audrey's hands and a glass of water into the other. "Here. Tums should help. There's also some Advil there and a gummy-vite."

Audrey took the pills and chewed her gummy-vite in complacent silence.

"Yes," said Lulu. "It was the Everclear that was the problem, not the draining of a flask in less than two hours."

Audrey blinked. "I did what?"

"Dude, you killed my flask, dropped it somewhere on the dance floor, and then puked your fucking guts out. I think you vomited for like twenty minutes straight. It was foul. Lulu had to undress you." Lo snorted.

At that, Audrey looked down. She was still half-undressed, half–in costume.

Lulu, however, couldn't laugh at Audrey's state. It would have been comical had last night not inflicted a great deal of pain on everyone involved. If she hadn't nearly had to take Audrey to the hospital. "Audrey. Last night was terrifying."

And Lo, having finished all practical concerns here, got up and went downstairs. Lulu, knowing Lo had reasons for everything, said nothing as she left.

"It's fine." Audrey pushed herself out of the bed with as much force as she was able. "I haven't had a night like that in ages."

This dismissal was worse than anything. Lulu had to make Audrey see how serious last night had been. "I nearly took you to the hospital. I can't believe I didn't. I should've."

"It turned out fine. Everything's fine." Audrey shuffled into the bathroom, splashing cold water on her face and rinsing her mouth out.

"But what if it didn't and you weren't?!" Lulu's voice cracked.

"But it did!" Audrey's tone brooked no what-ifs or hypotheticals. "And you're one to talk!"

"Me?"

Audrey rolled her eyes meaningfully. "You run around anyone's house with God knows who doing God knows what, and you're mad that I drank a little bit too much last night? You believe boys keep telescopes in hall closets."

"Excuse me?" Lulu croaked.

"Come on, Lulu. You know you play a dangerous game."

Lulu shook her head. Her ears rang. The room grew hot. A spinning sensation took over her head, and a voice in the back of her mind reminded her to take a deep breath. "No. I'm not having this conversation right now. We're talking about you. And the insane amount of alcohol you consumed last night."

"You're so insensitive." Audrey moved back to the bedroom and dug into her dresser, grabbing a large T-shirt to cover herself with.

"*I'm* insensitive?" Lulu's voice barely came out at a whisper—it was a stifled shout. Lulu shook off her desire to take on that argument. No reason would permeate Audrey's conscience right now. And right now, Lulu was more concerned Audrey wouldn't accept the realities of last night. Even if the bile clawing at Lulu's throat warned her that Audrey was right, that Lulu had played with way too much fire last night and lost. "Lo and I were worried half to death about you. I've never been so scared. Not since the last time. You promised."

Audrey flinched. "I doubt Lo was worried. She's been laughing at me all morning. She'd probably have enjoyed watching me get my stomach pumped."

"Don't you dare, Audrey." Lulu wielded her index finger like a sword. It was keeping the tears that threatened at bay, to focus her anger on a source outside herself. "Lo carried you over her shoulder last night, like a goddamn fireman. Lo did. While also keeping you ducked under the crowd, so no one would call your mom. Just 'cause she's not Little Miss Sunshine doesn't mean she doesn't care. You of all people know that."

"Fine. Sorry." But Audrey didn't sound all that sorry at all.

Lo reentered the room, ignored Lulu, and looked at Audrey. "I talked to your mom. She thinks you got up early for a run. So climb out your window in some workout clothes and you can come back as dehydrated and 'sun-dazed' as you want. You're welcome."

"She can't climb out her window!" Lulu felt cartoon smoke ought to be steaming out of her ears.

"She better. At least in the next twenty minutes, before her mom checks to make sure I'm not a liar. And I don't want her thinking I'm a liar. She should use our leaving as cover." And before she heard any further opposition, Lo put up a hand. "Lulu. Go take a walk."

Lulu opened her mouth, baring her teeth. That quiet voice in the back of her conscience reminded her to take a deep breath.

"I am not messing around. Go take a walk. Now." Lo grabbed Lulu's car keys off Audrey's dresser and shook them until they made a light jingling noise. "I'll be in the car. Go walk it off."

"You know what. Fine. I'm out of here." Lulu threw her parting shot over her shoulder. "Enjoy nursing your hangover alone."

Audrey flinched as Lulu slammed the door on her way out. Lo rolled her eyes, then helped Audrey out the window. It was only later, when Lulu was stomping around the block, that she realized that, at some point last night, they had totally abandoned Emma.

———

"You're a piece of shit, did you know that?" Lulu slammed the driver's side door as she got in. Lulu interacted with the inanimate objects in her vicinity with greater force than necessary: she flung the book on her seat into the rear seat with a thwack, she smacked the driver's seat with her back, she jerked the keys in the ignition. She left no energy in her body as potential. The car rattled with Lulu's frustrations.

Only a keen observer like Lo could tell that the walk had calmed Lulu down.

"Whoa. Aren't we Little Miss Cranky Pants this morning?" Lo was perched in the front seat, her knees up, her hands on her knees. She had actually gotten out a bottle of nail polish and was finishing up a coat on her left hand.

With overly forceful pokes, Lulu rolled down all the windows in the car. Everything smelled like plastic and fumes.

"I didn't eat breakfast. Didn't get up in time. And now I can't eat until dinner." That wasn't what was bothering Lulu. Her hunger was only making everything worse, taking all her gray-scale feelings and making them technicolor.

"Not my fault, babe." Lo blew on her wet nails, stashing away the bottle of polish.

Forty-five minutes earlier, she'd still been dressed as a ladybug, her makeup smeared across her face. Now she looked like she belonged on an editorial about casual brunchwear—a floaty dress, properly scuffed-up ankle boots, and neatly disheveled hair. Lulu wanted to lick her finger, reach out, and smudge Lo's eyeliner. She wasn't sure what point that would prove, but Lulu knew she would have felt better if she did. She took a deep breath, aware the voice that reminded her to do so was Emma's. Poor, abandoned Emma.

"You abandoned me in there." Lulu's statement held an unasked *why*, and Lo knew it.

"Yelling at her won't get what you want, Lulu. It never has." If Lulu wanted a concession, Lo had none to offer. She'd done what she thought necessary to mitigate the damage. Lulu would have to deal with that.

"Yeah? Then what will? She's blacked out before, but never like this."

"I'm not sure," Lo said. "I don't think it's up to us. She's in charge of herself."

"Brilliant." Lulu gave up on the conversation, instead focusing all her energies on the road. As she drove, a wind built inside the car, whipping air through their hair.

Lo faced out the window, allowing the artificial breeze to jostle her further awake. When she next spoke, she didn't turn to face Lulu. "So, are we gonna talk about how you hooked up with Anderson last night? Or are you going to pretend it never happened?"

Lulu continued to stare straight ahead of her. But she wasn't focusing on the road anymore. She was driving by memory.

"I see." Lo thrummed her fingers along the side dash. "Are you going to tell Audrey or Emma?"

"Wasn't planning on it." Particularly not after the vicious judgment Lulu had already faced that morning from Audrey.

"Fascinating."

"Lo, please. Just—don't." Lulu's voice squeaked. She hated that little tell.

"Your secret's safe with me, Lulu-cat. But outright lying is so unlike you."

"I'm not lying," Lulu said. But it was no good.

"That's a pretty big thing to forget to tell anyone, particularly 'one of your best friends.' And you know it." Lo had a sardonic grin as she watched a traffic light turn green.

Lulu gripped the steering wheel tighter. The tires squealed as she put the car back in motion. Lo thought she'd had Lulu. She thought she'd herded Lulu into a direction and would force Lulu to go through the gate, into the pen. Lulu refused to be corralled. She swallowed a lump in her throat. If she used her steadiest tone, maybe she could get the information out without it being a big deal. Facts, Lulu told herself, would ground her—plain language, nothing flowery, none of her usual hyperbole. Maybe it would make it all sound, and feel, better.

"It's just—I didn't want to."

"What?" Lo's voice was steady, but it was the eye of a hurricane—deceptive, threatening more menace.

Lulu gulped. "I thought I wanted to. And then I didn't. And he wouldn't stop. Not totally. I mean, he stopped. Eventually."

Lo was so still. Lulu had never seen Lo so still. It was unsettling.

Lulu reached for words, the ones that would set Lo in motion again. "But I'm fine. Everything's fine. Seriously."

"I'm going to murder him." Lo didn't sound remotely squeamish about the prospect.

"Lo, no. It's not that bad. I mean. He didn't, you know. Get anywhere he shouldn't." But Lulu, seized in a sudden flash of the memory of his fingers prying along the line of her underwear, shuddered. "It's not a big deal. Please, Lo."

Finally stopped at a red light, Lulu looked imploringly into Lo's eyes. Lo stared at Lulu for a long while. Lulu held still, a specimen under a microscope.

Lo let out an exhale; she'd been holding her breath. "Fine. But if I see him anywhere near you, I'm not responsible for what I do."

Lulu laughed a shaky laugh at that. "Aren't you?"

"No, I'm not. I take kickboxing for a reason." Lo was dead serious. Or maybe Anderson would be dead and Lo would look anything but serious.

"I thought that was because you said it gave you killer abs and the legs of a stuntwoman."

Lo smiled, like she was so proud to be capable of such great violence, that her muscles made her dangerous. "That, too."

"Remind me never to piss you off."

"You piss me off plenty." Lo said this like she'd tell someone the time, or report the traffic, or notice it was already raining. A statement of fact.

Lulu giggled—Lo's honesty was a relief. "Then what keeps you from chopping my head off?"

"I love you. Always have, always will." Lo shrugged.

"Well," Lulu said, a bit startled.

"Oh, don't say it back if you don't *mean* it, Lulu." Lo pouted her lips and puckered her eyebrows together, transforming the pretty paint on her features into a tool for the ridiculous.

"Shut up, Lo. You know I love you. Even if you're a bitch and a half." Lulu swatted at Lo.

Lo nodded assuredly. "It's one of my best qualities."

———

The weather crisped. Around these parts, there was a joke that there were only two seasons—summer and August. But Lulu could always feel the shift to fall. The breeze smelled different. The rush of cool air in her lungs changed, however slightly, the way breathing felt. Just because the switches were small, well, that didn't mean they weren't happening. Summer was so oppressive, Lulu appreciated the subtlety of fall.

Lulu took a deep inhale. She could see the whole neighborhood from up here where she sat. Outside her bedroom window rested the roof to the porch. It had a gentle, forgiving slope. It wasn't too high up, only one story. As a child, she had often found herself sitting up here, taking in the neighborhood, watching cars and cats and dogs and other passersby. It was like a really boring reality TV show that she didn't know why she watched. But there was a solitary romance in it, like she was the all-seeing eye of the neighborhood. The cooling air whipped through her hair; she heard a knock at the bedroom door. She ignored it. She wanted to be alone with her thoughts. She felt as though she hadn't been alone for ages.

An errant june bug bumbled across the lawn, unaware of the date. She wondered at it, solitary thing that it was. It ought to have buried itself deep and taken cover in the soil long ago, along with its brethren. But, then again, who was she to tell a little beetle what it ought to do. If it wanted to risk exposure, let it fly pathetically across the grass, all by itself. Another knock rapped across the wooden door frame, followed by the squeaking noise of her old door hinges.

"Honey, I'm coming in." It was her mother.

Lulu didn't turn around.

"I haven't seen you out there in forever." She walked over and turned Lulu's loud music all the way down. Not off, mind you, but down so low that only a hum of noise could be heard emanating out of Lulu's speakers. "Always gives me a fright."

Lulu sighed. She sat—knees up, back against the windowpane—on the roof of the porch.

"Lord, I remember the first time I saw you out there. On the roof playing with your little pony dolls, chatting up a storm like there wasn't a care in the world. Or like a dozen mosquitoes weren't about to fly into your room." Her mother chattered along casually, with a friendliness and brightness that Lulu saw right through.

"What do you want, Mama?" asked Lulu.

"I'm remembering how you used to be. And sometimes still are." Her hand reached through the open window and stroked the back of Lulu's hair.

Lulu shifted ever so slightly toward the caress. The pacing of her mother's movements had a soothing effect on Lulu. She wondered if all mothers had this magic, or simply her own. She didn't turn around.

"I came up here to sit with you. Seemed like you might need company. Plus your radio was so loud it was rattling in my office downstairs. Though I think I'll sit on your bed. I've never been the rooftop type."

"What does that make me?" Lulu turned to face her mother.

She had perched herself on the edge of Lulu's bed and looked newly aware that she had somehow wounded Lulu. "My little cat."

"I'm not a cat, I'm a girl." Lulu's response was hard around the edges, carried along an unsteady voice.

"I'm afraid you're not a girl anymore, either, darling. Not all the time, at least. You're in between. The good news is, you'll never feel this way again, so best take it all in now. The bad news is most people spend their lives trying to grab that feeling again." Her mother smiled.

Lulu wasn't sure of her voice, so she waited a full minute before continuing on in a hoarse tone, "I know." She hugged her knees to her chest, rocking almost imperceptibly back and forth.

"Could you maybe come in if you're going to do that? I don't mean to barge in and be a nag, but I am about to have a heart attack watching you teeter around on the roof."

Lulu raised an eyebrow and ducked under the window frame in response. She sat on the sill, legs swinging in her own room, with her shoulders propped up by the partially opened windowpane.

"I guess that's something." Her mother's mouth slanted across her face.

Lulu could have laughed, but she didn't have the heart at the moment. So she sat there, swinging her legs up against her wall. Her heels thudded rhythmically. "Do I have to?"

"Do you have to what?"

"Grow up," Lulu said.

"No, you don't have to," her mother said quietly. "You can stay here forever, eat takeout, and listen to your father's history lessons at the table. And I won't lie, Lulu, I would let you. I wish I wouldn't, but I would. But then I'd be so sad for you."

"Why?" Lulu startled at the look on her mother's face. Their typical interactions were either bombastic or silly. There wasn't much middle ground left over for earnestness.

"You only get one life in this body. You're going to charge headlong into everything. And I don't mean anyone, I mean you. You were the only one of my children who bare-handedly grabbed the same hot pan twice. I know you. Don't be afraid of yourself."

Lulu stared at her unmanicured toes. The edges of her toenails were crooked and uneven, and she raised her left foot up, picking at them, trying to repair them as best she could, with movements that would only make the situation worse. She remembered grabbing that pan, too. The first time hurt like all hell, though she wouldn't have phrased it like that at the time. She remembered wondering if it would feel the same a second time. It hadn't. It had felt infinitely worse.

"How can I fix it? I can tell something's wrong. Tell me how to fix it, honey."

"You can't." Lulu's eyes glistened. She blinked several times.

"Let me try."

Lulu shook her head. It had taken her fourteen years to figure out that some breaks were beyond repair. And what a rude awakening that had been.

Her mother sighed as she stood. She grabbed her daughter's chin delicately, and looked into her eyes, as though she was trying to read behind them. "You've always been my independent one. You hold so much in. You aren't who anyone decides you are. You aren't how anyone treats you. You have to find peace in that. It's not easy, but you do."

"Mama?"

"Yes?"

Lulu didn't know what to say there. She wanted to hold everything tight inside her, but she also wished she could unload the burden onto her mother.

So she reached out and grabbed her mom for a hug, feeling the release in such a simple touch. Lulu cried, in a small silent way. She hoped her mother couldn't feel her tiny sobs. Lulu wiped at her eyes and her nose while she still clung to her. She held in a sniffle. "Thank you."

"Honey, are you sure you don't want to talk about whatever is on your mind?"

Lulu shook her head to decline. "I'm all right now, thanks. I just had a bad week. I needed that. It was perfect. Thanks, Mama."

"Let me know if you change your mind. I'll be downstairs if you need."

Her mother was not one to force a confidence, and, resultantly, usually got more out of her children through her restraint rather than through assertion. Lulu, as the youngest, was too practiced in her mother's techniques. She took advantage.

"Sure," Lulu said. "Mama?"

"Yes?"

"I love you."

"Love you, too, little cat." And with that Aimee shut the door behind herself.

9

Collateral Damage

During her morning break on Monday, and unconscious of her untucked shirt, Lulu walked into the library. She was looking for a book for French. Instead she found Ms. Huntley, a uniform violation, and a detention. She had been distracted, hungry, and wondering if Dane would or would not show up to class the next period. That her fears proved unfounded— Anderson hadn't made an appearance—did nothing to quell Lulu's uneasy feeling. His absence confirmed that he regarded her as small, discarded, and insignificant. Rejection never felt good. Rejection after what had happened that weekend seemed somehow worse.

Lulu had planned on apologizing to Emma, but she had been conspicuously absent from her usual haunts. She was not reading in the cubby under the stairwell. Nor was Emma outside by the palm trees in the last of the fall sun. She hadn't even gone into the newspaper room to work on an assignment. Lulu could only be baffled. Emma hadn't held a grudge in her life.

Luckily, Emma appeared at the usual table at lunch. She sat between

Audrey and Lo. But even then, Audrey managed to mangle what had been on Lulu's mind all morning. Namely, to find Emma and apologize.

"Emma, honey, how dreadful!" Audrey said. "I can't believe we left you all by yourself at the party!"

Lulu arched an eyebrow but said nothing. She was trying to keep the peace. Or at least, keep her fight with Audrey from spilling across their entire friend group. But the declaration still irritated her. As though Audrey had been conscious for the leaving. As though Audrey could exculpate herself in the same breath that she implicated Lulu and Lo. Lulu wasn't particularly notable for her own apologies. But Audrey's current one was a tour de force in avoiding culpability. Emma caught sight of Lulu before she'd had a chance to rearrange her face to a pleasant expression. Emma shook her head, then looked away.

Emma's expression gave Lulu the distinct impression that a valuable piece of information had gone missing. Lulu had no idea where she might find it, though.

Audrey continued her verbal tap dance, equal parts flapping and flailing, as long as the rest of the lunch table would let her. "How about, to make it up to you, we have a movie fest at my house, but like an Emma-fest. So only your favorites! *Sixteen Candles*! And Disney princesses! A slumber party! This weekend! At my house! How fun would that be? Tell me it wouldn't be fun. Tell me."

Confusion washed across Emma's face. "It could be fun."

Audrey lit up with relief. "See! I knew it! It's going to be so fun! You can't wait!"

At that, Lulu finally cracked. "We left you because Audrey was falling-down drunk. She nearly didn't make it to the car. It was still horrible to forget you. Sorry."

"You're making fun of me," Audrey said, before Emma could answer Lulu's apology.

"This isn't about you, Audrey Louise," said Lulu.

"You're making it about me!"

"You're both making it about you! And y'all all ditched me." Emma covered her mouth, as though she couldn't believe she'd said it. But something unstoppable must have cracked open inside Emma. "I've got a newspaper assignment about a freshman on the girls' varsity volleyball team." And with that Emma stood, her chair scraping against the floor, and left.

Nobody could believe it, especially not Lulu. The table broke apart soon after.

———

The last bell couldn't save Lulu's mood. She had texted Emma repeatedly, trying to fix her earlier apology. No response. Lulu, ready for the day to at least be over, trudged to her locker, only to see Audrey waiting against it. Their eyes locked, removing all possibility of a graceful exit.

"I texted Emma." Audrey let out a cough. "Nothing."

If Audrey was waiting for a confirmation of the same from Lulu, she would remain disappointed.

Audrey stayed in place, but she looked away, over Lulu's head. "Are we still fighting?"

Lulu stared. Audrey finally looked back down and made eye contact.

"I'm sorry. I didn't mean to scare you or anything. I had no idea you would be so freaked out. It won't happen again, I swear." Audrey held her breath. Then she held out her pinkie.

Perhaps Lulu's anger the night of Halloween had simply been residual anxiety, left over from the dance floor. Lulu didn't like feeling helpless, and she didn't know if she'd been fair to Audrey during their fight the next morning. Going a whole three days without Audrey had been terrible enough. Lulu harbored no desires to prolong the experience. She took Audrey's pinkie in her own and swore by it. "Fine. You win. I forgive you. You always win."

"It's because I'm adorable, isn't it?" Audrey flashed an approximation of a charming smile, which she carried off in a hopelessly goofy kind of way.

"No, it's because you would be so helpless in the wild without me. I'm your only hope for survival." Lulu dialed in the combination on her locker, shaking her head.

Audrey slapped playfully, but overly enthusiastically, at Lulu's arm. "Shut up. I would so survive in the wild. I'd be, like, Queen of the Jungle. No, Queen of the Whole Wild."

"Okaayy," Lulu drawled. "Sure you would."

"Just you wait, Lulu Saad. Just you wait."

Lulu's breath caught. Today was no day for inciting curses. If she'd had any on hand, Lulu would have thrown salt over her shoulder. Atman Rai looked over at the sound. He continued to eye the two girls warily, unsure if theirs was a fight likely to spill over into his small bit of territory. He retreated quickly. Lulu regretted that he had learned to fear her anger.

Lulu turned. "Wait for what, exactly?"

Audrey put her hand on her hip, but with that move, her half-on, half-off backpack slid totally off her shoulders and crashed onto the floor. "For me to prove I'd do quite peachily without you."

Audrey slung the backpack onto her shoulders, her posture overly correct. Lulu suppressed a stubborn urge. She would fight for the lightness again between them. She flicked at Audrey's ear. Audrey swatted at Lulu again, this time too lightly to be taken seriously by a casual observer. No one turned to watch; no one slunk away from their playful pugilism.

"Don't say that, darling. You'll break my heart." Lulu fluttered her eyelids.

"You have a heart?"

Lulu barked a laugh. She and Audrey stared at each other for a long instant, both wondering what came next.

"I got a uniform violation. From Huntley. I've got a detention to serve in the next two weeks. Six a.m. time slot of my choice. Like that's a consolation prize."

"She's heinous; everyone knows it." Audrey soothed Lulu's wounds with dismissal.

Lulu had yet to find the tactic consoling. She slammed her locker shut.

"I know, it happens to the best of us. Happened to me like three times already. Don't let it get you down. I mean, blow it off until the last possible moment."

"What, like they'll forget I need to serve it?" Lulu couldn't believe that.

"They did for Lo."

"Lo could get away with murder if she was still holding on to the weapon and her hands were covered in blood, and you know it."

"I know, it's so unfair."

"Maybe," Lulu said. Lo's ability to get out of trouble made different demons for her to battle. "Besides, you'd think the administration would be way more worried about educating us than making sure our shirttails were in order. Fascists."

Audrey laughed. "Adults, can't live with them . . . until you go to college, then you don't have to!"

Audrey skipped a few paces ahead, then turned. "Do you need a ride?"

"Nah, I've still got to find that stupid book in the library. After all that, I left without it. I'll see you later, darlin'."

Lulu waved and Audrey waved back with a lightheartedness she would not have thought possible ten minutes earlier. Lulu looked at the stairs that led to the library and groaned. She dropped her bag, tucked her shirt into her skirt all the way around, despite its being after school hours, and then, grabbing her bag back up again, walked up the upper hallway stairs. No need to tempt fate with two violations for the same offense in the same day.

Lulu turned the corner into the stacks when she saw Dane about halfway down the same aisle. He was bent over and looking through a book. Her stomach dropped. She hoped he wouldn't look up and notice her there, so she busied herself with finding the book she needed. She felt a pull at her skirt.

She turned to face Dane, and her stomach knotted further at the memory of him from the Halloween dance. She carried the wild hope that his mind had been too hazy to form a full memory of his actions. Though another part of her wanted to remind him, painfully and acutely, of what he had done.

"What?" Lulu mouthed the word, trying to indicate that this was no space for a conversation.

"You don't have to be so quiet, you know. It's not like anyone's here after school." He spoke a shade above a whisper, loud enough to carry beyond the stack—loud enough for her to know he totally disregarded her wish for privacy.

She put her hand on her hip, instinctively drawing on her strength, as she continued with her near-silent whisper, using her other arm to direct his gaze across to the other students she saw sitting behind him. "Other than the people studying, you mean?"

He kept his attention focused directly on her, despite her attempts at deflection. He leaned in. "What are you doing here?"

"Looking for that Ronsard book for class." She turned back to her incomplete chore.

"So touchy." He poked her in the ribs.

She stepped away to give him a wide berth. "Not touchy."

Lulu moved back toward the call number of the book she needed, maintaining a gap between herself and him as best she could. Her response was curt, rude. The clippedness of her speech felt wrong. But prolonging the moment did not feel safe. Her nerves were on edge; she was sure there was a right response to the situation, she simply didn't know it.

She felt breath tickling her ear before she knew what it was, and then heard, quieter than her own whispers, "You didn't seem to mind so much last time we were this close."

His speech finished in his clear, audible whisper, "And you can't say it was because you were drunk, 'cause we all know you were sober, like the good little girl that you are."

Lulu's body went rigid; she stared with such intensely focused animosity that Dane couldn't laugh his way out of it. His lips were so close to her own, she could practically feel them.

"That night wasn't a yes, Anderson," Lulu said, her voice as steady as she could make it. She took a step sideways, giving herself breathing room. "Once isn't always or everything."

If Dane was put off, it wasn't for more than an instant. He leaned forward, over the threshold of her personal space. "You wait, Lulu," he said. "You'll want it again." Dane winked, like he knew her little secret. He took the book in his hand and pressed it against her chest, both a mockery and an insinuation.

At his lewdness, anger flashed through Lulu.

"But I'll let you get back to the Romantics of the Renaissance." And with a lecherous grin, he turned the corner and left.

Lulu looked down at the title of the book she held. She swore as she exhaled. He'd had the book she had been looking for the entire time. Once at the checkout desk, she presented the book to the librarian, who appraised her with an unfriendly eye and then sent her on her way.

As she walked out, Lulu looked over to the tables behind the stacks. She saw Emma with a freshman, the one with the bangs. Emma was leaning in and whispering what was clearly a joke, as the other girl giggled in response. Here Emma was joking and laughing with another friend. Leaving them all early from lunch and ignoring Lulu's texts. And Audrey's. Emma could have been keeping the peace. She could have been in the library *with Lulu*, beside Lulu not moments before, providing a buffer against Dane. Lulu swore, moving swiftly out the door before the librarian would decide to do anything more than glare in her direction.

Lulu wouldn't think on the feeling calcifying in her chest. The hard pangs that constricted her breathing. She'd have to solve this problem. She'd have to message Lo.

10

Love Notes from the Edge

"I know what you did," Lulu said to Lo. They both sat on the floor of Audrey's living room. "But I'm still serving the detention."

Audrey and Emma were focused on the TV. Lo didn't look up. She maintained her focus on the base coat she was applying across Lulu's nails. Lo had managed to get them to all agree to this slumber party, despite the tension at the lunch table throughout the week. She framed it as a necessary make-up session. Lo finished the base coat and started shaking a bottle of nail polish, making sure the color was thoroughly mixed.

"I can't believe you turned down the opportunity to skip a d-hall." Lo looked back down at Lulu's nails; she uncapped the polish bottle and set herself to painting. "It was supposed to make you feel better."

Lulu's smile spread across her whole face. She had been right.

After school on Wednesday, Lulu had gone to Mrs. Carly's desk to sign up for a detention slot next week. Mrs. Carly could be described as the Sealy Hall office receptionist, but that would be doing her a disservice. If the dean of students' office had come to life, if student files were the inner workings of a person's mind—then they only could have in the form of Mrs. Carly. She hadn't looked up from her work when Lulu had asked for the detention sign-up sheet.

"Miss Saad, you've already served your detention." It had been a dismissal. At Lulu's continued presence, Mrs. Carly had looked up and frowned.

"I have?" Lulu asked.

Mrs. Carly had pulled out her book. *The* book. A binder filled with class schedules of every student and teacher, and office hours of all the administrators. A student's most-recent-quarter attendance and detention records. The book was legendary. As a freshman, Lulu had been told that it was a shortcut for the files each student inevitably had, the ones in the dean's office. Those had full attendance, behavioral records, a list of friends, known associates, past and current relationships. The scariest part was that Mrs. Carly didn't need the book; she knew. Mrs. Carly was aware of what a student had done that weekend, probably before they'd done it. Lulu's current situation had proved most unusual to Mrs. Carly.

"Right here." But Mrs. Carly looked skeptical. She appraised Lulu, like she'd never gotten a good look at the girl until that moment. "Says you served under Medina."

And that's when the wheels had clicked into place for Lulu. Because Lo had Medina for advisory. And Lo could, however Lo did any of the things she did, easily persuade Medina to give her all the attendance sheets to take down to the desk. Including his detention hall attendance sheet. No teacher was supposed to do that. But Lo heard *cannot* and had taken that as a challenge for *would*. This was exactly the sort of surprise Lo would plan for Lulu. Lo was full of half-cocked plans and ironic pranks. Lo had clearly wanted to give Lulu freedom. Lulu had wanted righteous self-flagellation. She wanted to serve out her punishment, because she felt detentions for uniform violations were truly stupid. And she wanted to prove she *knew* how stupid they were, from firsthand experience.

Lulu had harnessed all her upbringing to not squirm under the scrutiny. "I think that must have been an error on Mr. Medina's part. He must have meant to check in someone else. I know I haven't served."

Mrs. Carly's frown expanded—giving off the effect that her extant frown had frowned. "You know. I didn't think you had been in early that morning. Well. I'm going to go check with Dean Knight's list. You wait right here." She scurried off into a side office.

Lulu drummed her fingers against the desk. She looked over—there sat a stack of detention slips. Probably for teachers to quickly grab and restock their supply. On pure impulse, Lulu grabbed a stack of detention slips off the top of the desk—not so many that the stack looked noticeably different—and stuffed them into her bag. The gesture was futile. But it made her feel like she'd stuck it to the man. Whoever "the man" was. She was going to serve her stupid detention. She was going to steal from the front desk. She was not going to be broken by stupid rules or terrible French assignments or dumb boys in libraries.

Mrs. Carly reentered with a huff. "I'm not sure at all. This is irregular. But, I suppose you wouldn't sign up for a detention you didn't have. When did you want, dear?" Mrs. Carly had decided, then. She took Lulu for the honest sort.

Lulu smiled, placating. "Next Thursday morning. Thanks, Mrs. Carly."

Mrs. Carly frowned again. "Well."

Lulu had skipped out of the room, flooded with relief. Lulu never wanted to come that close to getting caught by Mrs. Carly again. Her hands trembled slightly with what they'd done. She'd stolen from the front desk. It was a petty thing, but it was still moderately exhilarating and made her detention feel worth it.

Lulu didn't feel quite so triumphant now, realizing that not only would she have to wake up before dawn next week to fuel her day, but then she'd have to run out the door and serve a morning detention. Pride had gotten the better of her, unfortunately. At least Lo's manicure was soothing. Lo finished the last coat of color, then swiftly painted Lulu's nails with a gel coat.

"I feel so, so, so, so, so much better. You give the best manicures in the whole wide world." Lulu smiled from her heart.

Lo preened under the compliment. Then, never one to let her feelings get the better of her, Lo waved Lulu away. "Emma, get over here."

Emma avoided eye contact with Lulu. But she complied with Lo's request. Lulu scooted over and blew on her wet nails. They were blue—blue like the pair of hot pants she'd found once in a thrift store and would always regret not purchasing, blue like a shining metallic muscle car, blue like Nightcrawler's naked, muscular thighs. That was Lulu's favorite shade of blue. Lulu continued to silently admire her friend's handiwork.

Sixteen Candles was playing on the old tube TV. Lulu loved the grainy look of it; it reminded her that she'd been watching the movie since she was a little girl. She liked that feeling of certainty. That she could find a way to make the movie look the same as it always had. All it took was a less-than-desirable television and an old VHS player. Even if she did cringe through half the movie now. There was already enough tension without telling Emma her favorite movie was fairly racist and that its romantic lead facilitated a rape. Maybe she'd tell Emma the next time, when everyone's tempers had settled down again.

"Doesn't she remind you of Diana?" Emma watched the screen from where she sat by Lo.

"Who?" Lulu responded.

"Randy," Emma said. She was referring to Molly Ringwald's best friend in the movie, a girl with black hair, olive skin, and a dark sense of humor.

"No. Not *Randy* who. Who-does-Randy-remind-us-of who?" Audrey said.

"I think she means Bangs," Lo said, not looking up from Emma's nails as she worked. She was a stickler for getting the paint just so. She flicked Emma for wiggling. "Bangs's real name is Diana Agrawal," said Lo.

"Ohhh, the freshman girl. With BANGS," said Lulu. "Got it. Totally up to speed. Really, you think Randy looks like her? Like a freshman? Bangs is darker, and her hair is straighter. I guess she kind of looks like her, but without a perm." Lulu tilted her head back and forth, trying to compare a fresh mental image with a stored one.

"Does Bangs wear that much purple?" Audrey asked.

"Nah, but she's got the skin tone to pull off a lot of color," Lo said, still focused on her polishing.

"You're so right. I bet she can wear goldenrod," Audrey said with a sigh.

"Dude, no one can wear goldenrod," Lulu said, ever the skeptic.

"I bet Bangs could," Audrey said. She was still in a defiant mood, at least when it came to Lulu.

Lulu had assumed it would take a little bit of time for Audrey to get over it. Lulu should never have questioned Audrey's autonomy. That would only spell more work for herself in the long run.

"Randy has *epic* bangs in this movie. Lulu, if you cut bangs and let your hair go natural, would your bangs do that?" Audrey asked.

"God. Don't joke," Lulu said.

"She has a name," Emma said.

"Who?" Lulu asked.

"Bangs," Lo answered at the same time that Emma said quietly, "Diana Agrawal."

"Bangs, Diana. Whatever, it's all the same," Lulu said.

Emma frowned. Lo looked up and shook her head at Lulu.

"Oh, Emma. Don't worry about it, she won't ever know we call her Bangs. She's a freshman." Audrey looked so sure of herself.

Emma didn't look appeased. If possible, she looked more insulted. Lo kept right on painting Emma's nails.

"True." Lulu was trying to hedge her bets. She could see Emma getting further agitated, but she wasn't sure why. Maybe Emma was caught up in a point of honor. But that didn't seem too like Emma.

But Audrey was, as ever, heedless and unobservant. "And a slutty freshman at that."

Emma's face went completely slack.

Lulu only had an instant to make a recovery. "Hey! There I'll take offense. One of your best friends was a slutty freshman. Remember Lo, the early years?"

Lulu finished with a puckish wink. Lo laughed high and wide.

"It's true. Only because Lulu didn't have the cojones to be slutty until she was a sophomore. Poor little Lulu-cat, you missed a whole year of fun." Lo, looking up from Emma's nails, winked back.

"No, you forget. I didn't have fun and was still a slutty freshman. Doesn't take much." Lulu shrugged. "See, you can't attack slutty freshmen, Audrey. You're among the juniors they grew up to be. It won't do."

And for the moment, the peace was restored.

———

A listlessness settled over the slumber party. All the nails had been painted. All the hair had been braided, then unbraided and placed back up into slack ponytails. The sleeping bags were in disarray across the floor, scattered and clumped thoughtlessly, despite having been set into a neat row earlier in the evening. The girls were tired, but not so tired as to want to fall asleep. Or so they thought. They were fading, in and out. Audrey dropped off to sleep first, followed by Emma, her phone still in hand. Lo got up and headed upstairs to lay claim to Audrey's bed. Lo had a light snore that would particularly wake Audrey.

Lulu was a little bit sleepy, but, more important, she was full—properly so—for the first time in ages. All it had taken were nachos, queso, Spanish rice, flour tortillas, chicken fajitas, guacamole, sour cream, cheese, and salsa. Not to mention some funfetti cake and iced brownies. And a chocolate chip cookie. Slumber parties meant lots of time after dark, mostly spent eating. During Ramadan, this was the best kind of party Lulu could imagine.

No one else was left awake. Lulu ought to have been conked out, but there were still problems left niggling at her conscience, keeping her up. She didn't know what was wrong with Emma. She couldn't keep Audrey from making it worse. But there was one problem she could solve. One piece of the rattling in her mind that she could take charge of. She got out her phone and began typing.

I left something w you last time I saw you. Lulu hit send. Considering it was one in the morning, she didn't expect an immediate response. She at least expected a "who's this." Her expectations were unmet on both counts.

James responded right away. *What was it*

Here Lulu preemptively smiled. She was about to be clever. *My dignity*

Did you lose a bet again?

Lulu didn't give up. *No*

Are you drunk?

Lulu should have expected that, given the hour. But the comment still stung. *No just wanted to thank you*

What for? James wrote back.

And that was the crux of her crisis of conscience. She wasn't quite sure. He could have pressed his advantage on Halloween. Not necessarily physically, though he probably could have done that as well. She barely cried in front of friends, much less acquaintances. She had wanted to reach out and connect to someone, quickly. If she was a performer on the high wire that night, she'd slipped on one foot, and balanced on the other—one falling shoe marked the distance downward while the other held her precarious balance. He could have done anything—it wouldn't have taken much—to get her to tumble over. To have the satisfaction of watching a rival fall. But he hadn't. And in his situation, Lulu might have. She sat, stumped, for far too long, before she could come up with any kind of response to the question.

For being so decent on Halloween There. She'd said it. It felt like a good deal less than she ought to have said, but it also seemed to reveal a good deal more than she intended.

James, apparently, wasn't buying it. *Praise indeed.*

If he wouldn't see the pains she went through to make these kinds of admissions, then Lulu wouldn't take care to make them any further. *Shut up*

After seven minutes, she messaged again, the suspense making her anxious and energetic. How could he take her so literally? *don't shut up, shut up*

Her phone buzzed. *Which is it?*

Lulu typed furiously. *Don't be literal*

You want me to figuratively shut up? He was teasing.

Are you always this infuriating?

Do you always have this bad a temper?

Lulu had an immediate response for that, at least. *Yes*

Then.

Well.

Lulu waited. Her patience was rewarded.

I think you wanted to thank me not yell at me.

She waited some more.

Your thanks are duly noted.

Lulu smirked. *Duly noted?*

Indeed.

Indubitably. She'd hit send then followed up quickly. *Undoubtedly. Positively. Smatteringly.*

Are you flirting with me?

Yes. *No*

You're definitely flirting. I asked Matt. He says you're flirting.

youre so irritating.

Should I figuratively shut up or literally?

Lulu couldn't click enough keys to convey her frustration. She sent the message prematurely, to prevent typing for the whole next millennium. *Ughhhhhhhhhhhh*

Youre cleverer than that. I'll give you a minute to come up with a response.

She needed some way to turn this conversation back right-side up. She felt her control slipping. *This Matt hes writing your responses isnt he?*

Could be.

maybe I should meet this guy

You can't. He's busy.

Lulu grinned, holding the screen close to her eyes under the sleeping bag. She flopped over onto her stomach from her back. *With what?*

Not hanging out with you. I'm free though.

Lulu absentmindedly bit at her thumbnail, tapping it lightly between her teeth without doing lasting damage to her fresh coat of paint. *Youre shameless*

Sure. But is it working?

Yes. *Possibly*

All right.

Id have to compare you both to know for sure

Name the date and I'll drag him along.

I will so call your bluff

Good. I dare you to.

Saturday? Lulu held her breath for a response.

Right now is technically Saturday.

Dammit. *fine*

Lunch?

Lulu held back the emotions of that. She hadn't told him she was fasting.

Lulu gave the details of her whereabouts and then closed her phone. For a moment she froze, recognizing the giddy smile on her face; this might be a problem. Lulu didn't much care for problems. She tucked that thought away as she drifted off to sleep.

11

Ben Saad's Little Sister

Lulu closed her eyes in the sunlight the next morning as she stood outside. She relaxed under the two degrees of warmth those rays provided. The days were getting too cold to wait in the shade. As the November air burst across her face, Lulu nearly abandoned her idea of waiting for the boys outside. She looked at the house—an enticing retreat to the warmth—when she heard a car approaching. A whomping, thrumming sound that could be heard before the lines of the car could be seen. A beat-up, tangerine-orange Datsun pulled up alongside her.

A shaggy-looking boy who Lulu hadn't seen before stepped out of the passenger side of the vehicle. "It is so damn early," he said, stepping aside, nearly resembling the kind of southern gentlemen who open car doors for their dates. But there was nothing of the gentleman about him. He spoke gruffly and overly loud. The personal satisfaction of having a topic about which to complain radiated across his body. He possessed a stooping posture and cranky demeanor.

Lulu liked him immediately.

"Why am I here again?" the boy asked.

"Lulu only asks me out when she's dared to. And I dared her to ask us both," James said, calm as you please. He smiled at Lulu.

Lulu blinked. She was being teased. Again. She didn't know James was capable of it, not in the pleasant sort of way.

"Fair enough," the disheveled boy responded. "But I don't see how we're gonna fit."

James leaned across the front seat. "Lulu, this is Matt."

Lulu held out her hand and Matt shook it. "Lulu Saad. Pleasure."

They released their hands. Lulu leaned around to inspect how much room there would be for her to sit in the car. Not much. Not much at all. Maybe Matt wasn't a grouch so much as a realist.

"You have got to be kidding me," Matt said.

Lulu turned to face the direction of Matt's gaze. Lo had bounded out of Audrey's house. She headed rapidly toward them, in the clothes Lulu knew Lo had slept in—short-shorts and a camisole—no more, no less. Lulu stared. She was cold just looking at Lo. Plus, she didn't know how to warn her new companions of what was to come. So she said nothing, standing uneasy and unsure. Noticing her behavior, James turned to the source of her and Matt's attention. As though by instinct, both boys bore the expression of a character in a movie who looks up right before a truck barrels him over.

"Lulu, did you take my flat iron with you?" asked Lo once she was close enough.

"What?" Lulu looked around her. She didn't have a purse with her— only house keys, her license, and a twenty burning a hole in her back pocket.

Lo maintained direct eye contact with Lulu. Lulu ought to have melted into the pavement under such a gaze. The boys continued to stare. Lo ignored them.

"My flat iron. You know I can't make waves without my flat iron." Lo might as well have been speaking Finnish, for all that Lulu seemed to understand her. Lo raised her eyebrows.

"No," Lulu said slowly. "No, I don't have your flat iron."

"Hm. Okay," Lo said, her voice bright and sunny.

And then she turned. She elevator-looked the boys up and down. Lulu couldn't believe how Lo could manage it, considering James still sat in the driver's seat of the car. After Lo gave them each a once-over, she sniffed the air.

"Who are you?" Lo trained her gaze on James. Her voice was still cloyingly sweet, but she didn't ask; she demanded.

"James Denair."

"Where are you taking her?" Another demand.

"Lunch," James shot back.

"Lunch?" Lo asked, hardly waiting to take a breath.

Matt's eyes flitted back and forth between Lo and James.

James, however, had had enough. "What are you, her mother?"

Lo sniffed again. "That's ridiculous."

"Lo, *you're* being ridiculous," Lulu interjected. "I'm going to lunch. You don't need to defend my honor. Lord."

Lo arched a sculpted eyebrow. "Lunch?"

Lulu couldn't answer that. She felt her stomach clench. Lo smirked. She turned to stare down James.

"Lunch. Nothing else. I find her terrifying. Honest," he said.

Lo hummed for her little victory and leaned over Lulu to give a kiss on the cheek. "Enjoy *your meal*." Lo's eyes glittered. She eyed both boys once more and then vanished as quickly as she had appeared.

"Fuck you, Lo," Lulu shouted.

But Lo either didn't hear her or had chosen to ignore the comment. Lulu sighed. She looked over at James and Matt. She opened her mouth, but she wasn't sure what she ought to say. She didn't want to apologize for Lo. Nobody apologized for Lo.

"Wow, she's a . . ." But James seemed to have lost the word.

"Don't finish that," Lulu said.

James had the good sense to look chagrined. She climbed into the car. There wasn't much of a back seat to speak of, so Lulu straddled the gearbox, one leg intruding into James's driving space, the other taking up a bit of room in the passenger seat. There was no other seat where a third person could take up residence in the tiny car.

"Abrasive?" Matt hopped into the passenger seat with ease. "Terrifying?"

"Maybe," Lulu said. "But when I was in seventh grade I didn't realize I'd gotten my period and bled right through my skirt. Lo saw. She could have left me. She could have pointed and laughed and told everyone in the hallway. But she didn't. She walked up right behind me and said, 'I've got a sweater in my locker. Move.' Then she tied it around my waist, after walking directly behind me the whole way. Doesn't matter what she does or how she does it, I knew from then on she had my back."

Lulu didn't know why she said it. Matt visibly tensed at the mention of periods. But Lulu didn't care, and she couldn't stop herself from telling that story. She felt defensive about Lo. People assumed so much, so quickly about her. She had such a tough, hard candy coating on the outside, they never checked to see what was at her core. They saw a bitch with a pretty face. Everyone always seemed to miss how much loyalty Lo had. Lulu didn't.

"Fair enough." James looked over at where Lulu sat and grimaced. Exactly like Matt had, unfortunately.

Then Lulu noticed the direction of his discomfort. The parking brake was nestled between her legs. Lulu held back a tiny smile. No wonder they hadn't gone anywhere. And she thought he'd just been listening to her story attentively.

"You don't have a ton of crap for a girl who spent the night," he said, still apparently doing the mental gymnastics of finding a tactful way to release the car from park.

Lulu found his expression endearing, now that she understood it. She grabbed for the brake and lowered it. James sighed a small relief.

Lulu tilted her head. "Am I supposed to?"

"My sister always has a bag of stuff. You've maybe got keys, and a wallet somewhere, I guess." James checked his rearview mirror.

Lulu grinned, pushing up her glasses. She'd thrown out her contacts the night before. "Your sister must still be early in her slumber party career. I use all of Audrey's stuff. Plus, I've always got dibs on her spare sleeping bag. The only thing I need are my glasses and a ride home."

"Toothbrush?" James asked.

"She lets me leave one in her bathroom. We're fully committed," Lulu said, nodding thoughtfully.

"Congrats," James said.

Lulu laughed. "In Arabic, we say *mabrook*. Instead of congrats."

"I'll remember that for next time." James put the car in gear.

Matt groaned. "I'm sitting too close for flirting. And you've already told a story about periods."

"Period, period, period period period. Period. Period," Lulu said, the perfect, smiling portrait of a lady.

Her words left a good deal to be desired for Matt. He groaned, managing to slump farther down in his seat. James remained unruffled. Maybe he was playing it cool in front of Matt. Maybe not.

"Period," Lulu said, simpering.

"Fine, you win," said Matt, turning on the radio.

Lulu was triumphant, all grin and hardly any girl at all.

———

Lulu watched. James had three bites left of his burger. Two if he took bites as big as Matt had been taking. Matt's burger had been laid to waste ages ago. Lulu's stomach rumbled lightly; no one but herself heard. She turned to stare out the window; the boys' reflections glimmered over her view of the parking lot. Matt grabbed some fries. It was torture, the smell wafting off them, particularly after they had been so thoughtlessly, wonderfully covered in ketchup. Lulu suppressed a groan. She watched concern grow across James's face. Lulu turned to Matt.

"How're you doing there, killer?" she asked.

"Better," Matt said through a mouthful of french fries. "I missed breakfast."

"Me too," Lulu said.

James froze midchew at her words. For a moment Lulu was unsure whether he'd choked. He gulped down the food, his Adam's apple bobbing up and down his throat. He turned and stared at her, wide-eyed with horror.

The edges of her lips turned upward. He'd figured it out—what Lo had been insinuating earlier, that he'd taken a girl out for a meal she couldn't eat. He looked so helpless Lulu nearly laughed. He was quicker than most people, she'd give him that. Matt, he continued right on, stuffing fries in his mouth at least ten at a time, with globs of ketchup. It was a murder of everything Lulu had ever been trained to do at a dinner table.

She couldn't look away—a mix of fascination and horror captivating her attention. "You eat like my brother."

"God, there's a male version of you? He must be an unholy terror," Matt said, as though he'd known her for ages instead of an hour.

"More than one, actually." Lulu laughed despite herself. "And Ben *is* an unholy terror."

At this, Matt threw up his arms in disbelief and protest. Matt turned to James and exclaimed, "Holy hell. Do you realize who this is?"

James looked at Matt with a look of intense concern. "Lulu?"

"No." Matt waved over Lulu. "This is Ben Saad's little sister."

She was glad he no longer had french fries in his hand. Lulu had a feeling Matt would have made the exact same move, regardless—exactly like Ben. No wonder they had found each other.

As the moniker of Ben and Reza Saad's little sister was so rarely forced upon her, Lulu took it up with the joy of novelty. "You know Ben?"

"I do," said Matt.

"And Reza, too?"

"The incomparable Reza Saad. Of course," said Matt. "We all played soccer together. I mean I played with Ben. Rez would help us out sometimes, after practice, when we asked for pointers. Small fucking world." Matt laughed. "He mentioned you a couple of times. You are exactly what I pictured in Ben Saad's little sister."

"But not like what you'd imagine for Rez," Lulu countered.

"Not quite." Matt smiled in a way he thought to be conspiratorial, though to the wrong viewer it might come across as suggestive.

Lulu took its true meaning. They were to be great friends. "No, never quite."

"I never thought Ben Saad's little sister would be one of those girls who doesn't eat," Matt said.

Lulu's jaw set. "I'm fasting. For Ramadan."

"Shit," said Matt, almost looking contrite.

"Cool," said James. He didn't break eye contact with Lulu or make a strange, sympathetic face. He didn't ask for explanations. He didn't apologize or make it weird, as he nearly had before. He just nodded, then turned to Matt. "Dude, seriously? Could you not ask before eating my fries?"

Lulu felt indescribable relief at these words. She looked at James, but he was staring pointedly at Matt, who had a handful of fries half in his mouth. Matt's expression was penitent, almost. He opened his mouth to speak, but he was swiftly cut off.

Lulu held up her hand, in an attempt to prevent Matt from spewing a sea of ketchup and fries across the table. "You know, I once started a food fight in the fourth grade." She directed her contagious smile toward James. "Never got caught, either."

"In that case, I'm glad you don't have any ammunition," said Matt.

"If you say so."

"I'd love to know what you mean by that," said James.

Lulu knew a challenge when she heard one. "Any self-respecting girl who's been in a food fight knows that you can't only use your *own* food as ammo. How do you think I've been raised?" She grabbed one of James's fries with a plotting smile. She moved as though to fling it, but dropped it before launch.

He flinched, much to her satisfaction. "Badly, from the looks of it."

Their eyes locked, neither one willing to show their unease or embarrassment. Out of the corner of her eye, Lulu caught a movement from across the table. She heard the sound of crunching. James broke eye contact, and Lulu wasn't sure if she had won or lost.

"Matt, dammit!" said James.

Matt had finished off all of James's fries. Crumbs scattered everywhere as evidence of his crime. Matt looked nearly contrite. Lulu laughed heartily. James and Matt joined in. Lulu often felt quite sure moments like these were precious. A person only got so much spontaneity in one lifetime. The trio piled back into James's tiny car, a merrier, less stifled crew than had arrived at the restaurant.

12

Drop Trou

James's house was smaller than the other ones on the street—the lone piece of midcentury ranch architecture left on the block. The home had one other distinguishing feature: a basketball hoop set up in the driveway that had perfect half-court lines painted in hot pink. There was a coziness about the house and its situation that engulfed Lulu immediately. The front lawn had an azalea bush that wasn't much to look at this time of the year. But come spring, it would be lovely. A little winding stone path led up from the driveway to a bright red door.

"Do you play?" Lulu pointed to the basketball hoop as she stepped across the threshold.

Matt made an immediate beeline for the kitchen.

"Always here for the manners, isn't he?" Lulu laughed to fill the silence from Matt's absence.

"He's made himself at home here," James said. "And I don't play, but my sister does."

"Your parents put in that whole court for your sister? That's pretty nice," Lulu said.

"My mom bought the house with her in mind, after my parents broke up." James shrugged. "She measured everything so we could paint the lines to women's standard for her."

"Oh." Lulu wasn't sure what to say. She felt her first misstep. She hadn't quite mastered how to talk to kids whose parents were divorced in a way that communicated that she didn't think it was a big deal. Or that she knew it was a big deal, but she didn't want to make a thing of it. She wanted to prove she didn't judge, but usually she stood uncomfortably, her hands clasped behind her back, trying to figure out what to say next. "That's still nice, you know?"

"I do." He responded in earnest, giving her a quick smile and nod.

Lulu took a deep inhale, pivoting on the front of her feet. Curiosity would get the better of her. "Where's your dad?"

"Somewhere off in Florida still. I think." He kept his back to her as he spoke.

"Oh."

"Yeah, it's all right, though. I mean, there was a time when it wasn't all right. But now it is. Or at least he's so many states away that it's all right."

"I'm sorry." Lulu paused in the hallway.

James turned around. "Don't be," but then he didn't finish his clause with another, more trite one like, "It's not your fault," or "You didn't do anything." Instead he continued on with, "I'd rather have my one mom than two parents I can't stand."

Lulu blinked several times. "How'd you figure out how to be so calm about it?"

"Practice, I guess. Your parents split up when you're eleven, you either stay angry forever or you figure it out pretty quick. I don't think my sister

134

remembers their being married. To be honest, I'm kinda glad. Is that terrible?"

Lulu looked around at the room, taking in the family photos, the state of the furniture, the placement of the old television. "No, I don't think so," she finally answered, her fingers trailing against the chipped end table beside her.

"Hey—" he said, but then a trilling ring started. "Dammit." James looked around the room for the house phone—first checking its cradle, then checking around the couch and under the coffee table—to little success.

"I'm going to get that; it might be my mom, but do you want a Coke or something? Matt has probably already helped himself to all the food in the house."

"Sure," said Lulu. She wasn't going to drink it, but she needed somewhere to put her hands.

"Okay, I'll be back," he said, still in a harried search for the source of the ringing.

"I won't go anywhere." Lulu wandered around the room. She stopped in front of some shelves. She had picked up a framed photo when she heard a squeak at the other end of the room. Her head whipped up, and she set the frame down with a quickness that revealed her guilt.

"Snooping already?" asked Matt, popping out of the kitchen.

"Guilty." Lulu shrugged. "Are you making pizza snacks?"

"Only for the worthy," said Matt.

"Do I count?"

Matt tilted his head. "Jury's still out."

Lulu nodded. "Fair enough."

"Hey, sorry about that." James walked in with the phone in one hand, a soda in the other. He was looking between Lulu and Matt. "Matt, are you preparing for hibernation?"

135

Matt shrugged. "Possibly." He ducked back into the kitchen.

James took that as some kind of a cue. A sly smile spread across his face. "You're not going to drink this, are you?"

Lulu returned his expression. James missed some cues on her fasting but managed to keep picking them up in the nick of time. "Nope."

He drummed his fingers against the can and set it down on a coaster on a mahogany sideboard that was already covered in dents and scratches. Like he took care of it regardless.

"Come on, let's go upstairs." James gestured to a small half flight of stairs.

Lulu did her best not to resent having to trail behind him.

At the top of the steps was a single door on the left-hand side. She followed James through the doorway and stepped into his room. As she surveyed its contents, her eyes fell to his bed, neatly made, though the rest of the room was suspended in a state of chaos. She tried to look away before he caught her staring there.

A question had been bouncing around in her mind since before lunch, and, unable to hold it in any longer, she blurted it out. "Do you seriously find me terrifying?"

"Jesus, you don't know you're terrifying?"

Lulu didn't know what to say. Yes. She always had known she was terrifying. Her father was scared of her. And his father—her *jedu*—had been, too.

When Lulu first met her grandfather, he'd come to their house. She was all of three, maybe four. She walked right up to him. "Come here," she said. He followed. "Sit," she said. He sat. Then she crawled onto his lap and handed him a sweet. He ate it without question. From that moment on, she owned him. He would defy as many dictators as he had all over again before he crossed his granddaughter. She had command in her eyes, he knew. But she wasn't idly grasping for power that wasn't hers. She had simply been born in charge. She'd known it for ages. It was only when people wouldn't stop describing their amazement at her potency that she realized there was anything strange about it. She'd simply always felt like herself, not like some rare exception. And that, she found, scared people most of all.

Lulu's silence reverberated through the room.

James sucked in a breath. "I mean, I feel like when I'm around you I am always saying the stupidest things. Don't you say stupid things when you're scared?" James registered the expression on Lulu's face and mistook its meaning. He scuffed his toe against the floor. "Oh, of course not. You only say brilliant things."

"I don't," she said. "When I'm afraid. I usually can't stop talking, or when I'm nervous. I mean, in terms of sheer volume, the ratio of stupid things to not stupid is pretty high. Like about your parents earlier. Or the basketball hoop."

"That's something, then. I guess you're not a cyborg."

"Yeah," she said. "Though it would be kinda cool to have a bionic eye."

James laughed. Not a self-deprecating laugh. A real, honest laugh. Lulu loved that he didn't withhold his appreciation of her humor. So few boys would appreciate a joke of hers so freely. They wanted to be funny. But so did she.

She inspected his room, carefully avoiding looking at the bed again. She picked up a perfectly solved Rubik's Cube. "You can solve one of these?"

"Yeah." James shrugged. "It's pretty easy, you—"

But Lulu already had her hands up, waving in front of his face. "No, no. Don't tell me. I know there's a trick. I don't want to know."

"Why not?"

Lulu put down the cube. "I like a little mystery in my life."

"Even for stuff that is in no way mysterious anymore?"

Lulu turned on her brightest smile, her eyes lit with possibility. "Especially then."

James stood carefully still under the spotlight of such attention.

Lulu turned away and began flipping through a stack of photos she found on his desk. "Oh my God, is that Anderson?"

"You mean Dane?"

"Yeah. How old are y'all here?" She held up the photo.

James leaned over Lulu, pinching the corner of the photo to angle it toward him. "I think we're eleven or twelve."

"Those are some braces you've got there." Lulu turned, realizing only too late that their faces were too close. The smell of soap and lemons fluttered into her space. Lulu bit the inside of her cheek, desperate to not lean in.

James immediately backed up. "You interested in Dane?"

"Lord, no. I hate him," Lulu said, as casual as she might be.

"Hate him? Why do you hate him?" James had the look of a woodland creature again—a baby doe or a little lost lamb. What a sweet expression to catch on his face.

Lulu decided the best answer was also the most evasive one. She spun her half truths quickly. "I used to like him, you know."

"Did you?" Every time he looked like he might gain his footing in the conversation, it slithered out from under him. "What happened?"

"Freshman year happened," she said, letting him fill in the worst sort of blanks. She wondered if Matt would come back anytime soon. She'd never known someone who could spend that long foraging for snacks. Maybe he would bring some of them back to the room. Her stomach grumbled, as she remembered she couldn't have any snacks until sundown. She was so close to the end, too. She'd have to make it all the way through her fasting. She couldn't come this far into the month and fail. "I sometimes forget you know him."

Lulu continued wandering about his room, picking up errant objects and setting them back down equally as listlessly.

"That's how I was at that party. When we met." James hunched his shoulders slightly.

"How could I forget?" Lulu whirled around to face him.

James stared at her. She could see her half smile unsettled him. His whole posture was trapped—somehow suspended between a clear desire to bolt and a need to stand perfectly still.

Lulu decided to state the obvious. "God, you pissed me off that night."

"Don't I know it." He let out a laugh, more breath than sound.

Lulu watched his shoulders unhunch, and she knew, despite what he had said, he didn't know. He had no idea. He only ever saw the effect, the after. He had no idea what he had done to her that night.

"You saw me. Said I was different. I stay visible, but I don't like to be seen. Not like that. Especially not by strangers. I don't know what they're capable of. I wanted to put my fist through your face. You were so…" She wasn't about to use a gentle word. "Frightening."

James absentmindedly rolled up his sleeves, and Lulu watched the lean muscles in his forearms tense and relax. Her irritation flared as she lost the thread of her thought. He wasn't even doing it on purpose, because that self-conscious look appeared again across his face. Her jaw went slack as all her effort was concentrated in not trailing a finger along his exposed arm.

"And here I thought you were gonna say racist," he offered.

"Yeah," she said, recovering. Lulu looked him in the eye. "That, too."

He had a sloping, self-deprecating smile across his face. She couldn't help but return the expression.

"Yeah. I get that now," he said. "That wasn't where I was going, but I can see it."

"Why did you say it?" She needed to understand the way his mind worked. She needed his answer.

"I saw you and I thought. I saw you with Dane. It seemed like something he would say. Like a line. You're different from other girls. Unique. Noticeable." James looked away. "It was dumb."

Lulu shook her head. "Oof. Promise me never to take any more flirting advice from watching Anderson."

James barked a laugh. "You did say you liked him."

"True, but it doesn't mean I'd recommend the example. Short-term gain, long-term loss. Wait, that's not right. Isn't it supposed to rhyme? I think it's supposed to rhyme." Lulu picked up a Magic 8 Ball off James's desk and shook it. She didn't ask a question, but she waited for an answer anyway. *Reply hazy, try again.* She set the toy down.

"Why are you so intent on not being seen anyhow?"

"Because it's safer," she whispered. She wasn't sure if he'd heard her. She turned around and his expression was so placid.

"I've never been ashamed. But I do get afraid. And when I blend, no one notices anything I don't want them to see. Not any more than they might. Just dark hair. Or dark eyes. But I blend. I need it. I can make them look where I want them to. I'd be too scared without it. Now you see me, now you don't. That's why I don't mind my uniform so much. Except in the winter." She squirmed a bit, uncomfortable with laying so much of herself bare.

"Why in the winter?" he asked.

"So. Cold. I don't know why I bother with the tights. And our 'regulation outwear' is about as thin as a T-shirt." Lulu shivered at the thought. She was grateful that she lived somewhere with so few below-freezing days.

"Can't you wear pants?"

"Sure, boys' pants from the uniform store. You think I can squeeze my ass and my hips into boys' pants, you've got another think coming."

He peered over and Lulu whacked him.

"That wasn't an invitation to look, you punk."

"I bet you'd fit into mine."

Lulu huffed pointedly.

"Seriously." James grinned a mischievous grin. "Twenty bucks?"

Lulu grinned right back. She loved a dare. And loved that he knew it. And from his expression he might not have realized a step in this dare that she was going to thoroughly enjoy. The anticipation shot a small thrill through her.

"You're on." And then she stared. Right at him. She tapped her foot, theatrically. "I'm waiting."

James squirmed under the scrutiny. "For what?"

"Your pants." Lulu held her hand out, palm up, expectantly. She had a knowing look in her eye. "Those pants."

He looked down at his jeans. And then, whirling around, he saw what Lulu had already realized. There wasn't a bathroom connected to his room. There wasn't a bathroom on this floor that she'd noticed. The second floor was an addition to the house, an afterthought. And he'd have to sift through all his dirty clothes on the floor to find another pair of pants. James flushed from his neck to his ears.

Lulu grinned a shit-eating grin.

"Do you want me to turn around?" she asked.

That was the last straw for James, clearly. He took a deep breath. "No," he said in a quiet voice. "I'm fine."

He didn't break eye contact, which made Lulu think him braver than she had realized. As unceremoniously as he could, he undid the buckle at the front of his jeans. For half a second, the smug grin on her face was wiped clean. All she could do was stare at his fingers as the buckle of his belt jangled in the near-silent room. He looked up and his eyes gleamed. His mouth turned up on one side. He dropped his pants and handed them over to Lulu. He had on red boxers with Christmas emojis all over them.

Lulu smirked. "*Joyeux Noël.*"

It seemed James thought it was his turn to smirk. "Indeed."

She knew what he was thinking, with that smirk. That she'd have to take off her own pants to try his on. And because he was so wrong, she smiled back, like butter couldn't melt in her mouth. She would win this round soundly. Wearing the leggings she had slept in, Lulu wiggled into his pants. She did up the button and zipped them closed. They were plastered onto her skin across her hips and her thighs, strangely baggy around her knees, and they came well past her feet. They were at once too large and too small. She probably couldn't walk in them, but they did, in fact, close. She arched her eyebrows. "I guess you're right. I can get into your pants. I owe you twenty bucks."

"That is so unfair." He sounded about twelve shades of defeated.

"Unfair? But you won," Lulu said coyly. She played innocent one tick too well.

James glared.

"Next time," Lulu said, "particularly if I'm involved—think about the logistics of your dare."

Her smile was thorough. She stared unabashedly as his long, lean legs. He tried to maintain eye contact, but it couldn't have been easy for him. Then a slightly distracted look crossed his face and he broke their gaze.

"That's nice." James pointed at her throat.

"What is?" she asked, still smirking in victory.

He stepped closer and gingerly grabbed her necklace between his index finger and thumb. Lulu's breath caught.

"I didn't notice it before," he said.

"I got it last Christmas." Lulu responded automatically. She hadn't moved.

"You celebrate Christmas?" he asked with a hint of surprise in his voice.

"Of course I celebrate Christmas; what kind of American kid doesn't celebrate Christmas?" Lulu said with as much annoyance in her voice as she could muster. The irony of the statement was not lost on her, considering the gifted necklace had a charm of gold in the shape of the Sword of Ali. She glared at him.

"Some don't." He tilted his head.

Lulu mirrored his movement. She'd never broken her fasting like this before. Lulu licked her lips. And then the door slammed open.

Matt burst into the room with his leg propped on the door somehow, holding a plate in each hand and one in the crook of his elbow. He hardly looked up. "So, I made several Hot Pockets, and one of the forty-eight packs of pizza snacks in your freezer. And a couple of Pop-Tarts—" He looked up and froze, midmovement.

James dropped the necklace.

"I am going back downstairs." He cleared his throat. "Maybe outside. I don't think I can ever un-see this."

Lulu stood inches away from James, still wearing his pants. James, in a shirt and boxers, wore such a look of mortification that Lulu couldn't stand it—she cracked, doubling over in laughter.

"No," she said, trying to respond. But she couldn't get any other words out. She flapped her hands at Matt. She was in too much pain, her laughter having gripped her so. She bent over at the hip, but the legs were too tight to bend at the knees. She half hobbled, half fell onto the bed. This only served to worsen her state. She gripped the sides of her ribs, still unable to control her laughter.

"Stay." She was stuck, halfway bent across James's bed, in pants that felt like a sports bra for her ass, laughing until tears started streaming down her face. "Stay."

Matt stood still in the doorway. James's face flushed through a rainbow of colors—from pink to red to purple and back to pink again.

"Close the door, man," James managed.

Matt shut the door.

Lulu took in big gulps of air, her breathing finally steadying her. She twisted herself upward, nearly tripping on the extra seven inches or so of fabric wrapped around her feet. She hopped and shimmied out of the pants.

"Oh my God, I'm leaving." Matt leaped for the door again.

"Wait up! No! I'm wearing another pair of pants! And I need a ride!"

Matt acquiesced, still reeling from the shock of it all. He hadn't even set down the snacks. Lulu tossed the jeans back at James, and winked. Matt exited, bounding down the stairs.

Lulu turned to face James at the threshold of the door. "Thanks. I had fun."

"Okay," James mumbled.

"I'll see you around, Denair." She threw him her most winning smile, which cracked wider when he made eye contact. She left, following Matt down.

13

The White Rabbit

Emma did not sit with them at lunch. The slumber party should have made everything better, soothing ruffled feathers and the like. Instead Emma sat three tables over, having mentioned something about a newspaper interview. Again.

A newspaper interview, Lulu's right foot.

Emma was avoiding them. That much was plain and obvious. Nobody did an interview during lunch unless their article was due that afternoon. And not only was Emma a photographer on a voluntary writing assignment, Emma's article wasn't due until next week. Emma might have been a girl who liked to prepare in advance, but nobody prepared that far ahead. Not even a diligent photographer looking to switch into writing. Maybe she just needed space. Lulu watched the back of Emma's head as her curls bounced. She was nodding animatedly and scribbling into her notebook.

"There's a party at Dixon's this weekend," said Audrey, interrupting Lulu's thoughts. "I thought we'd all go together. Like Halloween."

Lo laughed. "Maybe leave the Daphne costume at home, though."

Audrey flushed from her neck to her hairline. "Obviously not *precisely* like Halloween. But the togetherness. Of before."

"We're missing a key ingredient to that recipe." Lulu pointed to where Emma sat. "Walker defected to the freshmen."

Lo rolled her eyes. "She did not defect. She's writing an article."

Lulu raised both her eyebrows. As if Lo believed that.

Audrey, who sat on the edge of her chair, popped up in an instant. "I'll get her."

And then Audrey was gone, over to Emma. She gesticulated wildly as she caught Emma's attention. As Audrey's speech quickened and intensified, so too did the frown across Emma's face. Lulu had never seen Emma's politeness fail so spectacularly before. Emma tilted her head for a moment, and her eye caught Lulu's. Emma's face was so blank, so unreadable, that Lulu guessed she was turning them down. Emma looked away, back to Audrey. Untethered, Lulu stared back at the empty spot on the table where her food ought to have been. Her stomach flipped. But she'd give Emma time. Sometimes, people just needed time. Lulu had learned that from her mother, of all people.

A scraping sounded just beside Lulu. Lo was up, her lunch tray in hand. "Gotta run."

Lulu held her hands up. "We've still got half an hour left of lunch!"

"I know. Nearly out of time." Lo tossed a fake kiss into the air.

"Lo." Lulu got up with Lo, having no food or trays to encumber her own escape from the dining hall.

There was such a weight in that one word. And Lo's response to Lulu's worry—which was more like criticism, honestly—had been to scoff and say, "Whatever, Lulu. He's smoking hot and I'm going to hit it."

Scumbag Luke. Lo was back to hooking up with Scumbag Luke. He didn't even go to school here with them. How Lo managed to find time in the middle of the day to rumple his gorgeous mane of hair, well, it was not only a mystery, it was damned impressive. Lulu followed quickly on Lo's heels. "Lo, you're fucking a racist!"

Lo had laughed at that. "I know."

"It's not funny."

"His pain is. I can see it. He hates the part of himself that's attracted to me. But he also hates the part of himself who thinks horrible, racist things. I can see that war. And maybe he'll battle that for his entire life. Or maybe he won't. I don't know; I doubt I'll be around." Lo shrugged her annoying, lilting shrug.

"So you're going to go around fucking racists trying to change their minds?" Lulu grabbed Lo's wrist. "What a volunteering spirit you have."

Lo snatched her wrist back from Lulu's grip. "God, Lulu, you're a riot. No. I'm not going to do that."

"Then, what?"

"People are complicated. I'm attracted to a racist. He's attracted to what he's been taught to hate. Maybe we're trying to play with power we don't quite have or understand. Or maybe it's a rebellion thing. I don't know. But I can appreciate the irony of the situation. I can laugh at it, at least."

"You're smarter than anyone gives you credit for," said Lulu.

"I know."

"That doesn't bother you?"

"Sometimes," said Lo. "I don't mind being underestimated."

"Why?"

"Because then those bastards never see me coming." And that was Lo's coup de grâce.

Lulu watched as Lo exited the dining hall, leaving Lulu to stand stupefied and alone.

———

Dixon Harrison had the sort of house made for profligacy—four floors, a plot of land with a wide berth from the neighbors, a swimming pool, and winding roads that concealed the number of cars parking in the neighborhood. Dixon would have likely sat atop the social heap without such amenities. But the house helped. Even Dixon knew that.

Lulu sat in the passenger seat of Audrey's royal purple cabriolet, parked across the street from the Harrison house. The soft top was up, increasing the cramped feeling of the car's interior. Emma had said she'd needed to stay home and do homework, and Lo said she'd get a ride from Scumbag Luke. So in the car were just Lulu and Audrey. Lulu stared at the house. She'd left her seatbelt on. And the heater was still running. The cozy comfort of the car was enough to satisfy Lulu for tonight. This did not bode well for an evening out.

"Here." Audrey dug a pair of dirty sweatpants out from behind her seat at the wheel. She unwrapped them to reveal a bottle of sun-warmed tequila. "Take a swig."

"I can't." Lulu wanted the sip, but she couldn't. She was tired of having a good humor about it. She thought about the sound the bottle might make if she smashed it against the pavement. It was a satisfying noise to envision. There was a small relief in that.

"It's after sundown." Audrey uncapped the bottle.

Lulu could smell its astringent pungency from across the car. She wrinkled her nose. "I know."

"So?" Audrey took a generous swig, winced, then sloshed the bottle over to Lulu, who shook her head and clamped her lips.

"So I'm not drinking. All of Ramadan. Not even at night. Like always." It was fine, really, that Audrey conveniently forgot the rules of Ramadan tonight. She forgot every year, at some point. Audrey had lasted longer this year than she had every other, before suffering a lapse of memory as to the rules Lulu followed during the month. The pattern was trending in the right direction.

Like clockwork, Audrey would grow bored of Lulu's fasting. And she would do her best to get Lulu to blur the rules. Lulu didn't budge. Neither would Audrey. Tonight was apparently the night this year for the rhythmic conflict.

"But you drink the rest of the time?" Audrey said, a hint of a whine on the edge of her throat. She must have needed Lulu to join her tonight. She shoved the warm bottle at Lulu one last time.

"Them's the breaks." Lulu shrugged, refusing to take the offered bottle.

Audrey returned the tequila to her lips and took a larger-than-average swill. She somehow produced a handkerchief to dab her mouth with when she finished. "You are so inconsistent."

"All religion is inconsistent. Think of me as accurately performing the human condition." Lulu raised an eyebrow. She'd been practicing that sardonic expression in the mirror. She thought she pulled it off rather magnificently. "Also what are you doing with a bottle of tequila under your passenger seat? What if you get an open container charge? You could lose your license."

Audrey snorted. "Doubtful. What cop is going to search in my car under my seat inside dirty sweatpants?"

Lulu took a clear look at her friend. There probably was a cop somewhere out there who would thoroughly search Audrey's car. The real odds of that happening in this neighborhood, or the one Audrey lived in, were so slim that Lulu had to laugh. Audrey had the air of a docile, white bunny rabbit. Lulu knew better than to fall for Audrey's resting expression of confusion. But other people, they saw that harmless white rabbit.

"Where'd you get the bottle anyway?" Lulu asked, switching the direction of the conversation.

"Sophomore in my music theory class." Audrey took a hulking swig out of the bottle.

"Which sophomore?"

"John? Alex?" Audrey tilted her head. "No, maybe it's David. It's a biblical name."

"Alex is definitely not biblical." Lulu gave Audrey a side-eyed glance. "Koranic, maybe, if you count Dhul-Qarnayn as Iskandar. And Iskandar is Alexander, obviously."

Audrey snorted. "You and your biblical knowledge of boys."

"That was low." Lulu flipped down the visor mirror in front of her. "Even for you."

"Sorry." Audrey shrugged. "I just don't even know how you keep track of them."

Lulu barked a laugh to keep her temper tamped down. "I keep a list of the boys I've hooked up with written down. So I don't lose 'track of them.' And I'm not telling you where I keep it. So don't ask. It's bad enough you know the list is out there."

Unfortunately, Audrey's expression grew sharp. "Who have you hooked up with that I don't know about?"

Lulu noticed her misstep immediately. She went coy. She hadn't told Audrey what had happened with Dane. She never meant to tell anyone else what had happened with him. "And why wouldn't you know someone I've hooked up with?"

"The only reason you'd keep the list from me is if someone was on it I didn't know! Spill!" Audrey swatted at Lulu's arm. Audrey was tenacious when she'd caught hold of a real truth.

Lulu dodged the hit and giggled nervously. She wasn't going to talk about Dane. She didn't have to talk about Dane. "Come on, Audrey Louise.

It was ages ago. I don't ask you about your embarrassing middle school crushes."

"Because those are crushes! I can't believe you're hiding someone from me! I'm your best friend!"

Let it not be forgotten that Audrey had a spectacular pout. It was a true glower, ready to teeter over the brink into a tantrum at any moment. Lulu admired that pout. Her own had been tainted by too many French movies. The *vedettes* had ruined her; her pout wasn't the least bit threatening. When Audrey pursed her lips, she was pure menace.

Another voice was muffled in the background. Must have been someone outside. Taking one last swipe at the edge of her lip with her finger, Lulu closed the visor up with a click. "Did I tell you, I invited James and his friend Matt to the party?"

"Don't you dare distract me—wait, James? From the belly dancing, James?"

"Yes. That one." One side of Lulu's mouth twitched upward.

"I knew it!" Audrey punched at Lulu's arm, but Lulu didn't dodge the blow. Audrey had never been taught to punch. "And since you now see how brilliant I am, I am going to let you know that I've an equally amazing plan for tonight."

"What is this amazingly brilliant plan?"

"Not telling. Looks like we all get secrets, don't we, Saad?" Audrey's voice taunted.

Lulu had no rebuttal to offer.

And Audrey, finally having drunk her fill, swung out of the driver's seat. Lulu got out of the car as well. The sound of their footsteps echoed onto the neighborhood street. Lulu thought she heard something behind her, but she didn't bother to turn around. Then Lulu heard a voice. A familiar voice.

"Should be fun tonight, don't you think?"

But Audrey hadn't said anything. Lulu stared at her. Audrey looked as confused as Lulu felt. To her eternal regret, Lulu looked to her right.

There, leaning out the passenger side window of a baby-blue Bronco with one hand still on the wheel, was Dane Anderson. Lulu examined the enormity before her—a hunk of steel and chrome. He hadn't bothered to park in a discreet location. Or facing the direction of traffic. He was a wonder to behold, Dane Anderson. Perhaps like gazing upon a circle of hell.

"Seriously?" Lulu said. "You're like a caricature of yourself."

Dane's smile was crooked, but its slope only made it all the more devastating. "Oh, Saad. How cute of you to notice."

Lulu, fuming, looked over to Audrey, who shrugged with overly practiced nonchalance.

Dane propelled himself out of the driver's side seat and edged his body in between the two girls so quickly that Lulu could still hear the car door's slam echoing into the night.

He looked Lulu directly in the eye as he slung his arm around Audrey. "Saad, you're adorable when you're angry."

Lulu watched Audrey's shoulders stiffen. Lulu opened her mouth, but she wasn't quick enough. Audrey had clearly had enough of being a bystander in this exchange. She looked prepared to do right by her friend.

"Why on earth would Lulu be angry?" Audrey raised a practiced eyebrow. Her defensive posture and the attack in her voice was obvious. Audrey meant to help. But she lacked critical information. Information Lulu had refused to give.

Lulu stood transfixed, the way she might watch a car stuck on a train track, a train rolling toward it with electrifying speed. Dane smiled a swift, malicious grin. And then Lulu knew what was going to happen before it did. She would have to put her body between the train and the car. She couldn't stop the train. She couldn't stop Dane Anderson. But Audrey would sit in that doomed car to the last. There was no shifting Audrey off her course.

Lulu threw herself in front of the train. She talked through Anderson, to Audrey. "Do you know if Lo is coming tonight?"

Audrey blinked. "Sure. She'll be here. She said she was getting ready when we left."

"Lo's got no personality." Dane interjected himself into a discussion obviously and inelegantly meant to exclude him and him alone. "I don't know why you're friends with her."

Lulu clamped her lips together, taking a deep breath through her nose. She would get through this, without Audrey the wiser. She was determined.

But Dane kept rolling right along. "She's all body. And face. Don't worry, Saad—no need to be jealous," Dane said with a surreptitious wink.

"Anderson, I don't know if you know this, but your dick doesn't have magical, personality-endowing qualities." Lulu cross her arms over her chest. A small knot formed in her stomach, clenching as she spoke.

Dane's triumphant grin returned. That feckless schoolboy one. "If it did, you'd have personality in spades, wouldn't you?"

Audrey's face scrunched again in confusion. "Why's that? It's not like you two have hooked up."

The small knot in Lulu's stomach hollowed out into a bottomless pit.

"Didn't she tell you?" Dane leaned in as Audrey's eyebrows puckered. "We consummated our mutual affection over Halloween."

The melodrama had nearly reached its inevitable conclusion. People didn't win against trains. Over Dane's shoulder, Audrey glanced at Lulu. Deny, and Lulu knew she would look guilty. Admit and she would sound as though she had slept with Dane and had failed to mention *that* to Audrey. That wasn't a win. There wasn't any win.

Lulu tried anyway. "There is no mutual affection. Or consummation."

Dane winked. "Just your tongue in my mouth." If it had been a bad teen movie, Lulu would have laughed out loud.

Audrey wrenched out from under Dane's arm. She shot Lulu a glare. "How wouldn't I know someone you hooked up with—that's how you put it, right?"

Lulu didn't have anything to say to that.

"And here I thought y'all were best friends," Dane said, the side of his mouth upturned.

"Same as a middle school crush, isn't it?" Audrey didn't wait for a reply. Instead she used her long stride to flee from Lulu without breaking into a run.

Lulu moved to follow her, but Dane snatched Lulu's wrist before she could move away. Lulu turned to face Dane. Whatever small joy Lulu had before, it vanished into the crisp, stifled air. She'd lost the battle, but she was going to win the war. She was ready to hit soft targets. "You are a beautiful piece of shit, did you know that?"

Dane's grin held. "Why, thank you."

"No. You don't get it. You are—and please do not take this lightly—absolute garbage. You're going to go through life getting everything you've ever wanted without any effort. It doesn't matter if you're as smart as you think you are. It doesn't matter that you're gorgeous. Every gift you've been given is wasted. You're a waste of human space. And you'll never amount to more than what you've already been handed. Ever." Lulu wrenched her wrist out from Dane's grip. "Stay away from me. Stay away from my friends."

Lulu was through the door of the Harrison house before Dane could respond.

14

Queens of the Wild

The air around Lulu was hazy and smoky; her chair was nestled in a small circle of chairs, most of which were empty.

Beside her sat Brian Connor. He was sitting close enough that Lulu could tell his aim was not mere sociability. But Lulu didn't care right now. She was using him, and if he had his own aim in mind, she wasn't in a position to try to stop him. Lulu was currently in possession of too many brain cells. Maybe a few hits would wipe the memory of her fight with Audrey from her mind. It was doubtful, true. But at this point, a temporary respite would help. It wasn't alcohol. It was probably beyond the gray area, to be honest. Lulu took a hit off the vaporizer. She was ready to float.

"Dude, it's two hits and a pass. You're not passing. Take your last hit or pass." Brian leaned toward the vape pen in Lulu's hand.

She was monopolizing the weed. Audrey had finally prompted Lulu to blur the rules of Ramadan. And she wasn't even here to enjoy it. "Brian, did you know?"

Brian's hand itched toward the pen.

"Did you know, that *hashish* and *assassin* are related words?" Lulu asked, taking a hit. "They say that the *hashashi'un* used to smoke up and assassinate political and religious leaders who didn't follow their ideas of Islam. Kinda like all those Christians who murdered one another over the oneness versus the three-ness of God."

Lulu laughed like she'd told a fantastic joke.

"That is a historical urban legend," said a scratchy, feminine voice.

"Miriam," Lulu said, a bit listlessly, as she looked up. "What are you doing here?"

"I could ask you the same question." Miriam plopped herself into a chair next to Lulu with all the presumption of friendship.

Lulu was glad to see her. Miriam didn't call out Lulu's smoking. She wouldn't. She understood instinctively, as many would not.

"Brian." Lulu held the vape pen like she had forgotten she held it. "This is Miriam. Miriam and I—we're cycle buddies."

"Is that period shit?" Brian demanded.

"It's a natural part of life, Brian," Lulu said, in a tone somewhere between a mother and an inebriate.

"That *is* period shit. That's disgusting." Brian frowned.

Sensing Lulu's target, Miriam drawled, "We share tampons."

"I'm leaving." Brian stood and stalked off.

Lulu smiled, wide. She took another hit. "And now, it's just us girls."

"How kind of him to leave his pen," said Miriam, taking it off Lulu's hand. She inhaled.

Lulu laughed. "Tonight. Is such a night."

Miriam grinned. "Isn't it, though?"

"Tell me about it," said Lulu, already experiencing a tingling sensation in her fingers. She smiled a sloppy grin.

Miriam blew out smoke and passed the pipe back to Lulu, who took it in a rote fashion.

Lulu looked back at the house. Lo had walked outside, through the patio doors. She was scanning the yard, squinting across its massive area.

"Lo," Lulu said in singsong. "Come sit. You're here. Siiiiiiiiiiiiiiiit."

Lo looked around the circle of half-empty lawn chairs skeptically. She closed the gap between herself and the chairs and stood hovering over Lulu.

"This," Lulu continued heedless of Lo's expression, "is my dearest, dar-lingest, most impressive-est family friend Miriam. She and I are halfsies. Which basically makes us best friends."

Miriam laughed. "It does, doesn't it?"

Lo huffed.

Lulu adopted a sober expression. She turned to Miriam. "Miriam, this is Lo. Do not fuck with Lo. She never says die. That's why she dates a superhot shitbag who already has a girlfriend."

"Lulu, you can't say that!" said Miriam, coughing.

"Don't mind Lulu. She grew up with too many boys. She's got no idea what is and isn't appropriate." Lo smirked and sat. She set the drink in her hand on the grass at her feet. "It's basically how she says 'I love you.' Besides. If I were Luke's girlfriend, he'd take me out on dates and then I'd never get an orgasm. He feels juuuuust guilty enough to go down."

Miriam took a long hit from the pipe. "This took a really personal turn."

Lo shrugged. "I know what people say about me behind my back. You'd probably hear it eventually anyway."

"She's right, you know." Lulu nodded solemnly. "I do try desperately, but I have no idea how to behave. I always manage to cock it up."

"Cock!" said Miriam, with a wild-woman cackle.

Lo laughed at that. " 'Never say die'! And I thought I was dramatic, Lulu-cat. *The Goonies* is classic, though, isn't it?"

"So classic." Miriam passed the pen.

Lo took it, one eyebrow raised.

"*Ahlan wa sahlan*," Miriam said, tipping her finger in acknowledgment of the pass.

Lulu giggled.

"What's so funny?" Lo asked.

"That's all the Arabic she knows," Lulu said, the giggles now laughter.

"Lulu. I can also say thank you. You bitch." Miriam shoved her hand in Lulu's face. "All the Arabic I know. Pshhhhh. Besides, between the two of us combined we've got the vocabulary of at least a three-year-old." Miriam huffed.

"Between the two of us," Lulu said, flourishing her hand, "we are at least one whole terrorist."

Lo wheezed, coughing on her hit. "You've gotta warn me before you say shit like that. Luke was one thing. That—that was beyond."

But Lulu didn't care. Tears of laughter were streaming down her face. Miriam shook her head; Lo passed the pipe along, back to Lulu, who took it readily.

"Everybody else is thinking it. I can see it on their faces. All the time. I'm just saying it out loud. Clearing the air," Lulu said.

"Too much weed in the air for it to be clear," Miriam said, taking two short hits in quick succession. "And I've never thought that."

"If white people can say it about me, why can't I say it about myself? Why can't I take it from them?" Lulu took one drag, considered another, then passed before she had time to reconsider her consideration. "And I am half-white, so I can at least half say it."

"You show the man you're more man than they are, Sister Comrade," said Miriam.

"Whoa there," said Lo. "There is no need to start the revolution. At least, not until we've sobered up. And I don't think your white half should say it any more than your Arab half. Save the racism for all the boys I half date."

There was a pause, then all three girls started laughing, hysterically. Sides were splitting, breath was catching, laughter fell straight into tears.

"What are y'all laughing about?" It was Nina Holmes. The laughter quieted down immediately. Nina scrunched her face and crossed her arms.

Lulu found her most sober expression. Nobody else could fully stifle their laughter. It was a suspicious circle of giggling. Nina's posture did not adjust.

"Here, join the crowd." Lulu offered up her seat, despite the plethora of empty ones. At the offer, Nina sunk into the chair. Lulu leaned over to Miriam and gave her three kisses on her cheeks. They both chuckled at that.

Nina squinted, still unsure. Lulu felt blamed.

"I bid you all adieu!" Lulu said, with a flourishingly little bow.

"I'll come with," said Lo, getting up out of her seat and grabbing her drink in one move. She must have sensed Lulu's tension. She linked her free arm through Lulu's, and they pranced through the grassy field of a backyard to the house.

Lo leaned in close, ready to tell Lulu a great secret. "One day, Lulu, we will be old."

"Oh, will we?" Lulu asked, laughing.

"Shut up. I'm not finished." Lo stopped moving.

Understanding Lo's protest, Lulu offered up her hands in supplication. She then took the invisible zipper at the right corner of her mouth and pulled it across to the left. She locked it and threw away the key.

Appeased, Lo cleared her throat to begin again. "One day, Lulu, we will be old. And we will say, remember when we were young and wild? Remember when we were queens?"

"Queens?" Lulu laughed again.

"Queens, Lulu-cat. We've crowned ourselves. We run ragged as we please. The only people who tell us what to do are each other."

"Won't we get to stay queens?"

"I don't know," said Lo. "We can't know. That's why we have to be them so thoroughly now. We have to take our crowns while they let us. While they're not watching."

"They?" asked Lulu.

"Exactly. They. You know—them."

Lulu giggled. She did.

"They will tell us we can be better than queens of the wild great something. They already told us we couldn't be fairy princesses or white knights or dragon slayers. They will tell us to grow up, be serious. They will tell us to get a job. To find our place. They will tell us to do our duty. They will tell us to fight for a spot at the table. But now, we don't. We desecrate their tables. We dance on tables. We take really big swords, and we hack those tables into tiny little pieces. Or whatever weapon you want."

Here Lo waved the drink in her hand so as to create a spectacular arc of fluid across the backyard that managed to hit absolutely no one. She'd fed the soil with her own debauchery.

"You," Lulu said. "Are high as a kite. I can't tell if you're being real smart or super dumb. If you hallucinate, tell me. I want to know what's coming."

"I can be high and tell the truth, Lulu-cat. Remember that."

"I'll never forget it. We're queens."

"Queens!" Lo said, her voice sailing high across her shriek. She lobbed her drinking cup across the lawn. She had no further use of it.

———

Lulu followed Lo to a patch of darkness in the back corner of the large lawn that was shielded by a stately portico. A group of boys surrounded the two kegs that had been placed there for apparent convenience and ease of access. But nobody could access the beer without crossing the border created by their bodies—clad in khakis and polos, with their unkempt hair held back by worn, white baseball hats. And here was Scumbag Luke, King of the Scumbags and ruler over all that the beer touched. He stood at the apex of their circle, the head of the worst kind of hydra.

Luke said nothing as they approached, though every boy knew to let Lo and Lulu pass to the kegs without incident. Lo smiled at him as she tilted her cup to a perfect forty-five-degree angle. It was not Lo's usual smile. Everything that was normally sharp with her had softened. Lulu hated to see her so. Lo passed the first drink back to Lulu, then began filling her own cup. Lulu took it, knowing she didn't have to drink it, knowing she could hold onto it like a crutch or an evil eye. Lo finished serving her own beer, but she didn't move out from the circle.

Scumbag Luke said nothing.

This ought to have been a mercy to Lulu, but the fact that he wouldn't speak first nettled her. Everybody knew what was between him and Lo. The boys had grown preternaturally quiet, speaking in half glances and stolen whispers and predatory smirks that Lulu wanted to wipe off their faces with a dousing of chilled, cheap beer.

Lulu could have used Emma at such a moment. Emma would have prevented Lo from coming this way at all. Emma would have distracted Lulu with a story about how Molly Ringwald convinced the director of *Pretty in Pink* to make sure Andie didn't end up with Duckie. Emma knew these things, knew they soothed, knew they were an antidote to the anger Lulu nursed. But Emma wasn't here and Emma needed space. Lulu tried to take deep breaths, but they caught in the back of her throat. They seemed to grow weighty at the top of her chest, expanding and refusing to be pulled farther into her lungs. She turned her gaze onto Scumbag Luke and stared with all her might.

Eventually, he looked up from his leering whisper to the ruddy-faced boy on his right. He stared back. But Scumbag Luke held no power over Lulu. She could not have explained why. There was, to her outward observation, little difference between him and Dane Anderson—minus the fact that they went to different schools from each other, they had the same kind of good looks and the same kind of easygoing charm. But perhaps the difference was the knowledge that Anderson had once gotten the better of Lulu. Scumbag Luke never had.

"It's Lyla, right?" Scumbag Luke grinned a Clint Eastwood grin—the kind where a person said a thing but knew another. He hadn't forgotten her name at all.

Lulu returned the smile, but hers was like Indiana Jones after he'd gotten punched in the jaw. Painful, but worth it. She'd made him talk first. "Yeah. I bet it's all the same to you."

Lulu could sense Lo glaring at her, a wind of hostility blowing from that specific direction. But Lulu refused to break eye contact with Scumbag Luke. *I know what you are.*

"I guess we've got another predator posing as a house pet here, don't we?"

Lulu fisted her free hand until she could feel her nail biting into the skin of her palm. The putrid tang in her throat receded a little. "Something like that."

"Where I come from, people say thank you when they've been offered hospitality." Luke gestured to Lulu's full container of beer. His challenge was evident.

"You're so right." The one side of Lulu's mouth twitched upward, but she bit the inside of her cheek to keep the expression from fully forming. She turned to Lo and, using the thickest version of her twang, Lulu said, "Thank you, darlin', for the beer. So kind of you."

The circle hadn't been particularly loud before. Now, it was still and nearly silent. Nobody knew the rules for this. These were uncharted waters.

Lo, however, turned and said, "Lulu, I know you're tired. Go find a ride home. Call you tomorrow."

Lulu wanted to scream. She wanted to wail. She wanted to throw a fit until at least three of those burly and soft-bodied boys had to haul her off the premises. But Scumbag Luke hadn't had the better of her before, and he never would. Lulu smiled half a smile. "All right."

Lulu pivoted as Scumbag Luke slung his arm around Lo—claiming his prize and offering his protection all at once—and the boys let Lulu out again with little fuss. Lulu released a breath she hadn't realized she was holding.

15

The Airspeed Velocity of an Unladen Swallow

Lulu wandered. It was not an aimless, pleasant wander. It was only direction-less insomuch as she did not have a good lay of the architectural land beneath her feet. She wandered because she did not know where she needed to go to find who she wanted. She wandered because her thoughts were absorbed with predicting Audrey's movements as much as with not getting lost in the Harrisons' cavernous, beautifully appointed home. So Lulu wandered—purposeful and without direction.

Lulu didn't remember greeting people as she moved through the house. She knew she did. She was raised too precisely to have ignored people she knew at such a juncture. But she didn't remember whom she waved to or hugged. Her actions were rote, if charmingly so. She smiled where required, she laughed when she felt the conversation swelling to a point. And then she wandered off again, searching.

When at last Lulu found Audrey, there was no exhale of relief in the discovery.

Audrey had one hand on the neck of a plastic handle of vodka. She poured what was clearly her fourth shot into a cheap disposable cup. Her eyes were glassy. Three-shot Audrey was wide-eyed and full of possibilities. Four-shot Audrey was aggressive and not at all alert. Four-shot Audrey was a bar brawl waiting to happen. Thank God they'd never been let into a real bar.

Lulu caught Audrey's hand as she finished the pour. "Stop it. We need to talk."

Audrey's face formed into a doofy half smile. "Cheers."

"Audrey, please."

Audrey threw back the drink, heedless. Her smile widened, grew toothier—sharper. "I'd offer you one, but I know you're the designated judgmental bitch for the night. Better than the designated slut, right?"

Lulu stared at Audrey. "Fuck you."

"Excuse me?"

"Fuck. You." Lulu took a deep breath. "I've been looking for you all over this house like a crazy woman, and the first thing you do is throw Ramadan and Anderson in my fucking face? Well, fucking fuck you very fucking much."

"Such a lady." Audrey managed to pour herself another drink without breaking eye contact with Lulu.

"No, I'm not." Lulu slammed her hand down on Audrey's drink cup, spilling the contents across the floor.

"That was totally unnecessary," Audrey said. Benign words, but Lulu could tell Audrey's rage had gone from a heated lump of coal to pure molten lava.

"I agree. That shot was unnecessary. I think you've had enough to drink for the night. Maybe for the century. I'm honestly impressed. Who would have thought you could accomplish so much in three short years?"

"What are you, my mother?" Audrey sneered.

"No. I'm your friend."

"I *thought* you were my friend." Audrey took a long draw directly out of the handle in her hands.

Lulu stared. "What's that supposed to mean?"

"You're someone who hangs around and makes herself feel better by comparing her life to mine."

"How could you say that?" Lulu didn't shout. She could barely take in the air to get her vocal cords vibrating. What a sucker punch those words were.

"You're so free from feelings. Must be nice to feel so brave, avoiding feelings. Sorry we can't all cut and run after we jump on a boy, Lulu. Sorry some of us get *attached*." Audrey brandished the bottle in her hands as the liquid within splished and splashed out of its mouth.

Cool vodka sprinkled across Lulu's face, waking her from her stupor. "Seriously, that's why you're pissed? Nothing else you need to get off your chest?" Lulu paused to see if Audrey would bring up the inciting incident. See if Audrey would ask about Anderson. About secrets and loyalty. But Audrey wouldn't and they both knew it.

"Nothing else." If anything, Audrey was a marvel at standing her ground.

"Super. Since we're on the honest train, you know what's pissing me off?"

"Enlighten me," Audrey said, continuing her downward spiral from sobriety.

Lulu watched the bottle slush as it went from Audrey's lips and back down again. Lulu had never seen six-shot Audrey.

"You're always like 'Lulu, be careful,' 'Lulu, watch out,' 'Lulu, they're not your brothers, Lulu.' I'm supposed to feel lucky when nothing happens. You always imply it. I'm afraid, deep down, that every warning I've ever been given is right. And I hate it. That I'm the kind of girl that should, eventually, have something horrible happen, like an after-school special. And I'm supposed to feel lucky when it doesn't. Because I take tiny pieces of the freedoms boys are given. And you remind me of that every goddamned time."

Audrey had nothing. Lulu's breathing hitched. She was losing balance at the precipice of her feelings. Lulu avoided this place, if she could. She wanted nothing to do with it. Her stomach roiled. Her head went light. And she couldn't remember how to breathe.

"So why do you keep doing the same thing?" Audrey breathed out.

"Because I want to. Because I won't let fear tell me how to act." Lulu shrugged. "At least, I wish it wouldn't."

"Jesus. You're intolerant—intolerant—toler—intolerable. Everything rolls off you. Nothin' sticks. How could anyone stay friends with you?" The plastic handle slid to Audrey's fingers, but she didn't drop it. Its lip dangled tentatively from the tips of her fingers.

Lulu wanted to speak. She wanted to tell Audrey about Dane, about Halloween. She needed the soothing balm of confession. But instead she opened her mouth and all that came out were shattered bits of sound. The noises scattered across the beautiful kitchen appliances and marble countertops. The shards of her heart went out with them.

"What? Nothing to say? You're always the chatty one." Audrey's breath heaved. "I know. Why don't you tell me about how you neglected to tell me about hooking up with *Dane*. And then *lied to cover your slutty tracks*."

Lulu opened her mouth and then closed it. How could Lulu explain she hadn't been able to put Dane on the list? She'd written the number *15* and then drawn a neat, straight line next to it. That wasn't a hook-up, though it had started out as one. It was the punishment implied at the end of every word of Audrey's concern. That one day she'd end up alone with the wrong boy, in the wrong room. And even then, that night on the dance floor was still only a slap on the wrist. A paper cut. Except. Except it had taken a small but not insignificant sense of Lulu's safety. Except it was now rearing its ugly head and separating her from Audrey. Except. Except.

Except now the paper cut was infected.

Audrey stood, smug and drunk and triumphant. Lulu grasped for the threads of her thought. She looked around them—they had drawn an audience. And who knows what everyone had heard. Lulu was too mad for words. She turned on her heel and fled back outside, away from Audrey and her punishing righteousness.

———

Lulu took the route that would take her around the side of the house, through a pretty garden path lined with knockout roses and a few other flowers that couldn't bloom in the cooling weather so Lulu didn't know what they were. As she made it out of the garden and onto some stones that lay along the side of a porch, Lulu stopped, immobilized. She stared. Hand to God, just stared.

Lulu had found Audrey again. Or, what was more accurate, Dane Anderson had found Audrey. They were wound up in each other, leaned against a set of french doors. Well, wound up together insomuch as Audrey couldn't stand on her own and Anderson was propping her up with any part of his body that he could.

Before Lulu could say anything, he turned. Anderson stopped trying to keep Audrey standing. He actually stopped. Audrey, whose body was already starting to slacken from the alcohol raging through her system, sagged against the wall. Then, lightly, playfully, Dane tucked a finger under Audrey's chin. He hadn't take his eyes off Lulu, as though they were trained to the magnetic north of her gaze. And Lulu stared right back. Then Dane pressed his mouth against Audrey's.

Lulu's skin burned. Her fury went straight to a blinding white flame. She acted on the only thought she had in her brain. The one compelling her to separate Audrey from this nightmare. She exploded from her stillness. She shoved Audrey aside, and Lulu thought she heard a faint yelp and the rustling of bushes in the background. She paid it no heed. Dane's smirk was too prominent in his face. And it was too like the ones she had just ignored by the keg. She held her forearm underneath his chin, threatening to press forward into his windpipe. For the first time, panic entered Anderson's expression.

He recovered quickly, though. "Christ, Lulu. You're fucking unhinged."

"Yeah. I'm fucking unhinged. So leave me and my friends the hell alone," Lulu growled.

"Look, honey, *she* found *me*. What am I supposed to do, say no to an open invitation?" Dane's charm was back, his half smile propping back up on the corner of his mouth. He'd smiled his way out of trouble too many times. "She does seem to be under the impression that my name is Clark, though."

Lulu pressed her arm forward. She was a hair's breadth away from him, her breath fanning across his face. "I will rip your heart out and eat it for fucking breakfast, Anderson. I will annihilate you."

"Aw, shucks, darlin'. You're so cute when you're impassioned."

"I'm not impassioned. I'm fucking furious." Lulu looked around for Audrey's limp body, but she saw nothing. She released her hold on Dane's throat slightly as she squinted into the darkness, trying to figure out where Audrey had got herself to.

"Good."

And in one swift movement, Lulu felt herself pressed up against the glass door, her lips in a sudden, hostile merge with Dane's. Lulu shoved him, hard. But the smile was still plastered across his face. There was only one explanation for it. She turned around, with dawning horror. There, on the other side of the glass french doors, was the main living room of the Harrison home. Everyone stood there, silent and watching. Everyone. She turned back to Dane.

"I think they enjoyed the show. What do you think?" said Dane. "Do you think they'll be saying come Monday that you defended your friend's honor? Or that you're a psycho bitch who's obsessed with me? Want the odds? Nobody will believe you, Saad. Nobody takes you seriously."

Lulu pointed a solitary finger at him. "Just wait, Anderson. Just you fucking wait."

Anderson made a swipe for her finger. "Looking forward to it."

Lulu dodged out of the way. Then Lulu did what great generals had done before her when faced with a defeat. She fled, hoping to live to fight another day. She rounded the corner, from the side of the house to the front, only to come colliding into a tall, slim frame. The frame grabbed her hand, holding her steady. Lulu felt like a malfunctioning circuit board, at once too much and not enough feeling across her body. She flailed, then stilled as she looked up and saw it was James. Unhesitating, Lulu wrapped her arms around him. Her hands tangled through his hair, her body flush up against his. His hands tested out their position on her hips, traveled upward to her waist, his thumb moving against her shirt at her stomach. Lulu was ready for his lips and for her own oblivion when James pulled away abruptly.

"What?" Lulu swayed slightly.

James stared into her eyes. He frowned. "God. You're high."

"No need to call me God," she countered. "And I'm not *that* high. Not anymore."

"Matt's still inside. I couldn't stay. Not in there." His frown deepened. "I can't do this. I can't."

Lulu's expression steeled. She took his meaning. He'd seen her through the window. She didn't know if he was taking his friend's side over hers. Or if he was just the type to stake a claim on a girl without consulting her first. Lulu found neither acceptable.

"Then *GO*," Lulu shouted with the final thread of her control.

James's shoulders stiffened. He gave a curt nod, then turned around and walked off. Lulu felt her breathing grow shallow. She propped one arm along the whitewashed brick, trying to steady herself. She could feel the hitch in her throat. She willed it away, but her body didn't listen. Tears came, unwanted and unbidden. Lulu held her breath, hoping to prevent any sound from escaping her lips. But she sniffled involuntarily.

A few paces away, James stopped. He turned around. He marched right back to Lulu and held out his hand. "You need a ride home."

All Lulu had to do was bridge the distance and take it. She paused for a moment. Then she stepped forward and took his hand.

———

They drove through the kind of neighborhood where people paid others to live their lives for them—walk the dogs, pick up the dry cleaning, push strollers, collect children from school. Those were the only people ever spotted beyond the hedges of the perfectly meandering roads. It looked like a grand neighborhood populated by luxury cars and members of the service industry. For the people who owned the homes, leisure had become a full-time occupation.

Lulu drew errant hearts across the light fog on the passenger window. She'd already texted Lo. *Find Audrey.* That was all she could say. Find Audrey. What else was there? Nothing. Just find her. Lulu turned to face James.

"What the hell is wrong with you?" James asked, breaking her reverie.

"I don't owe you anything." Lulu turned away again, placing her entire back to James.

"No, you don't owe anyone anything, do you?"

Lulu's head whipped around, her voice warbling. "I owe it to Audrey to find her. God, I don't know where she is now. I owe it to Emma to figure out what the fuck is wrong and why she's not here with us. I should be in her car, not yours. Not here. I owe it to Lo—I don't know. I owe Lo things I don't understand. And I owe myself a deep fucking breath, but how could you understand that?" Her friends were all different, and they were all ripping apart at the seams. Lulu couldn't stop it. Couldn't stop it at all.

"Because you won't let me! You don't trust me."

"Don't trust you? I don't trust *me*, you asshole. Do you know the kinds of boys I find attractive? Horrible people. Awful people."

"I'm not like that, Lulu."

"Oh, really, you're different? You're not like the other boys? You don't want to make me playlists with Drake on them? Full of blame and longing?" Lulu watched James's expression fall.

"Would you like a list? Michael Rossi, in the eighth grade, asked me if I had to marry one of my cousins. Because I'm Arab. Brian Connor, mind you after going through the trouble of asking me to dance and pull his sweet, sweet moves on me." Lulu arched her eyebrows to indicate they were anything but. "He told Nina that I was good for some fun, but I wasn't the kind of girl you date, *you know*. And you, when we met, you were pulling crap about my not being like other girls. Do you fucking get it? How can I trust myself? Would you trust yourself? And Dane. Jesus Christ. The first guy I had an honest crush on. The last one I let myself, too. You want to know about Dane?"

"What, did he dump you freshman year?" James's scorn sliced through Lulu.

Lulu felt as though she'd been spat on. She heaved a great breath. She tried to focus her thoughts, she tried to let go of all the guilt and the pain. But that felt nearly impossible now. "No." Her voice went as quiet as a whisper. "He didn't dump me."

"Jesus, Lulu, I saw you. I saw you come on to Anderson."

"Fuck you," she said, more breath than sound.

"Fuck you, too. I'm not a notch on your belt. You can't treat people like that."

"I'm not going to give consent for my heart. I don't trust it. You want my fucking body? You can have it. It's here, for the fucking taking." Lulu gestured to the whole of her.

James stopped at a red light and stared, slack jawed.

"You must know all there is to know about me. I'm a girl, so I must be jealous. And I'm wild and a bit slutty, so I must have been used. You think Dane broke my heart. Fine. You're right. He did."

James croaked out his next question. "How?"

Normally this was where Lulu would hold back. Where she would save face and guard her pride. But Lulu was too angry. The levee had broken, and the contents of her heart would pour out, whether she willed it or not. "Freshman year. I don't know. It was lunchtime."

"So what?" James asked.

"So I checked my phone. And it was everywhere," she said. "That shooting in Paris."

Lulu couldn't escape the news, couldn't escape the dread clawing up her throat. So many people, living their life with joy, with youth and freedom, gunned down. Lulu had stood there staring. Trying not to crumple in on herself. Trying to ease her mind around a gruesome reality. But there was no way to ease it. She couldn't imagine the kind of someone to do such a thing. But they had. And nothing had been the same since.

"Yeah," he said, as though he were at a loss for words himself.

"It was awful." Lulu didn't have another word for it. She'd thought about other words, but they weren't enough. Though sometimes, they were too much. "Everything was strange and unreal."

Lulu, much like the student populace around her, had spent the whole time staring at her phone in a daze. But then Lulu had gone toward the dining hall. And that forward momentum had changed everything.

A wave of nausea swept through Lulu. It must have been the weed, that was all. But even Lulu couldn't lie to herself that well.

"Yeah."

"They said it was my fault." Lulu was looking back out the window, drawing hearts absentmindedly. "They said. They said that since some crazy Arabs did it, or maybe they meant crazy Muslims, since they were Belgians, who knows. But since they did it, it was my fault. Like I'd done it."

Lulu breathed out onto the window, fogging over her earlier work. But the outlines and the traces of where she had been were still there. Her voice came out at a whisper. A secret between herself and this old pane of glass. "Like I could even think of such a thing."

The memory flashed, still fresh, still acute. She had passed by a group of freshman and sophomore boys on her way to Audrey's locker. And they had called out to her. They had told her the attack was her fault. She was Iraqi, wasn't she, they had accused. They knew she was Muslim. Her fault, they had kept on, the dirty little terrorist, the conspiring towelhead. Lulu had stood, for the first time in her life, at a loss for words. Worse than hearing the words from hateful strangers—she had stood hearing the poisonous words from boys she'd grown up with, boys she'd kissed, boys she'd had crushes on, boys she'd tasted her first alcohol with, boys she'd wrestled with for control of the TV remote.

Strangers, at least, she could have ignored.

She should have felt punched in the stomach. But she hadn't. She should have screamed, and yelled back at them. But she hadn't. Instead, she had stood there, dazed and stupid, while wondering if all those years she'd thought she belonged there that she had been terribly, horribly mistaken. The relatives who died fighting tyranny had choked the words in her throat. Her heart had shattered that day, into thousands of selfish pieces. The one she had now, the one she had put back together, had slivers missing in the strangest of places.

"And?" asked James.

Lulu realized she hadn't said anything for a long moment. She tried shrugging, but she couldn't quite pass it off as casual. It was too forced a move. Too strained under the weight of her memories. "And Dane was one of them."

She looked over to James. And she could see the recognition in his eyes. In that moment, he knew what Dane was capable of. He knew that Dane was not just one of them. The horrible pity in James's eyes spoke volumes. Dane had galvanized the troops and led them into battle. He had organized the horrible parade of hate in her honor, and even Lulu underselling his role could not hide this truth.

A new wave of nausea crashed through Lulu's body. She took a deep breath, willing the sensation away. It was the weed, the weed, not the terror or the memory. Not the pain in her chest. Not the heavy biting around her eyes. She remembered that the boys had started laughing then, at the end of their torment—razor-sharp-teeth-filled laughter—but she couldn't hear them for the ringing in her ears. She knew she hadn't started crying in front of them, but she didn't quite remember how she'd gotten to the bathroom on the far side of campus by the art rooms.

They had found her there a few minutes later. Lo and Emma and Audrey.

Lulu had never thanked them for that. For helping Lulu clean up her face. For being a friend to her when she'd needed it most and probably deserved it the least. That fact always hung around her memory like a guilty conscience. They had taken care of Lulu when so many seemed ready to abandon her. And now they were all splintering apart.

Lulu closed her eyes. The wave of nausea passed. Her head throbbed. She pressed it against the window, hoping the cool temperature outside would bring relief. "I'd had a crush on him, you know. But that wasn't it, really. It was something else. Something worse than that."

Her whole life, Lulu had been warned that boys would break her heart. That they would destroy her. But no one ever warned her that they would do so in this way. Everyone told her boys would hurt her only if she let them. No one ever told her that boys would break her heart for nothing more than being born as she was. "Make good choices," was the refrain. But that didn't apply to being Arab or Muslim. Those had been branded upon her at her birth. She'd inherited her mother's hair and along with it her father's religion. She could ignore it, but she carried that mark on her breath, in her skin, in her eyes, everywhere.

Lulu looked back at James. He was staring, a bit stupidly, at her. She regretted opening her eyes. She couldn't control the nausea anymore. It was a waiting game now.

"Do you know what that's like? To be attracted to someone who hates you for being born as what they see as less than?" Lulu didn't wait for an answer. "Someone who wants to make you hate yourself? It's like a nasty poison in a beautiful bottle. And if you are tempted to take it, even a tiny sip—it's your fault. Everyone'll say it. Because you know—and everyone knows—there's a poison in there and you shouldn't have been tempted in the first place."

James opened his mouth, then closed it, like he couldn't imagine what to say to that. Tears threatened in earnest. She would prefer to vomit in James's car than cry in front of him again. The car slowed as it made a turn into a new neighborhood. Her neighborhood.

"And then everywhere: I am Paris. *Je suis Paris*. But I'm not, am I? Everyone saying I am Paris and they mean themselves but specifically not me. Even though I learned how to pout like a French girl and when to *tu* and when to *vous*. I am not their Paris." Lulu cleared her throat. "Anyways, nobody I know died. Nobody my French teacher knew, either. And those boys kept on for the better part of a year, but nobody hurt me physically. Eventually

I told. And somehow, it stopped. The administration believed me, and the boys stopped. I know how lucky I am. But I hate myself a little bit, every time I see him. It feels, I don't know. It feels like I've lost. Like I never had a chance to win in the first place."

Lulu looked over and saw what James meant by his silence. She turned back to the window. She hadn't been able to readily admit to anyone new since that afternoon that she was part Arab and all Muslim. She choked on the words before she could get them out. She wasn't ashamed. She was deeply afraid. She didn't know how to counter such a set of terrible assumptions right as she met someone. She'd built a shell around herself, so she couldn't be hurt, so their prejudice would not be her pain. So only the people she thought she could trust would see her.

The car stopped in front of her house. Lulu pushed out of it, nausea clawing through her stomach and up her throat. She slammed the door and practically ran to the door. She needed to get inside. But as she clamored through her purse, trying to find her keys, the feeling was too much.

A hand was at her shoulder. "I don't want to startle you, but I'm right here." James swept his hand across her forehead and held back her hair. "Can you stand on your own?"

Lulu nodded faintly. The nod was a bad idea. The nausea surged again. His hand went lightly to her hip. Lulu thought to laugh; the gesture was nearly romantic. Then she turned to the side and retched in the bushes. Several times.

"It's okay." James kept her hair back in a gentle grip, kept a hand lightly on her hip. He seemed to be waiting for her to indicate if she could stand back up again or not. "It's gonna be okay."

"I'm not sure what your definition of *okay* is, young man, but this is certainly not mine," said Lulu's mother as the door swung open.

Lulu groaned. She couldn't believe James hadn't dropped her. It showed backbone to not be immediately terrified of Aimee Saad when the woman was in such a state. She was like an ancient sorceress turned into a dragon. She was power and wrath; vengeance and fury. She would direct her rage at anything that crossed her path. She wouldn't think to ask questions later. A righteous Aimee Saad was her worst and best form all at once. "Leila Margot Saad, you are in *deep* shit."

Lulu looked up from the bushes. Her mother stood in perfect silhouette in the doorway. Lulu groaned, before heaving into the bushes again. She felt too ill to think about the irony of finally being caught vomiting when it had fuck all to do with the substances in her body and everything to do with the riotous play of memories across her heart.

"And you," said her mother, turning to face James. "Who the flying fuck are you?"

Again, it was to James's credit that he did not flee from the premises. "I'm a friend. I was giving Lulu a ride home."

"A friend? You expect me to believe that? Do I look like I was born yesterday?"

"Don't answer that. 'S'always a trick question." Lulu coughed and spat into the shrubbery.

"Thanks for the tip," he said, as though he and Lulu were in some kind of private joke together.

"Have you been drinking?"

"Mom, if you have to ask that, you *were* born yesterday," said Lulu, resigning herself to her fate. She would not wail at the unfairness of the world. She'd gotten off scot-free too many times to think this bust wasn't somehow justified. Lulu heaved again. Then she spat the unpleasant taste of bile out of her mouth and hoped she had vomited her last.

"You're in enough trouble as it is, daughter o' mine. Don't push your luck." Her mother used her threatening finger point.

"Luck." Lulu laughed ironically at that. This time, the nausea passed without the upchuck reflex. Lulu sighed her relief. At least that part was over. A dizzying spin took over her head. The dehydration was kicking in.

Aimee turned to James. "I was trying to ask if you had been drinking. Not her."

"No, ma'am," said James. "I have not."

Her mother maintained her eagle-eyed gaze on James. "Are you going to release your grip on my daughter?"

Lulu felt James's fingers twitch, but he didn't let go. He did look a bit like a deer caught in the headlights, but he always looked like that to Lulu. "As soon as she tells me to, ma'am. I'm worried she can't stand by herself."

Aimee narrowed her eyes. Lulu felt James's tension through his gentle hold on her hair and body, but he didn't let go.

"Can you stand?" he asked her, leaning close to Lulu's ear.

Lulu nodded. James guided her to her feet and released her. Lulu swayed forward—her whole body, drained of adrenaline and fluids, had gone limp.

James caught her. "I think you need to get to bed."

At the mention of bed, Aimee Saad had finally reached her upper limit. She snatched Lulu out of James's arms. "If you think you're helping her into bed, young man, you've got another think coming. What's your name?"

"I—I didn't think that. I wanted to help. Ma'am. It's James." He stumbled through his words. "James Denair."

"Get the hell out of here, James Denair."

Aimee was about to shut the door when James said, "I'm sorry you found her like this. And I'm sorry you don't like me. I was trying to get her home. She's had a really rough night."

Aimee shut the door without another word.

16
Eidia

A familiar, worn compact car pulled into the driveway. Lulu heard the engine before double-checking out her bedroom window. She had to squint to see it, as the sunlight pulsed against her tender eyes. She made an approximation of a leap out of bed—stumbling across her floor until she could find her glasses.

"Rez!" she shouted as she trundled downstairs. She was desperate for company. Her mother was giving her an icy treatment—refusing to punish her, true, but also refusing to acknowledge her.

Reza Saad was there to give her an enormous hug and swing her in an arc before putting her down. Reza wasn't tall, but he had an imposing build. He smiled broadly. Reza was the eldest and the best of the Saad siblings. "How's everybody's favorite spoiled brat?"

"She's all right," she lied. Emma's responses to communication were monosyllabic texts. Audrey wasn't messaging, and Lulu was too proud to beg for Lo's attention.

Reza gave her another squeeze and Lulu winced. Reza had yet to learn his own strength. Or perhaps he never thought of Lulu as weak.

"Rez, don't encourage her. She's bad enough as it is." Ben entered, standing in the frame between the kitchen and the hallway. Where Reza was broad, Ben was skinny, still lanky. His hands hung like great weights at the end of his lean arms, and his face hadn't quite achieved the hardened edges of manhood. Ben was the middle one and the most reckless among the Saad trio. At least, that's how the family told it.

"Ben!" Lulu enveloped her second brother in her significantly shorter arms. Ben was distant with everyone. Lulu learned to never take it personally. "Both of you home at the same time? I thought you weren't due until tomorrow, crazy!"

Ben gave Lulu a good-natured pat on her back. "Nah, I decided to change my flight last minute. Rez swung around to the airport before he headed home. Figured I'd score points with the maternal unit."

"Does Mom know you're home? What about Baba? When did you get in? Where's your suitcases and stuff?"

"Slow your roll, little sister," said Ben.

At this, Reza put his arm protectively around Lulu, who stuck out her tongue at Ben.

"What a witty comeback." Ben smirked. "Glad to see that expensive education is paying off for you."

"Bite me," said Lulu.

"You two." Reza frowned. "Stop."

"He started it!" Lulu pointed at Ben.

"And you took it to a higher plane," said Ben, a single eyebrow arched.

Reza wiped a hand over his face, like he'd seen this scene too many times.

"Rez isn't Baba, little sister. He's not going to automatically take your side. Besides, I've got leverage."

Lulu stilled. "What leverage?"

Ben leaned in but then shouted in Lulu's ear. "A little bird told me you were very, very grounded."

Lulu jumped back. "Mom told? She's not even talking to me."

Reza glared at Ben. "Mom told *me*. She called worried you were going down Ben's darkened path. Her words, not mine."

Lulu sighed a great, burdened sigh.

Ben pulled Lulu into a headlock and rubbed his knuckles onto the top of her head. It was not done gently. "Well, shit, little sister. You are screwed."

"Ben." Reza used all the authority his older age afforded him. "Leave her alone. She's suffered enough. Probably."

Ben's expression of innocence was belied by the fact that he doubled down his efforts with his knuckles on Lulu's head. She yelped.

"Benyamin Saad, you're home for less than two minutes and you're already starting trouble." The front door swung open and through it came their mother, her arms laden with binders and papers and two laptop cases. She got on her tiptoes to give Ben a kiss on the cheek, then Reza. "Hello, Reza, sweetheart."

But there was no greeting for Lulu.

Ben released Lulu from the headlock instantaneously. He smiled, easygoing and open. "Me? I would never."

Lulu found a small but interesting stain on the wall. From the looks of it, it was a smudge of ink. She couldn't say *nothing* to her mother, though. "You're home early."

Aimee glanced at Lulu. She looked back to Ben. "Reza called me when he was at the airport waiting for Ben. I thought I'd come home now to see you all before heading back to the office for a late night. Well," said her mother. "Who wants to grab some lunch?"

Lulu turned to glare pointedly at Aimee.

But her mother just set down her work bags. "You know Ben isn't participating in Ramadan. And you're clearly playing fast and loose with the rules yourself. You don't mind, do you, Reza, honey?"

Reza shook his head. Their mother walked back out the front door to her car. Ben followed her with long strides, catching up to her quickly. Ben was not one to look a gift horse of food in the mouth. Lulu sighed. Ben was their mother's favorite. Lulu was their father's. Reza was nobody's favorite, but he was too good to seem bothered by this.

Lulu got her phone out of her pocket to message Audrey what a horrible bitch her mother was being, because if anyone could understand, it was Audrey. The time stamp from their messages glared up at Lulu. The ones she'd tried sending to find Audrey. The ones Audrey hadn't responded to.

Yesterday Delivered 11:42 p.m. Seen 11:46 p.m.

At least Audrey was alive. Lo had even confirmed that. Not that Lulu had cooled off enough from Lo abandoning them all for Lulu to respond to Lo, really.

Lulu put her phone back in her pocket. She'd kept it there today in case it buzzed, but as many times as she imagined it going off, her notifications stayed oddly mute all day.

Reza put his hand on Lulu's shoulder. "Come on. We *will* be able to eat Thanksgiving dinner. Fasting ends tonight. Let's go have one last miserable nonlunch."

Reza smiled. It wasn't charming. It was earnest. It was comforting. It reminded Lulu of their childhood—the three of them a solid fortress against their parents.

"Fine." Lulu threw up her arms for good measure. "Let's go watch Mom and Ben eat lunch."

"*Bismillaah ar-Rahman ar-Raheem. Alhamdulillaahi rabbil 'alameen.*"

As her father spoke, Lulu felt the rhythm of his speech reverberate through her body. The words washed her with calmness. She closed her eyes, trying to soak in as much of that feeling as she could. Reza nodded along with his father's words, mouthing them wordlessly in unison. Ben's face remained unreadable and placid. Their mother bowed her head respectfully. They were all there to finish Ramadan together.

At the beginning of their marriage, Aimee wanted to understand her husband's customs. So, of course, she had blended them with her own by asking how to pray at the table to break a fast. Ahmed explained, quite directly, that he'd never prayed over a meal in his life. Aimee explained, quite calmly, that she didn't know of any better place for a Muslim and a Christian to pray together without incident. He laughed. And on the end of that first Ramadan of their marriage, they had made the holiday their own. It was now as solid a tradition as any.

"*Ar-Rahman ar-Raheem Maaliki yaumiddeen,*" Lulu's father continued on in a deep, unyielding voice.

Lulu's eyes were still closed. There were so few times in Lulu's life, so few moments, that the sacred reached out and touched her. Sitting here, she felt it in her bones. It didn't matter that this was two old customs married together in a strange, new thing that only belonged to her family. That was what made it so special to her in the first place.

"*Iyyaaka na'abudu wa iyyaaka nasta'een. Ihdinas siraatal mustaqeem.*" Her father's voice was both lower and projecting farther than when he started.

Lulu didn't know how her father did it. He wasn't a particularly religious man. He hadn't even taught his children how to pray properly. As a professor, he cared more for the historical side of his religion than the spiritual. A religion he had given his children more out of duty than faith. But when he spoke the words of the opening surah of the Koran, he made magic.

"*Siraatal ladheena an 'amta' 'alaihim. Ghairil maghduubi' 'alaihim waladaaleen.*" He was almost finished, and Lulu wished she could trap the serenity this moment gave her. Religiosity or steadfast devotion did not belong to her family, did not belong to her. But this moment did.

"*Aameen*," Ahmed concluded, breaking the spell.

Ramadan was over. The Eid could begin. There would be a party. And food. And lots and lots of people. But that would be tomorrow. Tonight was for her family. Tonight was theirs.

The whole Saad family began to speak with rapidity and intensity. A single breath meant another had a space to interject, interrupt, and intercede in the conversation. Reza brandished his fork several times, mostly in the general direction of the potato salad. Ben continued to eat and talk, so his argument held equal parts discursive qualities and bits of food rolling along his mouth. Ahmed shook his head and argued with his sons. Aimee interjected herself when she found the others' arguments lacking, which happened more often than one might suppose.

Lulu stabbed a green bean. She chewed the single pod thoroughly. "Did you know that chimpanzees will go to war with other chimpanzees over territory and cannibalize their kills?"

"Little sister, aren't you a disappointment tonight? You so got that from the Discovery Channel ten years ago." Ben was too fun to fight with, and he knew it.

"Not as disappointing as your sorry ass," Lulu countered with the particular brand of sarcasm she saved for Ben alone.

"Leila Saad, you apologize right now." Her mother sat up with unintentional primness. "And do we have to talk about cannibalism at the dinner table? I hardly think it's good for anyone's appetite."

"Mom, it's not *human* cannibalism. It's monkey cannibalism," Ben replied quite thoughtfully.

"Chimpanzee." Reza nodded.

"Oh, excuse me. *Chimpanzee* cannibalism." Ben laid his hand over his heart. "You're quite right, Rez."

"My darlings, did you know," their father started, and Lulu was quite sure that she did know, whatever it was that he was about to communicate, "that during a bad winter the most vulnerable people in a medieval European village were likely to be cannibalized?"

Aimee set down her fork loudly. Reza coughed into his napkin. Ben snorted soda.

Lulu laughed with unexpected pleasure. "No, I didn't."

"That can't be right," said their mother, her nasal twang coming out in full force.

"There's evidence. And here, during the harsh winter in Jamestown. There's more than circumstantial evidence." Their father turned his attention to Lulu. "So your ancestors were, during the height of Baghdad, you know, writing treatises on the Qur'an, while the people of Europe, with their kings and their 'Holy Roman Emperors,' which, as you know—"

But he was interrupted by Lulu, Ben, and Reza in chorus with one another, "—weren't holy, or Roman, or emperors!"

"Yes, yes, exactly." Their father smiled, appreciating the teasing. He had an audience and little could ruin his thrill. "These people, they were starving and eating one another. And you, your people were writing philosophy."

"No, they weren't!" exclaimed Ben in mock surprise.

"They were!" said their father.

Reza shot Ben a glare. "He's kidding, Baba."

"You know." Their father took a bite and chewed thoughtfully. "Your grandmother still carries a gun."

Lulu's mischievous grin was reflected back at her in her father's face, particularly in his eyes. It was a non sequitur to anyone outside the family, but Ahmed was full of these.

"We know, Baba."

17

Spectacular, Spectacular

Lulu had spent the week off from school staring at her phone. Willing it to buzz. Hell, even willing it to ring. And Lulu hated picking up phone calls. But Audrey maintained her silence, and Emma maintained her newfound distance. And as for James, Lulu had gotten an *are you okay?* Which she'd followed up with a *super* that had garnered no response but a series of three dots hovering every few moments, only to be bounced back to nothing. When Lulu had broken down and messaged Lo, her phone filled with cryptic one-word answers and petty GIFs raising their eyebrows sardonically.

Better to go without a response at all.

Lulu was coiled—pent up with memories of her friends choosing boys over her, and boys groping her friends, and other hands altogether gently helping her find her balance again.

She was angry and she wasn't quite sure with whom. It could have been Audrey and her drinking, or Luke and his leering. Lulu wanted it to be Lo and her questing for unattainable boys. Or even James and his inability to keep his nose out of other people's problems. Or her mother's unwillingness to punish her and get the damned thing over with.

But it wasn't any of that. It was just a rage that had been simmering, waiting for the right moment to boil over. Hovering on the edge of the pot. A readiness that sank into Lulu's bones and told her the world was her enemy and would never be her friend.

So, of course, she had to paste on her old, pretty smile and go and celebrate a holiday.

The Alkatis had pulled out all the stops, including but not limited to at least a hundred people piled into their home, a modern credenza that functioned as a mere side buffet, and a live musician playing the oud for this large party in honor of the Little Eid.

Lulu made her way through the throng of people clumped at the entryway. Lulu had already lost her brothers somewhere in the crowd and she could barely make out her parents—her mother was kissing Auntie Salwa's cheeks and her father was already shouting with Amu Yusuf, Miriam's father. He reminded her of a big, friendly bear. He clapped, singing a famous Iraqi song about a beautiful girl named Leila when he saw Lulu.

Lulu waved and smiled, then ducked away—all the while cursing musicians who had the gall to fall in love with women named Leila. She ran from the sound of his discordant singing as quickly as she could without giving offense. Lulu had been cursed twice over with her name. White boys sang Clapton and old Arab men would sing this. She couldn't win.

Lulu emerged from a throng of people into a secluded piece of hallway before the rear entryway to the kitchen. She took a deep breath, but the relief didn't come. The strange lonesomeness of the crowd only increased when Lulu finally had a moment to herself. She pushed through the hallway, longing to be embraced by the rich cardamom and saffron wafting out from the kitchen. Lulu stepped into bright light ahead of her and let herself be enveloped in the sounds of chatter and the friendly clink of metal on china.

Ali and Thabit and Mustafa stood in a clump in the back of the large, warm kitchen. Reza and Ben had found them, and Ben had already started an animated story that required the full length of his arms to tell. Reza kept smacking Ben's hands down so he wouldn't inadvertently hit anyone as they walked by.

Across the kitchen, Lulu's mother had joined Ame Nadia. Auntie Farrah went right on chattering around Lulu's mother. Ame Nadia kept trying to include her. It was nearly funny, watching her mother be spoken over and purposely included at every other turn. One of the crowd broke away— Auntie Salwa maneuvered around the party, mistress of the house and the consummate hostess. Lulu admired her, working the room as well as Queen Noor might have in that monarch's heyday.

Lulu was so busy surveying the kitchen, she ran headlong into Miriam.

"*'Eid Mubarak, Lulu!*" Miriam said, grasping Lulu for balance. Neither one of them toppled over, and Miriam went in for the requisite three kisses across the cheek.

"*'Eid Said, habibti.*" Lulu avoided eye contact. She didn't want to be reminded of the weekend. She didn't want any memories flooding back now.

"Don't start habibti-ing me yet," said Miriam. "We've still got three hours to go."

Lulu laughed—a relief. "I like the word. Better than *sugar*," said Lulu. "My Mimi used to always call me sugar. But she'd drop the *r* somehow, and it came out more like *shuga*." Lulu clicked her tongue in disapproval.

"Fair enough." Miriam snorted. "I'm dying for a smoke."

Lulu turned away, not wanting to be reminded of smoking at all. "You've got like two hours before you can inhale the secondhand fumes of the hubbly bubbly. Pace yourself."

"You're a buzzkill tonight." Miriam absently picked at her teeth. "Dina alert, eight o'clock."

Lulu turned, her smile painted back on. "*'Eid Mubarak, Dina! 'Eid Mubarak, Tamra!*"

"*'Eid Mubarak, habibti,*" said Tamra.

Miriam raised her eyebrows at Lulu over Dina's head as they hugged. Lulu held in her laughter as she endured another smattering of kisses across each of her cheeks.

"Hungry?" asked Miriam.

Dina laughed, bright and sunny. "Starving!"

Dina picked up a plate and started adding food to it. Tamra followed behind her, circling the buffet table, followed by Miriam. Lulu trailed behind them all.

"Lulu, habibti! You don't have enough food on your plate! Here—" Dina added a full serving of rice to Lulu's plate. "There you go!"

Lulu smiled through her gritted teeth as graciously as she could. As the oldest of the four, Dina had such rights. Lulu put a spoonful of the rice back on the platter once both of the girls' backs turned. Miriam mimed a tongue clicking, as though Lulu had been naughty.

It was meant to be a joke, a gentle teasing, but Lulu bristled under the criticism. Even if it was fake criticism.

"Oh, and you have to try these," said Tamra, turning back and adding five grape leaf–wrapped rice nuggets to Lulu's plate. Tamra was younger than Dina but still older than Lulu. "My mother made them special for tonight. Took her all day yesterday."

Lulu stuffed a dolma in her mouth and hummed her appreciation. Tamra preened. And as Lulu's mouth was full, Auntie Salwa swooped into their small band, with three kisses each for the four girls. Lulu did her best not to spew grape leaves and rice onto her hostess.

"Habibtis, how are you? *Keifich, keifich, keifich?*"

"*Ziena, Amti. Wa anti?*" was Dina's reply.

"*Alhumdulillah, habibti. Alhumdulillah,*" said Salwa, squeezing Dina's cheeks between her index finger and thumb.

"*Allhamd'Allah,*" parroted Tamra.

"I'm good, *shukran,* Auntie," said Lulu.

Miriam smiled. "Same."

Auntie Salwa appraised them all for a moment before grabbing Lulu by the chin. "Always you have the look of your father, mashallah."

"*Shukran, Khala.*" Lulu wasn't sure why one of the Arabic words for auntie had slipped out. It was unbidden, as though Lulu had something to prove. As though she were Audrey tap dancing wildly for approval. Lulu needed no one's approval.

"Of course, habibti." Salwa pinched Lulu's cheeks. "But what are you girls doing here by yourselves? You should be mixing. Go and say hello to Auntie Farrah. She's been asking about you. She's very worried, you know. Her daughter is stuck on immigration. She wasn't born here, the eldest. We're all worried for her, inshallah. An engineer, too. Khala needs girls to dote on."

"Of course, Amti," said Dina, with all the respect in her voice.

"Ya, Mama, of course we will," said Tamra.

"Sure," said Miriam, on a shrug.

A tightness wrapped around Lulu's chest. These women knew how to look after one another. But they never extended the courtesy to her mother. And they only gave such consideration to Lulu when they saw her father in her. Lulu had built her own allies, and last time they had failed her. Or maybe she had failed them. And these ones, this family that should have been ready-made for her eyed her warily, as though she might prove unworthy at any moment. Lulu couldn't quite swallow the feeling, giving her voice a coiled, unsteady tenor. "Do you think she would want a baklava?"

"*La*, habibti, she has her own. You are such sweet girls, aren't you?" But Auntie Salwa couldn't seem to help herself and decided to add, "Despite everything, *ay wallah*?"

Salwa's eyes flickered to Lulu's mother in the distance. It was unconscious, Lulu could tell. Then Dina and Tamra glanced toward Aimee as well. Lulu bit her tongue hard enough to taste the tang of metal in her mouth. She held on to that taste, that sensation. Miriam, trying to break the spell, gave Lulu a good flick on the leg. Lulu nodded her thanks in return.

Auntie Farrah, apparently impatient, fluttered over to their small group. She greeted Salwa and launched into the middle of a conversation Lulu knew they had been having earlier. They spoke to each other in a rapid-fire Arabic that was difficult for Lulu to follow clearly. But Lulu could always pick out important words, no matter how fast the speakers might talk.

Lulu munched on one of her baklava, knowing it was impolite to interrupt. Dina and Tamra also listened attentively to the older women. Lulu watched as Salwa relayed Lulu's concern for Farrah. They both looked to Lulu, with kindness in their eyes. Farrah pinched Lulu's two cheeks with her forefinger and her thumb. It was a loving kind of pain that Auntie Farrah delivered. Lulu did wish her mouth hadn't been full of baklava when Farrah had chosen to do it. Lulu swallowed, then smiled.

The two women moved on in their conversation. They glanced over to Aimee. They continued to talk, their expression meaningful, their words slightly more hushed. The same, like always. The same whispers and looks Aimee would always get. The same whispers, if she was lucky, Lulu would get for the rest of her life. Everywhere was whispering. She'd never be free of it. Not here. And especially not at Sealy Hall. She'd been so foolish to think she could have built something unbreakable of her own there. Something impenetrable. Something that couldn't, wouldn't shatter. Lulu gritted her teeth.

"And her," said Auntie Salwa meaningfully, still in Arabic.

Auntie Farrah clucked distastefully. She answered in Arabic that Lulu could follow. "La, no, I know. *'Sharmoota.'*"

Lulu turned her head; she stared at the two women. Her attention drew the attention of Miriam and Dina and Tamra. But Lulu couldn't think beyond the ringing in her ears. *Sharmoota. Whore. Slut. Same slur in any tongue.* Lulu was haunted by it.

"*Ey*," said Auntie Salwa, with wide, knowing eyes.

"*Limadha?*" Auntie Farrah shook her head.

"Because *hoom niswangi. La*," said Auntie Salwa. Then she made a remark about a man like a tree, with the mind of a goat. They were speaking too fast to follow directly.

Auntie Farrah wiped her hands theatrically. "*Khalas.*"

Lulu watched knowing smiles grow on Dina's and Tamra's faces. They thought she didn't know. They thought her quiescence was ignorance. They thought Lulu's placidity equal to docility. Lulu could still taste the blood in her mouth. She was done biting herself. She would show them she knew how to snap.

"My mother may have made me a slut." Lulu's gaze flickered to Tanya and her fiancé. "But at least she didn't sell me to the highest bidder."

The air around them went still. Tamra flinched. Dina froze. Miriam looked ready to crawl under a rock. Auntie Farrah turned to stare, slack jawed.

Salwa, though looking as though she had been slapped, had a bit more presence of mind than anyone else. "Excuse me?"

"She doesn't understand. She doesn't know what she's saying," said Auntie Farrah, with as much force as she could. As though her pronouncements could rewrite reality and the truth in one fell swoop. Salwa's eyes narrowed at Lulu.

Lulu knew she was drawing a crowd. She didn't care. She heard the din of the room around her grow quiet. She'd lulled the women and girls around her into a strangled silence. But she couldn't back down. Not now.

"Oh. Is that not what you meant by sharmoota?" Here was the warped logic and beatific smile of Sealy Hall—an expression that belied Lulu's words. Her rage had finally boiled over. But instead of the blinding hot sensation that typically flushed through her, Lulu shivered, like she'd been hollowed out and frozen. She was finally who everyone thought she might be. Who she feared she was. It was nearly prophetic, this feeling, and she gave into her villainy willingly. "My Arabic is a bit rusty. Translation is so slippery. I always thought it meant *slut*, but I can tell by your expression that it means *whore*. Can you say the same of your daughters? Is that why you sell them so quickly? So you *do* think my mother is willing to profit off my short skirts and American ways. You're not so different from her, after all."

Auntie Farrah's jaw had found the floor. Auntie Salwa was sputtering. Lulu didn't break eye contact with her, though. Out of the corner of her eye, Lulu saw her mother whip her head around so fast, Lulu assumed she'd have a crick in her neck the next day.

Lulu's mother stood beside her in a flash. "Leila Margot Saad. You will apologize. This second."

"No. I won't." Lulu turned and walked away from the small crowd.

"You will go back there and apologize. Do you hear me." Her mother snatched her up by the arm.

Lulu yanked out of the grip almost. "No. I said I won't. I meant it."

The crowd's gaze followed them.

Aimee's mouth formed a hard line. "I have been so lenient with you. I've let things slide. I was giving you time to act like a grown-up after this weekend. I can see now that was a mistake."

"Mom, she was practically calling you—" but the look on Aimee's face quieted Lulu. And the phrase wasn't "practically" anything, but Lulu didn't need to repeat the insult for her mother, word for word.

"No, Leila. No. I've had enough. I'm a grown woman, and I decide what I can handle in this world, not you. I chose my life with my eyes open. This is nothing to what my own family does. You think you're proving a point? All you're doing is confirming the worst." And with no further ado Aimee clamped her hand around Lulu's elbow and yanked her. "You're making life so much harder for your father, did you know that? And me. I hope you see that. And if you don't, you're going to see it. You won't listen to me, you're going to have to listen to your father. He's going to be so disappointed."

Aimee had always explained the rules. Ahmed had always encouraged Lulu's wildness. This was what made the threat of revealing the truth to Ahmed so incisive. Aimee would be mad when Lulu violated the rules; Ahmed would be heartbroken. Anger was easy to deal with. Disappointment was not. Lulu was being sold out. Aimee had always threatened it, of course, but Lulu never thought she'd see the day when her mother would make good on that threat. She was abandoned. All she had been trying to do was defend her mother. And now, she would reap her reward for that.

Her mother yanked Lulu the final way to her father, calling him over. He had been in the middle of a jovial argument with Amu Yusuf. Aimee explained the situation with Tamra's mother succinctly. Lulu watched Ahmed's face fall. Lulu watched, knowing she hadn't only broken a piece of his heart. She'd broken the piece of his heart that he guarded the most.

"Leila," he said, his voice a quaking whisper.

"Yes, Baba."

"You will go apologize to Mrs. Salwa."

"No," Lulu said.

"Lulu. You will," he said, his evident misery hardening into anger as he spoke.

"I won't."

Ahmed moved to speak, but Aimee held up her hand. "If you're incapable of acting like a civilized adult, you will go wait outside by the car until we can leave."

Lulu opened her mouth.

"No, ma'am. I don't want another word out of you. You either apologize like we said or you go outside and wait. You've got two options. Decide."

For a moment, Lulu glared. Then she turned and stalked out the front door. Once she got to the car, Lulu kicked the front bumper for good measure. Earlier, when getting dressed, she'd wrapped a scarf around her neck to protect against the chill in the air. She yanked it up to her mouth and screamed into it. She kicked the back tire. She screamed again, her throat raw from the exertion. At least she could feel that. That scratching in the back of her throat. That was more sensation than she'd had all evening. It reminded her she was real, that she was alive. That everything was totally fucked.

"That bad, huh?" said a voice behind her.

Lulu whipped around. She knew her parents would follow her out here eventually. But it wasn't either of them.

"Mustafa. You scared me. What are you doing here?"

"Eid party. Same as you." Mustafa shrugged.

"If it's same as me, you'd know you should be shunning me right about now. I'm pretty sure I've got social pariah status."

"You talking about Tamra's mom?"

Lulu sighed. She knew word traveled fast, but somehow, the reality of it was more unpleasant than her imaginings. "Yeah."

"Don't worry. I'm sure it'll blow over." Mustafa hopped up onto the trunk of the car, his long legs firmly planted on the ground.

"Easy for you to say. I think I might have started World War III in there."
Lulu looked over to the doorway. Her impending sentencing would come
through there eventually.

"Maybe," he admitted. "Why didn't you apologize?"

"I can't. I couldn't." Whatever happened now, she had earned. An apology couldn't undo what Lulu's anger had done.

"No reason to stress over it." Mustafa patted the trunk beside him. "Won't
do any good now anyways."

Lulu was a dog on a lead. She hopped up beside him, her legs dangling
against the bumper. "You're tall."

"I like to think everyone else is short."

"You would."

"Not everyone can be such a perfect human specimen." Mustafa gestured across his whole body. "You know you used to call me Tofi."

Lulu opened her mouth, then shut it.

"What, no clever retort? Lulu Saad always has a clever retort."

"Fresh out of clever retorts at the moment," said Lulu.

"Why's that?"

Unbidden, the truth came to her lips. "You're too good-looking. It's kind
of a personal problem."

Mustafa stared, then shook his head. He smiled with what he had to say
next. "You're not so bad yourself."

But Lulu was on a roll, and she couldn't be stopped now. "No. I don't
think you understand. I've seriously had a crush on you since we were about
eleven. I mean, look at you."

Mustafa barked a laugh. "Who is he?"

Lulu blinked, startled. "Who is who?"

"Whoever it is you like."

"How do you know I like anyone?"

"Come on. You wouldn't say what you're saying if you didn't think I was safe from you. You're more careful than you ever let on. Recent events aside. And even that. I'll bet you've been planning to say that for years."

"How—"

"I've known you since you were eight years old. Give me some credit," said Mustafa.

Lulu looked him in the eye. He didn't flinch. He sat there, steadily looking at her right back.

"Do you think it ever would have worked? You and me?" Lulu asked.

Mustafa shrugged. "It still could. But not till we're twenty at least."

Lulu laughed at that. "You think you won't be living at home when you're twenty?"

Mustafa laughed in return. "You're right. Make that thirty."

"Not anymore," said Lulu. "I think I recently made the official unwanted daughter-in-law list."

"Don't be so hard on yourself. You could be forgiven in fourteen years."

Lulu swatted at him. They laughed, their eyes crinkling and their humor in perfect harmony.

Lulu reached out, toward him, then stopped. "May I?"

Mustafa shrugged, leaning back onto the palms of his hands. "Sure. Why not?"

Lulu touched his face. He had a light shadow across his cheek, though she could tell he must have shaved that morning. He felt like everything she thought he would. She felt nothing—no tingle, no pull. Only a sharp, beautiful jawline covered in stubble.

Mustafa laughed. "See, Lulu. It's too late for us. Or not soon enough."

Lulu socked him in the arm lightly. "Shut up, Tofi. Just because you're good-looking doesn't mean you know everything about everything."

Mustafa gave a wide and wicked grin. "I know. But it's why you've been in love with me since you were eleven. You're not thinking straight."

Lulu swatted at him again. "I never said in love with. I said I had a crush."

"You were in love with me." Mustafa waggled his eyebrows.

"I'm never going to live this down, am I?"

"Nope." Mustafa was still smiling as he looked at Lulu. Then he looked up and his face went slack. He hopped off the hood immediately.

Lulu watched him, refusing to acknowledge that the inevitable had happened.

"See you around, Lulu." Then Mustafa turned and said, with a nod, "Professor Ahmed."

Lulu watched Mustafa retreat back into the house. Her father coughed. Lulu refused to move.

"We have made your apologies for you. Mrs. Salwa has been very understanding. Do you understand me?"

"Yes, Baba," Lulu said, mechanically. She continued to stare off into the distance.

"You cannot behave like this. You cannot do as you say and you want. We are not like the others."

"What others?"

"You're Arab, Lulu. We don't talk this way to our family."

"She's not my family. That woman is—"

"Leila," Ahmed warned. "She is like family. Here, she is family."

"Do you know, Baba? Do you know what she said?"

"It doesn't matter."

"She called Mom and me a whore."

"How did you—"

"How did I know that? When I haven't been taught Arabic since I was a little girl? Since you gave up on me?" Lulu lashed. "You pick up words, Baba.

Common words. Hot, cold. Bread, chicken. Kisses, good-bye. Oh, and whore."
Lulu laughed a humorless laugh. "Hell, I don't need them to say it out loud.
I've learned when they say it with their eyes."

"Lulu, habibti. Even if she did, that doesn't make it good. You cannot call
names because you were called names. But that is not what she said. She was
repeating a story. She was calling that man—and no, I won't repeat who it
is—who used that word, one without family and honor. It is an old saying."

That truth sliced through Lulu like a dirty, blunt knife. Not efficient, but
gutting all the same. The wound was not deep, but it would likely fester and
grow septic. She bit the inside of her cheek so hard she could taste blood
again. So she could cling to that cold, unforgiving rage left inside her.

"News flash, Baba—we're not in Baghdad. We're in America." Lulu wasn't
yelling, but there was an unstable quality to her words that she couldn't
contain.

"Hayati," Ahmed started. She looked up into her father's eyes, feeling the
impending tears, not knowing how much longer she could hold them in.
"I came here for you. And I stayed here knowing my children would be
American. I could have gone back and started my family there. But I didn't. I
stayed so you could be American."

Lulu couldn't help but be reminded of countless conversations she'd
had, over and over again; they played out in her head. Of strangers asking
her over and over again, what she was. Like a piece of flora or fauna. Like she
was missing her proper taxonomy. That her father had planned this kind of
life for her was a new idea for Lulu, and the reality of it took her breath away.

She shouted, letting the full force of her anger crash over her father. "So
you wanted me to fit in nowhere? You wanted me to never be Arab but have
people look at me like I'm not actually born here?"

Lulu was breathing hard. She'd never yelled at her father before. Panic lit
through her—a flash of terrified lightning. "You say I need another weapon

to fight back. You say I misunderstood. I don't have any weapons. I was thrown into a conflict without any. I had to find my own. I had to make my own. I had to learn on my own. You never gave me any help there. You gave me books and articles. You keep telling me not to forget I'm Arab. But it's not just the white people reminding me who I am, Baba. Arabs remind me I'm not one of them, too. They look at me wary-eyed. And maybe they're right to, considering what I've just done. But you've never taught me how to deal with that. You wouldn't even give me the words I need to defend myself. I have old curse words picked up off silly boys. This world may never let me forget I am Arab, but it will also keep me from belonging as one of them. How can I know anything with everything you leave unsaid?"

Lulu stared at her father and he stared back.

The sound of a door slamming reverberated through the air. Lulu looked to the source of the sound. Aimee tromped down the pathway from the house, toward where Lulu and her father stood. Ben and Reza were quick on her heels. Aimee unlocked the car. Lulu opened the door and climbed into the middle of the back seat. She crossed her arms. Reza and Ben took their places on either side of her as their mother got in the driver's seat. Lulu wouldn't say another word the rest of the drive home.

18

And Hell Is Just a Sauna

On Sunday, Lulu turned on her computer—the one she had inherited from Reza when he'd left for college—and checked her e-mail. A message from one of her paternal cousins sat rather innocuously in her inbox. It was a cheerful missive about the end of Ramadan. School would be starting back up for her little cousin again. Rana asked if Lulu would also be headed back to school, not yet old enough to understand that school holidays did not work the same everywhere in the world. Lulu couldn't bear looking at it. Not after last night. She deleted it. A moment later, she moved the message back into her in-box.

A soft knock sounded at Lulu's door and Reza entered. "Mom said you were up here; I've come to say good-bye."

Lulu pushed away from her desk, her feet dangling off the edge of a chair that also used to be Reza's. Neither Ben's furniture nor his electronics ever lasted long enough to make it into Lulu's hands.

Lulu got up. And for a moment, she just stared. "See you."

Reza hugged her stiffly. "I'll be back for Christmas."

"Travel safe now." Lulu's voice muffled into a generous expanse of shoulder. Her arms were trapped at her sides by the awkward embrace.

Reza released his hold and walked out the door without another word. For the first time in her life, Lulu had been publicly shameful. And apparently Reza didn't know how to cope, except with silence.

"Take care. Love you," Lulu called after him, but it was no use. Lulu sat back down at her desk. She closed her eyes, attempting to banish Reza's rejection from her thoughts.

A loud, demanding knock rattled through her door. "Mom told me to say good-bye to you." Ben leaned casually against the doorjamb.

"I'm sure she did." Lulu waited for another perfunctory farewell, another awkward embrace.

But Ben continued to lean against her door frame, watching her.

She rolled her chair away from her desk. "Well, bye. Try not to die on your way back."

Ben should have left. But he kept leaning on the door frame, kept his watchful gaze. "Remember that time I put glue in your hair, just to see what would happen?"

"Yes?" Of all the times for Ben to bring up the time he had glued her hair together, this was a strange one.

"It got everywhere and ruined your clothes, and then Mom yelled at me because she had to cut your hair, because the peanut butter wasn't working." Ben shook his head.

"I remember," said Lulu. Reza had been the one to keep Lulu calm, telling her nobody could see the missing chunk of hair anyway. Lulu hadn't talked to Ben for a month.

"You forgave me, though." Ben didn't break eye contact.

Lulu took his meaning. "I think there's a significant difference between gluing your eight-year-old sister's hair together and effectively calling a bride-to-be a whore."

Ben frowned. "Give it time. Glue's a mess 'cause it's trying so hard to stick everything together. But you'll find a way through. You gotta know that."

Lulu tensed, ready for a fight. "Am I the mess, or is what I did the mess, Ben?"

"Both."

Lulu turned away, trying to look anywhere else. "Thanks."

"I mean, I sure as hell couldn't do it."

"Obviously." Lulu snorted.

"Lulu."

Lulu turned her chair back to face him. Ben moved from the door and reached out to pull her up and envelop her in his long arms, practically squeezing the air out of her lungs. She tried to resist her own response, but she hugged him back, reciprocating with a life-stealing clutch of her own.

"What's going on?" he asked. "You can tell me. I know you don't want to, but you can."

"You'll make fun," she said.

"No, I won't," said Ben.

Lulu pulled back and gave him an incredulous look.

"Okay. I might." Ben smirked. "But I have to say my stellar advice is worth the risk."

"I don't know how to be so in-between all the time."

Ben laughed.

Lulu huffed. "It's not funny." Not when the consequences had been so dire. Audrey had been attacked. Lulu had said unforgivable things. Emma had virtually fallen off the grid.

"No," Ben said, still laughing. "It's hilarious. And you know it. Nobody knows how to be in-between. Nobody knows what they're doing. We're all making it up as we go along."

She gave him a quelling look.

"Fine. I'm sorry I laughed."

Lulu could still hear the snicker that he stifled, but she tried for one last confession. Maybe if she said it out loud, the thought would stop bouncing around in her head, distracting and destroying her with equal measure. "I fucked up."

Ben watched her for a minute. "Not just last night?"

Lulu nodded. "Not just last night." She'd fucked up with Anderson, with Audrey—hell, even with James. Every time she replayed the memory from that night in her head it got worse, grew sharper teeth, became more monstrous.

"Tough break."

Lulu had been scared enough admitting to Ben that she'd been a total screw-up all week. His response did nothing to coax further confession out of her. "That's not advice, Benyamin."

"You didn't ask a question, Leila." Ben put his hand on his hip, just like their mother would.

Lulu groaned. "Never mind."

Ben took a deep breath, his expression turning at once to seriousness and concern. "Look. You don't have to be self-sufficient all the time. I mean, you don't need to be. Like, don't ask for my help, fine. But ask for someone's. That's all I'm saying. Ask. With a real question."

Lulu arched her eyebrows.

Ben sighed, then pinched the bridge of his nose.

Lulu swatted at him. "Get out of here."

Ben moved to the door, finally.

"And Ben?"

He turned around.

"I'll think about it," said Lulu.

———

Skipping out on the morning scene on Monday appealed to Lulu's lesser nature. After all, whatever she'd have to withstand, it wouldn't be good. It couldn't be. But she'd have to face the crowd and its stares and its rumors and its preconceived conclusions eventually. Better now than later—rip it off, like a Band-Aid. Seeing Lo approach purposefully down the hallway, however, did not provide Lulu with any reassurance on the tenor of the morning gossip. And this time, unfortunately, there wasn't a sweater on earth that could cover the incident.

"We gotta talk." Lo grabbed Lulu lightly by the elbow and steered her toward the bathrooms at the far end of campus. The ones by the art rooms, where a girl only went into to cry alone.

Lulu's feet shuffled and squeaked across the thin, synthetic carpeting as they rounded a corner fast. Lulu nearly got whiplash. "Slow down, crazy."

Lo came to an abrupt halt. She released Lulu's arm and looked over both her shoulders. Then she continued her speedy march to the bathrooms. Lulu had to follow. Once the bathroom had been reached and secured, Lo began.

"We have a problem." Lo didn't face the mirrors. She didn't fix her makeup. She looked Lulu dead in the eye. That's how serious Lo was.

"We?" asked Lulu.

"You didn't think I'd feed you to the sharks, did you?" Lo took a step back, her whole posture affronted.

"Wolves," said Lulu. "I'm pretty sure it's 'throw you to the wolves.'"

Lo took a step forward again. She reached out and put a hand on Lulu's arm. "Sharks, Lulu-cat. You're chum. Social chum."

"It can't be that bad," said Lulu, a sickening stillness washing over her.

"Worse. Now tell me everything."

"I thought you knew." Lulu crossed her arms.

"No, I've heard. I want to hear it from you," said Lo. "You've been on radio silence since last Saturday. It's spooky."

"You saw me. Outside. Then I headed inside. I saw Dane with Audrey. God, she couldn't stand. She couldn't stand, Lo. And. I lost it. I just lost it." Lulu stared. The tiles in the bathroom wall were uneven. The tiny blue ceramics that made a repeating pattern across the white were improperly aligned in the corner. It threw off the whole room.

"Holy fuck. Then why is everyone saying you hooked up in front of the whole party? They're saying you were fighting Audrey over him. It's a disaster. Di-sas-ter." Lo tried to catch Lulu's eye. "You know how Audrey is about this shit."

"When. When I lost it. He." And then Lulu lost her words. She tried using her hands, but those seemed inadequate as well. Lulu shrugged.

And Lo, bless her, seemed to understand intuitively. "When I get my hands on him for putting his hands on you. And Audrey. God. I'm going to cut them off. I'm going to cut off his fucking hands. He won't have hands. It's the only option left."

"Yeah. See. I already tried that. That's why I'm in the mess I'm in now."

"I'm not suggesting you smoke a j and then try to choke him when you find him propping up one of your best friends." Lo crossed her arms. "I'm saying you need to hit him where it hurts."

"How am I supposed to do that? Do you have a brilliant plan? Get me out of a d-hall, then egg his lawn with dyed-green Easter eggs? Punch him in the face? Those are the only revenges I've ever seen you get. Either violent or fantastically ironic. And since I've already tried the first, I'd love to know what your wonderfully ironic prank is. Because that'll really scare him off."

"Quit being such an asshole. I'm trying to help."

"Stop. Stop trying to help. I put my fucking elbow to his throat, and he's still not quitting. I've got nothing. Fucking nothing. And before you get all high and mighty, you're no better than me," said Lulu.

"The great Lulu Saad and her fucking defense mechanisms. She's never the problem as long as someone else is first."

"You're not the problem!" said Lulu. "Luke is!"

Lo clapped at that—in her slow, steady, patronizing rhythm. "Brava. Please, keep going."

"You know what I mean!" Lulu threw her hands up in the air.

Lo stopped clapping. She was an irresistible force, an immovable object. Lo was the mountain; Lulu was Muhammad. Lulu never had a chance.

"Do I?" Lo's lips curled as though in a snarl.

A lump formed in Lulu's throat, and she wanted to shout it away. If she screamed, she didn't feel that horrible stillness. If she stayed in motion, she didn't have to stop and absorb anything. "You left me to run off and play his fucking girlfriend. Not even that. A side piece. And if you'd been there, none of this would have happened. Dane couldn't have attacked us both like that. You could have prevented it all. If you weren't with Scumbag Luke. If you had stayed with your friends."

Lo shook her head. Her voice went quiet. "You coward."

Lulu flinched.

"So ready to pin the blame. So ready to throw anyone else under the bus. So ready for anyone else to be at fault. Fine. I'm done. I'm not cleaning up after your disaster. See what I care. Fix it yourself." Lo whirled around, slamming the bathroom door as she left. The door bounced against the latch twice with the force of her effort.

Lulu was alone.

19

Les Quatre Cents Coups

Throughout the week, rumors continued to circulate. Lulu Saad had attacked Audrey Bachmann in a jealous rage over Dane Anderson. Lo Campo wasn't talking to Lulu because she'd picked Audrey's side. Dane Anderson didn't even *like* Lulu; he just thought she was easy pickings. *You know Lulu.* Audrey Bachmann was avoiding Lulu Saad for a whole week. They didn't even usually go a whole five minutes without contact.

Those were just the repeatable rumors Lulu had heard. The others were worse. Much worse.

And Emma, she was missing—sidestepping the fight altogether to sit with one of the freshman girls who had made the varsity volleyball team. Emma was many things, but a coward wasn't one of them. It was just that Lulu didn't know what had gone wrong there. None of this helped douse the flames of gossip. But it was Lo's anger that gave real legitimacy to the talk. Lo didn't get mad at nothing, and Lo wouldn't even look Lulu's way anymore. Lo had proved herself to be wild, but also just. Lo's careful construction of her own image was coming back to bite Lulu in the ass. Because of course it would.

Just like being caught vomiting on her doorstep, not because of substance, but because she'd made herself nauseous when she'd explained herself to James. But Lulu refused to go down that rabbit hole.

Review week before finals was, therefore, especially delightful. Lulu was trying to keep her head down and get her work done. It was about the only thing she could do, and it wasn't helping much.

Madame Perault walked into the room and declared that as long as they stayed quiet and did not disturb her peace while she graded, the class had the period to themselves. She must have been in quite a good humor. Or at least, a state of personal ennui. But then she assigned ten chapters of a seventeenth-century novel to read, due the next day and definitively going to be on the exams, and everyone got out their copies knowing there was no way to complete the assignment without a substantial head start. Some teachers did not know the meaning of "review week."

Lulu hunched over her copy of *La Princesse de Clèves*. She read along with her finger, mouthing the words to herself as she went. After a few lines she would backtrack and go over them again. She held a pencil in one hand for underlining words, but she didn't have a dictionary out. She was giving herself context. She was following the rhythm of the words. She needed to get a handle on them. She needed them to make sense. Every sentence she deciphered gave her a sense of small accomplishment. Every paragraph she untangled gave her a piece of control back in her world. She was master, at least, of this small corner of her destiny. This book was at her command. It would be. It had to be.

Dane leaned in from behind Lulu and whispered in her ear, "I can't believe I showed up to class for this."

Lulu jumped. She hadn't heard him come in. Lulu wanted to make a clever remark on how tragic it must be for Dane to have to actually do his homework. To actually have to do anything in this life that was inconvenient to him. But of course, Perault had seen her jump. Fifteen minutes spent in diligence and Lulu was caught in her one moment of legitimate distraction. Besides, talking to Dane wouldn't do anything. Lulu ducked farther over the text.

Having not gotten the desired reaction, Dane tried again. He leaned in farther. "You been to any good parties lately?"

Lulu moved her hand as if to swat at the fly by her ear. Dane grabbed her wrist, gingerly but firm. A tension zipped through her body—electric, terrifying. Lulu freed her wrist from his grip, still staying firmly hunched over her novel. Dane poked the back of her shoulder blade. He began gingerly at first, then with increased aggression.

Lulu twitched. She scratched her pencil across the blank page at the front of her book. She tore this bit out as quietly and inconspicuously as possible. She jerked it back in Dane's direction. *what do you want?*

Lulu frowned at the jagged edge of her book, taunting her with its imperfection. The damage was done. Lulu could hear Dane unfolding the paper. She heard the pause. Then she heard the light scratching of his pen across paper. The slow tearing of paper fibers.

Guess ;)

no

Its easy

shop elsewhere.

Ur a self-absorbed bitch. U no that?

fantastic. stop talking to me

We aren't talking. We're writing.

Go. Away. Lulu printed this time so there would be no mistaking. No question of handwriting. No misspellings or reader errors. Nice, clean print.

Make me

Dane stuffed the paper down the back of her shirt so that Lulu had to untuck the back of her uniform polo to get it out. She read the note, crumpled it, and threw it on the floor. She stood up, quite immediately, grabbing her book and pencil. She walked briskly to a seat across the room, leaving the rest of her things behind. Dane managed to have the good sense to hang his head over his own book. Lulu was sure it was the result of shock. She took a deep breath before plunking herself in the seat. She took another deep inhale, opened her book to the appropriate page, and went back to reading.

Madame Perault looked up from the papers she was grading. She pierced Lulu with her gaze, arching one eyebrow in the process, but said nothing. She went back to her grading, satisfied.

Lulu ripped through the page with her pen as she attempted to underline, her hands still shaky and uneven in their movements. As soon as the bell rang, Lulu retrieved her belongings and fled from the room.

Headed away from the cafeteria, Lulu overheard a group of boys talking across the hallway. She couldn't make out the words, but she could hear them laughing. As she walked, she nursed a cornbread muffin and a box of chocolate milk, the most delicious and most portable foods on offer at the dining hall. Lulu rounded the corner and nearly ran headlong into Brian Connor. He was at the center of a group of boys, clearly regaling his friends with a story of some delight to him. They all went quiet as she passed.

Lulu suffered the instant awareness that they had been talking about her. Brian met her eyes then, and he turned away with a shrug. He continued with her still in earshot. Her ears rang and she walked away from them as fast as she could without breaking into a run. She had unfortunately failed to spare herself from the graphic description of what she looked like being manhandled by Anderson. She couldn't bear to hear the rest. She threw out her food in the first trash can she passed.

Lulu spent the rest of lunch in the empty freshman corridor. It seemed easier that way. She got out her copy of *La Princesse de Clèves* and continued on with her trusty pencil. Eventually, the bell that signaled the end of lunch rang. She'd gotten through six chapters. She should have gone straight to class, but she didn't. After a lunch period spent basically hiding out, she knew what she had to do instead. She went to the hallway where Audrey usually sat to study during her free period. She was there, propped up against a pier, reading.

"I need to talk to you." Lulu stopped in front of her. "We have to talk about what happened on Saturday."

"I already heard everything. And Lo is mad at you. Lo doesn't get mad over nothing. You stole a boy right out from under my arm. What kind of friend does that? Over a boy? You don't get it, do you? You'll never get it. You were jealous. That I had what you wanted. And you never told me." Audrey glared, her fantastic pout hardening her features.

"I'm not jealous of you," said Lulu. "You're my friend."

"Girls *are* supposed to be jealous of their friends. It's normal," said Audrey, her voice taking on that parroting quality Lulu knew well. Mrs. Bachmann could always come between them.

"Just because a thing's considered normal doesn't make it right or true." Lulu watched Audrey for a moment. "Do you remember what happened? Answer me honestly."

"You hooked up with Clark. You shoved me out of the way. And then you got into a fight with Dane Anderson so you could make out with him, too."

And Lulu knew. Knew in her bones, that Audrey had simply believed the first story she'd heard. She hadn't thought to verify or validate. She'd found the gaps in her own memory and filled them with the first bit of reporting that could seam them together. Lulu looked at Audrey, really looked at her. Saw her the way a stranger would see her. Saw her as a girl rather than as a person she knew. The effect was startling, dizzying. Lulu had thought Audrey's loyalty had been worth something. Perhaps Audrey was on Lulu's side in the long run. But so was Audrey's judgment. So was Audrey's righteousness. And those were pointed toward Lulu as well.

Lulu couldn't take it anymore. She'd scream. "Is that what you remember?"

Audrey jutted out her chin in response. "Yeah."

"Right." Lulu nodded. There was no Lo to send her outside. No Emma to remind her to take a deep breath. Just Audrey and her judgment. Just Lulu and her rage. "Tell me why I'm angry. Tell me."

"You're angry? I'm supposed to be angry." But Audrey's surety was shaken.

"No, I'm not angry. I'm furious. Livid. I'm beyond. If anger were the circles of hell, I'd be sitting there in the ninth one with fucking Lucifer himself. No. I'd kick Lucifer out. I'd be too angry for Lucifer. For fucking Satan. Do you get me?" Lulu grew. Six inches. A foot. Half a centimeter. She'd never know. But she grew—taller and broader, ferocious and feral. "You are beyond judgmental. Don't talk to me until you figure out why I'm mad. Do you hear me? Don't fucking talk to me."

And with that, Lulu walked off. She rushed outside, eager to breathe the biting, chilled air. The wind whipped across her plaid skirt and through her itchy polyester tights. The prickling sting felt good. Maybe not good, but a feeling more than numb. It was a familiar pain, that stinging itch. She yelped as the wind pulled through her hair, shivering as she waited for a way out of this mess.

———

Lulu ducked off campus, knowing the best ways to not get caught. She didn't skip except in an emergency, and today was definitely an emergency. She blocked her number and dialed into the office, impersonating her own mother and saying she was home sick for the rest of the day. She moved her car off campus, to a nearby plant shop so that the illusion was complete. But skipping wasn't worth much if Lulu had to do it alone. Alone. It was a funny concept for Lulu, who grew up in a house full of noise with two siblings. Lulu who was next to always within a circle of friends. *Alone.*

Lulu had a flash of inspiration. Matt. She could message Matt. She'd gotten his number when she'd grabbed a ride home with him. And she didn't have to worry about screwing anything up, because they had next to no history. Matt was a blank slate, and right now, Lulu desperately needed one of those. *beignets?*

always was Matt's response.

Lulu walked behind a row of bushes in the back alley of someone's home before she reached the beignet shop to wait. It was only a two-minute walk from campus and about five from where she parked her car, but she took the longer, more circumspect route. Lulu didn't need to get caught trying to sneak back across campus. That effort took ten minutes at least.

Hi Lulu wrote to Emma when she'd arrived. But she got nothing in response.

I'm sorry she sent to Lo who of course had read it and knew Lulu could see she had read it but said a glaring nothing in return. Lulu got on her phone and scrolled through some old photos as she waited, but she noticed there were fewer of them tagged than usual. She kept scrolling through—Lo was removing her, one by one. Lulu locked her phone and stashed it back away in her bag.

Lulu leaned against the brick wall on the side of the strip mall as Matt approached. The last Lulu had seen of Matt, they'd been walking to his house to grab his dad's car—just around the corner from James's house. Everything had felt new and possible then. A beginning.

"You know, that uniform...," Matt said when he got close. His dark hair was rumpled. Lulu got the sense he was never not disheveled.

Lulu arched an eyebrow—a dare.

"... is the most unattractive thing I have ever seen. Seriously, I feel duped." Matt had the air of a young man let down by the world as a whole.

Lulu could only throw back her head and laugh. She needed that laugh, which reached its peak pitch at a high cackle before settling back down again. Laughter kept strange memories at bay. Kept Lulu in the present moment. She couldn't think about what-ifs and laugh at the same time. They walked through the doors of the beignet shop, a light bell jingling in their wake.

"They're supposed to be equalizing, not tantalizing. This isn't porn." Lulu stared at the menu—more out of habit than necessity.

"Hey, not only porn. Like movies. All movies." Matt tapped his feet as he read.

They ordered beignets, a regular coffee granita, and a mocha one. They pooled together their small bills and loose change to pay and waited. Despite her uniform Lulu received nary a sideways glance. She'd figured out the art to not getting caught—maintaining the air of one who belonged. If she learned nothing else from Sealy Hall, Lulu could forever credit her education for that trick.

Their order popped up on the other side of the counter. They grabbed their respective drinks; Lulu grabbed the paper bag. She rolled down the folded-over top and offered the contents to Matt, who snatched a beignet greedily. Lulu popped a bite of piping hot fried dough into her mouth. She spoke with her gob half-open, trying to cool the bite as she spoke.

"The uniform pants are worse," she said, because she was apparently a masochist and could not keep her memories in line.

"Why's that?" Matt hadn't wasted time, either. His mouth and its entire circumference were dusted in powdered sugar.

"Remember James's pants?" Lulu pulled apart her beignet with the tips of her fingers. She waved her bite in the air, flinging powdered sugar this way and that. She was definitively *not* thinking about James and his holiday emoji boxers. Lulu licked a bit of dough that had stuck to her index finger. *Keep it together, Saad.*

"Oh God," Matt said, nearly choking on the remains of his beignet.

"Worse. They're all boys' pants. With pleats." *Emoji boxers. Emoji boxers. Emoji boxers.* "Khaki. Pleats."

"You're all right, you know that?" he said.

He offered her a sip of his mocha granita. She slurped it down with the last of her beignet. Mocha was Lo's favorite. The flavor was sticky sweet, mostly chocolate with a hint of coffee. Lulu was the one who preferred the more bitter flavors, to everyone else's amazement. She handed back Matt's granita and looked into the bag—one beignet remained.

Lulu tore a hunk out of the remaining beignet, then tore that in two and handed Matt one of the pieces. "You're an asshole. But I find it endearing."

"You don't mince words, do you?"

"When most of your friends are assholes, you kind of learn you can't. You'll be trampled otherwise." Lulu divided another hunk of the beignet. They settled into a rhythm of this. Ripping, tearing, sharing, and eating.

"Still not a very nice thing to say about your friends."

"They're loyal assholes. And that's what matters to me. I'd rather have assholes on my side than anyone else." She offered him her coffee granita.

He took a sip, winced, and went back to his mocha. "I think," he said, with his all-knowing voice, "you put on a tough act. And you'd die before you'd admit it. How right am I?"

Lulu slurped her granita. "And why would I admit that?"

Matt took the first step back outside, the bell jingling again at their exit. Lulu followed, shivering in the cold air. She took another sip of her granita, regardless.

"I parked by the flower shop. Closer to Sealy." Lulu flashed a winning smile. Down the block, Lulu spotted the fence she had parked her car behind that morning. "Thanks, by the way."

Matt angled the paper bag over his mouth, trying for one desperate bid to eat the last of the crumbs. His T-shirt collar was dusted with powdered sugar. His drink was empty. He tossed his containers into the trash. "For what?"

"Hanging out. School's driving me crazy today. My friends are driving me crazy."

"The assholes?"

"Sometimes when I'm around them for too long I forget why we even like each other."

"Yeah?" he asked.

"You really wanna hear about my bullshit?"

"Why not?" Matt shrugged.

And it was all that Lulu needed. "It's Lo. And Emma. And Audrey. All of them. Like, Audrey's the best when she lets her guard down. There's a version of herself she practices real hard to be, and then the parts of her that slip through when she's finally relaxed. I think she was raised to be a lady too much."

"Wait, you *weren't* raised to be a lady?"

"Not like Audrey was."

Matt tilted his head, clearly not understanding.

"She's so wacky. She's got the zaniest sense of humor. It was her idea for these super-rad tattoos on Halloween. Old sailor-type mom-in-the-heart tattoos, but for each other. Because we love each other so much. But she's been trained her whole life to be this prim and proper lady. And when she swears, it still sounds awkward, from years of castigation, you know? But there's a wild woman inside her. A real one." Lulu left off the problems that popped up when Audrey drank. That didn't seem like a fair mark against Audrey, before she'd even met Matt. Audrey had her faults. They weren't all for everyone's ears.

"Did you say castration?"

"God, you would pick that out from my entire rant."

"What else?" Matt bumped his hip against Lulu's. "Or, who else?"

"Lo, you've already met."

"She seems—"

Lulu arched her eyebrows. Nobody could talk bad about Lo except for Lulu.

Matt sensed this immediately. "—tough to get along with. Even if she's loyal."

"There's something about her, though. You want to follow Lo. To the ends of the earth. She's fearless. But not a fiery fearless. More, a tornado isn't scared of a house, you know? Lo's the tornado. We're all in her path. She's an Amazon. I know, that sounds insane, but she is."

"Jesus." Matt shuddered. "Would she chop off her boob?"

"If she thought it would improve her aim, she would. And she'd make everyone want to have only one boob, like bodies were meant to be that way." Lulu laughed. She would make up with Lo. One day. Maybe Lo would cool off in a decade. "Someone tried to call her Lolita once."

"Only once?" Matt asked.

Lulu nodded. "Lo has the meanest right hook I have ever seen." Nobody then had thought it from looking at her. They'd been wrong to underesti-mate her. *Lulu had been wrong to underestimate her.*

Matt's eyes went wide.

"Afterward she leaned in and whispered something to the guy."

"What was it?"

"No idea. But nobody ever snitched." Lulu grinned. "And no one ever called Lo anything else ever again."

"Christ," said Matt.

"And then there's Emma. She's the kind of person who doesn't look rebel-lious, but she is. This one time she shoved her ice cream in Nina Holmes's face because Nina started a horrible rumor about Lo. She made Nina go around and apologize to everyone and say that she'd lied and take it back."

"What does Emma look like?" Matt asked.

"A Powerpuff Girl."

"Sugar and spice and everything nice?"

"Exactly! Except, no one sees the drop of Chemical X. They only see the sweetness and light. She'll knock you off your socks, if you're not paying attention." And Lulu hadn't been paying attention. Emma had gone rogue and Lulu had no idea why. Lulu squinted in the distance. The florist was just up ahead.

"Question," said Matt. "Why'd you call on me and not James? You're not playing hard to get, are you?"

"I've never been hard to get, to be honest." Lulu chewed her straw absent-mindedly. "Just last time I saw him I was vomiting into my own lawn."

Matt whistled, like an old man in a Western. "That's too bad. Why never been hard to get, though?"

"I like the chase too much. How could anyone give that up? Seems so unfair for the boys to have all the fun."

"You chase boys…" Matt's voice trailed off, more unfinished thought than question.

"Hah. Maybe. Or maybe I don't run away when they catch up to me. I haven't quite figured it out yet. All I know is, once I pounce, or let them pounce, the fun's all gone. Usually."

"Usually?"

"Okay, so, like, every day last spring, I'd run for training. I'd run by the boys' lacrosse team, you know, to keep it interesting."

"And?"

"And a friend of mine. Let's call him Brian, he accuses me of running by the team on purpose," said Lulu.

"What did you do?"

"I denied it, of course."

"You lied."

"I didn't lie. See, Brian accused me of running by the boys on purpose, so they would check me out."

"Weren't you?"

"No. I was running by the boys to check *them* out. But Brian assumed the reverse. Boys are the subject; I'm the direct object."

"That's a technicality."

"It might seem like a technicality to you, but I like being the subject of my own sentences." Lulu kicked the curb with her shoe. The rubber of her sole made a satisfying squeak.

"Who cares what some idiot thinks of you?"

Lulu slurped the last of her granita. "If everything you did in life was constantly about that same misunderstanding, you'd be pissed off, too."

Lulu dug into her bag, pulling out her keys. She looked up, then froze. Across the street, the flower shop had closed early and locked the fence around their property. Her car was snugly, safely padlocked in for the night. Of course it was. Lulu pointed to behind the fence. "That's my car."

"Impressive," said Matt. "How'd you manage that?"

"Obviously the gate wasn't locked when I parked it," Lulu said, a shrill edge to her voice. Then, "Dammit, Matt. How are we going to get home?"

"I have an idea. You might not like it, though."

20
Hard to Get

A burnt orange Datsun parked in front of the curb of the plant shop, where Lulu and Matt sat. Under her breath, Lulu swore in all the languages she knew.

"Thanks, man," said Matt.

"No problem," said James, his elbow leaned out his opened window.

"Isn't it a little cold to roll your window down like that?" said Lulu.

James looked at her then. He smiled. "Are you going to accept the ride, Lulu Saad, or are you going to stand in the cold with your pride intact? It's totally your call. I do need to know. So I can plan."

"I plan on getting in the car *with* my pride intact. Thank you very much." Lulu pulled her shoulders down and kept her chin up.

Matt opened the passenger door. Lulu slid into the middle and swung her leg over the gearbox. Matt climbed in beside her.

As Lulu looked out the front windshield, she watched a purple cabriolet pass by on the street. Audrey had driven by with nary a honk or a wave. Not that Lulu wanted her to honk or wave. Lulu grabbed the parking brake. "I think I'll do this, if you don't mind."

"Thank God. It was weird enough when you weren't wearing a skirt," said James.

"Man, you know how to make a girl feel flattered," said Lulu.

"Could you start the car? Much as I'd love to watch you two flirt, I wouldn't. James, your heater is absolute shit."

James blushed. He rolled up his window and put the car into gear. Lulu dropped the e-brake and stared firmly ahead, out the front windshield. They rode in silence as James drove. James wouldn't say anything. Lulu couldn't. And Matt didn't seem to care one way or another. He leaned across Lulu and messed with the old dial radio until he found a station that wasn't playing a commercial. Lulu let the guitar chords and the rhythm of the road wash over her.

When the car stopped, Matt unbuckled, hopped out with not much more than a "thanks, man," and disappeared into his house. Lulu slid over into Matt's vacated seat. James put the car into gear and drove. Lulu drew shapes in the condensation on the inside of the window. James should have dropped her off first, not Matt.

James rolled down his window again. "Sorry, I know it's cold. But it's the only way to really defrost the windows in here."

Lulu shrugged into her sweater. " 'S'okay."

"I'll close it in a minute," he said.

The resulting silence threatened to devour Lulu whole. She had to fight it, to fill it. "You know, *Reza*'s a Persian name. And *Ben* always seems so Old Testament, so everyone thinks it's Jewish. And then I got the world's most generic Arabic name." Lulu watched the shapes she drew slowly fade out with the blast of cold air entering the car. "But Rez shouldn't have been named Reza at all. He should have been named for my grandfather. First son of a first son and all that."

"But he wasn't," said James. "He wasn't named for your father."

Lulu looked over. He had a firm grip on the wheel. His knuckles were going white from the cold. She could see his breath coming out of his mouth in little puffs. "No, he wasn't. He was named after my dad's best friend."

"Why?"

"He was killed the year my brother was born. Or at least, my father heard he died the year my brother was born. And without any children. So my dad gave him a legacy. He was Iraqi, but his family had been Persian, way back when. Nobody over there forgets these things. So they kept a lot of Persian names in the family."

"Lulu," said James. Like he was going to start something important.

Lulu breathed across the window, fogging it briefly one last time. She hummed, ignoring the urgency in his tone.

James pulled the car over. Lulu looked back at him.

"Lulu," said James again.

She couldn't ignore it now. "Yes?"

"I'm sorry," he said, still looking her dead in the eye.

"What?" Lulu shook out her head, like there was water trapped in her ears. "No."

"I'm sorry. I jumped to conclusions that Saturday. I know that wasn't fair. I just saw you through the window, and it was like the floor came out from under me," said James. "And that's not an excuse."

" 'S'okay. You get a freebie for holding back my hair while I puked and standing up to my mother."

"I'm serious," he said. "Don't play this off with a joke."

"Not a joke. I just believe in restitution more than I believe in apologies."

225

"I don't believe in excuses. Just in reasons. I've had enough excuses for one lifetime. I don't need to give anyone else more of them."

"Simple as that?" She realized the condensed white puffs were coming out of his mouth in shorter, smaller bursts. His lips looked soft. She leaned in, following the trail of his breath.

"Simple doesn't mean easy. It means uncomplicated," he said.

"I'm afraid of uncomplicated," she said.

"Lulu," said James.

Lulu hummed in response. The gap between them was closing, slowly, inevitably.

"I want to kiss you. But I won't unless you say that I can."

Lulu took a deep intake of breath. Her whole body came alive at the question. How many times had she been kissed? She'd lost count. How many times had someone laid their desires so clear before her? Never. She could say no, she knew. But she didn't want to. She wanted to hold on to this moment for a second longer—where anything was possible, where her imagination could only heighten her anticipation. Their lips were millimeters apart. Lulu couldn't see his breath anymore, but she could feel his eyelashes on her cheek. Both their eyelids were lowered, but they were still looking at each other, still hesitating. James, man of his word, would not move.

Lulu put them both out of their misery. She closed her eyes, took a leap of faith, and leaned in. Their lips met, softly. His hands tested out their position on her hips, and she made no indication for him to remove them. Her hands tangled through his hair. It was so soft her fingers slipped through faster than she had anticipated. One of his hands traveled upward to her waist. As his thumb moved against her shirt at her stomach, Lulu temporarily forgot she needed air. And then the kiss was over. He'd pulled away. Lulu was confused, a little disoriented. She had anticipated more, much more.

"We're right outside your house, by the way. That's why I pulled over. I thought you should know that," he said.

Lulu looked out the window to see her house, set exactly into her block as it always had been. That was a sobering, steadying sight. She closed her eyes for a moment. When she reopened them, she faced James. "Good call."

"I do have my moments," he said.

"I'm learning that," Lulu said, a sly grin pulling across her mouth.

James's expression mirrored hers. "Get out of here. I'll call you."

"I might pick up." Lulu opened her door and slid across the seat as she grabbed her book bag.

"Come on. Have a heart, Lulu."

Lulu grinned, blew a kiss, and slammed the car door. She practically skipped to her front door. She unlocked the dead bolt and turned around. He was still waiting, his car idling, to watch her cross the threshold of her own home safely. She entered, waving, as he drove off.

It was only later, when she was in her room and reliving the moment, that Lulu reached for her phone and realized she had no one to tell.

21

The Price of Freedom

Lulu was upstairs, working her way through those chapters of *La Princesse de Clèves* when the front door slammed shut and the sound of trudging could be heard up the stairs.

The door to her bedroom swung open. Aimee Saad startled. "Leila Margot Saad, what are you doing home so early? Why don't I see your car? How did you get home?" Her mother took a deep breath. "Don't you dare roll your eyes at me. Answer the question."

Lulu sighed. "I *didn't* roll my eyes."

"You were thinking about it."

"Am I going to be in trouble for having thoughts now?" Lulu crossed her arms.

"Answer the question."

"Which question?"

"Why are you home early?"

"Early dismissal." Lulu shrugged.

"Says who?" Aimee narrowed her eyes.

"Says me."

"Don't you dare get cute with me, Leila Saad. And where the hell is your damn car?"

"Locked up in the plant shop parking lot," said Lulu.

Aimee pinched the bridge of her nose. "What is it doing locked up in a plant shop? Actually, never mind. Don't answer that."

"There's a perfectly reasonable explanation," said Lulu. "I parked my car at a plant shop. They closed up for the day. The fence is now locked."

"You skipped class and got your car locked into a plant shop?" Aimee put her hand to her hip and took a deep breath. Lulu believed it was meant to be calming. She could tell it hadn't worked out as her mother had planned. "Do you realized how ludicrous you sound? Don't you already know how in trouble you are?"

"Go ahead and ground me some more. It's not like I have any friends left. Hell, at least I can blame being grounded on my lack of a social life. You'd be doing me a favor," said Lulu, all bluster.

Aimee gave Lulu a hard appraisal. Lulu stared back, unflinching.

"Fine," said Aimee. "You're ungrounded."

"What?" yelped Lulu.

"You're ungrounded. If I'm doing you a favor grounding you. You're not grounded," said her mother.

Lulu narrowed her eyes. "What's the catch?"

"The catch is Tamra's older sister, Tanya, is getting married, and you're going to help make centerpieces."

"I can't apologize." Lulu knew no one could apologize for what had happened. It had been too feral of an attack, the wound inflicted too deep.

"You don't have to apologize, darlin'. It's too late to apologize and have that make everything right. You just have to do penance."

Lulu groaned. "Come on, Mom. They don't want my help."

"Mrs. Salwa is being remarkably Shiite about the whole thing. Your baba got her great-uncle to issue a minor fatwa on your behalf. So you better thank Sheikh Fadi when you see him. And your father. Thank both of them. Profusely. This is also part of your penance."

"You are so Catholic," said Lulu.

Her mother glared. And eventually, under the weight of such a stare, Lulu flinched. "Fine. I'll make the dumb centerpieces."

"And give thanks."

"Yes, and that," said Lulu.

"Profusely," said her mother.

Lulu took a deep breath. "Profusely. I will make centerpieces and thank Sheikh Fadi and Baba profusely. I promise."

"Excellent. I'm sending you over during winter break. She's got about fifty of them. Plus five hundred gift bags to fill up with Jordan almonds."

"Fifty centerpieces? Five hundred bags?! That's practically child abuse, Mom."

"Oh, I'm sorry, is that going to be a problem for you? Do you have something more pressing that you needed to be doing?"

"No, ma'am," said Lulu at a low grumble.

"Good. When I tell you to jump on this one, you'll say 'how high?' Is that understood?"

"Loud and clear." Lulu fought the urge to salute.

"Excellent. Now finish your homework. I'm going to call the school and say you weren't feeling well and you forgot to sign out. You put a toe out of line again, and I'll make you work so many weddings you won't want to go to your own."

Lulu didn't bother to tell her mother that she'd already faked her own sick day. That would only make everything worse. Besides, Sealy Hall thought of working mothers as frazzled. It was a holdover from the days when only the right kinds of families attended and none of the upstarts could wriggle through the admissions system. Two calls wouldn't strike them as particularly odd.

She went for the retort of, "Then you wouldn't have any legitimate grandchildren, would you?"

"Don't test me on this, Leila, so help me God."

"Aye, aye, Captain." Lulu turned back to her French. Some things weren't worth finding out the hard way.

———

Squinting, Lulu walked out of her last exam into the overly bright sunlight. She pulled down the sleeves of her thick knit pullover. The light in December looked colder, somehow sharper than it did when compared to the sunshine of a few months previous. Physics might have been able to explain this to her. But, right now, Lulu didn't care about Science or Explanations. She didn't care about English or history or French. She breathed the free air. A stretch of next to nothing lay ahead of her. She wasn't sorry to have lost the distraction of her studies. Reza and Ben would be home soon. True, Reza was avoiding her, and Ben was still sending odd, cryptic encouragement about adhesive materials. He was trying, at least. Even if Reza wasn't. Having them home ought to be comforting, though. She wouldn't have to be quite so alone. Better than when she'd gone into her English exam and Lo had glared at her briefly, then sat three rows away.

But the house was empty when Lulu got home. And the only smell was the lingering astringent of fake lemons from the bathroom cleaning solution that had been used that weekend. Lulu sat on the couch, trying to enjoy being the master of the remote, when her phone rang. It was her mother. Lulu didn't dare screen the call.

"Leila." So she was still mad, then.

"Yes, Mama?"

"Are you back home?"

"Yes, Mama."

"How was your last exam?"

"Went fine."

"Good, good. You're expected at Dina's house at two o'clock. Be on time. Not Arab on time. Not inshallah time. On time, on time."

"They won't expect me to be on time, on time, Mom."

"I don't care what they expect. This is what I expect. This is your mess. You're cleaning it up. Be on time. Keep your mouth shut. Mrs. Salwa will be there. It's her daughter's wedding, after all. For once, please do as you're told."

"I do as I'm told all the time," said Lulu, though she couldn't even convince herself of that.

"I've got to get back to work. I'll hear if you're given anything other than a glowing report. Understood?"

"Understood."

"Please don't be difficult about this."

"I'm not being difficult!" said Lulu.

"Leila."

"I promise not to be difficult. Am I dismissed?"

Her mother sighed. "Dismissed. Please drive safe. I love you."

Lulu hung up the phone. She knew it was the petty thing to do, and yet, she had done it regardless. She needed that pettiness. It gave her a sense of control. She lumbered up the stairs to change out of her uniform.

Dina Alkati lived in a home with more understated elegance than her aunt Salwa and her cousin Tamra did. Her family's residence was a one-story affair, with the original dark wood paneling across the walls. And while its furnishings were not necessarily in current fashion, they had clearly all been imported. It was the sort of furniture you wouldn't notice, unless you could spot the craftsmanship. Lulu wished there was more light in this room, to watch the damascene inlays shimmer across the chairs, the way they did on the small precious boxes in her own home.

Lulu had not precisely expected a warm reception at the Alkati home. But she had not been quite prepared for the icy level of greeting she had received. Dina, with her least-most civility, had led Lulu into the parlor room of the home. The room had gone still in an instant. Tamra wouldn't even look at Lulu.

But this was all for Tanya, the bride. And the sheikh had spoken. So Lulu would be ignored but not shunned.

Lulu sat down at the seat offered her. She watched the other women—some hijabi, some with big roller-curled hair, some with sleek, ironed strands—as they were putting together Tanya's centerpieces. Lulu copied the movements. If she'd learned one thing in her time at Sealy Hall, it was how to keep her mouth shut and follow the motions of others. Not knowing wasn't necessarily wrong, but admitting to a lack of knowledge was greeted with merciless silence. Better to fake what she didn't know than to admit to such a defeat.

Eventually, the conversation picked back up. The elder women spoke mostly Arabic and the younger women spoke mostly English. All their speech was peppered with foreign words, regardless of the base language. Lulu spied a table with trays of spices, a small dish of salt, a mirror, white lace—good luck for the bride. Too bad there wasn't a traditional table full of good luck for calling the bride a whore and ruining one's life in the process.

Lulu could dare to dream.

"Hal anti jo'ana?"

Lulu looked up from her work. It was the third sister—Auntie Salwa and Auntie Farrah's.

"*La, shukran, Khala.*" Lulu shook her head. As if she could eat in a situation like this.

"*Jo'ana, habibti?*" The third sister wasn't accepting Lulu's answer as possibly true.

"*La jo'ana, shukran, Khala.*" Lulu was starting to feel legitimately bad she couldn't remember the woman's name. As though she needed to add to her list of sins.

The third sister didn't seem fazed in the slightest, as happy to be called Auntie as to be called by her given name. "*Bidik tishrabee shi?*"

"*La shukran, Khala,*" Lulu said. Even liquids didn't seem like they'd settle well on her uneasy stomach. Lulu was too tense. "Thank you, thank you, Auntie."

The third sister patted Lulu on the knee. She got up from her chair. Lulu went back to work on the centerpiece in front of her. A demitasse of tea rattled in front of Lulu.

"Work makes thirsty. You drink," said the third sister. "*Tishreeb. Tishreeb.*"

"Thank you, Khala." Lulu added three sugar cubes to the tiny glass and drank. No sense in fighting it.

The third sister sat beside Lulu. She watched and waited till Lulu had finished a good third of the piping-hot glass. Satisfied, she turned back to her work. The atmosphere of the room was less hostile after that. Lulu was unsure whether she had simply gotten a stamp of female approval of her presence or whether the room seemed better after a warm, sugary cup of tea. Lulu was midsip when Dina finally deigned to speak with her again.

"You're lucky Khala is so forgiving," she hissed. "You shouldn't be here ruining my cousin's day."

Wide-eyed, Lulu swallowed her last mouthful of tea. Her hand rattled as she set the demitasse down. Her cup was instantly refilled; Lulu looked up to see Tamra's older sister—Tanya the Bride.

"Piss off, Dina," said Tanya the Bride. "My mom is a bitch and you know it."

Lulu stared. Dina's eyes went wide.

"What? Mama's a survivor. You don't make it through what she has without sharpening your claws. And don't forget to add sugar, hayati. Mama made it so strong this time. She always makes it too strong. She likes it bitter." Tanya the Bride hoisted the teapot up. It looked heavy, the precarious way she balanced it. "Khala Zeena likes you."

"Khala Zeena doesn't know what's going on," said Dina, still hissing.

"Bad English doesn't mean a bad mind, Dina," said Tanya.

"I didn't mean that—" started Dina.

Tanya raised an eyebrow at her cousin. "Khala Zeena knows exactly what's going on. She's forgiving. War does that, I think. Makes you harder or makes you more understanding. No middle ground with war."

Lulu startled. Tanya was guilting Dina on Lulu's behalf. And nobody could guilt half so well as a bride and an older cousin to boot. The relief of having these tactics used on her behalf rather than against her was a new and wonderful feeling for Lulu. She inhaled it like a person starved of air. Nobody had ever done that for her.

Except for Lo.

Lulu jumped into this tenuous conversation rather than think about Lo. "I thought Dina meant Auntie Salwa hadn't told Khala Zeena what I'd done out of forgiveness for me."

Here Tanya laughed. "No, hayati. But she wouldn't dare go against Amu. Mama will remember what you said for the rest of your days. Or her days. Whichever comes first. You've got to respect her for that."

"And what about you?" Lulu asked on pure impulse.

Tanya leaned in close. Her voice was at a whisper. "I think it's hilarious. I've never seen anyone snap so spectacularly. You should win an Oscar for the best public scene made at a cultural affair. But if you tell anyone I said that I'll call you a liar and deny it until my dying day. I'm happy to be a bitch, too, if required."

"Are you in the majority on that one?" asked Lulu, almost hopeful.

Tanya laughed. She had a good, friendly kind of lilt when she laughed. "God, no. But who wants to be in the majority?"

"Why are you being so nice to me?" Lulu asked.

"Getting married makes one quite magnanimous, I've found. But mostly, I felt sorry for you. You normally look so tough. I knew you must have been really beaten if you didn't look tough. If you couldn't keep it together."

Lulu didn't know what to say to that. Then Tanya became Tanya the Bride again, and went back to letting all the aunties and young cousins touch her hair and pinch her cheeks and kiss her forehead. Lulu watched. And thought it was a stellar performance, there was an air of real happiness under the veneer of Tanya the Bride that made Lulu smile.

After a couple of hours, about a quarter of the centerpieces were done and none of the bags of almonds were filled. Lulu promised to return at the same time tomorrow.

Lulu checked her phone as she left Dina's house. Zero notifications. She wasn't sure what she expected: for Audrey to apologize or for Emma to message or Lo to at least stop untagging Lulu from group photos. It was unreasonable. But she had hoped for it all the same. Lulu's hopes inflated again when she saw she had a new message in her in-box. However, disappointment was to be hers this evening. The e-mail was from her cousin Rana.

Hello dear, How are you? We miss you very much. How are Auntie Aimee and your brothers? My studies are going well inshallah. I am glad the fasting is over. We had holiday

for Ramadan, then eid, and we can sleep instead of
studying. Kisses for you.

Love,
Rana

Lulu put away her phone. She got in her car, cracked her knuckles, and
told herself to drive home. But she looped down the big boulevard around
the park, the way she would drive to Lo's house. Lulu didn't slow as she
passed the home, but a zinging sensation, suspiciously reminiscent of longing, surged through her chest as she drove by.

22
The Legend of Billie Jean

Christmas was a layered smell. First, the tree would come in, bringing a deep pine note to the house. Then there were the cookies—gingersnaps and chocolate chip with pecans. There was a mild tang of dust, from when the box full of ornaments was eventually gotten down and unpacked. Then, come Christmas morning, the whole house would smell like a gumbo, two pots cooking low and slow on the burner. Reza and Ben had arrived home after the ornaments but before the gumbo.

"Hey," had been all Reza could say. He'd just stared at her for a long while after that.

Ben had taken Lulu into a headlock, as though nothing had changed. "How's the glue holding up?"

After that, Lulu had avoided them. She wanted no more advice from Ben and no more censure from Reza. She'd settled into a new pattern over the winter holidays. One she begrudgingly enjoyed, strange as it was. But Lulu was used to shuttling between her house and Audrey's, Lo's, or Emma's. Lulu couldn't have said when those girls had become integral to the rhythm of her life. The switch in routine—to Dina's home—gave Lulu the impression that she either got one or the other, never both. Lulu's visits to the Alkatis were an orchestration of her father's making, which only made Lulu wish she could orchestrate her own way to bring her friends back together again.

Lulu went up to her room with the intention of binge watching *Murder, She Wrote* on her laptop and feeling sorry for herself. Strictly speaking, Lulu wasn't supposed to have a television in her room. But it was an old rule, a holdover from her mother's childhood on what good parenting used to entail. Lulu had a laptop and Wi-Fi. There was no stopping television in Lulu's room any more than there was stopping time.

She flipped open her computer. She didn't want to watch anything on her queue, so she began scrolling through genres. Then subgenres. She was about to close out of the window, when her perseverance was rewarded: *The Legend of Billie Jean*.

There was only one person for it and that person was Emma. And that was the problem. There were things where only Emma would do. But there wasn't an easy, understood solution here. There wasn't a sheikh to issue a fatwa for their friendship. There was just Lulu, alone and with good reason.

The Legend of Billie Jean with a giant play button hovering over it lit Lulu's screen. She'd have to take the plunge and live with the consequences. She couldn't wait around for anyone else to save her from her own problems. She'd fix them or die trying, socially. Lulu dialed. The phone rang twice. Three times. Four times. Then the other end, mercifully, clicked. Lulu held her breath.

"Hello," said Emma.

Lulu detected a note of hesitation. That wouldn't do. "*The Legend of Billie Jean* is available. And we should watch it."

For a long beat, Emma said nothing.

"I fucked up. I know I did the wrong thing with Brian. I don't know what else I did wrong, but I know I fucked up. I wish I could fix it," said Lulu. "I wish I knew what I did."

She had to make things right. She had to ensure that restitution would be paid. Except Lulu also owed Lo restitution. And Audrey owed Lulu. And they all seemed to owe Emma. And Dane, he had been taking pieces from the people around him since Lulu had noticed him. It was too many problems, too many overcomplicated threads to untangle all at once. Lulu held her breath, hoping she could at least fix this thing between her and Emma.

"I can't believe I didn't know it was on streaming before you did." The sound of Emma fumbling with her computer, trying to queue up the movie, sounded through the phone.

Lulu felt relief all the way down to her pinkie toes. "Ready?"

"Ready," said Emma.

They clicked play at the same time.

Billie Jean's epic runaway road trip began. Emma cheered as Christian Slater pulled a gun on that old creepy dude who tried to assault Billie Jean in his office. That was where all of Billie's troubles started, and Lulu could feel her heart in her throat as she watched. Eventually the scene was over and Lulu could breathe again. She and Emma could gasp as Billie Jean cut off her glory of golden hair. They awed at her desire for justice. They laughed excitedly at all the glorious eighties' fashions. They had found their easy way with each other again, both wanting to relish this moment together. Their peace was tenuous, but it was not gone.

"You know," said Lulu, "this movie is pretty terrible."

"No. It's incredible," said Emma. "I mean, what other heroine chops off all her hair and wears a scuba suit as evidence of her total righteousness? Or takes a stand at the beach because a creepy old dude was being creepy as shit?"

Lulu's breath caught. Her heart rate kicked up, like she was running, fleeing. But she sat on the phone, watching the credits roll. Emma *would* find the heart of a matter. The same way that Audrey reminded Lulu how to find her backbone, how to stand ramrod straight, no matter what. Or the way Lo wouldn't let Lulu get away with anything.

Emma filled the silence. "Did you know that for years you couldn't buy this movie because Pat Benatar hated it?" Emma was a force of pop-culture knowledge to be reckoned with.

Lulu took a deep breath. In and out. That helped. "How do you know that?"

"She totally wouldn't sign over the rights to her songs so whatever studio it is, like, couldn't distribute the movie. Like years. Decades." Emma sounded as though she couldn't believe that one of her favorite eighties' music icons would deprive her from owning this movie in all its glory.

"Wow, Emma. You take bad-movie watching to a new low. Or high."

"I know. I mean, I can't believe she wouldn't release her music, all because she doesn't like the movie. I mean, you don't see Britney doing that with *Crossroads*, do you?" Emma's voice rose as she worked herself up to the point of righteous indignation.

"Emma?"

"Yeah?"

"I love you. Never change."

There was an eerie quiet on the other end of the phone. Then Emma said, quietly, "Seriously?"

"Of course, seriously," said Lulu. "Why, did you commit a murder or something?"

"No. But, I have something to tell you."

"What is it? I know it's been off, but I swear I can make it better," said Lulu. She had to. Everything had gone sideways; maybe if she could get this one thing right, the sensation that her world was sliding out from under her would stop. Lulu wasn't sure if that was the superstition or her lousy hope threading through her again.

Lo would be good at this. She would be fantastic at making a plan. *I'd love to know what your wonderfully ironic prank is.* Lulu had thrown that in Lo's face when she'd been mad. But now she needed a wonderfully ironic prank. When she had screwed up with Auntie Salwa, Lulu had been told to show up and make amends. She wished she could prove she was willing to show up for Emma. For Lo. And even for Audrey. Hell, she wished she could get Dane not to show up, at school, in her life anymore.

"I'm sorry. I've been awful to you. I've left you guessing when you were in such a mess. I was being selfish," Emma said.

"No, really, you don't owe me an apology. I've been such an asshole to you recently. If I were you, I'd avoid me, too. And hang out with freshmen. Scratch that, and hang out with literally anyone else. I set you up with Brian. I left you with him. Alone. I abandoned you at Halloween. Then I forgot you. And then I let being mad at Audrey keep me from honestly apologizing. God, that's stupid when I say it out loud. I'm sorry. For all of it. Please let me make it right."

"I'm not avoiding you. Not to hang out with freshmen. I mean, I have been avoiding you. And I have been hanging out with a freshman. Oh, shit. Lulu. I'm not hanging out with Diana. We're dating."

"Diana?" asked Lulu. "Who's Diana?"

"The freshman. Bangs. At Battle of the Bands. You saw me looking over, and you were right to assume I had a crush, but you got it wrong with who it was. Not Brian. Diana Agrawal."

Lulu could only think of everything she'd ever said about Bangs. A running, horrible catalog of the things that had flown out of her mouth from *B*: calling her Bangs to *S*: implying she was slutty. Lulu said the only thing that made sense. "She does have great bangs."

"Lulu, be serious."

"I'm totally serious. She has great bangs."

"I'm dating a girl," said Emma.

"Okay." Lulu could hear the faint murmur of an ad for some new series running.

"Okay? That's it?" said Emma.

And Lulu knew she had to say something real, something serious, so that Emma knew that Lulu was on her side. "Look, I'm figuring out I'm a self-absorbed asshole most of the time. Now that you've told me about Diana, it all makes sense. I feel like kind of an idiot for not figuring it out sooner."

"You are kind of an idiot," said Emma. There was a pause. "Please don't tell anyone yet."

"Okay," said Lulu.

"I'm serious, Lulu."

"I promise," said Lulu.

Emma sighed her relief. "I thought you were going to make me fill in Lo or Audrey."

"Who, me? Sometimes secrets need to belong to who they need to belong to." A pit welled inside Lulu—not guilt. Another feeling Lulu had no name for. She should tell Emma. About Halloween. About Dane. About the fight with Audrey. Emma's brave honestly threw into stark relief Lulu's own cowardice. But she held on to it for a little while longer.

"Can I ask you a question?" said Lulu. "Which you don't have to answer, by the way."

"Sure," said Emma.

"How long have you known?"

Emma laughed, breezy and relieved. "God. Ages."

"Then," Lulu wanted to phrase the next bit carefully. "Is there a reason you didn't tell any of us? Did we do something? I hope I never said anything that made you uncomfortable."

"Apart from making fun of my girlfriend's bangs?" Emma laughed. "Honestly? It's always been hard, when you've assumed I liked guys. It made the truth get stuck. Like I was coughing on it."

"I'm so sorry," said Lulu. "And for trying to set you up with Brian. I'm just so sorry."

"I know," said Emma. "I'm not mad anymore. I was. I didn't like anyone, not really, and I thought I could make it through high school and I could go off to college and be safely anonymous."

"Well, if you do tell her, Lo's going to be so insufferable. You totally bagged the hottest freshman girl."

Emma laughed. It was a good sound to hear. "Lulu!"

"What? You know that's exactly what she'd say." Lulu ached to hear Lo say it. She ached to have Lo heckle Emma and then have Lo run her hands through her annoyingly perfect hair. She missed Audrey piping in with an irritating correction. She missed their camaraderie; she missed their fighting. She'd missed their fierce friendship for much longer than she'd wanted to admit, even if it also drove her to contemplate drinking warm tequila in the back of an ugly, cramped car. If she'd been honest with herself, she'd have thought it ages ago.

She missed it, but she wasn't even sure how it had all broken in the first place.

"You know, now that you say it, I do know that's what Lo would say." Then after a long silence, Emma said, simply, "I'm scared."

"It's okay to be scared," said Lulu.

"Easy for you to say," said Emma. "You're not afraid of anything. You've faced down Audrey's mom after taking shots. You jump into pools to save people from drowning. You called me when you were done waiting for a reason why I'd run away. You're the bravest girl I know."

244

Lulu yearned for that to be true. "Emma. I'm terrified. All the time."

"You are not."

"I am. I'm afraid we're not all going to be friends again. I'm afraid I messed it all up. I'm afraid everyone thinks I'm a big slut because I make out with every boy who comes along. I'm afraid that means nobody believes me anymore. I'm terrified of being alone. I mean, I fucked up with you, with Audrey. With Lo. I've been miserable. What if I pushed you all away forever? And you, you keep the peace. We're at each other's throats half the time, and you break the tension like a puppy. Okay, that was a terrible metaphor, but..." Lulu took a deep inhale. "You're the glue, Emma. None of us work right without you."

Emma was quiet for a moment. "I've seen you say no."

Lulu laughed. "Thank you for that rousing vote of confidence."

"Lulu, this is different," said Emma.

And Lulu knew it was. *Circumlocution* was the big, fancy Sealy Hall way of saying what Lulu had done. Talking around what you didn't have clean, direct language for. "What are you going to do?"

Emma sighed. "What's gonna happen to me, Lulu? This is still Texas."

"I don't know. But I do know you can't give in to fear." Lulu had done so too many times recently to count. She didn't know how she would be done with the fear, but she knew deep in her bones that she needed to be. That she had to find peace or she would be at war with herself forever.

"What do you know about it?" asked Emma.

"Nothing. Everything. I don't know yours, but I know mine. Live your life, Emma. I mean, if you want we can give you a big fanfare and throw a parade. Or you could live your life the way you want to. Sometimes that is big and scary enough."

"It's not that easy."

"I know. For the rest of my life, people are going to think I'm a terrorist," said Lulu, trying to explain. Neither was interchangeable with the other, but she couldn't use a borrowed language to speak of what she knew.

"Only crazy people," said Emma.

"True. But those people are loud, and they can be violent. And I'm afraid of them." Lulu had never admitted as much out loud. It made her a little jittery. And then she took a deep breath and she felt calmer, more stable. The fear didn't stop waving through her, but it was becoming slowly more manageable. She was more than her fear. "I can't go around proving I'm American to everyone I meet. That's too exhausting. And I'm Arab, too. It's in-between. I'm in-between. It doesn't come with a neat package or a name or a support group. It just is. I can't change it. And even if I could, I wouldn't. Not really."

"You wouldn't?"

"No. I don't fit. And sometimes that's the worst—knowing I'll never fit; nowhere will ever feel comfortable and nowhere will ever accept me all the way. There's no rulebook, and I have to make it all up as I go along. But it also means I don't have to play by anyone else's rules. Play by your own rules, Emma. You may get hurt and people will probably still be awful regardless. I can't tell you to risk your safety. I can't tell you when. But I do know at some point, you've got to know where you stand with yourself. At least then you won't regret that you played by everybody's rules but your own."

"You make it sound so easy. You're so good at that. At speaking up."

"Me? I'm shit at it." Lulu's stomach lurched in that familiar way that made her close her eyes and take a breath. "I've been trying for ages to work up the nerve to tell you Dane put his hands all over me on Halloween and that's why I left you. I was too dazed and hurt to process anything more than what was right in front of me. That he toyed with Audrey to get back at me for saying no. That at the end of the day, if I'd left him alone, none of this would be happening. And we'd all still be able to sit together at lunch."

"No," said Emma. "That's not true. That's not your fault."

"I played with fire," said Lulu. "I know I did."

"I refuse to let you feel sorry for yourself, Lulu Saad. We gotta make a stand on the beach. Both of us."

Lulu groaned. "Like in this stupid movie? I tried that—that's why Audrey and Lo aren't speaking to me. I tried to *choke* him. You make a stand. I'll stay safe in my room."

"This movie isn't stupid. You know it isn't. And from what I heard, you're not speaking to Audrey, and Lo isn't speaking to you. I won't make a stand if you won't. You don't get to talk a big talk at me and do nothing."

"Don't hitch your wagon to mine. It won't work. And even if it did work, no plan would work without Lo."

"Thank *you* for the rousing vote of confidence," said Emma.

Lulu sighed. "Unless you know how to fake a teacher's signature, we're up a creek. Lo's the only one I know who can. I've thought about it six ways to Sunday. I can't attack him openly. And he's got social advantage. His only weakness is his attendance record."

Lulu could swear she heard Emma smile. But it didn't matter, because a moment later Emma broke into a laugh.

"What?" asked Lulu. "What is it?"

"Where do you think Lo learned to forge teachers' signatures?" asked Emma, and Lulu was reminded to never underestimate Emma Walker.

Lulu stood up and dug through her schoolbag. Inside were all sorts of items—scissors, notes, hair ties, books, folders, receipts from tacos she'd eaten and milkshakes she'd drunk, movie ticket stubs, and a couple of shampoo bottles stolen out of hotels. Lulu kept all sorts of crap. She told herself she liked to be prepared for anything, but she knew that was an excuse. She simply collected the debris of her life with little thought and less care.

But it was finally coming in handy. Lulu found the slips she had been looking for—the ones she had filched from the office all those weeks ago on a whim—and told Emma her plan.

23
Midnight Madness

The plan was this: to win on a technicality. Dane Anderson had looks, good breeding, and money. What Dane Anderson lacked was an attendance record. It wasn't much of a weak point, true. He was the sort of boy who was not so much seen as blameless but more so that he was easily forgiven for his sins. But the sin of truancy was the cumulative kind. The kind with compounding interest. One missed class was nothing. Ten missed classes, after four years of spotty attendance, in the semester leading up to graduation— well, that was something Lulu could work with.

But she couldn't work with it alone.

Lulu's plan was much like setting up a trail of dominoes. Too close together and she would topple her own structure. Too far apart and none of the falling dominoes would knock one another over. Emma had some theories about that. She said she'd enlist Diana's help. The magnitude of Emma's forgiveness made Lulu's heart swell and gave her the sensation that anything was possible.

Even revenge on Dane Anderson. And possibly a way to bring the gang

249

back together again. Because she could pull them all back together with this play. Everything had started going sideways at Halloween. She saw that now. And Lulu knew the best way to get everyone working together.

It was a wonderfully ironic prank, at its core, and Lulu hoped it would make Lo proud.

And just as Lulu hung up with Emma, she got a message. *Hey.* It was James.

Lulu typed, *this is so much better than a call.*

I know he sent back followed quickly by *That and I'm afraid your phone will ring around your mom*

Lulu laughed. *scared?*

Petrified

Lulu nodded. *understandable*

Excellent because my mom's sick, but she had tickets to go see Monty Python and the Holy Grail at the midnight movie tonight, wanna go?

is there an answer other than yes?

I mean. There's no.

i'm not saying no

Are you saying yes?

yes. if I can get out of the house.

You in trouble? From the other day?

:) Not from the other day. from life in general? all sorts of trouble

I'll pick you up at 11 if you're out on good behavior

excellent. good pick btw

I know.

That smug son of a bitch. Not only did Lulu love that movie, she had missed out on its past two midnight showings, due to each being sold out. *howd you know*

I figured if you're into weird arty French movies, you might be into weird British humor. Plus, I got the last two tickets.

Lulu had him now. *thought they were your moms tickets*

See you at 11, Lulu

At the top of nearly every roller coaster she'd been on, Lulu closed her eyes as she heard the final clicks ticking down. In that moment, when the car hung suspended by the gravity that pulled on either end, Lulu felt more nervous than at any other point in the ride—worse than dropping or looping upside down, worse than careening to a halt and getting stuck on the ride during unscheduled maintenance. It was the only point on a roller coaster she thought she might vomit. The feeling was remarkably similar to the one she was experiencing as she thought about her date.

Her mother had eyed Lulu suspiciously when she'd asked to go to the midnight movie that evening. But school was out for winter break and Lulu had been ungrounded.

"I thought you didn't have any friends," her mother had said.

"This isn't a friend," Lulu had said.

"Then who is it?"

"A boy," had been Lulu's response.

Her mother hadn't liked that. "You want me to let you out with a boy for a midnight movie when you should be grounded? Do I look like I was born yesterday?"

"I figured as much. But it was worth a shot." Lulu had turned to go then.

Her mother sighed and pinched the bridge of her nose.

"I didn't say no. You've held up your end of the bargain. And as long as you keep going to Dina's to help with Tanya's wedding, you're allowed to go out." She didn't sound happy about it, but Lulu's mother was a believer in fairness and bargains. A lawyer through and through. She'd not go back on a contract, even a verbal one. That was where Lulu had learned to respect the spirit of the law, over the letter.

And so Lulu was going out. She was sure she'd gotten away with something, but she knew she'd pay for it tomorrow when Tamra was ignoring her and Dina was hissing at her and the aunties who weren't her aunts were feeding her food she wasn't hungry for and tea she wasn't thirsty for.

James was on time. Not early, not late. Right on time. There was something unnerving about that. Unnatural, even. Lulu hopped into the passenger seat of the old Datsun. She buckled herself in.

"Wanna grab some food beforehand?" James turned, and his eyes were focused on her so intently Lulu had an impulse to look away.

"I really like movie theater popcorn. Like, I love eating so much of it I make myself sick. So I like to save room."

"All right. I won't make you share." James smiled. It was a warm, wide expression that gave Lulu the impression she was understood.

But can he be trusted? whispered that slithering part of her mind. Lulu shook off her nerves. "What's your mom like?"

James barked a laugh. "I think you might be the best weirdo I've ever met."

"You said we were using her tickets!" said Lulu, rather lamely.

"Nah, don't feel bad. You're full of surprises, that's all. She's strong. She's quiet, so it's not always obvious to everyone."

The idea of that made Lulu laugh herself. "Lord. And my mom's a spitfire. Or a pistol. Maybe both. It's very obvious."

James nodded, because he'd seen Aimee Saad in action. "What about your dad?"

"I used to eat oranges with my dad," said Lulu.

"Used to?"

"When I was little. I'd curl up on his lap and get him to peel one for me."

"Did he ever get a bite?"

Lulu laughed. "Yes. But I did take most of it." There was a pause, and Lulu thought she should tell him. About making up with Emma. About what she was about to do to keep Dane out of her life for good.

"You do know how to take advantage, don't you?" His voice teased, but it took the buoyancy out of Lulu's thoughts.

"I guess I do." Lulu shrugged.

"Sorry. That came out all wrong. Again," said James.

"You've got a talent for it."

"Luckily it's not the only thing I've got a talent for." And then James winked.

Lulu blinked several times. "What's that supposed to mean?"

"I guess you'll have to wait and find out."

It was a long movie.

———————

Lulu fidgeted. She had been fidgeting the entire car ride home. James had spent the whole movie actually watching the movie. Not that she didn't enjoy the movie. But she was starting to think she had made up the last time they had kissed. She hadn't even been able to tell anyone about it. Lulu huffed.

"What's up?" James's concentration was maddeningly on the road.

"Nothing." Lulu crossed her arms.

"Doesn't look like nothing," he said.

"It is. Nothing." Lulu blew a wisp of hair out of her eye.

"Okay, now I really don't believe you."

Lulu exploded. "Aren't you interested in me at all?"

James smirked. Lulu's eyes narrowed.

"You son of a bitch." Lulu swatted at his arm. Then play slapped over his head.

"Hey, hey," James said, using his arm to guard his head. "I'm driving."

"Fine." Lulu went back to crossing her arms.

"You look like someone with experience," James began.

"I don't have *that* much experience." Lulu was tired of having to explain this to people. More than some but less than others. Enough to know herself but not enough to know everything. If anyone could know everything.

James picked up on what she meant. "No, not like that. Experience with attention. I thought it might be nice. For you. To not always get that kind of attention. You know. See a movie, no pretense."

They were stopped at a light. For a moment, Lulu stopped along with it. Then she was in motion. She unbuckled her seatbelt and leaped onto James. She grabbed his face in both of her hands. James's arm went around her waist. Her mouth was on his, greedy. He responded in kind. He gripped the back of her shirt with his fist. Lulu tested her tongue against his lips. He opened, ready. They were locked together like there was no tomorrow, like only the apocalypse could stop them. And even then, only maybe.

A horn blared behind them. Lulu jumped, falling over onto the e-brake. James yelped.

"Christ. You're not safe to be around." James squirmed out from under her and drove, the light already yellow again.

Lulu grinned as the tires squealed against the pavement. She buckled herself back in.

When James pulled up to the curb of Lulu's house, his breath was still quick and short. "Get out of this car, Lulu, or so help me God, I'm probably going to get shot by your mother."

"Why my mother?"

"She seems more likely to own a gun than your father."

Lulu gave him a long stare. "It's not just my mother, is it?"

"No," he said. "It isn't."

Lulu looked James in the eye. A pit welled in her stomach. He looked relieved and frustrated all at once. Lulu would have put money on having a similar expression on her face. This energy between them was fresh, and fragile. Was there anything beyond wanting each other? Was there trust or only two people who caused traffic jams with their lust? Lulu opened the passenger door, needing to put air and distance and space between them. Before she hopped out she gave James a swift, chaste peck on the lips, then leaped from the car.

"Sweet dreams," she said, with a purposeful amount of honey in her voice. It was her turn to wink.

James shook his head. His eyes narrowed, and Lulu would have taken him for being annoyed if the corners of his mouth hadn't turned upward into an ironic smile. "You'll get yours, Lulu Saad."

"I'm going to hold you to that." Lulu shut the car door. She could feel her heartbeat in her throat.

James waited for her to cross the threshold of her home before driving off. The front door to her house slammed shut behind Lulu. She didn't bother with attempts at noiseless movements. She knew her mother would be waiting up for her on the couch. She always sat up waiting for Lulu, a Diet Dr Pepper in one hand, a magazine in the other, with the television on low in the background.

The predictability of it comforted Lulu. She enjoyed knowing what she was going to get when she arrived home. She would sit by her mother and watch twenty minutes or half an hour of some procedural drama. These moments gave Lulu her unabashed love of murder mysteries. Watching them felt like a piece of home, no matter where or when she was. Jessica Fletcher, Magnum, P.I., Shawn Spencer, Brenda Leigh Johnson, Sherlock Holmes—they were all to Lulu the image of her and her mother, curled up together, with her mother accidentally wired from caffeine and Lulu warm and fuzzy from her nights out. Her mother could always figure out the murderer. Lulu never could.

Lulu stepped into the living room. Her mother's spot was empty. She looked over to the television, but the screen was off, not on mute. No magazine set aside, no Dr Pepper can in sight. The downstairs bathroom looked empty from Lulu's position, so she was momentarily at a loss to figure out her current situation. She turned slightly on her heels, and there, in his chair, sat her father.

Ahmed must have noticed the surprise on Lulu's face, but he didn't acknowledge it or her disappointment. He was peeling an orange. He offered the slices to her; she declined with a shake of her head. When she had been little, the simple act of sharing an orange had seemed like enough. But now, she couldn't just share an orange with him. She felt as though she had bungled everything. When Lulu thought of oranges, her heart broke.

She sat across from her father's chair, next to where her mother would have been sitting on the couch, had Aimee been the one in the room.

Lulu opened her mouth to speak, but Ahmed beat her to it. "Mama told me you went out to see a movie. She said it was your favorite." His tone was purposefully calm, as though he always spoke thusly to his daughter about being out at two o'clock in the morning. His was a steady stream of facts, delivered with an as-yet-to-be-determined judgment.

Lulu responded in kind. "Yeah, they were showing *Monty Python and the Holy Grail,* and you know how I love it. It was great, really, to see it up there on the screen like that." Her father had been the one to introduce her to the Python's humor some years ago.

"Yes, I remember," said Ahmed.

Lulu knew what came next.

"My Aimee said you went with a friend. What friend?" There was no mistaking his intent now, as he looked up from his orange, directly into Lulu's eyes.

"Oh." Lulu had been holding her breath, and here she finally exhaled. "Not a friend. A boy. James."

"What James?" Ahmed's eyes squinted.

"James Denair." Lulu's bottom lip sulked forward from her face.

"Who is this James? At midnight?"

Lulu wasn't sure whether her father was muttering to himself or shouting at her. His orange was finished now, and it looked like the last bite had been an unpleasant experience, all sour tang and no refreshing sweetness to balance out the flavor. Lulu was tired, from the hour, from the tension between her and her baba recently, from the number of times she had already had iterations of this discussion in her life. She felt a tiny scream welling up in her throat, one she knew would never get out.

"Your mama, she knew this?"

"Yes. She knew."

He grimaced. It was an ugly, twisted version of his face. Lulu didn't know whether she disliked these looks as such because they were so exaggerated or because she had incited them. It was like watching a physical manifestation, a visual hyperbole, of all the disappointments she knew she was forever incurring with him, whether he realized it or not.

"Well." He spoke the word of a man who had nothing left to say but desperately wanted to speak.

"I know, Baba," said Lulu. "I know."

On her way out of the room, she leaned over and kissed his forehead lightly, part apology and part resignation. It bore the same kind of respect as the self-flagellation Lulu imagined in an Ashura procession. Lulu turned to leave the room.

"All right," said her father, his voice behind her.

Lulu turned. "What?"

Ahmed nodded. "It's all right, habibti."

Lulu understood. Her father could have been referring to the dating, or the coming home at two o'clock in the morning. Or the vomiting in the front bushes. But he wasn't, not really. He wasn't even talking about the scene she'd caused, the mess she'd made. She was all right. She would be all right.

"Thank you, Baba. For getting Sheikh Fadi on my side. I know it helped."

Ahmed shook his head. "Don't thank me. He was on your side. He came to me."

This was news to Lulu.

"Thank him, hayati. Thank him and be done with it." Ahmed got up and kissed Lulu on the forehead as he left the room. "Clean the mess."

And on that cryptic note, Lulu slumped onto the couch. Lulu had gotten Emma to talk to her. She'd gotten her involved in the plan. Everything else would have to wait until school on Monday.

24

Khalas

Lulu wasn't sure how long she had been stuffing candy-coated almonds into tiny boxes. She was sure there was a way to buy them prestuffed into these tiny boxes. Yet here she sat, grabbing almonds with the tips of her fingers and letting them fall into the absurdly small containers. She wondered, briefly, if stuffing the almonds into sachets would be better or worse. It didn't matter, not really. But Lulu wondered anyway. Wondering about Jordan almonds kept Lulu's mind off kissing James and making up with Emma and what was going to happen when school started back up in two days. Anticipation made Lulu jumpy. She had a plan, if it would work. She had a friend, if she could see the rest through. She had a start, a beginning. The way was dark, the path was murky, but Lulu could just start to see how to take the next step forward, and the next, and the next.

Lulu had to hope it would be enough.

Despite her grumblings, Lulu liked her rhythm at the Alkati house. She got tea from Khala Zeena and dirty looks from Auntie Salwa. They were sincere looks and Lulu—as someone who could feel deeply herself—appreciated their sincerity. Plus the wedding preparations kept her from the long hours at her own house, filled with her brothers' discomfort and her mother's disapproval and her father's bewildering behavior.

Lulu didn't even mind Dina's snide comments. She had, at first. But now, somehow, they felt like comfort. They'd become part of the fabric of this home, of this aspect of her life. Radical acceptance from Dina would have thrown Lulu for a loop. Perhaps, here, she would always be an outsider. But she was also no longer a trespasser. That had been a combination of her own horrible handiwork and their magnanimous forgiveness. Lulu had been forged in this fire. She would neither regret nor begrudge it.

"Lulu, you're hogging the sugar," snipped Dina.

Lulu passed the sugar. Khala Zeena pinched Lulu's cheeks with a smile. Lulu gritted through the pain and smiled as best as she could. Who was she to change an expression of love centuries in the making? She wondered idly if she would pinch her own nieces' and nephews' cheeks, or surrogate nieces' and nephews', as the case currently could be. If the gesture was merely a byproduct of culture and age or if she'd be able to resist the impulse.

Lulu might never be accepted fully into the homes of these women or admitted comfortably into the fold of Sealy Hall. But Lulu had been given the gift of fluency. Lulu was not French, but she could speak with them. Lulu was not from old WASPish money, but she could converse among them as well. That was what her parents had given her. The gift and the curse to move between people, languages, and cultures. Not to blend so much as to be able to communicate clearly across invisible borders. She was a traveler, a go-between.

Lulu remembered the day she had first gotten a joke in French. To her that was the ultimate test of fluency—to understand humor. Well, she understood the stiff, cold humor of Sealy Hall—their merciless irony and wit. And she cackled at the near-black humor of the Iraqi immigrants, the choice to laugh at torture and loss rather than to cry about it. They laugh at their troubles rather than sink into them. Why, oh why, she had kept biting her tongue until she tasted blood in her mouth, until all that was left to her was to explode in a spectacular fashion, Lulu suddenly did not understand. It was her one gift in this world. To speak on behalf of strangers and to strangers, at all times. To talk to more than one world, simultaneously. To think in more than one way and to know of many ways to live a life.

"Lulu, do you have all the boxes?" Dina snapped to make sure she fully interrupted Lulu's thoughts.

Lulu passed a large stack from her own pile of flattened gift boxes.

Khala Zeena patted Lulu's hand. Zeena took the sugar from Dina and lumped two spoonfuls into Lulu's tea. They had run out of sugar cubes by now. Lulu said shukran and kept filling bags of almonds. She tried to keep her mind on the task at hand—but it was a mechanical one. The kind that lent itself to wondering about Emma and her girlfriend or reliving the feeling of James's mouth or replaying all the daily markers of Aimee's frustration. Then her thoughts bounced back to James's mouth. He had a distracting mouth and he wasn't even here. And then forward, to how she could get Lo to talk to her. How Lulu could find her own forgiveness for Audrey. Lulu sighed and the expression went entirely over Khala Zeena's head. Zeena wasn't magic, after all. She couldn't read minds. She just understood more English than she spoke.

"Lulu, you don't have to skimp on almonds. We're not cheap. Inshallah, this is going to be a beautiful wedding. This isn't like other weddings you might have been to," said Dina.

Lulu imagined Dina was implying something about Aimee's people. Lulu let more almonds drop into the boxes.

"Not so much, Lulu! You'll not be able to close them!" said Dina.

This made Tanya the Bride laugh at the other end of the table. "Give her a rest, DeeDee," said Tanya. "She's suffering enough. I mean she's made like fifteen centerpieces and filled at least a hundred of my party bags. She's done enough."

And here Tanya looked Lulu dead in the eye. "I declare your penance complete. I am a satisfied bride. Khalas." Tanya wiped her hands against each other to emphasize the point.

"'Azzizati,'" said Bibi Hookum, Tamra, Tanya, and Dina's grandmother. Bibi Hookum's large, wrinkled hands pinched the hollow of Lulu's cheeks between her index finger and thumb. Then she gave a guttural trill of a cry and clapped a couple of times, bobbing her head back and forth with joy.

"Ey, Bibi," said Tanya to her grandmother. Over her grandmother's head, Tanya winked at Lulu.

"Tanya the Merciful," said Lulu.

Tanya laughed again. "Get out of here, Lu. You're dismissed."

Lulu looked up from her work, slightly alarmed.

"But if you miss my henna party, I'm taking back all my forgiveness," said Tanya on a final, magnificent laugh.

"Thank you." Lulu stood still for a moment, unwilling to leave.

"You heard me." Tanya swatted the air. "Get!"

Lulu got up, grabbed her bag, and walked toward the door. She waved lamely to the group of women, who clucked and half waved her off. Lulu should have gone straight home. But she didn't.

"I've got an hour," she said when she stopped her car in front of James's house. Her window was rolled down.

"Cool." James had a tentative expression on his face. He opened the door and hopped into the passenger seat. "Where to?"

"Milkshakes?" asked Lulu.

"Milkshakes," said James. His expression clarified, and Lulu saw that it was joy.

Lulu drove. She chatted as she went. She talked about Tanya the Bride and Zeena the Auntie and Dina the Bitch. She talked about hotel ballrooms and Jordan almonds and cutting wedding cakes with enormous saber-length swords. James laughed exactly when he should have and sipped his strawberry milkshake as he listened to the rest. Lulu wondered if that meant his lips would taste like strawberries. But he didn't try to kiss her. He just listened while she talked and laughed when she told a joke. She didn't tell him about her plan for Dane, though she felt herself nearly say it at least twenty times. But every time she thought she would, she managed to hold back. She wondered if she was dating him, if she wanted to be. It was strange, this thing, where they were like friends, but not at all.

Idly, Lulu wondered if Lo would still stare him down. Or if she'd approve. It didn't matter. Because Lo hadn't returned one of Lulu's calls or messages. And Lulu didn't have a single picture left where they were tagged together. Audrey would likely not approve. But since Audrey's opinion didn't matter, Lulu didn't need it. But then James cracked a joke about the airspeed velocity of swallows, and Lulu couldn't help but wonder if that would have made Audrey laugh or not. Emma, Lulu decided. She would tell Emma about James.

"And I can't figure out anymore if Ben or Rez drives me more crazy," Lulu said. "Ben thinks he gives the best advice in the world ever, even though he doesn't, and Rez just stares at me like I've grown a third arm out of my head or something."

"Why don't you tell them that?"

"Nah, Ben sees things the way he sees them, and it won't do much good to try to change it. And Reza doesn't seem to be able to compute anything I say anymore." Lulu turned away, trying to figure out why she was explaining this at all. "I always wanted a sister, you know."

"They're not all they're cracked up to be," said James.

"That's exactly what my brothers would say, too."

"Besides, I've heard you talk about your friends. It sounds like you already have sisters. Whether you wanted them or not." James took a last slurp of his milkshake, then looked at the dash. "Damn. Hour's up."

———

Lulu prayed to God for three simple things: an empty house, time to herself for a good hour, and Coke in the refrigerator. The fridge was nearly devoid of anything, except for an assortment of condiments, a couple of jars of pickles, and one last, shriveled-looking fruit that probably used to be either a lemon or a grapefruit.

And then her father called her from the other room.

"Ya habibti, how did your day go?" Her baba was sitting in his chair in the living room, casually eating an orange and reading a piece from this morning's paper that he hadn't had a chance to finish before leaving for work.

"Fine."

"I sent in the final draft of my book," he said.

"Great." Lulu swung the fridge doors between her hands, like it was a magic trick that would manifest food.

"Are you hungry?" asked her baba.

"Sure," said Lulu unthinkingly.

"Good!" Her father clapped his hand onto his knee, then stood up forcefully. He wasn't a large man by any standard. Indeed, he had the slight build one might imagine of the bookish one that he was. But his physical presence was imposing, impossible to ignore.

And that's how Lulu found herself in her car, driving her father to grab a second milkshake. Lulu drove, wondering if she would wake up soon, or if this is what people referred to when they talked about out-of-body experiences. As Lulu moved into the left-hand lane to turn into the drive-through, a purple cabriolet pulled up and began turning right. It could have been anyone's ugly, impractical, purple convertible.

But it wasn't. It was Audrey's.

Lulu turned, her car trailing behind Audrey's. She watched Audrey's brake lights go on, then back off again. For a moment Lulu just stared. Then a horn sounded behind her and she realized she was holding up the whole line. She pulled her car forward to order. Lulu turned, giving her baba a deer-in-the-headlights look.

"Vanilla," he stated plainly.

"One vanilla, and one chocolate, please." Lulu pulled her car through as instructed, all the while wondering if Audrey, still in front of her, was also getting a milkshake. But Lulu couldn't see what was being handed out the next window before Audrey pulled away.

Lulu's father graciously handed her cash. She paid, then drove forward to the window Audrey was just at. Lulu took the shakes and exited the lot. She slurped hers steadily, at a loss for what to do or say next. Her baba sipped his and remained quiet.

Lulu wanted to be brave. She wanted to be the girl who could talk to her father again. She didn't want to hurt him, but she was too wounded for too long to be sure of how to begin. She spoke for all these reasons and despite them all. She spoke what she had to, what she had always been afraid of, what she thought belonged to no one but herself. "You know. I'm sorry. That you had to deal with me. With what I said. To Auntie Salwa. To you."

"No," he spoke with quiet command, in a language he had made his own.

Lulu stared over at her father, her mouth gripping her straw and her eyes wide.

"I want you to know who you are, Lulu. Not for myself, for you."

"But, Baba, how am I supposed to learn who I am from articles? Why can't you tell me? Why can't you talk to me?" She chomped down on her milkshake straw, and she focused with such determination on the road that she began to lose sight of it.

"Do you know why I named you Leila?"

Lulu was too busy holding on to the tears pooling at her eyes to shake her head yes or no, though she thought she knew the origin story of her name. Four blocks from her house, Lulu pulled over. She could no longer see much beyond the wheel in front of her. She missed Audrey. She missed when talking to her father was easy. Or at least simple.

"I told you about the story of the lovers, Leila and Majnoon, when you were a little girl. Our older version of Romeo and Juliet. I told you it was that famous story throughout the Muslim world. I told you about that beautiful Iraqi song. But I never told you why I gave it to you." He paused for dramatic effect. Professor Saad knew how to draw his audience in, luring them with enough detail to make them wonder what might come next.

Lulu sniffled loudly, blinking away as many would-be tears as she could. She would not cry. She was fine. She was going to make sure everything was fine. She had to.

"I nearly named you Zeyneb. Both of these women cut a tragic figure. They have so much pain in their lives. But they are also eternal. They live on. People speak their names with reverence, with awe. I wanted to give you such a name like that, one with power, a name with history, a name with some weight—with baggage, I think." He looked his daughter directly in the eye, so there would be no mistake about what he said next. "I wanted that for you, because it gives you something to build on, to take and make your own. Everyone needs a foundation. Your name is yours, Lulu. Make it your own."

Lulu, belted into her seat as she was, jumped out, reaching across the center console and the gearshift to hug her father. Surprised, though pleased, he reciprocated. She pulled away, wiping her eyes with the back of her hands. She sniffled back snot.

"Mama's never going to let us go out alone together again, when she sees us."

"Luckily, she is at work," said her father. He grinned a conspiratorial grin.

They had a secret now. Funny that Lulu had been allowed so many with her mother and none with her father.

"You know, my baba and I, we used to go and get ice cream together, in the summers. There was this one ice cream shop." Her father launched into a story that Lulu had heard a million times. Now a million and one.

She was thoroughly annoyed as she listened, wanting to jump in and correct him where he changed details, or when he missed important plot points. She could appreciate her annoyance, though, in a way she hadn't before. She thought then that irritation is sometimes the most honest way of expressing love.

25

Goddess of the Hunt

The end of winter break should not have surprised Lulu. It had been marked on the academic calendar for a full year in advance. And yet, the rhythm of school again was startling, nearly painfully so. Audrey was still mad enough at Lulu to continue to refuse to apologize. Or, as was likely the case, think about what she'd done. Lulu might as well have been dead as far as Lo was concerned. But that was to be expected. Photos of Lo started to crop up. Lo with a group of boys, Scumbag Luke beside her. It was a bold series of photos—they had never been seen together so flagrantly before. But perhaps Lo was growing bold. Or perhaps she just wanted to rub her absence in Lulu's face. It worked. A new pang of regret and longing hit Lulu squarely in the chest every time she saw a new photo.

Currently, Lo was half the hallway down and refusing to turn her body in the direction of Lulu's locker. Lo had even said hello to Atman Rai as she'd passed. Atman looked at Lulu, startled and concerned, as if to say, "Why, oh why, do you continuously put me in the line of fire?"

It was an excellent question.

"Come on. Pining longingly isn't going to change anything." Emma leaned against Lulu's locker.

"I'm not pining longingly," said Lulu.

"You're staring over at Lo's empty locker with the saddest puppy dog of a look on your face. It's incredible you ever play it cool with boys."

"Shut up," said Lulu.

"Just letting you know. Do what you will with the information," said Emma.

"I'm still without a plan as to how to apologize to her."

"You'll think of one. I believe in you," said Emma. "Try something along the lines of saying 'I'm sorry' to her and seeing how that goes."

Lulu could have nearly cried, the belief was so endearing, so energizing. Emma's faith was a bolstering thing. No wonder she had such a stellar girlfriend.

"Emma. Lo has erased me from anything she can get her hands on. And clearly deleting my texts. And ignoring me in the halls. Should I hire a skywriter?"

"You'll figure it out," said Emma. "Exactly like you figured out what to do with Anderson."

Lulu sighed. She had taken open swings at Dane. She'd thrown her punches. It had all backfired. It was time to take a page out of Lo's book. It was time to fight dirty.

"Lunch?" asked Emma.

"I'll meet you there," said Lulu, swept up into the crowd of students rushing toward the dining hall. The melee gave Lulu the necessary cover. She ducked through the crowd into the back door of the school office. Lulu looked over her shoulder, twice. Mrs. Carly was nowhere in sight. No one was anywhere in sight. It was the shuffle toward lunch. The storm before the calm. *Now or never, now or never, now or never*—it was a mantra, a

269

benediction. Lulu kissed her fingers, then touched her forehead. She ducked behind Mrs. Carly's empty desk.

Here, right before her, was the Book. Lulu had a second to decide, possibly less. She stood at a crouch, which would only make it that much worse if she was caught. No smile or eyelash batting or faux innocence would be able to get her out of this one. There was a giddiness that overcame Lulu for a moment, so much power and information at her fingertips. But Lulu focused again—she had no time to waste. She flipped through until she found Dane's page. She scribbled a series of numbers—a student ID to be specific—across her forearm, momentarily thankful for the colder weather. She pulled her flimsy uniform sweatshirt down over the marks.

Lulu snagged a piece of candy as she slid out from behind the desk. She took a deep breath, then headed for the office door. She opened it and nearly bumped into Mrs. Carly. The woman gave Lulu a suspicious look. Lulu shrugged and popped the lollipop into her mouth, like she was merely in need of a sugar fix. This seemed to satisfy Mrs. Carly.

As soon as the door shut behind her, Lulu ran outside the building, taking huge gulps of crisp air. She'd done it. But that was the easy part.

During lunch, Lulu approached her usual table. Emma and Diana were already seated. As Lulu got to a seat, so too did Audrey, right across from her. They both stopped and stared at each other, mirror images of distress and horror. Lulu set her tray down but didn't sit. Audrey's eyes went wide. She turned on her heels and fled the dining hall. Lulu had won, and she wished she hadn't. It was a Pyrrhic victory, and nothing Diana or Emma said for the remainder of lunch could pull her from her miserable stupor. And as Lulu left, she realized that she hadn't seen Lo there at all.

Scumbag Luke was turning into the big, bad wolf, ready to devour Lo whole. Lulu shuddered at the thought.

After school, Lulu texted Matt and waited by their usual spot next to the beignet café. She handed him his mocha granita when he arrived. They began to split the bag of beignets she'd bought. Her campus was farther, but she always beat him there. Must have been the hallways, Lulu decided. She hadn't thought before of the privilege of an uncrowded school hallway, but she couldn't stop thinking about it now that she met Matt after school with a bag of beignets in one hand and two granitas in the other. Lulu liked beignets with Matt because it was easygoing. They ate and they drank and they bitched and there was nothing ever more than that. The same could not be said for James, but Matt said he'd invited him anyway.

"How's it going, killer?" Matt asked, hopping onto the roof of her car. Lulu had learned her lesson with the plant shop quite thoroughly. She parked her car right out front from the café forevermore.

"The same," she said. "Except I'm talking to Emma now. And her girlfriend."

"Honestly, makes sense why she was ignoring you," said Matt.

"You're a real treat sometimes."

Matt shrugged. "You know I'm right."

"And so am I." Lulu took a long sip from her coffee granita to hide the sheepishness that crept over her. When she looked up again, she saw Lo approaching with Luke from across the street. Lulu choked on her drink, before finally managing to get it down. Lo gave Lulu a cutting glare. She grabbed Scumbag Luke's hand, and turned them in the other direction, toward the other school's parking lot.

Lulu was about to get up and honestly chase after Lo when James stopped in front of them both with a "Hello, Lulu."

Her heartache was temporarily distracted by the sight of him. Lulu offered him a wordless sip of her granita. He took it. Lulu tried not to stare at his lips. She'd have to add sharing food to a list of things she could no longer do with James and maintain her sanity. It was already too long of a list.

"Thanks." He hopped up beside Matt on the hood of Lulu's car.

Lulu stood where she was, not trusting herself beside him, not that close. James smiled like he knew what she was thinking. Lulu scowled, but that only made his smile widen.

"Friends of yours?" asked James, pointing behind her.

Lulu turned. Emma and Diana were waving and headed to the beignet shop, away from the Sealy Hall campus. Lulu waved back. Emma and Diana stopped in front of Lulu's car.

"Hiya," said Diana.

"Emma, Diana," said Lulu, pointing at the girls respectively, "This is James and Matt," she finished, again pointing.

"Charmed," said Diana, a wry smile on her mouth.

"Likewise," said James, laughing. He was never one to withhold his laughter because a girl had told a joke. This, Lulu had learned and liked about him from the first.

"*The* James?" asked Emma. "Of nearly-drowning-in-the-pool fame?"

"Kind of," said James. "More like I pretended to drown and made Lulu jump into the pool just to see if she would."

Diana laughed. "I like this guy."

Lulu playfully socked Diana in the arm.

"We were going to get beignets," said Emma.

"Here," said Lulu, passing the bag over. "There's one left."

"Hey!" protested Matt, but it was too late now.

Emma took it off Lulu's hands happily. She and Diana shared.

"So," said Diana in between bites of fried dough. "Have you heard Lulu's totally brilliant plan for revenge on Dane Anderson?"

Lulu gulped. She hadn't told James. And now that she was put to it, she wasn't entirely sure why. She dared a glance to him, and he looked exactly as she'd feared. Doe-eyed, deer in the headlights, the works. Emma threw an elbow in Diana's rib.

"Oh, shit." Diana turned to Lulu. "I assumed—with everything—you'd told him."

Lulu said nothing, her eyes wide and her guilty feeling plainly written across her face.

James managed to keep his tone even. "Is there a reason you're planning revenge on Dane Anderson?"

Emma and Diana gave each other a pointed look.

"You know," said Emma. "I think we're going to run in and grab our own beignets." Emma grabbed Diana's hand and they vacated into the building.

"Yeah," said Matt. "Me too. Y'all owe me one." He practically ran after them.

Lulu and James were left standing, staring at each other.

Lulu took a deep breath. "He kind of sort of felt me up, against my will while we were also originally mutually hooking up. I mean I said no. But not at first. Then he definitely forced himself on Audrey. Who thought he was Clark Kelly because she was blackout. Then threatened me in front of an entire party after I kind of went for his throat. And you saw the rest. And then he told me no one would believe me. So. Rather than trying to choke him in public, I've decided to ... pivot."

James's face was unreadable. But she watched him clench his fist. He was definitely angry. He must have been mad she hadn't told him. She'd wanted to tell him. But she hadn't quite figured out how to break the news. She could watch the gears of his mind putting the story together with what he'd seen that night through the living room window. Like he saw the missing gaps and went from looking at an unsolvable jigsaw puzzle to seeing a fully formed picture.

James unclenched his fist, shook it out for a moment, then reclenched it. He looked like he was on the brink of deciding something, of speaking, when he turned on his heel and marched down a side street next to the café.

"Wait," called out Lulu, chasing after him.

James stopped.

"I'm sorry," she said. "I'm really, really sorry."

"Sorry?" James took a deep breath. He was clearly trying to manage his anger. "You have nothing to be sorry for."

Lulu, who had been racing after him, trying to catch up to the strides of his long legs, stopped short at the words. "I don't?"

"No. I just." James unclenched his fist again.

Lulu waited, knowing he was looking for the right words.

Then he looked up at her, his gaze piercing hers. "Is this what it feels like, to want to put a fist through someone's face?"

Lulu sized him up. "Yeah. I mean. You definitely look how I feel when I want to punch someone in the face."

"I can't believe he did that. No, scratch that. I *can* believe it. I can't believe I ever thought he was a harmless jerk." His expression softened. The anger in his eyes deflated with a sad helplessness. "I'm sorry you didn't feel like you could trust me. That I gave you stupid ultimatums. That I didn't punch him in the face sooner."

"Hey." Lulu reached out to touch his face, and James went very, very still. Lulu made sure he was looking her in the eye for this. "You weren't giving me ultimatums. You were giving me space. Space I needed. Space I still need. But I've got this. I don't need anyone to fight him for me. I tried that. It didn't work. I've got something else in mind."

James swallowed, his throat bobbing as he did so. "All right."

"Besides. I'd hate it if you broke your hand."

"Why's that?" He tilted his head, away from Lulu's hand.

Lulu lowered her arm. "Because I've been promised you've got hidden talents. I'd hate to miss out if it's your hands with the talents."

A wide, mischievous grin broke out across James's face. "Not my hands. Not exclusively."

Lulu did blush this time. She didn't know she could until that moment. But she felt the heat flushing across her face. And she could see the satisfaction spreading farther across James's.

"That is," she said, her throat somehow feeling suddenly dry, "quite the image."

"Ball's in your court, Lulu Saad." He took her hand.

"Resisting a lot of ball-related humor right now," said Lulu.

"Come on," he said, tugging lightly at her hand, like she could let go and not follow at any time. "I want my own bag of beignets."

Lulu let him lead her into the shop, like she didn't mind being pulled along at all.

26
The Tenth Day

Today was Ashura, and that meant today could not be a good day. Thirteen hundred years ago was a tragedy. Today was a tragedy. Lulu ought to have been used to distant-but-related tragedy by now, but she still wasn't. It was a senseless bombing. Not that Lulu had ever heard of a sensible bombing. It was Ashura, and it would not be a good day.

It had started out as days usually do—with morning first followed by afternoon then evening. It was a day Lulu held her breath during. She could have fasted. She could have refrained from many things—food, water, swearing, sex. But instead, she stopped breathing. She held her breath and walked through the day. She was a few days shy of her birthday, so she couldn't give blood. She could only tense up and wait. Crying was for holidays everyone else understood. There were places to cry about cultural memories. School was not one of those places.

It was evening by the time Lulu could process the news. And when she did, the first thing she did was run upstairs to her computer. She turned it on and heard the slow whirl of her machine booting to life. She clicked and she waited and she clicked and she waited. Finally, her e-mail was up. She found the one from Rana. The one she had never answered.

I hope you are safe. I hope you are well. I hope Amu and Auntie are well. I think about you always. Love, Lulu.

She clicked send before she could think better of it. Before she could think about what it would mean to not get an e-mail back right away. She simply logged off. That was all she could do. Send out messages into the void, and hope they were returned as promptly as possible.

And then, Lulu turned off her computer. And then she cried.

She wasn't sure why she cried. Whether it was for those who died on this day or those who died thirteen hundred years ago. They died in the same place, all of them. Same place, separated only by time. Millennia of time, but still, only time. She cried because she was not there, and she cried because in all likelihood she would never be there. She cried because so few things seemed to belong to her, but for some reason this was one of them.

And then, Lulu finally took a deep breath. Her tears settled. She wiped them away. She went to the bathroom and cleaned off her face. The cool water stung, all while making the most satisfying swish of a noise as it splashed across her face. Pilgrims had become martyrs—today was unfortunately the day for that.

Lulu was neither.

And in that moment, Lulu was resolved. Perhaps a rapid decision, or a rash one. But it was the quick explosion at the end of a long fuse. She couldn't prove this kind of thing to anyone. But she knew it for herself. She knew she didn't want to wait. Didn't want to live her life not trusting, with her tongue cut out and with armor around her heart. Perhaps because her revenge was in sight. Perhaps because the violence of the day reminded her that life was short and she must live her own as she ought. Perhaps she needed to take her own advice, like she'd given Emma. She needed to live life by her own rules. She needed to trust her own judgment.

Lulu walked downstairs.

Her mother stood in the kitchen. "The decorations look pretty for Tanya's wedding." She was clearly trying to distract from the day's sad news.

"They do, don't they?" said Lulu. She was shoring up her courage.

"Auntie Farrah sent me photos. Tanya picked pretty designs for the centerpieces."

"She did, didn't she?" said Lulu. Her courage was faltering, considering how decisive she had felt not minutes before. Her mother was still intimidating. Especially when Lulu considered what she was about to ask for.

"Lulu."

"Yes, Mama?"

"Stop it."

"Stop what?"

"Lord preserve me. You are such a contrary child, and I can't even blame your daddy because you get it from me."

Lulu maintained a wide-eyed expression. "Contrary?"

"For fuck's sake. Stop asking parroting questions," said her mother. "Out with it. What do you want?"

"I wanna go to the clinic."

"The what?"

"Or the gynecologist. I wanna go to the women's clinic. For birth control."

"Jesus, Lulu." Her mother reached for the cross that was no longer around her neck. She promptly sat on the nearest surface she could find. "I'm going to go gray early because of you."

"Then you can dye your hair blue like Mimi did. Blue is very in right now."

Aimee pointed her finger solidly. "Don't you dare, Lulu. Don't you dare."

"I hate that you don't trust me anymore!" shouted Lulu, the full force of her feelings coming to a head.

"You got your car locked up in a plant shop! You're asking for birth control on a random Tuesday! You won't tell me why! Probably for some boy you're sneaking around with!" And then, much more quietly, "Trust is earned, baby girl."

"Fantastic. I'll never live that one down." Lulu squared her shoulders. "I'm trying to be responsible, Mom."

"Really? Because I didn't know you had a boyfriend."

"I don't," said Lulu, with ruthless honesty.

Aimee stared. "That's a lot to take in, Lulu."

"What, so I can only want to have sex with boys who are my boyfriends?"

Her mother wiped her hand across her face. "Lulu. I was raised Catholic. In the South. Please give your mama a minute."

Lulu watched the war on Aimee's face. Between progress and safety. Between what she had been trained to do and the kinds of freedoms she had never had but wanted for her daughter.

It softened Lulu, a little. "I like him. But he's not my boyfriend. He could be. But I'm okay that he's not."

Her mother sighed. "Have I even met him, Lulu?"

"Do you mean, '*Is he good people?*'" said Lulu, in her twangiest of twangs.

Her mother gave Lulu a stern look.

"You've met him, Mama. He held back my hair when I was puking that one time."

Her mother groaned. "Of course. Of course it's that boy. Lulu Saad, you're going to be the death of me."

"You survived Ben, Mama. You can survive me." Lulu breathed in aggressive little spurts. But she wasn't finished, not yet. "I showed up every goddamn day of break at the Alkatis' for the wedding decorations. I didn't whine. I didn't complain. I let them be cliquey the whole time. I let it go. You're the one not moving on.

"I want birth control because I want to be ready. I don't know if he's my boyfriend. I don't know if he wants to have sex with me." That Lulu realized, was a stretch, but she plowed through the rest of her speech, not knowing when the confidence she felt would run dry. "I want to know I'm ready for myself. And I'm not sneaking around. I told Baba about him. I went to the movies with him."

Lulu was out of words.

"I see." Her mother stared. Then, "Fine."

"What?" Lulu shook her head out. She must have heard wrong.

"Fine. I'll go to the gynecologist with you." Her mother went over to the little forest-green Rolodex she left in a corner of the kitchen. It had to have been at least thirty years old, that creaky, plastic thing. She flipped through it. She started writing on a sticky note. She handed the note to Lulu. "Here. Make the appointment. And remember, if you break my trust again, it will be beyond repair. Do you understand me? Not for a long while."

Lulu held out her hand. "Shake on it?"

"Jesus Christ. Fine." Her mother took Lulu's hand and shook. "You drive a hard bargain."

Lulu shrugged as she started to walk out of the kitchen. "I learned from the best."

Her mother called after her. "Make sure to put the appointment in the calendar."

The family calendar. That lived in the kitchen. Aimee Saad did not fuck around.

———

A week later, Aimee picked Lulu up from the carpool lane. Lulu got in the car quietly.

"You sure about this?" her mother asked as Lulu buckled herself in.

"Sure," said Lulu as the metal clicked in through the plastic.

"All right." Her mother put the car into gear. They rode in silence.

Once inside the exam room, Lulu nestled her feet into the stirrups. Her mother was waiting outside, so Lulu could have her appointment on her own. Lulu wanted to text Lo and tell her that she was wearing a paper gown and her bare feet were nestled into fuzzy stirrups that had definitely seen better days. She was cold. She wanted to snap a picture and send it to Audrey, the worry etching lines across her face. Audrey's judgment would help in a moment like this. It would steel her. Lo might tell her what to expect. She missed them both so much in the moment. She had an acute pang in her chest. She sent a snap of her face to Emma, who sent a concerned selfie back.

Lulu took a deep breath. None of them were here right now. She couldn't message Lo, and she couldn't chat with Audrey. And Emma's apprehensive look hadn't helped Lulu much, either. Judgment, knowledge, abrasion—those were Lulu's current list of requirements. She tapped her foot in the stirrups and looked over on the counter. The speculum did not look particularly inviting. She looked away. A knock rapped at the door.

"Ready," said Lulu.

The doctor walked in, washing her hands in the room's sink. She was in her late thirties, maybe. She wore practical hair and practical shoes. She had a kind face. "How are we doing today?" The doctor flipped through her charts. "Leila?"

"Great. Fine," said Lulu. "Great."

"Great," said the doctor. "So what are we in for?"

"Um." Lulu wiggled her toes, letting them grip the fuzzy fabric. "Checkup. And. Birth control. I would like birth control."

The doctor flipped through her chart one more time. "All right, Leila. We can do that. Are you sexually active?" The doctor sat and wheeled over on her little stool toward Lulu.

"No," said Lulu. "Not yet."

The doctor started a breast exam. Her hands were frigid. "All right, Leila. I don't technically need to do a full pap with the speculum yet. But it's good to get a baseline on your tests, if you want. Totally up to you."

"All right," said Lulu, still holding in a yelp from the doctor's cold hands.

The doctor rolled her stool back to her desk, its wheels squeaking against the linoleum floor. She snapped on a pair of latex gloves, grabbed the speculum, and returned. "Might be a little pinch, all right. Deep breath."

Lulu took a deep breath. In went the speculum. The sensation was cold. Out came a swab. Lulu tensed, waiting for pain that never quite arrived. Her feet were cold. She was seminaked. And now the inside of her vagina was cold. She didn't know quite what to do with that information.

"All done," said the doctor, inserting the cotton swab into a plastic tube. She snapped off her latex gloves and wheeled over to her station one last time. She flipped through Lulu's chart. Then she scribbled. She held a small slip of paper.

"I'm prescribing low-dose Ortho Tri-Cyclen. Side effects should be mild. But call my office if you experience any intense versions of adverse side effects—nausea, tender breasts, headaches are pretty normal, but if they're unmanageable you call. If you have unexpected or serious mood swings—you call. You're going to need to take this at the same time every day. So set an alarm. You need to take it in the same two-hour window, or it's not as effective. The last seven pills are only reminders; they're basically sugar pills. And you're going to need to use a secondary form of birth control for the first month. If you get sick and take an antibiotic you might also need to use a secondary form of birth control. You should experience lighter periods. If you miss a pill, take it when you remember it, but remember to use a secondary form of birth control for the rest of the month. Do you understand?"

"Yes," said Lulu.

"Do you have any questions?" asked the doctor.

"No," said Lulu.

The doctor nodded. "Call the office if you think of any questions. Either I or one of my nurses can help you out. We can also talk about switching birth control if you don't like the way your body reacts to this one. All right?"

"All right," said Lulu.

The doctor handed her the small slip of paper—Lulu's prescription. "Take this to the front when you pay. Have a great day, Leila. See you next time."

"Bye," said Lulu lamely.

The doctor left her alone in her paper gown in the cold room. Lulu scrambled off the chair and got into her clothes. She took a deep exhale. She'd done it. She felt oddly vulnerable and oddly invincible.

She had one thing to take care of, before she talked to James. She had to go see about a boy.

27

Mess with the Bull, You Get Bit by a Shark

Lulu was waiting. She had a plan. She had her confederates—Emma had additionally pitched in by offering Diana's help. Lulu appreciated that. Both the offer and Diana's acceptance. And three, three was a good number of conspirators. Fewer, and Lulu would worry that the plot would be overly repetitive. Too much of a pattern. Lulu would have preferred four, even five of them. But she was still working on that part of the plan. So Lulu waited, as the slips were passed to the front office at an undisturbed pace. Enough to be believable, not so much as to arouse suspicion. She was not made for inaction, but if ever there was a time for it, it was now.

Exactly three weeks into her plan, Dane Anderson was called into the office during French class. He did not return. Lulu did her best to keep her features placid. It was a good sign. But no time to gloat. And no longer the time to turn back. The only way out of this mess was forward.

At lunch, the crowds still whispered, but Lulu had grown accustomed to ignoring it. Lo was still conspicuously absent from the dining hall, but Lulu had to ignore that as well. At least for now. Not that Lo would have sat with

Lulu. Not that Lulu had stopped texting the words *I'm sorry* to Lo. It was partly a plan of erosion and partly a hope that her ploy would draw Lo in like gravity. So far, nothing. But Lulu wasn't prepared to give up. She wasn't particularly good at waiting, but she was trying, and that was better than not trying at all.

Today, Lulu sat by Emma and Diana. Lulu was taking a large, luxurious bite of her slice of dining hall pizza when she saw Audrey startle into the room. Their eyes locked. Lulu swallowed her bite and put down her slice. Audrey squared her shoulders and, with a few false starts and a couple of run-ins with some unaware underclassmen, made her way over to their table.

Audrey reached out and touched Lulu's shoulder. Lulu froze. Their table went silent.

Audrey cleared her throat. "I'm sorry I didn't believe you. That was a shitty thing to do. I'm sorry. For all of it. Lots of things."

"It *was* shitty," said Lulu.

She and Audrey stared at each other for a long moment.

"Look," said Audrey. "I'm trying not drinking. I don't know if it will last. I don't know how I'm going to do it. I know I can't be this version of myself without y'all. Without you." Audrey's eyes went glassy.

"Don't you dare cry." Lulu was shouting. Maybe she was pulling the attention of everyone around her. She couldn't know. "Don't you dare."

Audrey sniffled. "I'm not crying!" But she was.

"I've nursed you when you're all vomity, and I've worried about your health, and I've kept you from getting in trouble with your mom. You don't get to cry!"

"I know!" said Audrey, who was audibly sobbing now. Several tables looked over. This was what Mrs. Bachmann would definitely call A Scene.

Lulu grabbed Audrey into a hug. "You're the worst, Audrey."

"I know." She had reached the point in her crying where she started to hiccup. "I'm so sorry."

"Let me finish!" said Lulu. "You're the worst. But so am I. Turns out I run away from all my problems."

Audrey slumped against Lulu. They collapsed against each other.

Audrey continued to cry. "I'm, so, so sorry," she said between sniffles.

"Shut up, Audrey. I accept," said Lulu, who sniffled herself. "But if you start drinking again I'm not keeping it a secret. I'm not your fucking caretaker anymore."

"All right," said Audrey, hiccupping again. "Sorry I called you a slut."

" 'S'okay," said Lulu. "I called Lo a slut and blamed her for Anderson attacking you. I better forgive you if I ever wanna be forgiven."

"Are we ever not going to be a mess?" asked Audrey.

"I have no idea," said Lulu. "But I hope so."

They sat there for a minute, with Audrey's head nestled into the crook of Lulu's shoulder. Then Lulu stuck out her pinkie and Audrey took it. They needed no words to swear. They simply twisted their thumbs and unhooked their little fingers, more benediction than promise.

"Besides," said Lulu, taking her seat again. She motioned for Audrey to do the same. "Dane Anderson is not your fault. He is not anyone's fault. But his own."

"Amen," said Diana with a fist pump into the air.

Audrey startled at the sight of the newcomer.

"I'm Diana. You used to call me Bangs." She lowered her voice into a conspiratorial whisper. "I'm Emma's girlfriend. But you can't tell anyone else that yet. Lulu's been sworn to secrecy and everything."

"Okay." Audrey rattled her head, briefly. "Nice to meet you, Diana."

"Fuck, you told her we called her Bangs?" asked Lulu.

Emma shrugged. Diana laughed at Lulu's embarrassment. Emma eyed Audrey. Audrey smiled overeagerly at Emma. And for them, for the moment, that was enough.

"Super sorry. What can I say? You've got spectacular bangs," Lulu tried. "I'm an asshole. Audrey's an asshole. We're all assholes. Don't let Emma fool you. She's an asshole, too."

At this Diana had a good laugh. "Same."

"Then you'll fit right in," said Lulu. "I am sorry, you know."

"We're all sorry right now," said Audrey. "Really sorry."

"You do know it's a problem, right? Calling the bisexual girl 'Bangs'?" said Diana, with an expression that indicated she had every idea how leading the question was.

"Fuck," said Lulu.

"Pass me your extra cornbread muffin?" said Diana.

Lulu passed her muffin over. "I take full responsibility for my idiocy. And I am sorry. Won't happen again."

Audrey, who was on the verge of tears again, said, "Same."

Diana pinched Audrey's arm. "No crying. You're all forgiven. Except I kind of like that you owe me one now. Feels appropriate."

Emma groaned.

Lulu snarfed into her carton of chocolate milk. She turned to Emma. "Were we this bad when we were her age?"

"Lo was," answered Emma. "You weren't till sophomore year."

"Why does everyone keep saying that?" asked Lulu, miffed that her freshman year was clearly overshadowed by her sophomore one. She knew why. But it was less of a sore spot, somehow. More of a fact. Like a bad haircut rather than a terror on her memory.

"Because it's true," said Emma and Audrey, in unison.

"You're awful chipper, all things considered," said Emma.

"I know." Lulu looked over to the empty chair where Lo should have been. It was a pity to share this news without her. To share any of this without her. "I think. That the plan is working."

"What plan?" asked Audrey on the last of her sniffles. She was dabbing her eyes with a thin, papery napkin.

Lulu looked at Emma. "Do you have it? The last one?"

Emma nodded.

"Have what?" asked Audrey, her exasperation overcoming her guilt.

Emma dug into her bag. She got out a signed detention hall slip, and handed it over to Lulu.

Lulu glanced around; nobody was paying them any attention anymore. "I think the final nail in the coffin belongs to you as much as it does to anyone. I think it belongs especially to you, honestly. Turn this in to the office today."

Audrey, her face scrunched up into a question, took the slip. She paused as she read it for a moment, then gasped. She said, quiet as she could, "This is for Dane Anderson."

"I know," said Lulu.

"How many of these did you do?" Audrey spoke in hushed reverence.

"Enough," said Lulu.

Audrey looked around the table. Lulu's eyes lit up. Diana smirked. And Emma, she kept right on eating her lunch, her face betraying nothing. Except the slight uptick at the corner of her mouth.

Audrey stuffed the slip into her own bag. "I'll do it today."

"Good," said Lulu. And that was that.

"I heard Scumbag Luke's having a party next weekend," said Audrey. "What do you think?"

"I'm game," said Diana.

"I can't; I have to go to a wedding," said Lulu.

Three heads swiveled to Lulu.

"You have a wedding?"

"Yeah, this weekend." Lulu shrugged. There was no way she was missing Tanya's wedding and living to tell the tale.

"No," said Audrey, rolling her eyes. "Not *this* weekend. The *next* weekend."

Lulu sighed. "All right, all right. I'll go. As long as it's not that Friday. I've got plans for Friday." She didn't, but she was planning on having plans. She didn't need to reveal that all quite yet.

"What kind of plans?" asked Diana.

"The kind you'll hear about from Emma after I've seen them through," said Lulu, giving Diana a light boop on the nose.

Diana wrinkled her expression at that. Emma laughed. Audrey smiled, half wonder, half relief.

"Saturday's your birthday," said Emma.

"Yeah, so?" said Lulu.

"So. Are your plans *midnight* plans?" Emma asked with far more coyness than Lulu knew her friend could muster.

"You know," said Lulu. "They might be."

But rather than feeling like laughing, she wanted to cry a little bit. The exchange was incomplete, unbalanced. This friendship was a four-headed beast, not a two-headed one or a three-headed one.

Lulu would have to figure out how to crack Dolores Campo.

———

Headed to French class the next day, Lulu was walking up the narrow stairwell in the back of the building when she heard a loud thunk from behind her. She nearly tripped, the noise startled her so. She looked down and behind her to discover Dane standing below, looking impish. A book rested on the step behind her. Dane must have thrown the book at her, missing her hips by mere inches.

"What the flying fuck was that for?" Lulu raised her shoulders, a cat with her back in a corner.

"I don't know." He took a step closer. "Why are you ignoring me?"

"You really have to ask that?" Lulu picked up the book. She took another step up the stairs. "No, seriously, stay back."

At the challenge, Dane lunged across her, clearly not aiming in the least for the book. He caught her waist in his other hand. His words were barely audible. "Make me."

Lulu could smell the Old Spice he used at some point in the morning. That scent was now ruined for her forever. She wiggled backward to little avail. She could taste his breath, not sweetened with peppermint or laced with alcohol. Just his smell invading her space, until there was a cloud of him surrounding her. Lulu shoved the book up against Dane's chest, pushing him back two feet.

The dazed focus in Dane's eyes broke. "You're such a fucking bitch."

Lulu took a deep breath. She stepped forward. "Did you know that the penalty for more than two unserved detentions is a Saturday work hall?"

"The fuck does that have to do with anything?"

Lulu continued to hold him at bay with the book. "You see, two or more unserved detentions is a Saturday work hall. And Saturday work halls are serious."

"Don't be cute with me." Dane pushed his body forward; Lulu stepped back, out of reach. She kept the book in her hand.

"Of course you knew that. Or at least, you probably learned that when you were yanked out of class last week. But did you know that if you've accrued enough detentions in a short-enough period, you've basically earned a suspension by proxy." Lulu tutted.

Dane's face hardened. With rage. With awareness. With a kind of violence Lulu would have feared before.

But she had an ace up her sleeve and she meant to use it. "And suspensions right before graduation never look good, do they, Anderson?"

Horror flooded Dane's eyes in earnest. He was piecing the puzzle together—a chat last week with the dean, his strange attendance record, his extra five detention halls in four weeks.

"I see you get my meaning," said Lulu, a smile playing at her lips. It wouldn't do to gloat. But she couldn't bite her joy back, not all the way. "You've got two months to graduate. And I'll bet your attendance record is already keeping you barely above the line."

"What exactly are you getting at, Saad?"

"You need me to spell it out for you?" Lulu paused. "I'm getting at the fact that if you don't leave me alone, if you don't leave my friends alone, you'll find that diploma hard to access come May. I'm hanging on to a last slip. I'll get it to you and not the office if you behave. If you don't, well."

Lulu handed Dane his book. Her eyes were glinting daggers, her smirk was razor sharp. He didn't reach out for the textbook. Lulu dropped it with a loud thump on the floor. Dane jolted slightly. Lulu turned, whipping her hair around as she walked away.

"Wait," Dane called.

Lulu stopped.

"Are you fucking with me?" His shock was palatable.

She wished Lo had been here to see the look on his face.

"No, I'm not." Lulu laughed with an indescribable lightness to her tone. "You better take me seriously. Get your shit together, Anderson. I'm going to class. You probably should go as well." Lulu walked out of the stairwell and into the upper hallway.

Freedom comes in many forms. Sometimes it's the emancipation of adulthood. Sometimes freedom is a car—transportation that all you have to do is load up with fuel and go. Money often offers freedom;

education, too. Lulu had the latter in spades. Today freedom was a well-delivered threat. It was unchecked, silent power—pure and simple. Lulu reveled in this kind. The air tasted cleaner. Her limbs swung more loosely from her sides. Her hair blew more lightly through the breeze. It was all meaningful, symbolic. Lulu, grand conqueror of the known world. Why aim to be a queen when she could be an empress?

But Lulu thought better of that. She didn't want to conquer anyone who hadn't already tried to subjugate. She would not use her newfound power to take away anyone's freedom that hadn't taken a potshot at her own.

28

Tanya the Wife

Lulu would be loath to admit that she loved weddings, but she did. On her mother's side they were all doom and gloom—wifely obedience and manly fidelity. They were the kind of services that boiled her blood. And still she loved weddings. Wedding ceremonies on her father's side—and any Arab that lived within the county limits was considered to be on her father's side—were intimate. Lulu was rarely invited for the ceremony. Those were for grown-ups and witnesses and holy men. But the reception—that was where the life was.

When Tanya the Bride walked in with her groom, Ali, she'd transformed from your average Arab American young woman into a frothy meringue to behold. Lace and tulle and beading and anything that could add volume and glimmer under the lights of the hotel ballroom. Here, subtlety was not a forgotten or lost virtue—merely a worthless one.

Tanya the Bride—no, she was Tanya the Wife now—and Ali the Groom took their seats at the head table for two, giving their attention to those who came and waited attendance on them. They were grabbed for hugs and kisses.

Envelopes of money were aggressively stuffed into Ali's pockets by jolly men. Big-haired women grabbed the bride's hair, her chin, her cheeks, while they trilled and clapped. Joy and sexism, ritual and finance, love and family all tied up in these small gestures.

Lulu *loved* weddings.

She loved watching two families come together. Loved the rites of it all. She loved getting dressed up and putting on the flashiest dress she owned. She loved to dance well into the night, until it was morning again, until she knew she'd ache from the effort the next day. Tanya had even invited Lulu to her henna party. Lulu loved to watch as the bride got all the best designs, all the most intricate work across her hands and feet. But first, at this wedding, Lulu had to find Sheikh Fadi. She'd made a promise that she intended to keep.

"Hello, Sheikh," said Lulu.

Sheikh Fadi kissed her hand and reeled Lulu in for a hug. "Hello, habibti."

"Thank you," said Lulu, pulling back, "for all your help."

The sheihk shook his head. "La. It is my job to help. You don't thank. You do."

Lulu shook her head. "I couldn't have done it without your help. Thank you."

"La, la." Sheikh Fadi swept his hand forward a couple of times and quickly, indicating that it was nothing, that Lulu was practically dismissed. "The work is yours, habibti. Opportunities are easy to give, where I stand. Not always easy to take."

"Thank you, Sheikh." Lulu gave him a quick kiss on the cheek.

"La." The Sheikh shook his hand again. "Go, habibti. Dance."

And so Lulu took her place on the dance floor among the women, many of whom still shunned her. Tanya had been right—Auntie Salwa would likely never forget what Lulu had done. But not all would be so stringent.

The younger ones were more forgiving. Tamra was actually standing within a foot of Lulu. Dina twirled beside Lulu, even if Dina wouldn't make eye contact the entire time. Miriam didn't dance, but she'd stepped onto the gleaming white polished tiles just for Lulu's benefit. And that was a glimmer of hope for Lulu. She had sequestered herself to the outskirts of her people for years. Then she'd alienated herself with a few choice but terrible words. And even then she was less alone here than she'd believed. Less alone than she'd feared.

Browns swirls of henna climbed and crawled up Lulu's hands, past her wrists. She watched them flash in the light as she moved. But as beautiful as the designs were, Lulu didn't care about them. Caring was for when she was still, when she was no longer in motion. She loved this dance. The insane beat of the drums, the impossible pace of her hips shimmying back and forth. Here she never danced the Dance of the Seven Veils. Here, she danced until she was exhausted. She danced until she couldn't feel her feet anymore. Then she danced some more. She took her turn with Tanya the Wife, and she was not shut out of the dancing circle. She was granted the same rights as anyone else. And at long last, Auntie Salwa turned and faced Lulu. She gave Lulu a curt nod, then turned away again. *There.* That was enough.

Lulu left the dance floor. Breathless, she plopped onto the seat beside Reza.

"You looked like you were having fun out there," said Reza, who along with Ben had flown back into town for the wedding. Smoothing more of Lulu's ruffled feathers. Everyone in her family was doing some degree of penance for her.

Lulu wiped sweat from her forehead. She grabbed the napkin she'd left at the table and dabbed at her upper lip. "Such fun."

"You always loved to dance at these things. I've always had two left feet," said Reza.

"I guess some things stay the same," Lulu said.

"I guess so," he said.

"Where's Ben?" Lulu asked.

"The buffet, I think," said Reza.

"Is Mom still off doing damage control?"

"Come on, Lulu," said Rez. "Don't be so hard on yourself."

"That's choice coming from you," said Lulu.

"Was I that bad about it?" said Reza.

Lulu raised an eyebrow. "Worse. You've basically shunned me since November."

"Shit."

Lulu tutted. "Now, Rez, you should know better than to use such language in front of me."

"Come on, Lulu. Cut me some slack. You're my baby sister. And I'm not perfect. You don't have to treat me like I'm perfect. I get enough of that from Ben." Reza gave his words force.

"Sorry," said Lulu.

"For what?" asked Reza.

"Thinking you thought the worst of me," said Lulu.

"Pardon granted," he said. "And I'm sorry, too. I freeze when I don't know what to do."

Lulu laughed. "Better than me. I run away."

"Is it that bad?" Somehow Rez knew. Maybe because Rez always knew. He was more intuition than logic, though he'd never admit that to anyone. Not even to Lulu. Especially not Lulu.

"Right now? No. I've survived worse. This is a definite improvement from like three weeks ago. On most fronts."

"Most?"

"I had a plan," Lulu admitted. "It hasn't worked all the way."

"A man, a plan, a canal—" started Reza.

And they shouted in unison, "PANAMA!"

Lulu laughed; Reza laughed.

"How embarrassing," she said once she'd caught her breath.

"Whoa. You're the embarrassing one. You're the one Mama and Baba will be apologizing for, for like the next three years."

"That's a *very* conservative estimate. These are a people who still haven't gotten over the first sacking of Baghdad," she said. "In 1258."

"You haven't destroyed the hub of culture and literature and leveled a city. Nor did you raid the museum of antiquities. You might fare better than the Mongols did." Reza shrugged. "No promises, though."

Lulu punched Reza's arm lightly. "Reza. Sometimes you are infinitely worse than Ben."

"I've always been worse than Ben. But nobody ever seems to notice."

"I have. You're on notice," she said.

"Lulu. Go back to dancing. Leave your big brother alone."

"I'll go back to dancing, but like hell am I leaving you alone. It's the dabke. You're not off the hook for this. No one is. Even Bibi Hookum dances the dabke."

Lulu grabbed Reza's hand and dragged him into the circle on the dance floor, where it was impossible that he would miss a step. They danced a circle, hands held. *Cross, step, cross, step.* They danced for life and love. They danced, sweaty palm clasped to sweaty palm, because that was what their forebearers had done and it was what they had been told they must. They danced the dabke and Reza only tripped once. They danced the dabke and Lulu laughed, smiling not only at Tanya the Wife but also at Dina the Just and Tamra the Unforgiving and Miriam the Wild. They all danced the dabke, and as the circle turned, their hearts were lightened.

———

Ancient Astronaut Theory is the belief that intelligent extraterrestrial beings have visited Earth and made contact with humans in ancient times—antiquity, prehistory, whatever. Proponents suggest that this contact influenced the development of humanity. The intelligent extraterrestrials became deities in most, if not all, early world religions as such visitors' advanced technologies were interpreted by early humans as pure divinity. In reality, it's a bunch of pseudoscientists with purchased degrees who believe aliens built the pyramids. Ancient Astronaut Theory is the honest culmination of truthiness, scientific interest with no method, and racism. And it once had its own dedicated time slot on the History Channel.

The men of the Saad family loved this show unequivocally.

None of them—not Ben, not Reza, and certainly not Ahmed—were built for more than six hours of sleep in a night. This gene had definitely skipped Lulu. Reza and Ben and Ahmed would invariable find one another, late at night or early in the morning, watching streamed reruns of *Ancient Aliens*. It beat going to the gym at four o'clock in the morning. It was a ritual. Not a sacrosanct one, but one born of habit—the kind that means more than one that has been sanctified by dogma.

"Rez! Rez! It's the guy with the hair," said Ben.

"Dude, I see him," said Rez.

"But he's your favorite! I didn't want you to miss it," said Ben.

"Yes, I like this one. What kind of hashish do you think he smokes?" added their father.

"The good stuff," said Ben.

"Excuse me?" asked their father, mostly paying attention to the theory that aliens populated the planet with ants. He chuckled.

"Nothing, Baba. This guy is funny," said Ben.

"I mean, so funny," said his father.

"What are you guys—" said Lulu, walking into the room. She was keyed up from the wedding. Her body was exhausted, but her brain was alert. "Oh no."

"Oh yes," said Ben.

Lulu flumped onto the couch.

"Can't sleep also?" asked her father.

"Basically." Lulu wiggled, trying to find a comfortable position.

"This show, Lulu. It is funny," said her baba.

"THIS DUDE WITH THE HAIR THINKS THAT THE EGYPTIANS WROTE ABOUT A MYSTICAL ANT WATER CEREMONY. THEREFORE ALIENS." This from Ben.

Reza, by this point, was beside himself. He was crying he was laughing so hard. Their father shook with silent mirth. Lulu sighed.

"Little sister," said Ben. "This man believes that ancient astronauts taught human beings about the construction of buildings specifically for the purpose of human habitation. He believes he has scientifically proved the existence of aliens from the existence of ants. And ancient mythology."

"We *are* kinda descended from bugs," said Reza.

"Different branch of evolution," said their baba, stressing the first syllable so it sounded like evil-lution. The pun was entirely unintentional, and Lulu had to hold in the laugh. She'd explain it to him later.

The program went on and the fellowship of three laughed again. Lulu snorted.

"Little sister, lighten up," said Ben. "It's hilarious."

"You three have the worst taste." Lulu tried to lean back onto the couch, but there was too much room behind her neck.

"Says the Saad sibling who watches *Murder, She Wrote* with Mom," said Ben.

"That is a good show!"

"I'm glad you couldn't sleep." Reza didn't look away from the television, but he threw her a cushion to set behind her back. He was paying attention, even if it didn't always seem it. He was learning to reconcile his idea of Lulu with the reality of her. It was a dance they would have to do many times over in this life. "Now you'll understand the joy of Ancient Astronaut Theory."

"Agreed," said Ben.

"Yes," said their father, though he was only half paying attention. "Love you."

"I love you three, too," said Lulu. "Even if you're all idiots," she added, under her breath.

But Reza was smiling. He turned and gave her a wink, before the show grabbed his attention—and laughter—again.

29

Seventeen Candles

"Do you want to have some friends over?" asked Lulu's mother, rifling through papers at her desk as she spoke. "I know your birthday's not technically until tomorrow. But it'll be your day at midnight."

"No," said Lulu.

"Are you sure?" asked her mother, looking up from her work. "You always have a sleepover on your birthday."

"Yeah," said Lulu. "I wanna do something different this year."

Her mother frowned, her eyes narrowing. "How different?"

Lulu raised her eyebrows. "I promise you don't want the answer. But nothing illegal."

"You," said her mother. She pushed up her reading glasses. "Are your father's daughter through and through. I have no idea what to do with you sometimes."

"Love me?" said Lulu.

Aimee sighed. Then a ping sounded on her laptop and she began typing. Lulu knew their conversation was over for now. Work Aimee had taken over.

301

Mom Aimee wouldn't be back for a couple of hours. Lulu trotted up the stairs.

hi sent Lulu to James.

Hello was his immediate reply

wanna hang

Sure. What do you wanna do? responded James.

pick me up in an hour?

sure thing

The orange Datsun rumbled down the street. Lulu leaped off her bed and rushed down the stairs. She gave her mom a kiss on the forehead. Work Aimee was still in. Lulu counted her blessings.

"Headed out, Mom! I'll let you know where I'll be."

Aimee pulled down her reading glasses for a moment, but she forgot to look up. "Where are you going again?"

"Dinner, remember?" said Lulu. "With James."

Work Aimee looked up over her reading glasses for a moment. Then a ping sounded on her computer. "All right, text me."

"You're the best!" said Lulu, and her mother waved her off.

Lulu swung the door open as she saw James reaching for the bell. He looked startled, but not unpleasantly so. He had on his usual jeans and a T-shirt. His hair was damp, still fresh from the shower. He had a small nick on his cheekbone from shaving. He looked like heaven.

"Hi," said Lulu.

"Hi, yourself," said James.

"You hungry?" asked Lulu.

"Starved."

"Excellent." Lulu grabbed James's hand and led him to his own car.

He trailed behind her, laughing. "Do you want my keys, too?"

"Can I?" asked Lulu, light in her eyes.

"You're joking, right?"

"It's almost my birthday." Lulu made her most pleading face.

James laughed at it. "When's your birthday?"

"Tomorrow."

"Tomorrow's only a few hours away." James folded his arms. "You can wait."

But Lulu couldn't. "Please," she began. "Please, please, please, please, please." She hadn't thought she'd wanted to drive his car until this moment, until she'd been nearly given the opportunity, then denied. Now she needed it. She was all raw energy and nerves.

"You're not going to give up, are you?"

"Never," said Lulu. "Never say die."

Lulu had a pang in her chest at her own words, but she put it away for later.

James tossed her the keys. Lulu caught them with her left hand. Glee lit her face. She leaned toward him and gave him a kiss on the cheek. Lulu hopped into the driver's seat. She started the engine and put the car into gear. It jerked forward. James grabbed the dash. Lulu grinned.

"Nervous?" she asked.

"Unbelievably," he said. "I can't believe I'm letting you do this."

"You must really like me," said Lulu.

"Yes. I do. That and you're incredibly convincing. How do you do that?"

Lulu shrugged. "I can't reveal all my secrets, James. I'm not a Bond villain."

"Fair enough," said James, bracing himself.

Lulu made a turn. "Holy shit."

"Yeah."

"Power steering makes a difference," said Lulu.

"Look, you're already learning," said James.

"I would have serious guns if I drove this all the time."

"Not necessarily. I drive it all the time, and I've got pretty skinny arms," said James.

"But they're muscular," said Lulu.

James blushed. "Um. Right."

Lulu laughed. She drove them to dinner. They talked as they ate, not realizing as time slipped by. They closed down the small neighborhood taqueria. Lulu tossed James his keys back. He put the keys in the ignition. He looked at the analog clock on his dash.

"It's nearly an hour to your birthday. Do I need to get you home?" he asked.

Lulu tilted her head thoughtfully. She had an impish smile tugging at the corner of her mouth. She grabbed him for a kiss. He accepted it gladly. They broke apart, taking in gulps of air.

"Or," said Lulu. She swallowed as a pause. She looked James in the eye. He seemed to understand her expression because he gulped right back at her. "Alternate idea. Do you want to have sex with me?"

James stared. He just stared. Lulu stared back at him, a wild panic running through her chest.

"You're sure?" he asked. "About everything?"

And Lulu knew he wasn't talking about sex. He was talking about relationships, and trust, and playing the field, and Lulu finally having enough space in her mind to process this.

"No," she said. "But I'm tired of being afraid. I'm willing to try."

"I wouldn't hurt you," said James. He still wasn't talking about sex. How Lulu knew, she couldn't say.

"You don't know that. And neither do I. I'm okay with that. I wouldn't do anything different." Lulu waited, wondering if he'd say yes. Wondering if her answers were satisfactory. At least, they were true.

"Me neither," he said. "But I'll try not to hurt you."

"Likewise," said Lulu.

"Okay," he said.

And Lulu knew it wasn't an okay as a filler, as a transitional statement. It was an answer. She could feel her heart beating in her throat.

"I gotta. I need to. To get a thing," he said.

Lulu nodded. Words were not enough. They were too much. They had fled the premises of her mind entirely. James drove. Lulu rode shotgun. He parked outside a drugstore. As he ran in, Lulu made a phone call. The phone rang twice, then she heard it click on.

"Mom?" said Lulu.

"Lulu, honey, are you on your way home?" asked her mother. Mom Aimee was back.

"No, Mom…I'm still with James," Lulu said. The words felt foreign on her lips.

"Honey, is everything all right? Do you need me to come get you?" said her mother, an increased tone of alarm in her voice.

"No, Mom. Everything is fine. I'm fine. I'm safe. I'm going to be home a little after curfew. Trust me, okay?" There was what was felt to be an interminable silence on the other end of the phone. Lulu's heart sank.

Finally, her mother said, "Okay."

"You don't need to wait up," Lulu offered.

"Darlin', if you think for a moment I won't wait up for you, then you've lost your damned mind." She inhaled. "But, come home soon."

"I will, don't worry."

"Like hell I won't."

"Love you, Mom."

"Love you, too, little cat. Please be safe."

Lulu hung up. A few minutes later, James got back into the car, clutching the plastic pharmacy bag like worry beads. He looked straight ahead.

"Want me to drive?" Lulu asked.

"Probably," he said.

Lulu scrambled across the seats, crawling over him until she sat in the driver's seat and he sat in the tiny middle area of the transmission. Lulu put the car into gear. James put his hand over hers. Lulu looked over. He was smiling. Lulu grinned back.

"My house," he said.

———

"Where's your mom?" Lulu asked as she parked.

"Midnight movie. They're showing *Pretty in Pink*." James jostled with his keys. His hands shook slightly as he tried to fit the key into the door's lock.

"Where's your sister?"

"Slumber party. Thank God." He finally got the key in.

Lulu heard the dead bolt release. The house was quiet, the only light inside coming from a switch left on in the kitchen. The house creaked with their movements, but quietly, as though it wanted to keep their secret as much as they did. They walked up the stairs, stopping at the top. James came within a hair's breadth of her; he reached out one hand toward her hip and another toward her neck, but he didn't touch her. Lulu could still feel the heat from his hands regardless.

"James?"

He wouldn't break eye contact. "Yes?"

A match had lit inside her, and now her whole body was going up in flames. From a flicker to a blazing forest fire. She had to remember how breathing worked. Inhale through her nose, exhale through her mouth. The tips of her fingers tingled. James's eyelashes were so long, so dark. She watched them flutter. Lulu's breath hitched. She'd always thought the moment before kissing someone, the moment where she wondered *if* they would kiss her, was the most exciting point. That had been the thrill. The game, the flirtation. It was nothing to this, this endless *when*. He wanted to kiss her. She wanted to kiss him. It wasn't if. It was when. It was how. Did he want the same kind of kiss she did—the same exploding need? Or would he be more patient than she could be right now? She wanted to run her hands through his hair and dig her nails into his back. She knew what she wanted before she was going to have it. It was exhilarating.

Still, he waited.

"Please," she said.

And they were entangled. Pressed and wrapped around each other. His lips played at hers and her fingers yanked in his belt loops, pulling him closer, still not close enough. James pulled Lulu through the doorway of his bedroom. She gasped for breath, pulling his shirt off. He played with the edge of hers, and she threw up her arms without hesitation. He obligingly removed her shirt, a smile playing at the edges of his lips. His mouth trailed down her neck. And then he whispered an act Lulu had, until this moment, experienced only mild curiosity for. She let out a shaky breath.

"God yes," she said, collapsing backward onto the bed. Then the rest of her clothes were on the floor. Kisses trailed down her neck, down her stomach, lower and lower. His mouth reached their intention. Lulu felt higher, and higher. Her toes curled at the sensation of his tongue on her. She whimpered and laughed. She moaned and she cried out. And then she floated back down to earth. Lulu hummed and reached out for James. She tugged at one of his belt loops. She dipped a finger beneath the band of his jeans. He went for his belt, a clanging noise rung through the room as his pants hit the floor. Lulu sighed. James covered it with a kiss. He moved away from the bed for a moment. He reached into the pharmacy bag that had miraculously made it up to the room. He fumbled with the condom. Lulu giggled.

"Not helping," he said.

"Did you want help?" she asked.

"I've got it." He fumbled for a few more moments before getting it secured.

"Are you sure?" he asked.

"Yes," she said. "Are you?"

"Yes," he said.

And then there was only skin on skin. Lulu touched him wherever she liked, feeling more exposed by this than by her nakedness. They were a jumble of limbs, his trembling lightly and hers filled with sensations that were unexpected and consuming. She nearly laughed at that. Instead she kissed him. There was no pain, only this wordless promise between them.

———

Later, Lulu lounged across the bed. James stared over at her. He'd curled into his boxers as quickly as he could. She, however, did not share in his modesty. Lulu was enjoying the feeling of his sheets up against her bare skin. It was a small, personal pleasure. Besides, she found his continued embarrassment harmlessly hilarious. He didn't know where to look.

"I like you," said Lulu, breaking the tension in the room.

James laughed. "I like you, too."

"How'd you do that? Go from Biggest Jerk Alive to the person I'm lying in bed naked with."

James blushed through to his ears. "I don't know."

"Don't you?"

"If I'd known how, I would have done it a lot sooner, trust me. I can't believe some of the idiotic things I said to you. I think I'll regret it forever."

"Don't. I like that you're capable of being an idiot. It makes me feel better that you can be so human. Maybe because your hair is so pretty. Or is it your eyes. I'm newly obsessed with your eyelashes." Lulu reached out and lightly dusted her fingers across his lashes.

James closed his eyes, allowed her the familiarity. Lulu kissed James again. It was a lingering see-you-later, not a good-bye. It was a kiss that was unable to stay the night. She crawled out of bed and slid her pants on.

"Hey, do you … do you wanna grab some breakfast?" she asked.

"Now?" James asked, popping up from his prostrate position.

"No, I mean, tomorrow morning. There's a special place in my stomach for potatoes and eggs."

"I'll keep that in mind. And I'd like that. Breakfast, I mean." He looked across the room at his clock. "You know. It is tomorrow morning. Happy birthday, Lulu."

James got out of bed and silently wished her a happy birthday. Lulu was smiling by the end of it. Then the sound of a door thumped below them.

"Shit," they said at the same time. It was definitely his mother.

"Window?" asked Lulu.

James opened his bedroom window. There was a small sloping porch roof that Lulu could lower herself down from. Thank God for Southern porches. Lulu crawled through the window onto the small roof.

"I can't believe I'm letting you do this," he said.

He would make a spectacular Juliet, leaning out his window like that. All he lacked was a balcony. She tugged his shirt for another kiss; it was soft and slow and melting.

"I'll be all right. I'm like a cat."

"Cats climb higher than they're able to get down from and get stuck in trees."

"There was a time before firemen, and cats had to get down from those heights all on their own. I'll manage." She winked.

Lulu grabbed hold of the edge of the roofing, then swung down. Her feet dangled, maybe three feet off the ground. She took a leap of faith and dropped down, landing relatively unscathed in a crouch. She walked out so she could see James, still in his window.

"Made it!" she said at a loud whisper. Then she dangled his keys in her fingers, waving them at him. "I'm borrowing your car. Again."

James shook his head. "See you in the morning, Lulu."

"See you," said Lulu, grinning.

Lulu arrived home to the dark of her house. She found her mother, dozed off on the couch while *Murder, She Wrote* hummed along in the background. Lulu crouched down low next to her mother's still form.

"Mama," Lulu whispered.

Her mother made a sound between a hum and a groan, a noise only those recently awoken are able to make sincerely.

"Mama, I'm home. I'm all right. You should go to bed now."

Her only verbal reply was to hum again, though she twisted herself back into an upright position. She mussed her hands through her sleep-induced hair. She reached out and lovingly grabbed Lulu by the chin and smiled.

"Mama, I'm going upstairs now," said Lulu.

Her mother looked over at the clock on the cable box. She nodded, following Lulu up the stairs. Lulu kissed her mother good night and went into her room.

Lulu's brain was full, full and tangled and complicated. She went through the motions of getting herself ready for bed, but she hardly started to brush her teeth when she went in search of her sweat pants. She went on like this, distractedly trying to ready herself for bed for a quarter of an hour. After finally getting her contacts out, she crawled into bed and fell asleep.

30
Bulletproof

Lulu should not have been disappointed. But deep within her, she had believed that if she'd pulled off the right plan, she would magically solve all the problems in her life in one fell swoop. She'd had her revenge, or, at least, delivered a great comeuppance. She had enlisted Emma's help, and gained a new friend in Diana in the bargain. And when Audrey had apologized at lunch, Lulu knew the plan was working, would work. Knew it was gaining mass and pulling the right people into its gravity. But Lo had not been drawn in. She hadn't shown even a flicker of interest in Lulu. Or any of them. She'd been disappearing at lunch since the start of semester, likely finding a way off campus during the hour and meeting up with Scumbag Luke.

It made Lulu feel as though her plan was ultimately a failure. She knew she shouldn't look at it like that. But she'd made her revenge so craftily, so carefully, that she believed it must have attracted Lo's attention.

Luckily, Lulu knew where to find Lo tonight, because Scumbag Luke was throwing a party.

Lulu and Audrey flanked around Emma and Diana. They were a united front—a protective guard against the world—and they would not break. Not this time. The atrium narrowed, and the girls had to walk single file to pass through. As Lulu walked by Michael Rossi, he muttered rudely under his breath, loud enough that Lulu could hear him, but quietly enough so that she knew he meant to be talking to the boy beside him.

"What?" Lulu shouted, surprised by the force of her own voice. It was wild and powerful, not like a jungle cat or a bird of prey, ready to pounce, more like the Grand Canyon, steady and wondrous to behold. "What was that, Michael?"

Michael was taken aback. He opened his mouth to speak, but no words came out.

"That's what I thought." Lulu turned then, as he stood gobsmacked in her wake.

"Holy shit, that was amazing," said Diana. "You've gotta teach me that trick one day."

"I learned it from Lo," said Lulu.

"Come on. Let's grab drinks," said Diana with a nod.

Diana's easy confidence made Lulu grin. Once in the kitchen, Lulu saw Nina Holmes, who clapped and handed Lulu a drink.

"Lulu! Drink! I missed you!" Nina must have been totally obliterated to be grabbing Lulu for a hug.

The drink was reminiscent of a lemon push pop. Lulu gulped her first two sips, then scrunched her face with the overtly sweet taste of the drink. Nina swatted at Lulu playfully. Lulu set the drink down inconspicuously on the corner. She needed the most of her faculties on this evening, birthday or no.

"You guys adopted a freshman?" asked Nina.

Lulu looked to Emma for an answer.

Emma took a deep breath. "No. She's my girlfriend."

Diana beamed and grabbed Emma's hand.

"Aren't they adorable?" said Audrey with a head tilt. Audrey was so proper she could make anything seem all right.

"Holy cow!" Nina took another swig of her drink.

"I know, right?" said Lulu. "Isn't it great?"

"It's amazing!" said Nina. She got out her phone, ready to demonstrate her ability to group message and talk simultaneously. The news would be across the party in ten minutes flat.

Emma reached out with her free hand and squeezed Lulu's for a moment before releasing it.

Audrey looked at Emma, at Diana, at Lulu. "What now?"

It should be noted that while Emma was making her declarations to Nina, the kitchen where they stood was not devoid of other human life. And while each girl might have had her own answer for *What now?* none of them were allowed to answer it. Because just as Nina Holmes was about to relay her fresh information to at least a dozen of her closest contacts, Scumbag Luke crossed the kitchen in less than three steps. Lo stood behind him, wary and unsure.

Having both seen and heard the scene with the inebriated Nina, Scumbag Luke did exactly what anyone would expect of such a boy. He slurred a slur in Emma's direction, though Diana, Lulu, Audrey, and even Nina were graciously included in his fear and his hate.

And while the kitchen was noisy, as soon as the words were out, the din quieted to nothing. Emma stared wide-eyed. Diana's face grew grim. Audrey swallowed her nerves. Nina and Lulu looked on in horror, as though they knew such a thing were possible but somehow still had not expected it.

But Lo, she had the good sense to yank her hand out from Scumbag Luke's. "What did you say?"

"You heard me," said Luke, who, unlike Michael, was clearly unwilling to back down.

Lo looked at him plainly. She made a quick, curt nod. And without any other warning, without any wind-up, she socked him straight in the nose.

"The fuck?" Scumbag Luke grabbed his nose, now streaming blood. There were involuntary tears in his eyes.

"Don't you ever, ever use that word again. We're done. Now apologize." Lo flexed her hand, resisting the urge to shake it out after her punch.

"What?" Scumbag Luke was more stunned than anything.

"You *heard me*. Apologize."

"I'm sorry," said Scumbag Luke, his voice warbled and nasal from the flow of his own blood.

"Not to me." Lo pointed to Emma. "To her. Apologize to both of them. Now."

"I'm sorry." Blood had dripped onto Scumbag Luke's pristine white polo shirt.

"Don't you dare use that word again. And if I ever even hear of you saying it, I'm calling your girlfriend."

"How?" he choked out.

"I stole her number off your phone. For emergencies. Don't fuck with me on this, Luke." Lo flipped her hair magnificently, triumphantly, grabbed a set of keys, and stalked out the kitchen, through the atrium, and, as everyone heard from the slamming of the front door, out of the house. For a moment everyone was too stunned to respond. Then the room erupted with chatter.

This was a night to remember.

31

The Sisterhood of the Uniform Pants

Emma looked around her, her startled state evident. "Did . . . did Lo just fight for my honor?"

"Uh. Yeah," said Lulu, equally flabbergast. "I think she did. To be honest, though, who hasn't wanted to punch Scumbag Luke in the face?"

Nobody had an argument to that.

"What a night," said Audrey to nobody in particular. She grabbed the drink that was in Nina Holmes's hand. But she caught Lulu's eye, and she poured the drink into an unsuspecting lady palm that was sitting in a large piece of decorative pottery.

Nina Holmes was still too stunned to relay her gossip at all. Everything that passed in the kitchen was already around the party in ten minutes flat, though.

"I'm going to go after her," said Lulu.

"Me too," said Audrey.

"Me, three," said Emma.

"I'll stay. In case she doubles back," said Diana, understanding that what needed to happen belonged to the other four girls alone. Emma leaned into Diana for a kiss. Realizing she was two seconds away from rudely staring, Lulu turned to give them privacy. Emma only had that kind of focus when balancing chemistry equations and shuttering photos from behind her camera.

The three girls went outside. And there, sitting on the stoop of the porch sat Lo, crying. Audrey, Lulu, and Emma stopped in their tracks.

Lo looked up. She wiped her nose across her sleeve. "Come to gloat, have you?"

"No," said Lulu, in motion again.

"Come to say you were right? Look at Scumbag Luke, a scumbag like you said all along?"

Lulu laid her hand on Lo's forearm. "No. We wouldn't say that. Especially me. Not anymore."

"Don't touch me," said Lo, yanking out of Lulu's grasp. "Nobody touch me."

But Lo didn't wait around for anyone to try. She got up, wiping her face against her other sleeve, and ran to a big black pickup truck across the street. She unlocked it and got in, speeding away into the night.

Dolores Campo had cracked.

Lulu's eyes went wide. She turned to Emma. God knows why Lulu turned to her, because she'd arrived at the party the same time as herself, but she asked anyway, "Has she been drinking?"

"No." Emma shook her head, at a loss for other words.

Lulu exhaled her relief.

After a long, long silence, Audrey coughed. "That's not Lo's car."

Emma and Lulu stared at Audrey. Then they pivoted and stared at the curb where the truck had been. And Lo didn't drive a truck.

"Does that mean," said Lulu. "Was that—"

"—Luke's truck," said Audrey and Emma in a deadpan.

"So. Somewhere out there." Lulu waved to the expanse of the neighborhood. "Is a crying Latina girl in the borrowed property of her white ex-not-quite-boyfriend."

Audrey and Emma stared, wide-eyed and terrified. Dolores Campo being pulled over in the car of a Luke Westin would not go over well, even under the best of circumstances.

"If Luke finds out." Lulu shook her head.

"He can't find out!" said Audrey.

"If he does. There'll be hell to pay."

"You think he'd report it as stolen?" breathed Emma.

Lulu nodded. And then she prayed to God, the prophet, and the other four saints whose names she blessedly managed to remember. Because they had to find Lo before Scumbag Luke realized his car was missing.

Emma put her fingers to her temples. "We need to figure out where she went."

"She's not picking up her calls," said Audrey, who had already gotten her phone out.

"Get in my car," said Lulu. "We'll drive around and find her. She can't have gone far."

———

But Lo was nowhere to be found. Not three blocks up, not four blocks over. And while a pickup truck might be conspicuous elsewhere, in Texas you couldn't throw a rock without hitting one. Lulu grew frenetic, turning, turning, turning around corners, ducking into strange alleyways, driving past the same houses at least half a dozen times.

"She's not here." Audrey, trying to break Lulu out of the searching haze, touched Lulu's arm. "She's gone."

"I'm trying again. I'm calling." Lulu pulled over. She got out her phone and dialed Lo one last time. Her Hail Mary. Her ninety-nine names of God. The phone rang three times. Four. Five, six, seven. Half of ring number eight started when the phone clicked over. Lulu thought the answering machine had picked up. But the only sound was static air.

"Lo?" said Lulu. "Lo, are you there?"

A quiet "Yes" followed.

"Ohthankgod." Relief washed through Lulu.

Emma and Audrey looked at her, bright-eyed, hopeful.

Lulu nodded and held up her hand. "Where are you?"

"I'm at Sam Houston," said Lo.

"The statue of Sam Houston?" Lulu couldn't believe it. "Lo. That's in Huntsville."

"I know," said Lo.

"How did you get to Huntsville?"

"I got on the freeway and I didn't stop," said Lo as though it were the simplest thing in the world.

Lulu didn't know what to say for a moment. "Can you even pull over at the statue of Sam Houston?"

"I dunno," said Lo. "I just did."

"Will you stay there? Please stay there."

"All right," said Lo. "I'm out of gas anyway."

"We're coming to get you. Don't go anywhere."

"All right," said Lo.

And Lulu drove to Huntsville, with Audrey and Emma in tow.

———

When they found Lo, she was sitting on Sam Houston's right foot, lit up by a set of floodlights. Towering over her was sixty-seven feet of Texas heritage.

The enormous statue of Old Sam was a monstrosity, but it was *their* monstrosity. Lulu leaped out of her seat, the car warning her with a repeating ding that her keys were still in the ignition. She didn't care. She clambered onto the platform and grabbed Lo into a fierce hug.

"That was so, so brave." Lulu couldn't believe Lo had taken Scumbag Luke's truck. "And stupid. Unbelievably stupid."

Lulu wouldn't let go of Lo, so when Audrey and Emma finally scrambled their way up the marble platform, they had to huddle around them both.

"What happened to the sneaky Lo?" asked Lulu, through a mouthful of Audrey's hair.

"She had a leave of absence, I guess," said Lo with a sniffle.

"Oh no, not you, too. You're too tough to cry, aren't you?" Audrey squeezed the group hug tighter.

"Says who?" said Lo, tears welling, sniffles again threatening. Nobody had ever seen Lo like this. Not when Michael Rossi had called her Lolita. Not when she'd gotten a black eye after her first kickboxing class. Not even when Lulu had blamed her for Dane Anderson and cruelly called her a whore.

"It's like the rules of our friendship." Emma's voice cracked. "Lo is too tough to cry or crack."

"You're supposed to be too nice to abandon us." Lo began to cry in earnest.

Lulu felt tears falling across her cheeks, but she refused to register them. "And Audrey's supposed to be too proper to get falling-down drunk."

Audrey sniffled loudly. "Well, Lulu's supposed to be too wild to care at all."

This renewed a fresh round of wailing for everyone. Luckily, Emma cried like Claire Danes, so her sobs muffled the sound of everyone else. She was an ugly mourner, Emma Walker was. And soon the sound of her howls caused Lulu to begin to laugh. Once Lulu laughed, Audrey had to laugh, and so too did Emma, and finally, wonderfully, Lo cracked a smile.

"Y'all are all idiots. But you're my idiots." Lo squeezed them all tighter. She pulled back and dried her eyes against her sleeve. She looked over the fuel-less truck and said simply, "That's Scumbag Luke's."

"Leave it," said Emma.

The other three girls went slack jawed. Emma held out her hands for the keys. Lo dropped them into her palm without a word. Emma opened the door, wiped down the keys with her shirt, then stuffed them up in the driver-side visor. She wiped down the steering wheel, then she closed the door and wiped the handle.

"Leave it," she said again. "Let's go."

Emma herded Lo into the passenger seat. Lulu got in the driver's side. Audrey and Emma climbed into the back.

"Lulu?" said Lo.

"Yeah?" said Lulu, ready to take the car out of park.

"Do you still have scissors in your purse?" asked Lo.

"I think so, why?"

"Can you not go for a second?" asked Lo, her voice unnaturally small and quiet.

Lulu left the car in park. She turned around and Audrey was already ready with her purse. Lulu dug in her bag and eventually pulled out a pair of craft scissors, blunted at the ends. "Will these do?"

Lo's gaze steeled. "They'll have to."

Lulu tried to hand them over, but Lo wouldn't take them. She shook her head and stared Lulu directly in the eyes. "I need you to cut my hair."

"What?!" screeched Audrey.

"My hair. I need you to cut it." And then Lo's bravado became truly bold. She pointed to her jawline. "To here."

Seeing the look of pure determination hardening on Lo's face, Lulu knew better than to protest. But. "Can't we at least find a beauty supply store around here and get some proper hair scissors?"

"No. They won't be open and you know it. No stalling," said Lo.

"But your hair!" cried Audrey from the back seat.

"Lulu." Lo was determined. That much was obvious.

"You have to promise to not be mad at me if I do it," said Lulu.

"I promise," said Lo.

"What do you promise?" Lulu had to cover all her bases on this one. She'd go with Lo to the ends of the earth, but she needed to hear the command clearly and from the first.

"I promise to not be mad at you if I change my mind after you've cut my hair. Satisfied?"

"Yes," said Lulu.

"Don't do it, Lulu!" said Audrey.

"God, Audrey. Quit being such an Amy March," said Lulu.

"I am not Amy March!" said Audrey.

"Yes, you are, with your 'Jo! Your one beauty!' and all that crap," said Lulu.

Lo raised an eyebrow. It was the only piece of her stalwart expression that had moved. "Amy's always been my favorite."

"You would," said Lulu. "Mine was always Jo."

"If she's Amy—" Lo started.

"—and I am not Amy," said Audrey.

"Whatever, so she's Amy. Then I'm Jo," said Lo.

"Oh, you're not Jo. I'm Jo. You're Meg," said Lulu. "Definitely Meg."

"Meg?!" said Lo.

"I'd rather be Meg than Amy," said Audrey, crossing her arms and looking out the window. She was in her protest mode. Her pout would be next.

"I'd rather be Lydia Bennet than Meg. Meg's insufferable." Lo had a definite huff to her voice now.

"Fuck you guys," said Emma. Three heads swiveled toward her.

"Fuck you guys, seriously. That makes me Beth. I am not fucking Beth. If we are the March sisters, I am not fucking Beth."

"Beth's good at the piano," Audrey tried.

"Beth dies. Beth is so good that she is too good to live in this world and she dies. Of a weak heart and a love of piano. I am not Beth. If I'm anyone, I'm Jo. She's clearly the lesbian." Emma raised an eyebrow in pure challenge.

After a sincere silence, all four girls broke into laughter—cramp-inducing, tear-springing, near-manic laughter. It took a full ten minutes to calm down again.

"My hair is no way my one beauty," said Lo once they had settled down. She looked Lulu dead in the eye. "Chop it off."

"Okay," Lulu said. "Also."

All eyes pivoted to Lulu.

"I had sex," Lulu said, as plainly as she might. "Last night."

Audrey was first to chime in. "With James?"

"With James."

"Belly-dancing James?" asked Lo.

"Belly-dancing James," said Lulu.

"I knew it!" said Emma.

"I told you so. Didn't I tell you so?" Audrey was positively triumphant.

Lulu loved to see her like this. "You did. You so told me so."

"Please tell me you had an orgasm," was Lo's contribution to the conversation.

"None of your business." But she winked, ruining any seriousness to her tone.

"Good on him. The white boy goes down," said Lo.

Audrey snickered. Emma giggled.

Lulu shook her head, then brandished the scissors in her hand. She took a handful of Lo's hair, held the scissors up to it, placed the locks between the sharp edges, and waited as decent a length of time as she could. "Here goes nothing."

Snip went the scissors. Another bold snip. Then several, all in a row: *snip, snip, snip*. She worked in silence. Nobody else in the car dared breathe too loudly.

Finally, Lulu stopped cutting. "It's done."

Lo continued to stare straight ahead. "How's it look?"

"Not half-bad." Lulu shrugged. "Not good, you know, but not *bad* bad."

Lo didn't seem ready to look. She wouldn't turn her gaze downward to see the pile of her hair now strewn across Lulu's car.

Lulu paused. "Do you want bangs?"

"What?" Lo picked up an enormous clump of her hair out of her lap, disbelief coating her face.

"Like, while I'm at it. Do you want bangs?" asked Lulu.

Lo closed her eyes. "Why not?"

And so Lulu leaned in close and began cutting in a fringe—a bit swept off to the side that seemed more forgiving than blunt and straight across. Lulu cut upward, trying to make a softer line. She wasn't particularly good, but she had enough skill that a professional could easily fix her mistakes.

"All right. You ready?" asked Lulu.

"As I'll ever be," admitted Lo.

Lulu flipped down the visor and turned on the front inside lights. "Voilà."

Lo's eyes went round, her mouth forming a small O and her hand quickly coming up to cover that expression. Lulu's stomach dropped.

Then Lo let out a laugh.

323

"Oh my God, Lulu. I love it." Lo ran her hands through her now-shortened hair.

Lo's looks were still uncommon. But when Lulu looked at Lo, she saw a girl who was more pleased than pleasing. And while Lulu had seen Lo self-satisfied many times, she had never seen her in that state for no reason other than for herself.

"It's amazing. May I?" Emma reached out and Lo leaned her head toward Emma's hands. Emma thrummed her fingers through the short, tousled cut.

"So cool," Emma said.

"I know," said Lo.

"It's almost doing that messy thing you like," Audrey tried. She had been raised to value her long mane of hair. But she was trying, even if she didn't get it, and that made Lulu smile more than had Audrey liked the haircut from the start.

Lo turned on a grin. She was wild-eyed—Heracles finally giving Atlas back the world. She looked free. "You're right. Almost. My mom is going to have a conniption fit. I love it."

Lo dug into her own purse, searching. She pulled out her eyeliner. "One last thing. Lulu, can you do that thing, with my eye makeup. The one where you look fearless?"

Lulu smiled. "Yeah. I can do that."

And so she did.

32

The Stars at Night
Are Big and Bright

Three months later

Lulu clapped. Then she whistled. James was on the dance floor with Emma at the moment. It was adorable watching them both move with awkward limbs and little sense of rhythm. Juniors were invited to prom, since the senior class was too small for a one-grade prom to be anything but an uncomfortably long night. Even Sealy Hall had its limits. Lulu smiled. James had undone his bow tie and taken off his rental jacket as soon as he was able. His sleeves were rolled up. But still, despite his many, many protests, the tux suited him.

Emma had, in an act of true bravery, lobbied to take Diana. Parents were in an uproar. Those parents on the planning committee had, initially, refused to let Emma take a student of the same gender as her date.

However, when Lulu had gone into Dean Knight's office asking for a quote on homophobic prom policies for an article in *The Sealy Examiner*, the administration's tune changed rather dramatically. Sealy Hall didn't want the smirch on their public record. One didn't build a lasting relationship with universities around the country only to squander it when it came to public affairs. No need to air that dirty laundry in public. It wasn't quite tolerance, but it was something.

Student-run journalism, it turned out, had its perks.

Emma had been given a grudging pass. The grudging nature of the pass annoyed Diana, but Emma counted all her victories. Audrey, in what can only be termed a flash of stupidity, had asked the sophomore in her music theory class. The one whose name she still had trouble remembering. It definitely wasn't Alex. The boy had been so shocked that he had agreed on the spot. That pairing for the night was already a tremendous disaster, but it was the kind of disaster even Audrey could appreciate. It was a funny tale in the making. Audrey wouldn't have any what-ifs left on that score. Nina danced with Brian Connor, and Lulu didn't know who looked more triumphant in that moment. She wasn't sure it mattered anymore.

Dane Anderson was on the far side of the room, giving Lulu a wide berth. He'd brought a sophomore, and Lulu felt a distinct pang for the girl. He'd received his diploma days before, but Lulu decided she must have finally shocked him into maintaining his distance.

Lo went stag and possibly enjoyed herself more than anyone. She made it seem like everyone else should have gone alone as well. And maybe they should have. Most of the boys and several girls were giving her longing looks. Lo ignored them all.

"Do you think we'll be old ladies one day, sitting around and still bitching?" asked Lo, collapsing into a chair next to Lulu. Lo glistened with sweat, her breath coming out in spurts and puffs.

"We can't know that," admitted Lulu.

"Okay, you can't *know*. But do you think it?"

Lulu looked at Lo. She looked over at the dance floor. At Audrey and

Emma and Diana and James. At the mass of everyone, dressed up and smushed together in a sweaty, elegant jumble.

"Yeah. I do," said Lulu.

"Me too." Lo smiled.

"How long do you think we'll feel like this?" Lulu asked.

"Like what?" asked Lo.

"Like sisters," said Lulu.

"Forever, Lulu. Forever."

Acknowledgments

When I was a little girl, my favorite fairy tale was Cinderella. It felt so real, so true to me. The world could often be a cruel, vicious place. You could work hard and scrub and toil tirelessly and so many forces would try to hold you back. But others, with a touch of love, could notice you and spread their own magic your way.

Reader, those who share their magic are the best kind of people.

My agent, Lauren MacLeod, understood this book from the very beginning. She knew Lulu and she loved Lo and she made me pull Emma forward and kept Audrey from slipping through the cracks. She was the greatest advocate for these girls and their story. She never asked me to temper their anger or soften their wildness. Her faith in this story still blows me away. Thank you, Lauren, you poetic, noble land mermaid.

And then there is my brilliant editor, Kat Brzozowski, who saw the potential for a horse-drawn carriage out of a pumpkin and several unruly mice. I'm beyond proud of this book and so much of that is because of her work. She pulled the best, realest, truest version of this story out of me. Thank you.

You have been an amazing champion for this book and a sheer joy to work with. Long story short: Kat's a genius editor with an impeccable eye. There are not enough superlatives for her. Feel free to @ me on that.

An enormous thank-you goes to the entire team at Feiwel and Friends/ Macmillan: Kim Waymer, Jean Feiwel, Alexei Esikoff, Patricia McHugh, Nancee Adams, and Khalid Zaid Abdel-Hafeez. My amazing publicist, Morgan Rath. You all helped bring Lulu to life. Special thank you to Hadeel al-Massari and Sharmeen Browarek for their wonderful sensitivity reads. Also, this cover. Michael Frost photographed, Tanya Frost styled. Liz Dresner did the cover direction and design. Thank you for giving the world the best cover to judge this book on. You h*cking nailed it.

With her fabulous #DVpit event, Beth Phelan still feels like my fairy god-mother. Thank you. You've made a world of difference to me. You've made a world of difference to so many readers.

And while I may have loved Cinderella, I am nothing like her: neither sweet-tempered nor able to pull all my hair back with the tug of a single, well-pressed ribbon. Steven has been my cheerleader through all of this. He never let me give up and for that I will be eternally grateful. He also dealt with more grumping and moping than any single human should. If y'all see him in the wild, buy him a donut. He likes the maple-glazed kind.

Shout-out to my family and friends, who have all been amazingly sup-portive of my being a writer from the get-go, despite being thoroughly and practically employed themselves. My baba, Hazim; my mom, Deborah; and my brother, Joe. Rachel Stoll, who read half of this book in iMessage form and totally out of order. My best friends and adoptive sisters, Selina Singh Hamill and Leslie Pfeiffer. Thank you for your faith in me. Y'all's belief is the wind beneath my wings. I don't care how cheesy that sounds.

Thank you to Jodi Meadows, who took me under her wing and answered every question I could ask about authordom. Your generosity is unparalleled and your taste in pens is exceptional. There's nobody I'd rather DM about the optimal writing paper.

Karuna Riazi has been a light in dark places. May the love you put out into the world come back to you tenfold. You have been the hero we all need.

The #DVSquad that came out of #DVpit has been the Dream Team of support groups. I am in forever awe of y'all's ability to rally and advocate. Karen Strong, Kat Cho, Meredith Ireland, Jennifer Zeynab Joukhadar, J.S. Fields, Cam Montgomery, J.A. Reynolds, Sarena Nanua, Sasha Nanua, Cindy Baldwin, Isabel Sterling, S.A. Chakraborty. My apologies if I did not name you. I love and see all the work y'all are doing. Your words will change the world. Never stop gif-ing on.

To my first readers, who read the whole way through this manuscript all those years ago, when it was certifiably unpublishable—Leigh Cooper, Alex Massengale, and Katie French. You are True American Heroes.

And finally—thank you to Ms. Gara Johnson-West, who taught my first women's studies class way back in the day. I wouldn't be the feminist I am without you, your wisdom, and your encouragement. Also—I'm still really sorry about that French Revolution paper.